STARSHIPPED

Also by Cat Sebastian

You Should Be So Lucky
We Could Be So Good

The London Highwaymen Series
The Queer Principles of Kit Webb
The Perfect Crimes of Marian Hayes

The Seducing the Sedgwicks Series
It Takes Two to Tumble
A Gentleman Never Keeps Score
Two Rogues Make a Right

The Regency Impostors Series
Unmasked by the Marquess
A Duke in Disguise
A Delicate Deception

The Turner Series
The Soldier's Scoundrel
The Lawrence Browne Affair
The Ruin of a Rake
A Little Light Mischief (novella)

PRAISE FOR *STAR SHIPPED*

"Cat Sebastian's writing positively sings. Filled with heart and humor, *Star Shipped* is an absolute master class in enemies-to-lovers yearning. I couldn't love Simon and Charlie more."

—B.K. Borison, *New York Times* bestselling author of *First-Time Caller* and *Good Spirits*

"Nobody does a road-trip romance like Cat Sebastian! *Star Shipped* has all the humor, found family, and quiet moments of agonizing tenderness that Sebastian does so well—and in Simon it also has the most spiteful and delightful wet-cat hero I've ever come across, and I'm *completely obsessed with him*. This book is a tremendously enjoyable tale of growth, vulnerability, and what it means to be trusted with someone's story. I'll be rereading it whenever I need a sweet, sharp-edged dose of joy."

—Freya Marske, *USA Today* bestselling author

"No one builds characters like Sebastian does. The amount of love and care that has gone into these men is unreal. I couldn't not fall for Simon if you paid me a million dollars."

—TJ Alexander, *USA Today* bestselling author of *A Gentleman's Gentleman*

"*Star Shipped* is a dazzling rom-com that makes you laugh through the banter and cry through the softness. With her signature warmth and wit, Cat Sebastian writes the love we all want: someone who knows every messy bit of your heart and stays anyway. The sort of romance that makes you fall in love with falling in love all over again!"

—Chip Pons, author of *Winging It with You*

Star Shipped

A Novel

CAT SEBASTIAN

AVON
An Imprint of HarperCollins*Publishers*

Without limiting the exclusive rights of any author, contributor or the publisher of this publication, any unauthorized use of this publication to train generative artificial intelligence (AI) technologies is expressly prohibited. HarperCollins also exercise their rights under Article 4(3) of the Digital Single Market Directive 2019/790 and expressly reserve this publication from the text and data mining exception.

This is a work of fiction. Names, characters, places, and incidents are products of the author's imagination or are used fictitiously and are not to be construed as real. Any resemblance to actual events, locales, organizations, or persons, living or dead, is entirely coincidental.

STAR SHIPPED. Copyright © 2026 by Cat Sebastian. All rights reserved. No part of this book may be used or reproduced in any manner whatsoever without written permission except in the case of brief quotations embodied in critical articles and reviews. For information, address HarperCollins Publishers, 195 Broadway, New York, NY 10007. In Europe, HarperCollins Publishers, Macken House, 39/40 Mayor Street Upper, Dublin 1, D01 C9W8, Ireland.

HarperCollins books may be purchased for educational, business, or sales promotional use. For information, please email the Special Markets Department at SPsales@harpercollins.com.

Avon, Avon & logo, and Avon Books & logo are registered trademarks of HarperCollins Publishers in the United States of America and other countries.

hc.com

FIRST EDITION

Interior text design by Diahann Sturge-Campbell

Spaceship illustration © DM7/Stock.Adobe.com

Library of Congress Cataloging-in-Publication Data has been applied for.

ISBN 978-0-06-342958-1

Printed in the United Kingdom

26 27 28 29 CPI 10 9 8 7 6 5 4 3 2

For the people who write the world's most gorgeous stories about television shows I might have seen one episode of twenty years ago. You're lifesavers.

STARSHIPPED

Chapter One

Every day this week, the air conditioner on set has woken up and chosen violence. Simon is not prepared to work in tundra conditions. He isn't built for Siberian gulags or ice fishing huts.

A production assistant brings him a blanket—actually just kind of tosses it in his direction and runs, because possibly some of Simon's discontent is showing on his face, and in his body language, and in the fact that he's said, "I guess this is how I'll die, not that anyone cares," fifteen times already—but the blanket is made of something scratchy, and his fried nerves can't take one more entry in the Bad column.

"You look like you're in a nursing home," Charlie says when Simon has the terrible blanket wrapped around his shoulders. "Or, like, you're doing a fashion shoot where the concept is sexy assisted living facilities in outer space."

After seven years, Simon shouldn't be appalled by the things that come out of Charlie's mouth. But before Simon can present Charlie with an itemized list of everything wrong with what he just said, the assistant director shouts that it's time for yet another take of this godforsaken scene.

He's spent the past three hours huddled up with Charlie behind the fuselage of a crashed spaceship. He's said the line, "Wait, I think they hear us," so many times the syllables have unraveled into a meaningless series of noises.

They shoot another take. And another one after that, Charlie's enormous arm a heavy weight around Simon's shoulders, his body a hulking and weirdly familiar presence against Simon's side. A disheartening percentage of Simon's career has been spent hiding behind spaceships, alien temples, and gigantic fungi with Charlie Blake.

There is not a single person on this set who wants to be here. They should have wrapped two hours ago. Lian, the showrunner, looks like she could light the entire set on fire using only her eyes. That would at least warm them up, so Simon's all for it. He catches her eye and tries to silently communicate that arson is a valid choice right now. She shoots him an extremely unimpressed look, which is unfair because it's not like this shitshow is *Simon's* fault.

They shoot yet another take, but when the actress playing the bounty hunter finally delivers her line the way the director wants, a piece of the prop tree thuds to the floor. Simon's never heard a more demoralized "Cut." There's an ominous throbbing behind his left eye, but maybe if he ignores it, it won't turn into a full-fledged migraine.

"Just fucking calm down," Charlie hisses while the crew sets up for another take.

"I don't know why I didn't think of that." Simon pitches his voice to maximal dickishness. Which, for Simon, is about twenty times the amount of dickishness a normal person can summon up. He knows his strengths. "That never occurred to me. You are *so* right. I *should* calm down."

Charlie clenches his jaw, a sure sign he's pissed. Anytime he isn't grinning vapidly is a sure sign he's pissed. He is not a man of nuance or depth. A little more work and Simon can get that vein in his forehead to pop.

"I mean," Charlie says, "you're stressing everyone out. I've worked with you long enough to know this is just your usual C-minus personality, but they think you're mad at them." He flicks a glance at the empty circle of space surrounding them. The crew has cleared a blast radius. "Maybe if everyone settles the fuck down, we can get out of here before midnight."

"That has nothing to do with me," Simon says. "Maybe they're afraid you're going to dump coffee on them." This is probably unfair, because it's been years since the coffee incident, but nobody's ever accused Simon of letting go of things too easily.

The vein in Charlie's forehead pulsates, and Simon's hit the jackpot—bells ringing, lights flashing, coins all over the floor.

Charlie opens his mouth but snaps it shut before saying anything.

"What?" Simon asks.

"Crew's watching," Charlie mutters.

Obviously everyone on set knows that Charlie and Simon loathe one another—after all this time, there isn't much the crew doesn't know—but Simon tries to keep it professional. Or professional-adjacent.

They aren't touching anymore, but they're still sitting close enough that they hardly need to speak above a whisper. They're basically huddling for warmth, after all. Simon wishes he'd taken advantage of the downtime to go someplace—anyplace—else. But the props people are nearly done fixing the tree, so there's no point in getting up now.

For the hundredth time in the past hour, Charlie slides a hand under his shirt and scratches his shoulder. To call it a shirt is an exaggeration. It used to be a shirt, but now it's some shredded fabric attached to Charlie's chest with double-sided tape in a way that's somehow more lewd than just taking the whole thing off. In theory, the shirt was shredded when they were attacked by knife-wielding aliens. In reality, it's because one of *Out There*'s real creative innovations is coming up with excuses to show as much of Charlie Blake's torso as possible. Simon would bet there's nobody in the history of network television who's spent as much time topless as Charlie has.

"Just take some Benadryl," Simon says.

"What?"

"You're allergic to the tape." It's happened before with mic tape and other adhesives. Just last fall Charlie got hives from the clear film they put on new tattoos. How on earth is Simon the only one who remembers this?

"I swear to God you're fucking telepathic when it comes to things that embarrass me," Charlie says under his breath, which makes no sense because the man is scratching himself in public. That's what he should be embarrassed about, not the allergy.

"Can you please just ask a PA for some Benadryl so I don't have to watch you paw at yourself?"

Charlie scrubs a massive hand over his big stupid jaw. "If I mention I have hives, we'll be here forever. Somebody will have to fill out paperwork. Fuck's sake, it's just a rash. Some of us don't have riders in our contracts about which brands of hairspray they're allowed to use on us."

"Okay, and stay with me here for a minute, Charlie, but allergies are *literally* why people have riders about that sort of thing." Something wonderful occurs to Simon. "Wait, you do know that allergies aren't good for you, right?" Charlie used to think New England was a state. There is no limit to the things he doesn't know.

"I fucking know that hives are—"

"Stop that," Simon hisses, swatting Charlie's hand away from his shoulder. "You'll be scarred for life."

Charlie grabs Simon's wrist, his fingers encircling it far too easily, then scratches his shoulder with his free hand. Simon attempts to wriggle free and, when that doesn't work, tries to pry Charlie's fingers open.

"You have five seconds before I bite you," Simon says reasonably.

"All right, mister workplace health and safety."

"Gentlemen," Lian says, looming over them, murder in her eyes.

"We're being good," Charlie says immediately, dropping Simon's hand.

"If I kill you both, every person on this set will give me an alibi," Lian says. "We'll finish the season with Alex and Roshni playing your roles and call it another alien body swap storyline. Am I making myself clear?"

"Yes, ma'am," Charlie says, the picture of innocence. Simon wants to drown him.

It's past midnight by the time Charlie's and Simon's characters are rescued from their hostile alien planet and they can all go home.

In the parking lot, Simon presses the button on his key fob, trying to hear his car beep over the pounding in his head.

"You can't drive," Charlie says, coming up next to him. His mouth is full and he has half a blueberry muffin in one hand. Simon would kill a man for some of that muffin. Every time he stops by craft services, they're out of muffins. Every time he sees Charlie, he's eating one. Simon suspects foul play. "You've been yawning for an hour. You'll be asleep before you get on the highway."

"And how exactly is this any of your business?"

"If you're dead in a ditch, we'll never finish this episode." Charlie crosses the parking lot. By the time Simon realizes he's following, it's too late to change course without looking like an idiot. "For the millionth time, how hard is it to just let the studio send a car when you know we'll be late?" Charlie unlocks his car. "Get in."

"No."

"I'm going to run you over if you don't get in." Charlie opens the passenger door. "I'll chase you across the parking lot until I've run you over and then I'll put the car in reverse and do it again, so help me—"

"Do you ever stop?" There's a blurry halo now around the LEDs illuminating the parking lot. Simon knows he can't drive with a migraine, but he also can't let Charlie be right. Truly a no-win situation.

Charlie sighs and looks up at the sky. "It's better for the environment," he says. "Only one car going to our neighborhood instead of two."

Somehow Charlie figured out that *It's better for the environment* is Simon's override code, not because he cares that much about carbon emissions or whatever, but because he can't disagree without sounding like more of a dickhead than he's willing to let even Charlie think he is.

"Oh my God, shut up." Simon gets in the car. It's ridiculously comfortable, something he forgets in the weeks or months between the times Charlie forcibly kidnaps him and drives him home.

"You should put something on that rash," Simon says after a

minute, when Charlie's basically driving one handed and scratching his shoulder with the other hand.

"It's fine."

Simon rummages around in his bag and hands Charlie a tube.

"Of course you carry around allergy cream." Charlie says this like he's discovered some filthy secret.

"My God, you've found me out."

"You've been in *GQ*."

"What does that have to do with anything?" Sometimes Simon worries that Charlie's thought process is fundamentally broken.

"You look like *that* and you still manage to be the least cool person I've met in my life."

Simon sighs pointedly. He's reasonably tall and fairly thin, and his cheekbones and jawline do a lot of work that his personality doesn't. All that, plus good clothes and a decent haircut create the optical illusion of charisma. The only reason Charlie doesn't understand this is because he's the kind of man who spends three hundred and sixty days a year wearing cargo shorts, flip-flops, and T-shirts that got shot from cannons at sporting events.

"Nobody says *cool* anymore," Simon says, which is something he learned from his niece and has been saving for the right moment to deploy against Charlie.

But Charlie just starts laughing—his real, ear-splitting, honk of a laugh; not the smoldery, square-jawed *ha* he does on camera. "Have you been watching TikTok unsupervised?"

Simon tries to breathe in slowly and breathe out even slower, or whatever it is you're supposed to do when you want to throttle your coworkers, and when that doesn't work, he focuses on the fact that he only has to put up with Charlie Blake for another month. One month, and he'll be done with *Out There*, done with Charlie, done with storylines he's already acted out a dozen times.

At the next red light, Charlie uncaps the tube and reaches under the collar of his T-shirt to rub some ointment on his shoulder.

"You can take it home and give it back to me tomorrow," Simon says, magnanimous, like he can't afford to just let Charlie keep some Target-brand allergy cream.

Charlie throws the tube across the car into Simon's lap.

Simon shuts his eyes against the glare of oncoming headlights. He doesn't mean to fall asleep, but the next thing he knows, Charlie's pointing the air conditioning vent directly in his face.

"What the fuck," Simon mumbles. "What is wrong with you?"

"I was trying to aim it away from your face, you paranoid weirdo. Shut up."

The next time Simon wakes up, they're in his driveway.

"Come on," Charlie says, flicking Simon's shoulder. "Get out of my car."

THERE'S A TEN-YEAR-OLD Prius chaotically parked in Simon's driveway, a notification on his phone that his home alarm's been disarmed, and a single word text from Jamie: "sorry."

Simon wants to pause outside his front door for a minute to get his thoughts together, but Charlie always waits to make sure Simon gets inside, like he's dropping Simon off after a playdate. So unless Simon wants to have a mini breakdown with Charlie's headlights turned on him like a prison searchlight, he has no choice but to open the door before coming to grips with what he's going to find on the other side.

Six cardboard boxes are piled in the foyer, each one of them battered and crumpled from all the other times they've been used to hastily pack Jamie's things and bring them to Simon's house. There isn't a right angle to be found among them.

On the sofa, Edie sits with her ears impatiently in the air, staring at the door like a parent waiting for a teenager out past curfew. She loves Jamie, so this is just drama, but Simon can respect the effort.

"Sorry," Jamie says. He's sitting cross-legged on the other sofa. There are purple circles under his eyes and his hair looks like it's been in the same ponytail for a few days, but he looks better than he did the last few times they went through this. "I didn't have anywhere else to go."

"You can always come here." Simon means it, but right now he'd very much like to pack a bag and stay at a hotel. He loves Jamie, loves him as much as he's capable of loving anyone who isn't his dog, but right now, all he wants is to take his migraine medication and collapse dramatically into bed without anyone asking whether he's okay.

With Jamie around, there's always someone to bear witness to exactly how far from okay Simon is. He's spent decades patching together something that looks like fine from a respectful distance, but once anyone gets too close they can see the seams. Simon has let Jamie see more of the seams than anyone else—and a lot more now than when they were dating—but nobody needs to see the full picture. Simon doesn't want to see the full picture.

"It'll only be for a week or two," Jamie says.

It's never only for a week or two. Simon doesn't even want it to only be for a week or two. He's told Jamie—oh, maybe ten or twenty thousand times—that he can move into the spare bedroom permanently. He likes having Jamie around—or, he does when he can keep his own shit together well enough that Jamie won't suspect how close he is to unraveling.

"The spare bedroom belongs to you. I don't know who else you think ever sleeps there."

Jamie opens his mouth and Simon knows that he's going to offer to pay rent, just like he does every time they have this conversation, and the ball of pain behind Simon's left eyeball might actually detonate if he has to go through it again. "I'm glad you broke up with him," he says quickly. "Now I don't have to go to jail for murder, so that's nice for me."

"Technically, he broke up with me."

Simon groans and covers his face with his hands. Jamie dates men who are objectively terrible—not violent or abusive, but dirtbags who get upset when he doesn't promote their YouTube channels or copyedit their screenplays.

Simon and Jamie were together for over a year. If Simon hadn't already known he was a nightmare at relationships, Jamie not only wanting him but staying with him would be all the proof he needed.

Simon sits next to Jamie and lets Edie climb into his lap. He matches his breathing to the rise and fall of her chest, focuses on the weight of her on his thighs. Somehow, a ten-pound mini dachshund does better work than the heaviest weighted blanket he's ever bought.

"I was going to ask you to stay here this summer anyway," Simon says. "I don't want to drag Edie to New York just for her to be alone all the time in a strange apartment."

After they wrap up this season, Simon's starting rehearsals for an off-Broadway production of *The Tempest*, directed by someone he went to college with. The role fell into Simon's lap when the actor who was their first choice broke his leg. He still can't believe he got it, and was convinced it was all down to stunt casting until he spent an hour looking up every production the theater had done and combing the casts for anyone who looked suspicious.

This would be the perfect time to mention that he isn't doing another season of *Out There*, but he doesn't know how to talk to Jamie about this. A few years ago, Jamie played a recurring character on the show. He tried not to act crushed when his character got killed off, but Simon leaving the show on his own terms will probably not be a great experience for Jamie.

"I always knew I'd wind up dog sitting for celebrities," Jamie says. He must notice how uncomfortable Simon looks, because he quickly adds, "I will happily stay in your very nice house with its very nice kitchen and the world's most perfect dog."

"Well. Thanks," Simon manages.

Jamie squints at him. "Do you need to take your migraine meds? Your eye is twitching."

"No," Simon says, even though there is no sane reason in the entire universe for him to lie about it. "I'm fine."

DURING SIMON'S MORE generous moments—nine hours sleep, no skipped meals, at least twenty-four consecutive hours away from Charlie—he can admit that a lot of the bad blood between them is because they got off to a terrible start.

After college, Simon landed a minor role playing a slightly villainous elf in the adaptation of a fantasy series he'd been obsessed with as a teenager. Working on *Tree of the Gods* had been a living nightmare, but he'd been nominated for a couple awards, even managed to win one, so he probably shouldn't complain.

When that show ended, he'd met with Lian Zhong, who'd been in the writers' room and was preparing to shoot a pilot about people stranded on a hostile planet after a shuttle crash.

"Think *Twin Peaks* in space," Lian had told him. "Leaning hard into the camp." She wanted him to read for the part of Jonathan Hale, the ship's doctor with a mysterious past.

All the other scripts Simon had been sent were for gritty prestige dramas. *Out There* looked like the opposite, weirdly out of step with the rest of the market. It looked *fun*, and Simon needed a break. Badly. He figured it would last one season, maybe two, and then he'd go back to more serious work.

"I want it to be a good experience for everyone," Lian had said, putting enough weight behind each syllable that Simon knew she meant it wouldn't be like *Tree of the Gods*. Simon trusted her to not be a fascist or a psychopath. He was right about that much, at least.

When they shot the pilot, he was mostly impressed with the rest of the cast. There'd been Alex Guttierrez, who'd just finished a stint as a villain in a superhero television series. There was Samara Jackson, who'd been on a Disney show and then a teen drama.

Then there was Charlie Blake, all of twenty years old, who'd done one season of a reality television show allegedly about restoring old cars but actually about Charlie taking off his shirt. He wasn't bad, but it was clearly a case of his personality mapping pretty closely onto the role. Charlie was playing Luke West, a hot-tempered former juvenile delinquent sent on parole to colonize a newly terraformed planet. And, well, Charlie—with his shaved head and his DIY-looking tattoos—looked like he knew a little bit about being a juvenile delinquent.

But when the network saw the pilot, they wanted more Charlie.

Presumably what they really wanted was more of Charlie's shirt off, because that's exactly what they got.

Simon had been livid. It wasn't just that he didn't have top billing or enough lines. It wasn't that he didn't want to share the spotlight—or not only that, at least.

The real problem—and Simon knows this makes him a snob, this isn't news to him—was that a former reality show star brought down the tone of the show.

Halfway through the first season, when Charlie started missing call times, showing up drunk, and generally acting like he'd read a book called *How to Crash and Burn in Hollywood,* Simon was annoyed. When Charlie punched the wall of his trailer and broke his hand, Simon was more than annoyed. When Charlie dumped hot coffee on a guest director who'd—admittedly—been a complete misery to work with, Simon expected Charlie's character to be written off the show. But Lian—for reasons Simon doesn't understand and officially does not care about—gave him a second chance. Or, really, a fifth or sixth chance by that point.

Simon never expects people to change—at least not for the better. And he's not sure Charlie did change, but his behavior did, at least on set. During the second season, he was professional. He apologized in person to everyone—even Simon—and basically went out of his way to be a total fucking delight and people *fell* for it.

If Simon were a better person, maybe he'd have let it go. Maybe he'd even have been impressed that Charlie managed to turn things around for himself. But all Simon's feelings were clouded by being stuck—with Charlie, with *Out There,* with a future that narrowed down and closed off before he even realized it was happening. Because the show turned out to be a hit, and Simon's fun little break has lasted seven years.

Hell, if Simon were a better person, he'd be grateful. He has steady work on a show that's never going to win awards but has a loyal enough following that the annual cancellation rumors never feel too realistic. He has a house he loves, a dog who tolerates being put in sweaters, and a friend he can list as his emergency contact.

But Simon is not a better person, and for the past few years, he's become increasingly nervous that the longer he spends on *Out There*, the harder it will be to find work on something different. Casting directors will look at him and think: midbudget science fiction show. They won't remember the award or the nominations; they won't remember the Shakespeare festivals or the projects he's managed to squeeze in when he isn't shooting *Out There*. He's tired of eleven-hour days, nine months a year, playing a role he could do half asleep. He's especially tired of Charlie Blake, who obviously is loving every minute of it.

That sounds shitty, like Simon's phoning it in on *Out There*, but he isn't. He has too much pride to let footage exist anywhere in the world of Simon Devereaux being a bad actor. But there are only so many times you can get rescued from space prisons, participate in love triangles with space diplomats, or heroically save people's lives from space viruses. He's bored. It sounds so petty, but that's what it comes down to.

And, honestly, that is kind of Charlie's fault. The show could have been something a little . . . elevated, maybe? Something character driven, at least. But Lian and the rest of the writers have to work around Charlie, who's very good at motivational speeches, heroic rescues, and a sort of constant smolder. He knows how to take big blue eyes and a six-pack and somehow make you think you're watching something special. Simon doesn't blame Lian for realizing she had something good on her hands and deciding to capitalize on it.

It's just that even if the rest of Simon's life is going to hell in a handbasket, at least he can fix his career, so that's what he's going to do.

Chapter Two

Simon's in his trailer, very much minding his own business, when Alex Gutierrez, who plays the captain of their spaceship, flings herself through the door and whispers, "Is it true? Tell me you aren't leaving."

Somehow, Alex is immune to all the please-go-away vibes that constitute Simon's only coping mechanism. She texts him for no reason Simon can discern, sails uninvited into his trailer, and beams at him without any provocation. At first, he worried she had somehow failed to notice exactly how gay he is and was attempting to flirt.

Simon isn't used to his general repellence not working. He's had decades to refine his strategy. He doesn't say much, but his face is naturally pretty bitchy—it's the cheekbones—so his silence gets interpreted as arrogance. He does nothing to contradict this assumption. And so instead of seeming awkward and anxious, he comes off as aloof. Bored. Kind of an asshole. People leave him alone. It's wonderful.

He's reasonably cordial with everyone at work. Almost everyone. He's polite. Well, he tries to be polite and maybe gets halfway there most of the time. Fact is, television sets are loud and the lights are too bright; the costumes are unbearable and there's always someone touching you. You'd think he'd be used to it, but maybe he's sliding toward a cranky middle age. Crankier. In any event, the fact that Alex is here at all boggles the mind.

"I'm not discussing this," Simon says, a little tartly and, case in point: not particularly nice.

Alex is in full makeup, green lines branching across her cheek because Captain Alvarez has been infected with some kind of space pathogen. Alex is spending the last two episodes of the season lying very still in med bay. "That's a yes. You're leaving."

"Nothing's decided." He isn't *lying*, exactly. So far, nothing's official. His agent keeps telling him to give it time, to think about it, and Simon can't seem to get across to him that he's done all the thinking he needs.

He's well aware that any other actor who hadn't signed a new contract by this point would have their character killed off before the season ended. He's seen it before: they've been mauled by giant space beetles, executed by space fascists, and devoured by space parasites. The next season, they're replaced by new characters on this ragtag band of conventionally attractive space explorers. It's the circle of life.

But Simon's getting special treatment, and he'd be lying if he said he wasn't flattered.

"That's not a no," Alex says.

"It was supposed to be a secret. Who told you?"

"Why keep it a secret? I mean, if you leave, it's not going to be a secret for long." She's looking at him intently, like she really wants to know his answer. Like she has opinions she wants to share. Simon wonders exactly how unprofessional it would be to shoulder her out of the way and flee his own trailer.

"Not while we're still shooting. I don't want people to..." Simon isn't sure how to finish that sentence. He doesn't want to have to say goodbye a hundred times? Accurate, but impossible to explain to people whose brains are wired normally. He doesn't want to notice that people are glad to see him go? Also accurate, but nothing could make him say that out loud.

"Yep," she says, like Simon just confirmed her suspicions, but she doesn't look mad about it. Simon is confused by almost every aspect of this interaction.

"Charlie's going to lose his shit," she adds.

The idea of how happy Charlie will be when he finds out he's rid of Simon makes him feel like he's lost a game he shouldn't even admit he's been playing.

"Well, you can see why I don't want to be around for that," he says.

"Hmm," is all Alex says, but then she takes out her phone and shows him a video of her dog, and he shows her a video of his dog. This is the level of interaction Simon can cope with, even when in the background of one of Alex's videos he can hear Charlie laughing.

"WHAT ON EARTH," Jamie says the following night. He's on the sofa next to Simon, looking at his phone.

For the past twenty minutes, a bowl of milk with seven floating cornflakes has been sitting on the coffee table, a constant irritation at the back of Simon's mind. He's counted the cornflakes a few dozen times because his brain has decided something dire will happen if he doesn't keep a weather eye on the cornflake situation.

"Hmm?"

There's an expression of unholy glee on Jamie's face. "Charlie Blake liked all your Instagram posts going all the way back to November."

Jamie's been running all Simon's social media for years. Jamie won't let Simon pay him, and at this point Simon's given up trying. Money is always lurking in the dark corners of their friendship. It's not that Jamie's broke—he makes a living off his YouTube channel somehow, in addition to residuals from old acting jobs. But Simon feels... not guilty, exactly, but something like that. Survivors' guilt, maybe.

"He shared that video of Edie in the sweater vest," Jamie says.

Simon slides closer to look at Jamie's phone. On the screen is a video of Edie taking a nap, snoring loudly, wearing a cable-knit sweater. Jamie posted it a few hours earlier, and Charlie apparently shared it along with a string of heart emojis. "Maybe he did it by accident?"

"You think he tripped and fell and liked twenty pictures of Edie?"

"Maybe his phone got hacked? Maybe he's having a neurological episode? Maybe it's a cry for help?"

Jamie gives him an unimpressed look. "You're better than this."

Simon counts the cornflakes again. Still seven, what a surprise. Would it be too weird to reach over and eat one to achieve a much more comfortable six cornflakes? He turns his entire body so the bowl is no longer in his field of vision.

"What I think," Jamie says, "is that Charlie has his notifications set so he doesn't see when people like his posts, and it hasn't occurred to him that you might not do the same thing."

None of this explains what Charlie was doing liking all those posts in the first place, but Simon's ready to file it away as one of life's unsolvable mysteries, until the next day when Charlie walks into his trailer. Simon's expecting Jamie, who went off to talk to somebody. It was probably unprofessional of Simon to bring Jamie, but he's convinced that if Jamie has five unsupervised minutes, he'll wind up eloping with the first dirtbag he meets.

When Simon realizes it's Charlie standing in the doorway, he's hit with the same reaction he has whenever Charlie takes him by surprise: he wants to push him out the door but in a way that involves at least a little groping. In the instant before Simon processes that this is Charlie Blake, what he sees is—

Well, Charlie looks the way he looks. It's just that Simon notices sometimes, and he'd prefer not to. The fact that Simon can catch a glimpse of Charlie Blake, a man who's just this side of feral, and think *hmm* is proof there's no sense in this world.

Then Charlie takes a huge, showy bite out of one of those blueberry muffins that keep disappearing from craft services. What the hell? Simon doesn't even like muffins, or blueberries, or foods that get crumbs all over the place, but these are surreal. They're basically brioche, and when Simon's migraines are so out of control that he thinks he might as well try avoiding gluten for the twentieth time, he decides that these muffins are gluten-free in, like, a spiritual sense. They would never hurt him.

And now it's been a full month of watching Charlie eat them while Simon can't find any. Nobody would blame him for reaching out and snatching that muffin right out of Charlie's hand.

Instead he asks, "Can I help you," dickishness cranked all the way up.

"Just saying hi."

"Saying hi," Simon repeats, because they do not have a *saying hi* kind of relationship. And then, proof positive he's been spending too much time around Jamie, his mind immediately supplies the messiest thing he could possibly say. "Thanks for liking all those pictures of Edie. You were so thorough."

Simon expects a comeback from Charlie, because this is the rhythm that's defined the last seven years of Simon's life. Instead, Charlie stands there and slowly turns pink. It takes Simon a moment to understand that this isn't a sunburn or yet another allergic reaction, but Charlie *blushing*. Simon isn't sure he's ever seen Charlie blush, not once.

Charlie casts his gaze around the trailer, clearly looking for inspiration to change the topic. Simon watches in bewilderment as Charlie studies the paperback Jamie left open and face down on the table, the bottle of nail polish (also Jamie's), the two half-eaten salads.

"Are all those yours?" Charlie finally says, gaze landing on the admittedly vast array of prescription bottles on the table next to the salads.

"*That's* what you're going with?" Simon asks, and he's blaming Jamie for that too.

"Are you okay?" Charlie's still looking at the bottles. Usually they stay in Simon's bag, but Jamie wanted aspirin and Simon's been turning his bag inside out trying to find it.

"Um, yes?"

"Because that's a lot of medicine for a person who's okay."

"Seriously?" Simon points at each prescription bottle in turn. "Allergy, migraine, another migraine, antianxiety, another antianxiety, antinausea. That's it. Do you want a doctor's note?

A treatment plan? Are you doing a drug sweep of all your colleagues' belongings?"

"You should keep those locked up," Charlie says. Simon searches his face for some sign he's being made fun of and comes up with nothing.

"They're usually in my locked trailer."

"Hmm," Charlie says, because he is actually, honest-to-God, accusing Simon of unsafe drug practices. "You should leave them at home."

"Are you under the impression that people can schedule their panic attacks and migraines for when they're at home? Genuinely curious. You can leave anytime, you know!" He makes a shooing gesture toward the door, not something he'd do to anyone else, not even Edie (especially not Edie).

Charlie flinches a little, and Simon enjoys the dopamine hit he gets whenever he cracks Charlie's facade of relentless cheerfulness. Then Charlie puts on the slightly constipated expression he uses when his character has just lost a crewmember. "Are you okay?" he asks, like he didn't just ask the same thing two minutes ago.

For one hysterical moment, Simon imagines answering honestly. No, he isn't okay. He left okay in the rearview mirror nearly a year ago when his migraine meds started fucking with his old anxiety meds, and since then he's relying on much-less-effective anxiety meds. He isn't okay, but he also isn't getting three migraines a week.

"I'm fine as long as I have my medicine," Simon says pointedly. "And as long as people don't barge into my trailer and accuse me of drug trafficking."

Charlie looks torn between embarrassment and offense. On

anyone else it would look ridiculous. On Charlie it looks—it doesn't matter what it looks like, because Simon's quitting this show and will peacefully live out his years not thinking about what Charlie Blake looks like. In a few weeks he'll be in New York, where he'll have a job that doesn't involve spaceships and where he won't have any coworkers he wants to sexily murder.

"I stopped by to ask if you wanted to come to the after party at my house. It's after the wrap party."

"I know how after parties work, thanks."

"You could bring Jamie."

Simon nearly says that of course he'd bring Jamie, because Jamie's been his plus one to everything for years. But Charlie speaks first. "Partners are invited."

"Jamie and I aren't together," Simon says before he can investigate why he needed to clarify that particular point.

"Oh God, I'm so sorry." Charlie looks at the pair of salads, like he thinks maybe Jamie dumped him midway through lunch.

"It's been a while." It's been five years, but Simon's used to people assuming he and Jamie are still together, because some straight people have a hard time with the idea that you can be friends with someone you've had sex with.

"Oh."

"We're friends," Simon explains.

"That's nice," Charlie says, sounding perplexed. Charlie isn't the kind of straight person who should need this explained to him, because he's friends with Alex, and also Bethany in the costumes department, and probably every other woman he's dated. He accumulates friendships like some kind of snowball of extroversion, always gathering and never letting go. It makes Simon—who has one friend and a handful of people whose texts he mostly returns—feel panicky, but also, maybe, a little ashamed.

Simon claps his hands together. "What a fun conversation this is. We should do it more often."

For a horrible moment, Charlie's face brightens. Then he seems to register the sarcasm and his expression closes off. Simon feels like one of nature's greatest monsters for the split second before remembering this is the same man who's spent the last month somehow depriving Simon of blueberry muffins.

"Anyway, you're invited. Jamie's invited." Charlie's hands are in his pockets, his gaze on the wall behind Simon's head. "People swim. So, like. Bathing suits."

"Thank you for explaining how to use a pool. Please go now."

When Charlie leaves, Jamie immediately enters, an expression of shit-stirring ecstasy on his face, and Simon doesn't need to ask whether he eavesdropped.

"Charlie Blake is the only living person who thinks you need to be told not to skinny dip," Jamie says, dropping into the chair next to Simon's. "Also, why did he invite you in the first place?"

"He always asks." This is the first time he's invited Simon in person, though. Usually the invitation arrives in the form of a message in the group chat Alex keeps re-adding him to. "He invites the whole cast, but he knows I'll say no."

Charlie's parties are probably loud and crowded, filled with various kinds of smoke and appetizers that've been left out too long for food safety purposes; the kind of parties where if you open the wrong door, you find your actual coworkers having sex with one another. Simon's policy about all these things is a firm no thanks.

"I'll come along if you want company," Jamie says, as if there's any question of Simon attempting a social event without him.

If the past is anything to go by, Jamie is right on time for a rebound. There is literally nobody on the cast or crew of *Out There* who would be a worse choice than whoever Jamie will pick if left up to his own devices.

"Okay," Simon says. "We're going."

IN THE LAST episode of the season, Charlie's character tries to rescue Simon's character from a hostage situation. Something's wrong with the escape shuttle, and Jonathan Hale is insisting that Luke West leave him behind and save himself.

"Just—just shut up," Charlie says while heroically shouldering open the shuttle door. He's wearing a whole entire shirt and his light brown hair is carefully disheveled. "I'm not leaving you here. I'm not getting in this damn thing by myself."

"I won't let you die here, you—"

"*Let?*"

Charlie grabs Simon's collar in a way that's fifty percent menacing, fifty percent affectionate, and will be cherished forever and GIF'd immediately by queer spaceship enthusiasts. It goes on like that, as it does at least once a season. Luke and Jonathan angrily-slash-sexily attempting to sacrifice themselves for one another is a core part of the show.

Nobody ever explicitly told Simon to play this kind of thing romantically, and so he doesn't. His character is too buttoned-up to play anything romantically, including actual romantic scenes. But sometimes he thinks Charlie *is* playing it romantically. Then again, there isn't anything Charlie could do to make the sentiment "I'd rather die with you than live without you" more romantic than it already is.

Occasionally, interviewers who think they're being clever ask Simon what he thinks about all the gay fanfiction being written about his and Charlie's characters. He always says he's thrilled fans feel inspired to write stories about *Out There*. Which is true enough—the fact that *Out There* is a show fans have that kind of relationship with is part of why he's stuck around so long.

For general sanity purposes, Simon doesn't let himself think too hard about what goes on in the writers' room. They do their job, he does his. But they've spent years writing lines and entire story arcs for him and Charlie that are pretty romantic. And yet, their characters keep getting paired with women.

He knows plenty about the history of movies and television shows depicting characters of the same gender in unusually close friendships, acting in a way that can only be described as romantic, but then becoming involved in straight romantic relationships. Somewhere in the bowels of the internet is all the *Lord of the Rings* fanfic he wrote in middle school, and also all the *Sherlock* fanfic he wrote in high school. Simon basically has an honorary master's degree in dubious homoerotic tension.

At the time, he had no problem recognizing that tactic as textbook homophobia. Now, though, he's less sure.

There's no shortage of queer talent on the show. For all intents and purposes, Simon is out at work. So is Alex, who's brought partners of various genders to events. Two of the writers are nonbinary. Lian has a bi pride sticker on her laptop and an ex-wife in Palo Alto. There are queer characters and a couple of storylines that are fairly overt metaphors for trans rights.

But it's network television, and a queer romantic relationship between main characters is probably a step too far. From the beginning, Lian's been negotiating a delicate balance between doing what she wants and making the network happy.

Simon doesn't think he'd ever recover from having to shoot a romantic scene with Charlie, so whatever's going on with the writers has worked out pretty great for him. And less great for, like, equal representation on slightly above-average science fiction shows. But Simon isn't looking a gift horse in the mouth.

The point is, he's done this before, this romance-but-with-plausible-deniability scene. This time, though, when Charlie's knuckles skim Simon's throat as he grabs Simon's collar, Simon hesitates before delivering his next line. When they lean together, their bodies fitting the way they always do, Charlie smelling like coffee and mints and whatever shampoo was probably on sale at Costco, it hits Simon that this is the last time.

Simon will be so glad to be done with this show. He doesn't know where this nostalgia is coming from.

"Don't you dare tell me to leave you," Charlie says, and Simon rolls his eyes. It's familiar and kind of dumb. As they reset the shot, Simon can't believe he isn't going to do this ever again.

From an *Out There* fan Discord

SpacePope: There is no plausible heterosexual explanation for "Don't you dare tell me to leave you." I will not be hearing any arguments at this time

SpacePope: Are you telling me someone wrote those words and expected me to hear them with my own gay ears and not come to some conclusions??

SimonDevereauxsCheekbones: My cousin's a PA (not on Out There but on another show at the same studio) and he says a third of the Out There writers' room is like. Very gay.

HowlsMovingSpaceship: Okay sorry to be Like That but you realize that queerbaiting is worse if it's done by queer writers who know exactly what they're doing, right?

SpacePope: How is that even queerbaiting? It's just plain queer.

HowlsMovingSpaceship: It's the literal definition of queerbaiting. If you judge by the words coming out of their mouths, Luke and Jonathan are basically in love. Meanwhile, Luke is always—ALWAYS—involved with at least one woman.

SupervillainApologist: guys, mom and dad are fighting

GalactoseIntolerance: Y'all. It's a network show. If anyone actually believes they're going to write a gay relationship between the two main characters, that's kind of on them.

SpacePope: That might have been true five years ago but IDK if it's true anymore?? Off the top of my head, I can name four successful mainstream shows that are super gay.

DeathStarJacuzzi: In my mind, they're established life partners in an open relationship, and the writers assume it's so obvious that it never needs to be stated

SimonDevereauxsCheekbones: Guys, my cousin says Simon is gay and is out to everyone, brings his boyfriend to parties, etc.

HowlsMovingSpaceship: Tell me exactly how you think this is relevant

SimonDevereauxsCheekbones: Just that it's less likely to be queer-baiting if there's an actual gay actor involved? Maybe?

SpacePope: Are we publicly outing actors now?

SimonDevereauxsCheekbones: It's not public! This is a private server.

SpacePope: It's public enough.

HowlsMovingSpaceship: Mods, can someone delete the last few messages please?

Chapter Three

Simon has rules: the cups go in the cabinet in a particular order, the car gets parked in a particular part of the driveway, and the laundry gets done in a particular way. They're so second nature that he sometimes doesn't notice he even has a rule until someone breaks it. With Jamie around, his rules are in shambles and he's constantly running into evidence that his mind was put together wrong.

He can't tell whether Jamie's noticed. Probably not, because if he had, he'd have insisted on talking about it. Or—worse—he'd have quietly started following Simon's deranged little rules because he doesn't want to be a bother. Which is all the more reason for Simon to make sure Jamie never finds out, obviously.

Simon's sitting on the sofa, trying to read a book while his brain is screaming that the cabinets are *wrong* and his groceries are *wrong* and also everything in the world is wrong because Simon didn't turn the doorknob the correct number of times and how can a person be expected to function under these circumstances.

Yesterday, his therapist gently reminded him that his rules have a name, a diagnosis, and a treatment plan; it isn't just that Simon's super bitchy about his surroundings. When he was living alone, he'd been able to delude himself into thinking he was cured. He doesn't want to admit how much worse he is now than he was a year ago.

The thing is, he likes having Jamie here, and he wishes the more malfunctioning parts of his psyche would get on board with that. There's some deep, pathetic part of Simon that wants to take the people he loves—who love him—and just, like, chain himself to them. Metaphorically, maybe. But also kind of literally. He'd cut out his own tongue before letting anybody figure that out.

At the other end of the sofa, Jamie gasps.

"What?" Simon asks, glancing over the top of his book. Jamie has the look he only gets when he has something a little mean and very messy to share. Simon's mood instantly brightens. Other people's drama is a thrilling change from the contents of his own mind.

"Did you recommend a book to Charlie?" Jamie asks.

"I'm not sure anyone's recommended a book to Charlie in his life."

"It's—okay, I'm just going to read the caption." Jamie drops his voice an octave and adopts a slightly country accent Simon gathers is supposed to sound like Charlie. "Having a blast reading this book my man Simon Devereaux recommended!"

"What the hell," Simon whispers. "My man?" Has Charlie had a stroke? Then his brain catches up with the rest of what Jamie said and he reaches for Jamie's phone.

On the screen is a selfie of Charlie with a book. He's lying down, the book open on his chest, the photo taken at just the right angle to make the most of his entire shoulder/biceps region. But Simon is strong; he isn't letting himself get distracted by any of that.

The book on Charlie's chest is *A Scorched Land*, the same book

Jamie was reading in Simon's trailer the other day, which—it's a free country, and Simon might have opinions on the books Jamie chooses to read but he keeps them to himself. Mostly. But that doesn't mean he wants his name publicly associated with books about dragons falling in love or whatever the hell is going on in that series.

"Can anyone tell me," Jamie goes on, leaning over Simon's shoulder and reading the caption in his fake-Charlie voice, "whether this girl is actually going to get together with this dragon or???"

"Oh my God."

"Charlie, God bless him, is over there fully believing you'd read a book about dragonfucking," Jamie says. "Honestly, you should be flattered."

"What are the comments?"

Jamie takes the phone back and scrolls. "Mostly recommendations for books with actual dragonfucking." He types something, presumably his own recommendation.

Simon takes his own phone out of his pocket and unlocks it, all the while knowing it's a bad idea. He opens Instagram, ignores his notifications, and navigates to Charlie's profile.

"I feel like I should take your phone," Jamie says. "I think you'd take my phone in this situation, but on the other hand I really want to see what happens. God, I hate hard choices."

"I'm only going to message him," Simon says. "Nothing public."

"That's not what I'm worried about. I think you're so obsessed with that man, you're basically under the influence. Double the legal limit. You have no judgment where Charlie Blake is concerned."

"Charlie Blake robs everyone of their judgment," Simon says. "He's like a walking injury to the prefrontal cortex."

"Welllll," Jamie starts, but Simon's already typing.

> **Simon:** That was Jamie's book. I haven't read it.

Dots appear almost immediately.

> **Charlie:** ok so can you ask him if the girl is in love with the dragon? comments are divided

> **Charlie:** also you should read it, 100% bugfuck nuts, why aren't all books like this

Simon squeezes his eyes shut, as if when he opens them he won't see a screen that's asking him to make bad choices.

> **Simon:** From what I understand, Jamie thinks everyone's in love with the dragons, but he isn't sure whether the characters or the author are aware of this.

> **Charlie:** ???

> **Simon:** Same

He immediately regrets it. It looks like he's trying to have a conversation with Charlie, something he affirmatively does not want, because he values his sanity.

> **Charlie:** tell him I liked the book.
> i read it in like five hours

> **Charlie:** first book i finished since high school

> **Charlie:** maybe middle school

"Jamie." Simon shuts his eyes again because he's pretty sure he'll start laughing if Jamie catches his eye. "Charlie wants you to know that he loved this book. It's the first book he's finished in years. He seems excited to have discovered books, as a concept, and is giving you a lot of the credit."

When Simon opens his eyes, Jamie looks deliriously happy with the mess of it all. "What does he talk about with the people he dates?"

"What do you mean?"

"Charlie was with Alex for a while. She's super smart. Didn't he also date Bethany in costumes? She has an MFA."

Simon opens his mouth to point out that intelligent women are perfectly capable of dating people for their looks, but something stops him. Charlie isn't book smart. Simon isn't sure he finished high school. Sometimes it seems like he might not even have finished kindergarten; Simon was eyewitness to the moment Charlie—delighted—learned that the rhinoceros is not a creature from the Mesozoic Era but something you could see at the zoo.

But Charlie learns his lines faster than anyone Simon's worked with and he's quick on his feet. "I think he's smart in some other way. Like, some mysterious way you and I can't recognize."

Jamie blinks at him. "That might be the nicest thing you've ever said about Charlie Blake."

Simon lobs a throw pillow in Jamie's direction.

IT'S *OUT THERE* tradition to have dinner at Lian's house the night after shooting wraps—just the main cast, no partners. It's a social obligation Simon doesn't actively dread. He sees these people nearly every day. They already know he's standoffish. Expectations are appropriately low. Simon could probably take out his phone and do a crossword puzzle and nobody would even think it was strange. He could put on noise-canceling headphones and dark sunglasses and simply astral project to some calmer, better place, the way he does sometimes on set. They'd all just say, that's Simon, he's an asshole, what can you do.

He sits next to Roshni, who's played a bounty hunter on *Out There* for four seasons. She's part of what Simon thinks of as the Calm Faction of the cast and crew along with Simon and Lian, as opposed to the Feral Faction, which includes Charlie and Alex. Somewhere in the middle are Petra, who plays a telepathic diplomat, and Amadi, who plays an alien prince.

The food is—well, Simon picks at it and spreads it around his plate, because he's had two migraines in the past month, which is a lot better than this time last year but it's still more than zero.

He's operating on the theory that if he avoids every migraine trigger in existence, he might get marginally fewer headaches. Not that he's noticed any kind of correlation between what he eats and whether he gets a migraine. It's more like he's hoping the universe will deduct a headache or two for his extra effort. This is—he is well aware—not rational, but neither is repeatedly counting the hoops in Alex's left ear, and he's already done that six times tonight.

Lian comes up behind his chair and leans down. "It's vegan," she whispers.

Which means (1) it doesn't have whatever aged meats or cheeses give some people migraines, and (2) Lian's been paying attention to what he eats. This gives Simon a strange feeling that he refuses to identify or dwell on, so he takes a bite of what turns out to be some kind of grain salad and arranges his face so it looks like he's paying attention to the conversations around him.

Charlie (wearing actual cargo shorts in a room full of adults eating an expensively catered dinner at their boss's house) is arguing loudly with Alex about something Simon thinks is a cartoon. They've been having this exact argument for seven years. Amadi is letting Petra monologue about her wedding plans. Roshni and Lian are whispering, their heads close together.

It's comfortable in a way he imagines isn't so rare for most people. He isn't going to miss the work, but he might miss this feeling of almost belonging. He'll never go to Lian's house for another dinner she insists is mainly for the tax deduction but is actually because—against all odds—most of the people on this show like one another. Well, they don't like him, but he's one of them anyway.

He's almost enjoying himself, despite the occasional displeased looks Charlie keeps throwing his way. Annoyingly, Simon doesn't even know what he did to bother Charlie this time. He likes a full inventory of Charlie's sore spots.

Usually Simon makes an excuse and leaves right after dinner, but tonight he hesitates. Still, not wanting to leave isn't the same as wanting to stay, so he slips out to Lian's backyard.

Someone else already had that idea, though—two people, actually. And they're kissing. He notices the cargo shorts first, and no surprises there—Charlie and Alex are back together. All that cartoon-based fighting was probably their idea of foreplay. They haven't noticed him, so he takes a step back toward the house, but stops short when he realizes that the person Charlie's kissing isn't Alex. It isn't a woman at all. It's one of the waiters from the catering company.

Back inside, Simon locks himself in the bathroom.

Simon's general policy about everyone else's sex life is that the less he knows, the happier he is. He hopes they repay the favor, because while he's made practically zero effort to hide that he's gay, he doesn't want to have to talk about it. He isn't famous enough for it to matter, except to a few dedicated weirdos who are niche enough that their speculation rarely leaks outside their own world of carefully curated, intensely homoerotic *Out There* GIFs.

Anyway, Simon tries not to pay attention, but there's some horrible, traitorous part of his brain that's always tuned-in to whatever Charlie Blake is doing. Simon notices if Charlie looks a little too long at a guest actor, or if he flirts back when the set design guy flirts with him. Simon's noticed, but he's never let himself come to any conclusions. It's none of his business. And—maybe he doesn't want to think about Charlie Blake being queer.

The problem Simon has right now is that Charlie isn't out, at least not at work. And even if he's out to some of the cast, someone else from the catering company could see him, not to mention Lian's teenage kids.

Simon doesn't have a lot of humanitarian impulses but he isn't letting people get outed, not even Charlie, not even when he's kissing a cater waiter basically in public.

He leaves the bathroom and stations himself by the back door, with no clear idea of how exactly he'll go about waylaying anyone who tries to go outside. He takes out his phone and starts playing sudoku, which won't raise any questions, since hiding in empty hallways and playing on his phone is pretty on-brand for him.

The waiter comes inside first, not sparing a glance toward the corner where Simon's lurking. Simon could go back to the living room now, but he doesn't, so he's still there, skulking in the shadows in the creepiest possible way, when Charlie comes inside.

"What are you doing?" Charlie asks.

"Reading," Simon lies.

"Did you start that dragon book?"

Bafflingly, Charlie sounds like he's attempting a normal conversation. He's talking to Simon like it's a natural continuation from yesterday's ill-advised messages. Simon doesn't like it. It makes him feel off-balance, much more so than the revelation that Charlie is apparently into men.

"No." Simon isn't sure whether he's rejecting dragon romance or civil conversation or something else, so he turns on his heel and heads back to the living room, where everyone's standing around in a way that means they're about to leave. Alex is giving Roshni a hug that's only slightly less violent than a football tackle. Simon decides to leave before it's his turn to get mauled. He thanks Lian for dinner and books it for the door.

"Do you need a ride?" Charlie asks, following him out.

"I drove."

"Good, then you can drive me home."

"No, I really—"

"Alex, keys," Charlie says, and before the words are even out of his mouth, he's taken his key fob out of his pocket and tossed it toward where Alex has just left the house. She catches it in one hand.

"Sweet," she says.

"Wait," Simon protests, trying to come up with an excuse not to drive Charlie home in front of a group of people who all know perfectly well that Charlie has driven Simon home dozens of times. But before he can think of anything, Alex is pulling out of Lian's driveway in Charlie's car.

"Door," Charlie says, pulling on the handle of the driver's side door on Simon's car.

"What?"

"Unlock the door," Charlie says, very slowly, like Simon's the one here who isn't making sense. "So I can get into your car."

"I can drive, you know." But even as he says it, he's unlocking the door. It's just because he hates driving, that's all, or maybe because he isn't tacky enough to argue with Charlie in Lian's driveway.

Charlie spends a full minute moving Simon's seat back and adjusting the mirrors and in general making it so the next time Simon has to drive, the car will feel like a rental.

"We're the same height. Why are you moving everything?"

"You're on top of the steering wheel," Charlie says, tilting the side mirror one fraction of one degree. "If the airbag goes off, you'll break your ribs and puncture a lung and die."

"Are my mirrors going to kill me too?"

"I mean, yeah, if you need them to reflect anything other than the side of your own car."

"My car has a backup camera." So does Charlie's car, obviously. This should not be a new concept for him.

Charlie looks at him like he's never heard anything so dumb in his life, opens his mouth, shuts it with a click of his back teeth, somehow managing to silently convey that Simon's basically using tarot cards and vibes to maneuver his car.

Charlie drops an arm along the back of the passenger seat, looks over his shoulder, and backs out of Lian's driveway in a way that leaves Simon feeling faintly insulted.

Heroically, Simon doesn't ask where all Charlie's opinions on vehicular safety were when he rammed his old truck into the car of a certain guest director six and a half years earlier.

"So," Charlie says, when they're heading east on Franklin. There's some weight in that syllable, enough to clue Simon into the fact that he's been cornered. At least now he knows why Charlie insisted on driving him home: Charlie's going to give him an insulting lecture about how Simon had better not tell anyone what he saw in Lian's garden. Simon thought Charlie hadn't seen him, but he must have been wrong.

"You're leaving the show, aren't you," Charlie says.

It takes Simon a second to recalibrate his irritation. "You see, the problem is that nobody ever told you how secrets work. Nobody was supposed to tell Alex, and Alex wasn't supposed to tell you, which means you weren't supposed to let me know that she told you. Hope that clears things up!"

"You really are leaving, then?"

"Nothing's set in stone," Simon says, even though it nearly is.

"You were going to leave without giving anyone a chance to say goodbye. What, we'd come back in August and you just wouldn't be there?"

"I guess there would have been a press release or something, like when Samara left."

"That isn't the point, Simon!" Charlie's hands flex on the steering wheel. "You've worked with these people—dozens of people—for years, and you weren't going to give them a chance to say goodbye?"

The idea of saying goodbye to everyone involved with the show makes Simon want to check himself into a special hospital by the sea. "Most people leave shows in between seasons. The cast and crew find out when they find out. This is very normal and you're the one making it weird."

Charlie pulls into a car wash parking lot, hits the brakes, and turns to face him. "But you had a chance to be better! You could care, just a little, about people's feelings."

And that hits too close to home because Simon *does*. He does care what people feel. He obsesses over it, getting so anxious that it's all he can think about. When he's super anxious, he stops being able to think straight about how normal people react to things. Other people's emotions become illegible. And then he really does fuck up.

Tonight at dinner, Simon probably spoke twenty words. Twenty *words*. And he wasn't even that anxious, at least on his own personal scale. It had practically been okay. But being in a group of people—or sometimes being around anyone, and sometimes just sitting alone in his house and remembering people exist—makes some fundamental part of himself shut down, and the best he can hope for is a quiet retreat into his mind, and that everyone will read his silence as dickishness and not literal mental illness.

"Uh," Charlie says, and Simon realizes he's been sitting still, his face in his hands, for a while now.

Simon makes himself lower his hands. "You do *not* get to judge me. Not about that."

"Do you—don't fucking kill me, Simon, but I have to ask—do you need medicine right now?"

What Simon needs is a time machine to go back and hide those prescription bottles before Charlie could see them. "What I would love is not to be in a poorly lit parking lot with a man who's yelling at me." Simon's just being a dick—he isn't afraid of Charlie—but he needs this to end.

Charlie recoils as much as he can in the driver's seat of a car. "Sorry," he mutters, and puts the car in gear.

"Jamie doesn't know I'm thinking about leaving," Simon says when the car is moving. "So if you and Alex and whoever else you told could just keep it together when you see him at the wrap party, that would be great."

He's expecting Charlie to pounce on that—Simon's being a bad friend, not even caring about Jamie's feelings—but he doesn't say anything, and the silence lasts until he's parking in Simon's driveway. It doesn't occur to Simon until he's letting himself into his house that now Charlie has to walk home.

SIMON CAN'T SLEEP, which is no surprise. Historically, it takes him five to seven business days to process one single unanticipated emotion, and tonight he's been handed a slew of them.

He's seriously considering borrowing Jamie's copy of *A Scorched Land* to see whether dragon romance might be the mental anesthesia he craves, when his phone buzzes. It's his niece. If it's one o'clock in California, that means it's four in the morning in Connecticut, but Nora is seventeen and has the sleep cycle of a bat.

> **Nora:** Dad wants to know if you're coming to my graduation

Other than Nora, Simon's family doesn't know he's spending this summer on the East Coast. He's going to have to tell them soon because not mentioning it will tip the scales from "distant but plausibly warm" to "estranged" and Simon doesn't want to be the one responsible for that.

> **Simon:** Is that an invitation or a warning?

> **Nora:** 50/50

> **Nora:** figured you hear it from me, give me the answer you know they want, and then you don't have to talk to my dad

> **Nora:** or YOUR dad

> **Simon:** This is bullying.

> **Nora:** correct

It's not that Simon dislikes his family. He doesn't, at least not most of them.

It's just that the Devereauxs are gregarious Connecticut football enthusiasts with jobs in investment banking and corporate law. Simon's bad at math, introverted, and gay—a combination they all treat like a delicate health condition. One of his brothers is the junior senator from Connecticut and the other's a partner at a top New York law firm. Both his parents are retired hedge fund managers and both his stepparents are retired doctors. Simon pretends to fly through outer space for a living; they just don't have many overlapping areas of interest.

There's a story Simon's brother used to tell as part of his stump speech, about how Simon struggled academically until his parents sent him to a school that focused on the arts. This was supposed to demonstrate Senator George Devereaux's commitment to education and arts funding, as well as to remind everyone that he has a semi-famous brother. The story's even kind of true. In eighth grade, Simon flat-out refused to do any schoolwork whatsoever until his parents agreed to send him to a high school with a decent theater program.

He'd been a wretched little goth child, grew into a wretched little goth teenager, and only thanks to a timely growth spurt, a late appearance of the family cheekbones, and a talent for looking handsomely judgmental was he spared the fate of becoming a wretched little goth adult. There's a fine line between being sullen and being superior, and it took Simon some trial and error to find that line and keep to the correct side of it.

Nora was born when Simon was in high school. He mainly knew her as a face on his oldest brother's campaign-curated social media until she was thirteen and started texting him out of the blue.

At first he couldn't understand why she sought him out. But then she sent him a selfie—not one of the campaign-approved shots of her in a school uniform, but a picture of her with inexpertly applied black eyeliner and no smile—and it all clicked into place. Somewhere in his mother's house, there are pictures of Simon with the same smudged eyeliner and scowl. She's a wretched little goth child and she thinks of him as proof of concept. Devereauxs can, with a little effort, avoid getting an MBA.

They don't look much alike, but he feels like there's a resemblance anyway, something that makes him almost understand what people are talking about when they talk about family.

> Nora: anyway, party's at the end of may. you don't even need to drive. metro north to greenwich or just go back to your roots and hire a car. dress code is generationally wealthy white people

> Simon: If I don't go, you know it isn't personal, right?

> Nora: yeah yeah whatever

Simon has nearly two months to wrap his mind around this, so he probably should reassure her that he'll be there. But he can't, so he just sends her a picture of Edie and tries to fall asleep.

IN THE MORNING, Jamie's up before Simon, which is a bad sign. He's lying in wait in Simon's kitchen, a full pot of coffee on the counter.

"Has Ken been in touch?" Jamie asks, which is a worse sign. Ken is Simon's agent.

"No."

"Okay, he's useless as usual, good to know."

"Hey—"

"So there was an article yesterday about *Tree of the Gods* and your name is mentioned."

Simon's face heats. That show made the worst day working with Charlie Blake seem like a peaceful visit to the library. The showrunner habitually screamed and threw things, which opened the door for every other sociopath on set to let loose. The lead actor was a Method pest who stayed in character in order to harass every woman under thirty-five and hurl insults at everybody else. Simon spent months wishing he'd gone to law school.

"That show ended eight years ago," Simon says. "Are they ever going to stop talking about it?"

"There are rumors about the second book finally getting adapted. That's why it's all getting dredged up."

Those rumors reappear every few years and never go anywhere, possibly because the entire former cast and crew are using the power of negative thinking to un-manifest it.

"Anyway," Jamie goes on, "it's the usual stuff about difficulties on set. Nothing you haven't seen before."

"Difficulties," Simon echoes. Jamie's being delicate. "What exactly does it say?"

"It mentions that you walked off set, and hints that now there are tensions behind the scenes on *Out There*."

Simon did walk off set while they were shooting *Tree of the Gods*, that much is true. But he'd bet the article says he stormed off set, which is—well, that's probably true too. His scene partner was crying, the showrunner was yelling at them, it was over a hundred degrees and his costume involved leather pants, and all Simon could think was that he needed to not be there.

Only after he got home—his ears still ringing, his nerves still jangling—did he realize he'd fucked up. He'd come back the next day, mortified.

Even before the first season aired, there were rumors about the set being toxic, full of feuding actors and drama queen behavior, probably because the show *was* full of feuding actors and drama queen behavior. The story about Simon walking off set—stripped of context so he was just a spoiled actor unwilling to take direction—fit that narrative and served as a handy illustration of why the show was behind schedule.

"I guess the implication is that I'm the common denominator," Simon says. "I'm impossible to work with."

Charlie's lecture about treating his coworkers decently feels even worse now than it had last night. Had Charlie read the article? Had everyone at Lian's read the article? They'd probably heard the stories already, so it shouldn't matter, but Simon wants to hide under a blanket and never come out.

Until now, he's assumed that all he needs to do is leave *Out There*, and the rest of his career will fall into place. He'll be offered some roles and at least a few of those will be interesting. Problem solved. But Simon isn't nearly enough of a draw to make up for being difficult to work with. Queasiness settles in his stomach.

"Anyone who's worked with you knows those stories don't mean anything," Jamie says, because he's loyal but deluded.

"A few weeks ago, I threatened to bite Charlie."

"On set?"

Simon nods miserably.

"Maybe don't do that again? For what it's worth, the article linked to an old story about Charlie getting into a bar fight."

That had been over six years ago, during *Out There*'s first season. The fact that Charlie's old sins are being dredged up too does make Simon feel marginally better. Getting into a bar fight is objectively worse than storming off set, right? Then he realizes he's judging his own behavior against Charlie Blake's and barely coming out on top.

"I'd tell you to call Ken," Jamie says. "But you'd do just as well to tell the dog."

"Jamie—"

"Or, like, write about it in your journal."

"I don't have a journal."

"And you hardly have an agent."

"I don't want to deal with any of this," Simon says. He's barely handling a basic, no-complications kind of day. Throw in anything else and he's hopeless.

"Ken or the bad press?"

"Yes?"

Jamie taps his fingers on the counter. He looks like he wants to say something but, in the end, he just starts making omelets. "Do you want me to email Ken?" he asks when they're eating. "I can cc you and say I'm your assistant."

Another thing that Simon doesn't want to deal with is that Jamie is, basically, his assistant. And, for the past few weeks, his personal chef.

"It's fine," Simon says. "Don't worry about it."

From an *Out There* fan Discord

GalactoseIntolerance: trying to figure out (1) if Simon Devereaux is actually a nightmare to work with and (2) whether I care

SupervillainApologist: I'm going with "probably" and "absolutely not" personally

SimonDevereauxsCheekbones: who is in here slandering my biological son simon devereaux

GalactoseIntolerance:

[link to *Variety* article]

HowlsMovingSpaceship: When "sources" talk about "tensions" on set, it feels like code for "in any other workplace HR and/or law enforcement would get involved" or "somebody's been sexually harassing somebody else"

DeathStarJacuzzi: nah, it can literally mean "someone was annoyed that craft services ran out of vegan options and made a cranky face about it"

SimonDevereauxsCheekbones: I don't know, it kind of makes me sad to think that actors on Out There hate one another?

SpacePope: That article was written in fifteen minutes by someone making twenty cents a word, maximum, and so they recycled two pieces of old news. That Charlie Blake bar fight story? Is six years old. In the last five years, he has no negative press unless you count people complaining about a badly tailored suit he wore to the Golden Globes last year.

DeathStarJacuzzi: that suit was worse than any bar fight

SpacePope: anyway, I wouldn't put too much credence in anything in that article

SimonDevereauxsCheekbones: I'm choosing to believe that if Simon stormed off set, it was to rescue a kitten, and that if Charlie got in a bar fight, whoever he punched just needed punching

GalactoseIntolerance: Can we talk about what on earth Simon Devereaux is even doing on Out There? Why is he on a show with a budget of like five cents instead of playing a sociopathic billionaire on HBO or a sociopathic vampire on AMC or a sociopathic line chef on Hulu? Everything he's done other than Out There is . . . fancy?

SpacePope: Lian Zhong, Out There's showrunner, was one of the writers on Tree of the Gods. My read is that she basically swept him away from that hellscape in a bridal carry and now he's loyal.

DeathStarJacuzzi: Fun fact, Lian Zhong is BFFs with Charlie Blake's agent, which also explains . . . a lot.

SimonDevereauxsCheekbones: BRB as soon as I update my red tape conspiracy wall

Chapter Four

After half an hour at the wrap party, Simon might bare his teeth at the next person who tries to hug him. His skin feels prickly with unwanted contact. The smell of perfume has lodged in that place behind his eyes where headaches start. The restaurant the production company booked is one of those places with too-high ceilings and terrible acoustics, where conversation dissolves into a buzz and there always seems to be a draft coming from somewhere.

Jamie gets him a glass of ice water with a lime wedge, which looks enough like a mixed drink that nobody ever asks him why he isn't drinking. Which, he does, but not when he's in an environment composed entirely of migraine triggers.

Wrap parties always have a little last-day-of-school energy, probably because of the combination of work finally being done and the knowledge that not everyone will be coming back. But this time it feels intense enough that Simon starts to wonder if other people know he's planning to leave, if all this hugging and earnest, teary-eyed, shoulder-grabbing I-love-you stuff is because they recognize it's the end of something. It's probably just the open bar making everyone act that way, but it makes Simon even more uncomfortable than hugging ordinarily does.

"Every party my parents went to," Jamie says, "my dad would

find the kitchen and start doing dishes. He never had to make conversation with anybody."

"Oh?" It's rare enough for Jamie to talk about his family that Simon's concerned they're about to have a heart-to-heart in public.

"I'm just saying you could do with a kitchen. Look, you don't need to do anything. You can't go to a party incorrectly. Just stand there and look pretty. Anyone who gets a chance to talk to you won't be paying attention to what you say."

Most people might not be reassured to hear that they're about to be objectified, but that's truly the kindest thing Jamie could have said. Simon squeezes Jamie's upper arm.

Something in the room alters, like the center of gravity shifted, and Simon doesn't even need to look to know that Charlie's arrived. Simon looks anyway. Charlie's wearing what he probably thinks of as nice jeans and a shirt with buttons. For Charlie Blake, this is basically a tuxedo.

Simon has on a dark suit, no tie, everything noticeably expensive and immaculately tailored—boring, except for the suit's deep plum color, dark enough to pass as black in pictures. Black but with a secret. And his shirt is lilac silk, unbuttoned just enough to be slightly louche. He's wearing barely tinted aviators to shield his eyes from the worst of the overhead lighting.

"You look like an old timey drug dealer," Jamie had said when they were leaving the house. "But in a sexy, upmarket, financially solvent kind of way."

"Thank you," Simon had said, touched.

"Wow," Jamie murmurs now. "I always forget what he looks like when he isn't wearing space clothes." Jamie means the vaguely military-inspired outfits Charlie wears on *Out There*.

Tonight, Charlie looks freshly scrubbed, like someone who could jump-start your car or chop firewood. If only he wore sweaters, he'd look like a plausibly rugged L.L.Bean model.

It's for the best—at least for Simon's peace of mind—that he doesn't wear sweaters.

"Don't worry," Jamie says, "you're still the prettiest princess."

As Simon watches, Charlie hugs someone, then someone else, holding them close while he speaks into their ear. He makes it look so easy, like he wants to be here, like he's genuinely happy to see all these people. Simon should look away—he should walk away—but he doesn't, and when Charlie catches his eye, his smile falters just a bit before it's back in place.

Simon winds up in a mind-numbing conversation with one of the producers. Out of the corner of his eye, he sees Jamie starting to fidget. Another five minutes of hearing about the producer's son's lacrosse team and Jamie will pull the nearest fire alarm.

This is why Jamie can't find steady work: he can't, or maybe won't, fake it. That, and he has a YouTube channel dedicated to making fun of movies. If you were trying to figure out the most efficient way to guarantee that nobody in this industry would ever hire you again, it would be fifty hours of footage of you mocking their friends' work.

This is also, probably, why he's Simon's ideal friend. Simon never has any doubt that Jamie sincerely enjoys being around him.

"Why don't you go and get us some more drinks," Simon suggests when the producer pauses to breathe. Jamie's gone before Simon even finishes the sentence, and Simon resigns himself to hearing more about the trials of having a child in a private school that costs sixty thousand dollars a year. It's not so different from the school Simon went to, so he really shouldn't judge. He's judging anyway.

Every minute or so, Charlie's booming laughter cuts across the buzz of chatter. Over the producer's shoulder, Simon sees Charlie talking to Jamie. This is fine. He's already decided it's fine. They know one another from when Jamie was on the show, and from dozens of events just like this one. But the other day, Simon told Jamie what he saw in Lian's backyard, reasoning that if Charlie's exes adore him, then he can't be a bad target for Jamie's rebound. If Simon feels weird about it, that's just because Simon feels weird about everything.

"There you are!" Lian says, coming up next to Simon and laying a proprietary hand on his elbow. "I'm so sorry, Will, but I need to steal him away." When they're out of earshot, she drops his arm and leans in close. She smells like champagne and is a little wobbly in her heels. "You're welcome."

He doesn't bother explaining that he's fine with boring conversations, because all he has to do is occasionally interject a syllable or two. She's clearly pleased with her rescue mission.

"Okay, what am I wearing?" Lian asks, holding her arms out.

What she's wearing is a black silk dress cut like a smock but with a lot of drape and a chic little tie at the neck. "Margaret Howell," he says.

She shakes her head, not because he's wrong but because she thought she'd stumped him.

"I've been trying to find a present for my niece," he explains. "And I happened to see it." It's partly true—he does need a graduation present for Nora, but he checks the women's collections of his favorite designers out of habit. Half the texts he sends his mother are links to clothes she might like.

"Lucky niece," Lian says, her smile broader than he's used to.

"You're wine drunk," Simon says, surprised by a wave of something like affection.

"I had an idea," she says into his ear. "It's about next season."

"I'm not—"

"I know, I know. That's what I have the idea about. I think you'll like it."

"We shouldn't talk about this now." Simon gestures at the sea of people around them.

"Call me tomorrow, okay?"

Someone comes up to them, and Simon doesn't have to turn his head to know it's Charlie. Maybe it's just that he's big enough to block the light, or maybe after seven years Simon's gotten used to the cologne Charlie wears whenever he considers it a fancy enough occasion to warrant shoes that aren't flip-flops, but either way, there Charlie is.

"I was looking for you," Charlie says. "Can we get a picture?"

Simon doesn't say anything because he assumes Charlie's talking to Lian.

"Simon?" Charlie asks. "Picture?" He holds up his phone, like the problem is that Simon doesn't know how pictures get taken.

"Why?" Simon asks automatically. Lian snorts.

Charlie frowns. "Why not?"

Simon can't come up with a good enough reason, so he puts on his work smile and lets Charlie take a selfie, but all the while he's suspicious. They haven't talked since Charlie lectured him in the car. But now Charlie's arm is around Simon's shoulders for reasons that have nothing to do with stage directions. It's strange to be this close when they aren't on set.

"He's up to something," Simon tells Jamie as they're getting ready to leave.

"I don't think Charlie Blake has ever been up to anything in his life."

"First that Instagram thing. Then he personally invited me to his party. And now this picture."

"Diabolical."

"Come on, he's never done any of that before."

"Maybe he's exhausted by all the psychosexual warfare and just wants to be normal."

Normal is out of the question for him and Charlie, and he needs to make Jamie understand this. "Just the other day, when he was driving me home—"

Jamie starts to laugh, loud and bright, and Simon throws his hands up in surrender. "Come on," he says. "Let's go to Charlie's party and get it over with."

SIMON'S NOT SURE what he was expecting Charlie's house to look like, but if he had to guess he'd have imagined one of those huge leather sofas that look vaguely inflated. Plenty of forest green. Probably a lot of the kind of art you only acquire when an interior decorator decides your walls are too empty. An over-reliance on ceiling lights. The design equivalent of cargo shorts.

There is a big leather sofa, but it isn't completely hideous. And there's plenty of art that somehow encompasses both dorm room prints and expensively framed generic-looking abstracts. For the most part, it looks like Charlie walked into a Pottery Barn and bought one of everything.

There are twenty people in the living room, and, from the sound of it, at least as many outside. People are relaxed, their feet up on the sofa, a pile of shoes near the door. This group is at home here, in Charlie's house, on his comfortable-looking furniture. Simon gets a few double takes when he walks in.

He shouldn't have agreed to come. He told himself he was doing it for Jamie, but Jamie is glued to his side like he's Simon's emotional support dog. The thought makes him wish he had Edie. Everyone would pet her and ask how old she is and compliment her sweater, and he'd hardly have to make any conversation at all.

"Go off and have fun," Simon tells Jamie, trying to sound like he means it. Through the open French doors, he sees Roshni on the patio, talking to a man he thinks is her husband. "Seriously. I'm fine."

Once Jamie is out of sight, Simon resists the urge to lock himself in the bathroom and do a crossword on his phone. These are people Simon sees every day—usually only for work reasons, and partly against his will—but still, he's used to them. They're used to him. It's fine. He's fine. He steps through the doors.

It's barely April, so the water can't be warm, but a dozen people are in the pool. It doesn't take much to identify Charlie as one of them. His hair, usually wavy and light brown, is dark and slick with water. His shoulders are—well. You'd think Simon would be used to the sight by now, but apparently not, because he has to look away.

There's an empty chair next to Roshni, and he sits in it before he can overthink whether she's saving it for somebody. "Now is the time to tell me about your children's tuition," Simon says, instead of being a normal fucking person and saying hello, "or why you think they should be captains of their lacrosse teams, because I had a lot of practice with those topics tonight. I have my lines ready. I'm off book."

"They're only two," Roshni says, "but I'll keep that in mind." She and her husband proceed to manage the conversation in a way that leaves Simon only needing to supply enthusiastic noises when they mention their twin daughters doing anything especially adorable, terrible, or clever. It shouldn't be a surprise that Roshni, who's never been anything but kind, is taking a little bit of care to make sure he's comfortable, or that she's married to someone equally kind.

"Is that Samara?" Roshni asks, looking over Simon's shoulder. Simon turns around to see Samara Jackson, who played a space diplomat on the first two seasons of *Out There*. After she left the show, she texted Simon to ask if he wanted to get coffee. Simon, aware that these offers don't actually mean anyone wants to have coffee with you, never responded.

Roshni waves extravagantly, even though she and Samara never worked together. Maybe they know one another from Charlie's parties, if Samara still comes despite not having been on the show in years.

He probably ought to say hello, but he doesn't have whatever it takes to walk a few yards and initiate a conversation with someone he hasn't talked to in five years. He's about to start feeling guilty about it when he hears the sound of someone dripping all over the patio next to him. It's Charlie, who apparently wrapped a towel around his waist without first using it to dry himself off, because beads of water cling to his shoulders and chest, illuminated by the strands of lights strung up overhead.

"You came," Charlie says.

"I did," Simon agrees. For a moment, they stare at one another. Simon stays perfectly still, like he's hiding from a *Tyrannosaurus rex* and not the existence of social norms. Then Simon remembers his manners. Or at least one manner. "Thank you for inviting me."

"I always invite you," Charlie says.

"I know, I just—" He doesn't know how to finish that sentence, because what can he say? He only agreed to come this time because—the truth of why he accepted Charlie's invitation hits him. He isn't doing this for Jamie. He's here because this is his last chance. Charlie won't invite him to any more parties because Simon won't be working on *Out There*.

"Thank you," Simon says. "You have a lovely home," he recites, rote, like it's a sentence he learned in a foreign language phrasebook designed for aliens wearing human skin-suit disguises.

Charlie's eyebrows shoot up, probably because Simon's being weird even by Simon's standards. "I have to . . ." Charlie says, then just stands there.

"Right." Simon's still looking up at him.

"Bye." Charlie hesitates another moment, then leaves.

"What was that?" Roshni's husband asks. Roshni starts talking about a book she wants Simon to read. Simon dutifully takes out his phone and orders it right away, because that gives him something to do.

After maybe twenty minutes, he knows he has to let Roshni and her husband talk to someone else. He makes an excuse and heads toward the kitchen, remembering what Jamie said earlier about his father hiding in the kitchen during parties. He can probably make himself look busy by getting a glass of water.

There's a side door from the patio that looks like it leads to the kitchen, probably through a laundry room or mud room for collecting wet bathing suits. He figures this is his best bet for a quick escape without running into anybody. The door is slightly ajar.

Once he pushes it open, though, he hears Charlie's voice. Or, rather, his laugh. It's quieter than usual, as if whoever he's talking to is very close. Simon steps through what turns out to be a laundry room and pauses at the door to the kitchen, steeling himself for seeing Charlie. But then he hears Jamie's voice, low and a little silky, and Simon *knows* that tone. Simon ought to go back out to the patio, but that might look strange to anyone who watched him walk through the door, so he's frozen in place.

Through the crack in the door, he can see one of Charlie's hands bracketed on the counter next to Jamie's hip. Behind them, a piece of kids' art hangs on the refrigerator door.

"Are you hitting on me?" Jamie asks, a little teasing.

"It's more like I'm making sure you know that if you hit on me, I'm good with it," Charlie says.

Slowly, making it obvious as hell and giving Jamie time to back off, Charlie lifts a hand and tucks a strand of hair behind Jamie's ear.

"I'm tempted," Jamie says, "but I'm trying to be a better person and I just don't think Simon would like it if I kissed you."

Simon doesn't like hearing that, largely because it's true. Maybe it's some old residual jealousy at seeing Jamie with someone else, but Simon feels hot and anxious at the sight of Charlie's hand resting on the counter near Jamie's hip.

Charlie takes a full step backward. "He said you weren't together anymore."

"We aren't."

"But he wants to be. Or you want to be."

"No, it's definitely not that."

"Oh," Charlie says, "he just wouldn't want you to hook up with me because he doesn't like me."

Jamie opens his mouth and shuts it almost immediately, then tilts his head to the side. "No," he says slowly, drawing the syllable out, "not that either."

Before Simon can figure out what Jamie means, he decides that it's time to make his exit. None of this is meant for his ears. He slips back out to the patio and hopes nobody notices him.

"I THINK I nearly kissed Charlie? Or something like that?" Jamie says as they walk home. They'd taken rideshares earlier, but it's too nice a night to get a Lyft for a five-minute walk, even if it's uphill the whole way to Simon's house.

"Why are you telling me?" Simon keeps remembering how Jamie said *Simon wouldn't like it*, and how he'd known right away that Jamie was right. But then why tell Simon about it?

Out of the corner of Simon's eye he sees Jamie turn his head to look at him, sharp. "Because I tell you everything? Besides, better to get it out in the open. Especially if it's something that could turn toxic, you know?"

Simon thinks of all the things he isn't telling Jamie—from how he's leaving the show to the way he feels on edge and twisted up when he sees his dishes stacked the wrong way in the cabinet. The knowledge that he's disappointing people is nothing new; even disappointing Jamie is nothing new.

They step into the street to avoid a bougainvillea whose branches are spilling across the sidewalk. It's late enough that the neighborhood is almost perfectly quiet, except for the chirp of crickets and the distant hum of traffic. The air is heavy with jasmine.

"It wouldn't be toxic," Simon says. "I mean—you don't need my permission or whatever." None of it feels like the truth, but he wants it to be.

"It's too messy, even for me. Fucking my best friend's work nemesis?" Jamie puts air quotes around *work nemesis*, like it isn't perfectly accurate. "If he were the man of my dreams, I'd probably do it anyway, let's be honest. But for a hookup? Big dumb golden retrievers aren't even my type. Not worth it."

Jamie's actual type is emotionally stingy and kind of mean, which is how he and Jamie got together in the first place.

They're in Simon's driveway now but he doesn't want to go inside. Some things are easier to say in the dark, side by side. "I know I'm not a picnic to live with. Or be near. Or—anything, probably. Just—thanks."

Jamie leans over and smacks a messy kiss on Simon's cheek. "Where'd that all come from?"

"I just—the past few months—" Simon doesn't know how to end that sentence that isn't a monologue of whining. He reaches out, just a little, from some sad old belief that a hug will make things better. He lets his hand drop, then sticks it in his pocket.

"Charlie's more of a rabid wolverine than a golden retriever," Simon says, and Jamie laughs.

Chapter Five

The next morning, Simon wakes to the sound of clattering coming from his kitchen. He finds Jamie using the stand mixer that Simon keeps forgetting he owns. Gobs of batter are all over the counter. Simon averts his eyes.

"I'm making pancakes," Jamie announces. "I don't even like pancakes."

Neither does Simon, but he takes one anyway and leans against a clean edge of the counter to eat it.

"So, I fucked up," Jamie says.

"Oh?" All Simon can think is that even though it's only nine o'clock in the morning, Jamie's somehow gotten back together with his ex.

"I told Charlie that I told you what happened last night, and now he thinks I outed him to you. I didn't want to tell him that you already knew."

"If something had happened between the two of you, did he think you wouldn't tell me?" Simon asks. He has some experience with super closeted actors. For a while, Simon was sort of seeing this guy from his old show, but even he wouldn't have expected Simon to keep him a secret from his best friend.

"I know! Maybe it was tacky of me to tell him that I told you, but

I was thinking that—well, anyway, I wasn't trying to stir up drama, I swear." He looks abashed, and Simon believes him.

"If he cares that much, he shouldn't be hitting on men in his kitchen when there are fifty people nearby."

Jamie pauses with a pancake on his spatula. "I didn't tell you it was in the kitchen."

"I was coming in through the laundry room," Simon admits, his face hot. "I was there for less than a minute."

"Hmm," Jamie says, looking at him very carefully. Simon resists the urge to hide behind his pancake. "Anyway, I feel like a bad gay. I know I'm a disaster along every possible axis but at least I've never outed anyone."

"And you still haven't."

"But he thinks I did."

Reasoning that if Charlie's been texting Jamie, he's definitely awake, Simon grabs Edie's leash and his darkest sunglasses and announces that he's taking her for a walk.

It isn't far, but Edie is old and her legs are only three inches long, so Simon carries her most of the way to Charlie's house. It would have been smarter to do this over the phone, but Simon can't handle another minute in the house with the kitchen in chaos.

Still, Simon should have texted to make sure Charlie was home and alone, which only occurs to him as he's walking up the driveway and steeling himself to ring the doorbell. But he's already probably triggered Charlie's doorbell camera, so he can't turn around now.

Charlie answers the door wearing a T-shirt with ARIZONA DIAMONDBACKS in faded script and which might have fit him at some point in his life, like maybe fifth grade, but is basically obscene right now.

"Simon," he says, looking exactly as surprised as anyone might when they see their least-favorite coworker on their doorstep on a Sunday morning.

"Are you alone?"

Charlie blinks. "Yes?"

"Jamie didn't do anything wrong."

"Okay. Come in?"

"I don't need—"

"You're letting all the cool air out."

Simon sighs and walks in. "Look, I saw you kissing that waiter at Lian's house." He takes off his sunglasses and tucks them into the neckline of his shirt.

"And you told Jamie."

Until now, Simon hasn't properly considered that maybe *he* outed Charlie. "Yes," he says. "I'm gay, Jamie's gay, and it didn't occur to either of us that a man who kisses other men in public would be so closeted that you need top-level security clearance to discuss that fact with a close friend."

Charlie scrubs a hand over his jaw. "It isn't. A secret, I mean. I'm not closeted," he says, a little defensively, like he thinks Simon would blame him for it.

"Fair," he says, instead of pointing out that you don't generally accuse people of outing you if you aren't closeted to some extent. He's here to clear Jamie's name, not to debate the gradations and nuances of outness. "Sure."

"Tell Jamie I overreacted. No, never mind, I'll tell him myself.

I can't believe you came all the way over here just to make sure I wasn't mad at Jamie."

"He's my best friend," Simon says. And then, "He's family," in case Charlie's the kind of person that means something to.

"And you brought Edie," Charlie says, getting onto one knee and holding out a hand to her. "Can I pet her?"

"Yes, Charlie. She's an elderly dachshund. She isn't going to hurt you."

"I didn't think she was going to hurt me. I just don't want to bother her."

The sight of Charlie's big hand scratching behind Edie's ears is a little more than Simon can take, so he glances around Charlie's living room. There are no beer bottles, no crumpled napkins, not so much as a stray pool towel. "You wouldn't know there was a party here last night."

"I had the cleaners come at eight this morning." Charlie's still kneeling, but he looks up at Simon and quirks a smile. "I always do. It gets rid of anyone who crashed."

That sounds like something Simon would do, or at least it would be if he had parties or allowed anyone other than Jamie to sleep at his house.

"What was going on with the pictures last night?" Simon asks before he can think better of it. "And the stuff on Instagram? Are you making fun of me in some way I haven't figured out yet?"

Charlie gets to his feet and crosses his arms in a way that threatens to rip that poor shirt apart at the seams. "When I want to make fun of you, I just make fun of you. For example, why are you dressed like a mime to walk the dog?"

Simon automatically glances down at himself. He's wearing

dark jeans and an orange striped boatneck that he stole from Jamie. The entire effect might be a little more Monaco Grand Prix 1955 than most people are comfortable with, but it barely even counts as a look.

"I run cold," Simon says helpfully, "in case you're wondering how a person can wear clothes that cover their entire body." He glances pointedly at the sliver of skin on Charlie's side where his too-small shirt has ridden up.

"Should I just take it off?" Charlie asks, too amused.

"Nothing I haven't seen a thousand times before. I'm contractually obligated to deal with your naked chest."

"Not anymore, you aren't. Anyway, with the pictures and stuff, I'm trying to do damage control in case people think it's my fault you're leaving the show."

"Why would anyone think that?"

Charlie laughs. "Why wouldn't they? People are going to hear your name, and they're going to think about *Out There*, and they're going to remember the last time they heard gossip about *Out There*, which was when I wrecked the trailer and went to rehab. Then they're going to remember every rumor they heard about us not getting along on set."

"They're just as likely to think that I got pushed out or that I flounced. There was an article in *Variety* last week."

"I saw it. It makes us both look shitty."

"Damage control isn't a bad idea. Not that I'm definitely leaving right now," Simon adds, not wanting Charlie to think he knows more than he does. "But one of us is going to leave eventually. What you did is a good start." Charlie preens a little. "If anyone looks us up, they'll see we interact. That's not what people do when they have longstanding professional grudges. But it isn't enough."

"Do you have a better plan?"

Simon absolutely does not, but he isn't about to admit it. "We have two weeks until I need to be in New York. I guess we should be seen together a few times. Lunch, maybe?" That isn't going to be enough either. He isn't sure how famous you have to be for pictures of you eating lunch to be so newsworthy they make the rounds, but Simon definitely isn't at that level. Still, it's a start.

They make plans to meet two days later for lunch at a restaurant that Charlie makes Simon pick because "you're the one with weird food issues." He isn't wrong.

"That place on Hillhurst and Price, the one with the patio?" Simon can't remember the name—he just keeps track of nearby restaurants that have outdoor seating so he can bring Edie.

"The one with the tiny pizzas or the one with the fancy fries?" Charlie asks.

"Fries." It shouldn't be a surprise that Charlie knows all the same restaurants. They're practically neighbors, after all.

Only when they're standing silently in Charlie's foyer, nothing left to say to one another, does it hit Simon that this was the first actual conversation they've ever had. Seven years of sniping and not a single conversation.

He scoops up Edie and makes an awkward retreat.

"As tempting as the offer is, no, I'm not coming on your friendship date," Jamie says. "I'm cooking."

There's a butter wrapper face down on the floor, eggshells in the sink, and four bowls on the counter, each containing something gloopy looking. Simon wants to hose the entire room down immediately, preferably with bleach.

"It's not a friendship date," Simon mumbles.

Jamie gives Simon a once over, pointedly pausing on each garment. Peach cotton shirt embroidered with tiny flowers. Cream colored pullover. Sandy twill pants. Penny loafers. A suede jacket that's too warm to wear but which Simon will bring in an emotional support capacity. Jamie's ability to communicate "you're wearing a mortgage payment's worth of subdued neutrals to eat sandwiches with your enemy" using only his eyes is kind of scary.

But all Jamie says is, "This is the best costume for today," and Simon tries to look like someone who isn't sagging with relief at the approval.

Simon gets to the restaurant promptly, which means he sits in his car from 12:50 to 12:59. But when the clock turns over to 1:00, Charlie's already there, sitting on a low wall outside the restaurant, wearing sunglasses and torn jeans, reading a paperback with a dragon on the cover. Somehow, in the past two days, Charlie's scruff has grown into an actual beard. Simon wasn't prepared for a beard.

"Oh, hey," Charlie says, pulling off his sunglasses. Inside, he flashes the hostess a smile that has Simon almost flinching from the sheer wattage of it. Simon's seen his fair share of that smile over the years, but off set and in broad daylight, it hits him like a mild concussion.

"Is that book any good?" Simon asks once they're seated, mainly because the sight of Charlie with a book is so incongruous that he has to say something. It's by a different author than the series Jamie was reading.

"Not as good as the other one, but not bad."

It turns out that "is that book any good" is the only conversational gambit Simon has to offer. Now that he's used it up, a hideous silence descends on the table. Simon reads his menu like it holds the secrets to the universe, instead of exactly the same sandwich and salad options it had the last dozen times he's been here. When the waiter comes to take their orders—a grain bowl for Simon, a hamburger for Charlie—Simon has to be reminded to let go of his menu.

"They didn't have anything on that entire menu you wanted to eat?" Charlie asks.

"I ordered—"

"If you have five substitutions, you're ordering off menu. Come on. That's asshole behavior. Even you know that."

Simon does not need to defend his food choices to Charlie or anybody else, but all his substitutions were mentioned at other places in the menu, so it isn't like he's asking for anything special. He's ordered the same thing a few times at this restaurant. The fact is he just doesn't have the emotional space for new food today, and since that sounds legitimately unhinged even in his head, he won't be sharing that fact with Charlie. "I'll leave a big tip," he says.

They descend into another long silence.

"So." Simon drags the syllable out just for the sake of filling dead air.

"So," Charlie agrees, and proceeds to say absolutely nothing else. And, seriously, this is all Charlie's fault because nobody who's ever met Simon would expect him to navigate his way through an awkward situation. Meanwhile, Simon has spent hundreds of hours watching Charlie smile and laugh and talk like it's *easy*. So, if you want to be technical about it, and Simon one hundred percent does, Charlie ought to be saying something instead of sitting there toying with the frayed edge of his T-shirt sleeve in a way that's very distracting but does nothing to improve the situation.

When Charlie's phone buzzes, he grabs at it, probably relieved to have something to do other than marinate in awkwardness. But when Charlie looks at the screen, his face falls.

"Expecting something?" Simon asks, not because he cares, but because he feels like he owes it to this little project to say something vaguely in the shape of a conversation.

"I was hoping it was my stepfather. It's been a few days, and he isn't picking up the phone or answering my texts."

Other than regularly scheduled phone calls with his mother, Simon doesn't call his parents or stepparents, but if he did, and they failed to answer in under three rings, he'd assume they were unconscious on the bathroom floor. He would literally call the police. He has enough sense not to say this out loud. "I'm not sure I've ever called my stepfather. My mother is the intermediary."

"He isn't with my mom anymore," Charlie says, which, yes, Simon could have guessed. Charlie would probably not be worried if he could simply have asked his mother whether her husband was alive and well. "And they were never married, so he isn't really my stepfather, but I don't know what else to call him."

In an interview Charlie gave a few years ago, and which Simon read in an incognito window on his browser, Charlie said he was raised by a single mother, and they moved around a lot. That's all he's ever said publicly about his family.

"If you think of him as your stepfather, he's your stepfather,"

Simon says, as if Charlie needs Simon's own personal blessing to call people whatever the hell he wants.

Charlie says nothing. Neither does Simon. Simon wonders if social anxiety can actually kill a person.

The waiter appears with their lunch and temporarily puts them out of their misery.

"This is good" and "Have you tried" get them through the next few minutes. When they wear out that line of conversation, Simon feels increasingly desperate. The problem, obviously, is that they're trying to be polite. When they're sniping at one another, conversation flows freely, but the entire point of this is to act like civilized adults in public.

"Want to see pictures of Edie?" Simon finally asks, opening an album on his phone.

Charlie drags his chair to Simon's side of the table. There's Edie in an array of sweaters, Edie pointedly ignoring every toy Simon ever bought her, Edie curled up on a pillow on Simon's bed.

Simon loves his dog with all his heart, but pictures of her living her ordinary, if highly photogenic, life are not interesting to anybody but himself. Charlie says all the right things, though, and Simon realizes he's seen Charlie do this before. Charlie bent over someone else's phone, admiring babies or pets or intricately decorated baking projects is not an unusual sight on set.

"Do you have pictures of her as a puppy?" Charlie asks. Does Simon ever. He opens that folder, and Charlie says things like "Look at her" and "I can't take it," and either he's a much better actor than Simon ever gave him credit for or he's just wildly wholesome. It has never once occurred to Simon that Charlie might be either wholesome or especially good at acting, so this is a very confusing moment.

Adding to the confusion is Charlie's forearm, resting on the table, and how he's leaning in the way people only do when they have no boundaries. Not that they're touching—whenever one of them moves, the other adjusts, preserving a firm inch of space between their shoulders, their arms, their hands.

"Your birthday's coming up, isn't it?" Charlie asks, apropos of absolutely nothing.

"It's next week," Simon says, startled into giving an answer instead of demanding how Charlie knows this. "I'll be thirty-four." Maybe if he keeps saying it out loud, it'll start sounding like a reasonable age for a person to be.

"Are you doing anything?" They're close enough that Charlie's voice is low, just for Simon, and Simon's trying not to have any thoughts about this whatsoever.

"I wasn't planning to. But since Jamie's there, we'll have dinner, I guess."

Charlie reaches across the table for one of the fries left on his plate. "You live together?"

The fact is, they practically do live together, except whenever Jamie moves out for a few months to live with some wretched boyfriend. "Sometimes," he says.

"Are you sure you aren't together? Or something like that? Because you said you weren't, and he said you weren't, but if you actually are then I'm going to feel like a dick for having hit on him."

Simon is annoyed that now both Jamie and Charlie have made this Simon's problem. What business is it of Simon's who either of them mess around with?

"There's nothing going on. Jamie's staying in the guest room. The two of you are adults and what you do is up to you. But," he adds, irritation giving way to something angrier, "he's just come off a bad breakup, and he deserves a hell of a lot better than he's gotten from anyone he's ever dated. If you do get involved with him, the bar is pitifully low but please try to clear it."

By the end he's whispering so nobody at any nearby tables will be able to make any inferences about Charlie's personal life. He doesn't realize exactly how far he's leaned in until Charlie turns his head and Simon has to practically lunge backward. He's still close enough to see the tiny crinkles starting to form at the edges of Charlie's eyes. It's unreal that nobody has ever told this man to wear sunblock.

"I wasn't going to date your friend," Charlie says, looking Simon dead in the eye, "or fuck him or do anything other than *briefly* flirt with him and occasionally ask him for book recommendations."

Hearing *fuck* from Charlie's mouth, low and at close range, isn't healthy for Simon's peace of mind.

"He has terrible taste in books, so good luck with that." Simon doesn't mean it as a joke, but Charlie laughs anyway. "What about that waiter at Lian's? You two aren't . . ."

"I wasn't just, like, making out with the waiter."

"You were definitely making out with the waiter."

"No, I mean we met on, you know . . ." Charlie taps his phone.

"The apps."

"Right. So when I saw him at Lian's and he seemed to want to go for it, I didn't want to act like I was too good for him. Like, there I am, semi-famous with my semi-famous friends, and there he is, washing Lian's dishes. I didn't want to be rude."

"You realize that fucking someone once doesn't mean they have a permanent subscription."

"I know!"

"It isn't like tenure."

"Oh my God, Simon, shut up."

"Would you have gone home with him, just to be polite?"

Charlie hesitates in a way that makes Simon pretty sure he would have done exactly that. "I mean, I wouldn't have been complaining."

Simon's face heats for no reason whatsoever. He takes a sip of his water.

When the check comes, Simon reaches for it, because paying for Charlie's lunch is easier than whatever math will be involved in sorting out who got what. He waves away Charlie's credit card.

"That's nice of you," Charlie says, sounding exactly as dubious as anybody should while calling Simon nice.

On the way out, they get stopped by two people. One of them is wearing an *Out There* T-shirt. Well—not technically *Out There*, but the symbol the space anarchists on the show use to identify one another. They don't even need to ask for a selfie before Charlie's offering one.

Simon rarely gets approached by fans. This is Los Angeles: people are used to minor celebrities. But Charlie's handling it with a practiced ease that suggests it does happen to him, and fairly often. It isn't like Simon's jealous—most of the time he doesn't want to be approached even by people he knows—but he kind of can't stand to watch Charlie handle it so smoothly, so happily, and in a way that will leave these fans feeling good about it. Simon's never managed that, not once, and Charlie's ability to do it effortlessly is just another annoying thing about him.

"I can't believe we saw both of you together," one of the strangers says, her hands clasped in front of her, like this has been a transcendent experience. And Simon's been a fan of things. He understands.

Simon smiles and leans in for a picture, trying not to think about Charlie's hand on his shoulder. Charlie signs some random piece of paper using a sharpie that he produces out of thin air, then hands it to Simon so he can sign too. Then Charlie compliments the girl's tattoos, follows her on Instagram, and follows her tattoo artist on Instagram, while Simon tries to remember where he's supposed to put his hands, what a normal facial expression feels like, how to cosplay as a functional person.

"You couldn't have *said* something?" Charlie asks when they're alone. "They'll think I'm holding you hostage."

"That is literally the best I can do," Simon says, and maybe he snaps a little, because when Charlie looks at him his eyes are narrowed. But something must be showing on Simon's face, because Charlie lets it drop.

From an *Out There* fan Discord

HowlsMovingSpaceship: So have Out There's producers or show-runners or whoever decided that "it's hot" is enough of a justification for whatever wild shit they decide to put on air?

HowlsMovingSpaceship: Because that's a tattoo of the Pegasus Coalition insignia on Charlie Blake's bicep. Needless to say, canonically it would be QUITE a plot twist if Luke West were affiliated with space communists

[image from *Out There* showing Charlie in character as Luke West with a ripped sleeve barely covering a tattoo]

SpacePope: holy shit what on earth

SpacePope: "It's hot" is an affirmative defense. Source: I went to law school

SpacePope: Although to be fair the Pegasus Coalition aren't space communists so much as anti-colonialist space warriors

HowlsMovingSpaceship: True, my bad

SpacePope: Do we think Charlie Blake understands the implications? I know three people with that tattoo and I've had to bail two of them out of jail MULTIPLE times but only for good reasons if you catch my drift

HowlsMovingSpaceship: I hate to say this but I don't think Charlie Blake has understood a lot of implications in his life. He strikes me as not exactly a thinker

SpacePope: oh god I feel really mean because he seems NICE. but yeah, same

Chapter Six

Simon's therapist—a semiretired seventy-five-year-old who works out of her home in Laurel Canyon and decided to let the entire concept of telehealth pass her by—wants him to sit with the discomfort. Instead of repeatedly counting electrical outlets and arranging objects at right angles and indulging every other whim his synapses throw at him, he's supposed to acknowledge the impulse and ride it out.

That is not working so well for Simon at the moment.

Hiding in his bedroom while Jamie uses every single bowl in the house to do a dry run of Simon's birthday cake, Simon looks into changing his ticket to New York. His sublet doesn't start until next week, but he could spend a few days at a hotel. Surely he can manufacture some reason why he needs to be there early.

But he won't lie to Jamie. Jamie would figure it out and then his feelings would be hurt, and he'd be even more hurt that Simon didn't tell him what was wrong. If Simon admitted that the kitchen mess bothers him, Jamie would stop making messes, but then Jamie would know that Simon is the kind of nightmare ingrate who complains about the mess someone makes while they *bake him a literal birthday cake.*

And the thing is, he wants the cake. He wants to like it, wants to be the kind of person who likes it. He wants to help Jamie make the cake and then sit on the sofa and judgmentally watch HGTV together without swatting away intrusive thoughts the entire time. He misses his old meds. They weren't perfect, but now he regrets every minute he didn't appreciate only being a moderate basket case.

So instead, he takes Edie on a walk. They've been doing this a lot, so many walks that she looks askance at her leash and also at Simon when he says the magic word *walk*. The sun is just starting to set, so the light is coming in at a brutal angle. He puts on his darkest glasses and hopes for the best.

If anyone asked, Simon would swear that when he bought his house, he didn't know Charlie lived less than half a mile away. He'd be lying, but he'd say it anyway.

It's just that he fell in love with the house. It's a 1930s Tudor with arched doorways and built-in bookcases so tall they need a ladder, and it's small enough to encourage his family to stay at a hotel when they're in town. He loves the house more than he dislikes Charlie.

Besides, it's not like they're next-door neighbors. They only bump into one another on the rare occasions that Simon's walking Edie while Charlie's out for a run. Once a month, maybe, because Edie isn't interested in exercise and neither is Simon. Still, in the four years Simon's lived here, he's learned to recognize Charlie from a hundred yards away. That gives him just the right amount of time to stir up a nice panic about what he's supposed to say or whether it's stupid to wave.

Tonight, when he realizes that the man jogging toward him is Charlie, his heart picks up immediately from the usual combination of irritation and reluctant attraction, but both of those things are now somehow informed by the experience of sitting too close at lunch. When they said goodbye outside the restaurant, it had been almost friendly, or at least closer to friendly than they've ever gotten. Maybe they trauma bonded over their failure to make conversation.

He attempts a smile that's maybe ten percent warmer than his usual "the social compact compels me to smile at my neighbors" smile.

Charlie stops running. "Oh, hey." He gestures at Edie. "Can I?"

"Of course."

Charlie kneels and holds out his hand to Edie, who sniffs it politely. His T-shirt is one of those fabrics that's supposed to wick sweat. It's soaked through and clinging. If Simon takes off his sunglasses, it's not because he needs an unimpeded view.

"I was going to text you," Charlie says, getting to his feet, "but I have to go to Phoenix tomorrow. I should be back in a few days."

"We're on a deadline here." Simon sounds peeved and insufferable even to his own ears.

"I still can't get in touch with my stepfather, so I'm going to go check on him. Or at least check on his house, maybe file a missing persons report. Shouldn't take too long."

And now Simon feels like a dick because missing relatives do take priority over whatever nonsense the two of them are up to. "I'm sorry to hear that."

"I've spent the day on the phone with every hospital in Maricopa County. Did you know that if you give someone's name, they'll tell you if that person is a patient? I thought that only worked on television. Thing is, if I call the cops to check on him, it's not gonna end well. So I'll just do it myself—"

"Okay," Simon says, because Charlie said that all in one rush, not pausing for air. He thinks about telling Charlie to take a deep breath, but Simon would personally knife anyone who tried that on him.

"I would've flown out tonight," Charlie says, a little defensive, "but there weren't any seats. I checked every airline that has a direct flight, and flying *standby* seemed—"

"All right," Simon says, taken aback. "Nobody's asking you to fly standby. Just go and find your stepfather and don't worry about the rest of it."

"Just don't worry, huh? How does that work out for you?" Charlie doesn't say it meanly, but he isn't joking either. There's something strange and tense around his eyes and the set of his jaw. Charlie isn't just worried, he's frantic.

Simon looks around desperately, like maybe he'll find a passerby who's more qualified to deal with Charlie's feelings than Simon is. But no, it's just the two of them, alone in a darkening street.

"Sorry," Simon says. "I'd be beside myself if anyone in my family went missing, even the ones I don't like." He has no excuse for adding that last detail except for how sheer proximity to Charlie's sweat-soaked T-shirt has put him into an altered state.

"There's another possibility, but it's stupid, so don't make fun of me." Charlie says this seriously, like he's afraid Simon's going to roast him about his missing stepfather in the middle of the street.

"Okay?"

"You could come with me. It'd be a shitty couple of days, but we could make it look like a vacation or something. We take a bunch of pictures, post them to socials."

Simon doesn't know what to say to that. He has loads of objections, starting with how spending a few days together will make them both homicidal and ending with his profound lack of interest in going to Phoenix.

But then he remembers what's waiting for him at home: a night of suppressing the urge to flick the light switches in multiples of three while wondering how long he'll feel like his kitchen is contaminated. The growing impossibility of hiding all this from Jamie.

The fact is, he'd much rather be annoyed by Charlie than by Jamie.

Besides, Charlie's right. A social media–documented trip is a good way to control the narrative about why he's leaving *Out There*. He has ten more days in Los Angeles. That's not a lot of time. This is probably their last chance.

"I told you it was stupid," Charlie says when Simon's been silent for too long.

"Let's do it."

"Really?"

"Unless you've changed your mind?"

"No," Charlie says, looking very much like a man who's changed his mind.

"Just tell me now, because if you're pissy with me because I barged in on your family emergency, you'll only have yourself to blame."

Charlie throws his hands up so suddenly that Edie takes a step backward. "I didn't change my mind! For fuck's sake. I'm just surprised that you'd want to come."

Want is not the word Simon would use. "What flight are you taking tomorrow?" He already has his phone unlocked.

Charlie tells him. Simon checks the airline app, but there aren't any seats left, not even in coach. "It's sold out."

They check a few other flights and they're full too. What on earth are all these people going to Phoenix for?

"Oh well," Simon says, certain that it isn't disappointment that he's feeling.

"We could drive," Charlie says. "I usually drive anyway. It's only six hours."

If filling the dead air during a half-hour lunch was bad, twelve hours round trip in a car will be excruciating, and that's not even counting whatever's waiting for them in Phoenix.

"When do you want to leave tomorrow?" Simon asks.

"Would six be too early?"

Six is a disgusting time to be on the road, but obviously Charlie wants to get there as soon as possible, and Simon isn't going to be so much of an asshole as to complain about that. "Unless you want to leave tonight," Simon suggests, because he has to offer.

"That would get us into Phoenix in the middle of the night. Someone will call the cops on us for breaking into Dave's house."

It was silly of Simon, really, not to immediately assume that any plan of Charlie's might involve breaking and entering. More fool him.

"Six o'clock, then." Simon walks home, trying to figure out exactly what he's gotten himself into.

Chapter Seven

"You know, not what I'd wear to drive through two hundred miles of desert, but okay," Charlie says when Simon steps out of his house. Charlie's leaning against his car, a bucket-size travel mug in his hand.

"Layers," Simon says with emphasis, because Charlie still hasn't grasped that this is the trick to looking civilized. He's wearing a tan leather jacket and a scarf and sunglasses, very twenties aviator, and he's pleased to have achieved this look on effectively four hours' sleep.

"Here." Charlie shoves the mug at him.

"Sure, Charlie, I'll hold your coffee."

"It's your coffee, dipshit. Just say thank you."

Then Charlie opens the trunk and loads in Simon's suitcase before Simon can point out that he could have done that himself.

In the car, Simon sniffs the contents of the travel mug.

"It isn't poisoned," Charlie says.

"Exactly what someone would say if they poisoned my coffee."

"For fuck's—it's your normal order, oat milk latte with no syrup."

Simon takes a sip. Maybe he shouldn't be surprised that Charlie knows his order. Charlie takes his own coffee black with four packets of plain white sugar.

"Thank you." Simon's mouth is strange around the words. Basic civility doesn't come naturally around Charlie.

"Don't hurt yourself there."

They're heading east, the rising sun blazing into their faces, so Simon puts on his darkest sunglasses, the ones he can barely see out of. He shuts his eyes, because it's six fifteen and all the coffee in the world isn't going to keep him awake.

When he opens his eyes, they're already outside the city. In fact, they're nearly in Palm Springs. The dashboard clock tells him he's been asleep for well over an hour. He peels his face off the window and sits up straight, trying to look like someone who wasn't just drooling all over his collar.

"Dolly Parton?" Simon asks, noticing the music coming from the car speakers. He can't remember Charlie ever putting on music before. They usually just sit in fraught silence, punctuated by occasional insults, until Charlie pulls into Simon's driveway.

"You have a problem with Dolly Parton, you can hitchhike back to—"

"I don't have a problem with Dolly Parton. Jesus. Calm down. I was just surprised because—"

"I deliberately put on a playlist that I didn't think would piss you off, and—"

"You're the only person in this vehicle who's pissed off," Simon says, aware that he sounds distinctly pissed off. "You're driving. You can listen to whatever you want. I have noise-canceling headphones if I get desperate."

"Fine."

"Also I like this song. I was just surprised because nobody ever plays it." Simon's not sure whether he's defending his taste in music or making sure Charlie knows he isn't bothered, or something in the middle.

"I think we're coming up on the last Starbucks for a hundred miles," Simon says a while later, checking the map on his phone. "So if we want non-gas-station coffee, this is probably our last chance, unless there's some other place you know about."

Charlie grunts in a way that Simon chooses to interpret as agreement.

"What do you want?" Simon asks. "I'll just order it now. Coffee with a bathtub full of sugar? Hot or iced? Some kind of muffin?"

"Iced. Largest possible size. And a slice of that lemon cake, if they have it."

Simon puts in the order. When he gets out of the car in the Starbucks parking lot a few minutes later, it's hot enough to take off his scarf and jacket. Charlie's watching him.

"Layers," Simon reminds him.

Charlie's wearing sunglasses, but he pushes them up into his hair just so Simon can see him roll his eyes.

Simon picks up their order and brings it out to where Charlie's leaning against the car.

"Thanks. I usually forget," Charlie says. "I wind up drinking cold, burned, gas station coffee in the middle of the desert."

Simon's about to tell Charlie exactly how disgusting that is, when a child materializes beside them.

"Hey there," Charlie says, immediately turning on his smile.

"Are you Luke West?" the boy asks. He looks older than Roshni's kids but not by much. Kindergarten, maybe?

"I'm Charlie, but it's my job to be Luke West on television," Charlie says, kneeling down. "And this is Simon, who plays Dr. Hale. Do you watch *Out There*?"

"With my dad," the kid says. There's something about the way he says it—proud, maybe, about getting to stay up a little late to watch a grown-up show—that makes Simon remember creeping into the living room in his footed pajamas to watch *Star Trek: Voyager*. It's a memory from the other side of the country, from before Simon was Simon, before he'd figured out how to keep himself safe, and it has no place in a sun-soaked California parking lot.

The kid's dad is inching closer, like he's waiting for an invitation, and Simon doesn't have a doubt in his mind that this guy sent his kid in first so Charlie and Simon wouldn't blow him off. Which, to be fair, would work on Simon, but he doubts that Charlie blows anyone off.

When the man asks for a picture, Charlie puts his coffee on the roof of his car and reaches for the man's phone. He subtly angles it so the car isn't in the shot. Simon leans in and smiles, then watches as Charlie discreetly reviews the pictures before handing the phone back.

"It's okay if you post them," Charlie says, zillion-watt smile still in place. That is, after all, the entire point of this trip, and pictures on other people's social media are only going to help.

Then Charlie gets into the car, effectively ending the interaction. It's all very smooth, very polite, even friendly, but Charlie did the whole thing on his own terms and in under two minutes. It annoyed Simon the other day at the restaurant, watching Charlie do this thing that Simon still can't get a handle on, but he tries to summon up something a little less petty. Charlie thanked him for the coffee, and Simon isn't going to let Charlie be better than him at whatever this is.

"I usually just flail," Simon says when they're in the car. "You're good at that."

"Nobody expects you to be friendly," Charlie says, his mouth full of poundcake.

"Oh, fuck you, Charlie. I was trying to be nice."

"So was I! What I mean," Charlie says, audibly wrestling his voice into something less frustrated, "is that friendly isn't your thing. You're—" He gestures in Simon's direction. "You're you. And that's not an insult. Or, like, not more than usual."

"I'm touched."

"What I'm trying to say is that people don't expect you to be a ray of sunshine. They want to be in your presence while you glower and chain-smoke."

"I don't smoke," Simon says, scandalized.

"Metaphorically."

"Do you know what a metaphor is, Charlie? Do you really?"

"You know, you're fucking impossible sometimes. All the time, actually. Literally every minute."

They aren't going to survive another four hours in this car if they're at one another's throats. Simon takes a sip of his coffee and a bite of his granola bar so he can't say anything. Charlie shoves the rest of his cake into his mouth, probably having the same idea. Or terrible manners. A flip of the coin, really.

"We should post a picture before we get back on the road," Simon says when he can trust himself to sound normal. "Or a video, or whatever."

Charlie takes out his phone. "Okay, come here. Closer. Lean

over the console, Simon. It's not going to work if you aren't in the picture." He wraps an arm around Simon's shoulder and hauls him in. "Smile, for fuck's sake. You look like I kidnapped you."

Simon rolls his eyes, but obviously he knows how to look like he's having fun on command, at least for three seconds. He pretends Charlie said something funny, glances at him, and laughs. He ignores the five spots on his upper arm where Charlie's fingers are holding him in place, pushes away the thought that in the past seven years, he's probably touched Charlie more than he's touched anybody else.

Charlie lets go, then holds out his phone to show Simon the pictures. Neither of them look like idiots. That's all that matters. "Fine," he says, then waits while Charlie types out a caption and posts it.

Charlie backs out of the parking spot, looking over his shoulder, his hand on the back of Simon's seat. He has to be the only person under sixty-five who does that. Simon's used to it, used to the way Charlie's hand sometimes brushes Simon's shoulder, used to the way Charlie swears under his breath at pedestrians who walk behind the car, used to a lot of things that he probably doesn't need to have any feelings about.

"I can drive," Simon offers once they're on the highway and there's no chance of Charlie taking him up on the offer.

"You don't need—"

"If you don't want me to drive your car, that's fine, but I've never been in an accident and—"

"Driving keeps my mind off shit. Also no offense but I'd like to get to Phoenix today and we both know you'll go fifty-five miles an hour the whole trip."

"Have it your way," Simon says, magnanimous, and settles back in the seat, his eyes closed. He can probably get in another nap or two before they reach Phoenix. It could be worse.

"I haven't had an accident either," Charlie says after a minute. "Not since I was seventeen, at least. And I know you're gonna bring up that thing where I backed into the director's car, but that was on purpose, so it doesn't count."

This was the same director Charlie dumped the coffee on. Charlie rammed his old truck into the guy's Tesla. The cops had shown up on set. So had Lian, who'd missed a week's worth of drama because one of her kids had gotten her appendix out.

"He called Alex feisty and told Samara to stop being so aggressive," Simon says. "And he helpfully reminded me at least ten times that Jonathan Hale is not A Gay and so I should butch it up. I didn't shed any tears over his stupid car."

"Really?" Charlie drums his fingers on the steering wheel.

"Has it somehow escaped your attention that I'm an extremely petty man?"

"No. I mean—you aren't . . ."

Charlie is apparently trying to be nice again, and Simon decides that it's time for some positive reinforcement. "I very much am. It's a feature." He takes a deep breath. "It shouldn't have gotten to that point. I knew he was toxic—"

"Abusive."

Simon swallows, because Charlie's right. He tries not to think about what role his silence played in the entire mess. "It's just that it wasn't as bad as things on *Tree of the Gods*."

"What the fuck, Simon? It's not, like, an abuse contest."

"No, fuck you, I mean that I think I was maybe a little desensitized to, uh, hostile workplaces. I was so glad *Out There* wasn't a total shitshow, and I didn't see how bad things were that week. Or I didn't want to." The truth is that Simon knew he couldn't handle another situation like *Tree of the Gods*. He would have quit, left town, and let his middle brother set him up with some non-job at his investment bank.

"Alex said that was probably what happened."

It makes Simon a little queasy, both at the idea that Charlie and Alex have talked about this, and the implication that Alex had to make excuses for Simon. There's also, in the tightness of Charlie's jaw and the dryness of his voice, the suggestion that Charlie didn't agree with Alex—that Charlie thought Simon didn't object to anything that director said.

"I thought you were the problem," Simon says, because *honestly*. He isn't going to pretend that Charlie was a saint. "When I agreed to do the show, Lian said it wouldn't be like *Tree of the Gods*, and all I could see was that she let you—you know."

"Show up blitzed? Nearly fuck everything up for all of us?"

Really, it was the trailer-punching that set Simon's alarms off. The coffee incident and rumors of bar fights didn't help. But that isn't the point.

This is where a better person would apologize—for misjudging Charlie or for being so in his head that he couldn't see what was happening around him.

"It was a long time ago," Simon says, which is obvious and meaningless and dumb. But Charlie just hums in a way that doesn't sound overtly hostile so maybe he understands what Simon's trying to say.

THE LANDSCAPE SHIFTS to reds and browns, set into relief by scrubby bushes on the side of the road and the bright blue of the sky. There are no more billboards for casinos and furniture outlets, no more palm trees. The highway dwindles to two lanes, stretching out across a terrain that Simon only knows from that week they needed to shoot a space desert on location and the time he picked Jamie up at Coachella. Except for the cellphone towers, it looks like a faded old postcard. Greetings from the wrong side of Joshua Tree.

"It's like this for the next three hours," Charlie says.

"How often do you do this drive?"

Charlie's quiet for a moment, drumming his fingers on the steering wheel. A muscle in his jaw ticks. "Not as often as I'd like."

Simon's phone buzzes, which means Jamie's up. He's sent a picture of Edie refusing to look at her breakfast, her head pointed away from the bowl, her nose in the air.

"Edie is on a hunger strike," Simon says, mostly because three hours of silence is not okay and dogs are a safe topic.

"Will she be all right?" Charlie asks. Simon has the impression that he'll turn the car around if Simon says so.

"She gets like this whenever I travel. She'll eat, but first she needs to make sure Jamie knows he isn't her real dad."

"Is that normal? Alex's dog doesn't do that."

Simon tells himself that Charlie isn't accusing him of animal abuse or implying that Edie is a psychopath. "Alex's dog is a hundred-pound lab mix who was raised by a normal, well-adjusted person. Edie is an overbred dachshund who was raised by me. They are not the same." Also, Alex's dog has, at most, one functioning brain cell, but Simon doesn't mention this in case Charlie won't recognize it as a compliment.

"Edie is perfect just the way she is," Charlie says.

"Nobody said she wasn't."

"I swear to God, Simon, if you start a fight over us both agreeing that your dog is perfect—"

"I'm not fighting!" Simon throws his hands up. "You know, I think our whole problem is that you take my bitchiness personally. I'm like this with everyone. You aren't special."

"Jesus Christ," Charlie mutters.

Simon takes his book out of his bag and attempts to read, but he keeps reading the same sentence over and over. This book requires thinking, something he's never been great at when Charlie's around.

"It isn't true, you know," Charlie says.

Simon gives up, closing the book. "What isn't?"

"You aren't mean. You're mean to *me*, but not in general. Usually you're quiet. Like, really quiet. You can't be bitchy if you don't talk."

"Not with that attitude."

"Alex thinks you're nice."

"Slander. And we both know Alex would never describe someone she liked as *nice*."

"Simon. You fucking idiot. Alex is your *friend*. She's been your friend for *seven years*."

Working together isn't the same thing as friendship, but Simon isn't going to be the one to explain this to Charlie if he doesn't already grasp the difference. Still, he remembers how he felt at Lian's, that sense of almost belonging. If they all actively hated him, they'd have figured out a way to avoid spending extra time with him. Maybe.

It occurs to him that if Charlie hated him, he'd have figured out a way not to spend six hours trapped in a car together.

It also occurs to him that if he hated Charlie, he maybe wouldn't be here either.

But, no. Simon is capable of nuance. It's never been about hate. He doesn't hate Charlie. He resents Charlie. Charlie annoys him. A lot of people annoy him. The whole reason he agreed to this trip is because Jamie, his favorite person, is on his last nerve.

"You aren't special," he says again, because it feels crucial that Charlie absorb this information. It might be crucial for Simon to absorb this information too, but that's a thought for later.

He makes another effort with his book. It's the one Roshni recommended. It contains zero dragons and zero implied dragonfucking, thank you very much. He is a man of sophisticated tastes.

He manages to finish the paragraph, but his eyes keep drifting to the left. Even though the road is straight, Charlie keeps adjusting his hands on the wheel. He's even more fidgety than usual.

Simon, having spent seven years learning the most efficient ways to press Charlie's buttons, knowns that all this fidgeting and jaw clenching is a sure sign he's getting pissed off. Based on how frequently he glances at the blank screen of his phone where it rests in the console, Simon can guess why. It turns out there's no satisfaction in watching Charlie get annoyed if Simon isn't the one making it happen.

Whenever Charlie shifts his hands, the muscles in his upper arm move, and the tattoo on his biceps becomes this mesmerizing presence in the corner of Simon's eye. Charlie got that tattoo between second and third season. At first glance it looks like a vine, or maybe barbed wire, but when you pay attention, you see that it's clusters of stars and planets.

"You haven't turned a page in forty miles," Charlie says.

"Well, that's about fifteen minutes the way you're driving." Simon doesn't actually have any complaints about Charlie's driving; he's just being difficult because that was Charlie's shit-stirring voice and Simon knows how to give an audience what they want.

"Because I'm doing a hundred and sixty miles an hour? In my Audi SUV?"

"Maybe I'm a slow reader. Maybe you hurt my feelings."

"Maybe you just hate that book."

"I kind of do." Simon sighs and closes the book again. "It's the book's fault for being so boring."

"I'm telling you, read *A Scorched Land*. Download it. It's like $4.99."

"I hate ebooks."

"Of course you do."

"The backlighting gives me headaches."

"Then get the audiobook." Charlie waves a hand at the car radio. "Or don't, actually, because I already have it." He unlocks his phone and hands it over. Simon scrolls through four chaotically disorganized pages before finding the audiobook app.

"I didn't agree to any of this," Simon says as he opens the book and starts it from the beginning.

Chapter Eight

They're still in the middle of the desert when houses start to appear. Before Simon's ready for it, Charlie's taking an exit.

Simon's experience of the world is mostly confined to a couple of affluent zip codes in California and the greater New York area, cities in Europe that have fashion weeks, and various beachy vacation spots.

He isn't avoiding the rest of humanity out of snobbery—which he's sure of because there are plenty of things he does avoid out of snobbery. It's just—new things make him uncomfortable, and since his baseline level of comfort these days is a two out of ten, maybe it isn't a terrible idea to do what it takes to prevent that number from sinking any lower.

The neighborhood Charlie turns into is rough, not just by Simon's standards. The lawns are a mix of dry dirt and weeds. A couple houses have boarded up windows.

"I tried to buy him a nicer house," Charlie mutters. "That didn't go over too well."

"Not judging."

"Yeah, right."

For the past half hour, Charlie's been cracking his knuckles, rolling his shoulders, gripping the steering wheel so hard his fingers go white. He's grinding his teeth loudly enough that Simon can hear it. He's worried, and if there's anything in the world that Simon understands, it's worry. After six hours in the car together, Simon can't just sit idly by, so he aims for distraction.

"When my mother tried to buy me a nicer house, I didn't talk to her for three months." This is a lie. Simon and his mother exchanged perfectly cordial texts and had their usual semi-monthly phone call in which they take turns monologuing at one another, but in his heart, Simon wasn't talking to her.

"Your house went for over two million dollars. What the fuck."

"Did you look up my house on Zillow?"

"Obviously."

Simon snorts. "This was before I bought the house." He'd been living in a perfectly nice condo in West Hollywood, but Simon's mother had been Concerned.

Charlie turns into a driveway that already has an ancient car parked in it, propped up on concrete blocks. Simon isn't totally sure about his role in this whole operation, but when Charlie gets out of the car, Simon follows.

It seems like a bad sign that the rusty mailbox next to the front door is overflowing. Charlie rings the bell anyway and radiates impatience for thirty seconds. Then he goes around the side of the house, uses his bare hand to scrape through the dirt in a cement planter, and returns with a key. "Fucker's hidden his key in the same place for twenty years."

Simon is absolutely abetting a felony right now. The only reason he isn't actively having a panic attack is the sheer novelty of crime.

When Charlie opens the front door, they're blasted with hot, stale air.

"Dave?" Charlie calls. "It's Charlie!"

Until now, Simon has managed not to think too hard about what exactly Charlie's expecting to find here, but he'd like to imagine that if there was any real possibility of—say, just for the sake of argument—a dead body, Charlie would have called emergency services days ago. Still, Simon stays by the front door while Charlie heads into the house, calling his stepfather's name.

Then, feeling like an asshole for letting Charlie find whatever there is to find—which is not a body—on his own, Simon begins to look through the other side of the house. The kitchen and living room are a mess, but there's nowhere amid the heaps of clutter a person could possibly be hiding. Through a pair of dusty sliding glass doors is an empty backyard. Well, empty of people. Three cats are perched on a concrete wall. Gas cans and oddly shaped bits of metal are strewn across the patchy lawn.

Inside, Simon looks at the dishes in the sink, the pile of newspapers on the coffee table, the loose paper clips and unemptied ashtrays and stray pieces of paper. He tries to push them to one tidy corner of his mind. They're none of his business. It's boiling in here, so he takes off his sweater and folds it neatly before putting it in his bag.

"His truck isn't in the driveway," Charlie says, coming into the living room. "And the AC is off, which means he probably planned to be out for more than a few hours."

"Has he ever done this before?"

"No."

"If he was going on a trip, who would he have told?"

"He doesn't really have friends. I checked the garage's Facebook page and messaged a few of the people who've interacted with it, but nobody got back to me. I think they're dead."

"Oh," Simon says, taken aback.

"They're classic car people. Average age is like eighty."

"How old is Dave?" Charlie's twenty-seven, so Simon's been assuming his stepfather must be in his fifties.

"Sixty something." The words come out strange. Charlie's fists are clenched and his face is red. This is how he looked all the time that first season, but back then Simon chalked it up to whatever array of substances Charlie was on, and also to Charlie being a giant asshole. Now, he's pretty sure that what he's seeing is anxiety, maybe the beginnings of a panic attack.

"Okay, you're going to sit down and have a glass of water and a snack, then we'll knock on the neighbors' doors and see if they know anything."

"Can't eat Dave's food," Charlie says in that same strained voice. He tugs at the collar of his T-shirt.

And, okay, there's a lot to unpack there, but for now Simon gets a granola bar out of his bag and Charlie's own water bottle from the car. He's expecting a fight, but Charlie drinks the entire bottle of water and eats the granola bar.

If someone hovered over Simon while he was freaking out, Simon would hate them forever, and since he and Charlie are just barely being cordial, he decides to play it safe and make himself scarce. Figuring that Charlie's mental state can't possibly be helped by it being at least eighty degrees in this house, Simon finds the thermostat, then fiddles with it until he hears the air conditioning turn on.

The house has two bedrooms. One contains an unmade bed, a full laundry basket, and an old television. The other has nothing but weight equipment that, even from the doorway, Simon can tell is covered in dust. There's no trace of a child ever having lived here.

There are no photographs anywhere in the house. Back in the living room, there's a bookshelf with a dozen or so Clive Cussler and John Grisham paperbacks, none more recent than twenty years old. There's a dog collar, just sitting there on the shelf, even though there's no other sign of a dog. Everything is covered in a layer of nicotine-tinged dust. It's like the set designers went overboard staging a lonely old bachelor's house.

"My hands are tingling," Charlie says. "That's new."

"This sort of thing happen often?"

"Been awhile."

"Does anything help?"

"Gotta ride it out. Distraction's good."

And that isn't exactly Charlie asking Simon to distract him, but it's close. "Don't look now, but three of the fattest cats I've seen in my life are staring at us through the back door," Simon says. Charlie, of course, looks immediately.

Small talk isn't a skill Simon has, but it's the only means of distraction he can think of, so he tries to imagine what Jamie would say. Jamie has a way of stringing together random observations into a narrative that blends into something like ASMR.

And so Simon reminds himself that he's an actor and sets about channeling Jamie. He narrates everything he does.

"I'm getting the mail," he says, as he steps outside and empties the overstuffed mailbox. "It's just bills and coupons." Next to the mailbox, hidden behind an empty planter, are a pile of rolled up newspapers. Simon counts six. He brings it all inside and stacks it neatly on the counter. The whole time, he keeps up his stream of dumb commentary about feral cats and junk mail and the sheer variety of allergens he's noticed in this house.

"Based on the newspapers, he's been gone six days," Simon tells Charlie.

Charlie nods, as much as he can with his head in his hands.

"Hey, this is probably a stupid question, but would your mother know where Dave is?"

"I texted her. She asked Dave who. So, no."

So much to unpack.

"What if he went on vacation and I'm being messed up about it for no reason?" Charlie asks.

"Wouldn't he answer his phone if he were on vacation?"

Charlie shrugs. "Probably."

Simon currently has over two hundred unread texts on his phone, mostly from group chats that he's not invested in and likely only got added to out of politeness. He hasn't listened to his voicemail since 2018. He's not exactly a shining star of keeping in touch with people. But he'd like to think that if someone called repeatedly, he'd respond. If Charlie's stepfather went on vacation and just turned his phone off with no warning, he's an asshole of a caliber that Simon can't even aspire to.

"Do you want to sit for another minute or go knock on some doors?" Simon asks when Charlie's hands finally unclench.

They knock on the doors of the six closest houses. A young woman holding a baby doesn't know who Dave is but wishes whoever lives in that house would get rid of the car that's up on cinder blocks. An older woman squints at Charlie and says she hasn't seen Dave's truck in a week—or, at least, that's what Charlie tells Simon after translating from Spanish. Nobody else answers the door.

As they walk back to Dave's house, Simon clears his throat. "Not to be grim—"

"I'm already there," Charlie says.

"You mentioned calling the hospitals. Did you call the police?"

"He'd hate having the cops in his business."

"He should have thought of that before deciding not to answer his phone," Simon snaps. "I mean," he says, softening his tone as much as he can, which isn't much, "either he's okay or he isn't. If he isn't, then he should be grateful that someone wants to help. If he's fine and just decided to fuck off, then he's a dick and he deserves what he gets."

Simon half expects Charlie to tell him off, but instead he just looks sad. "Yeah," he says. "Yeah, that makes sense."

"Before we even think about going to the police, we need lunch. Do you know anyplace near here or should I find something?"

"Do you like tacos?"

"Everybody likes tacos."

Charlie gives him a skeptical look, which is a huge improvement over anxious and tragic, so Simon will take it.

"I THOUGHT YOU were vegan," Charlie says as soon as they order.

Simon makes a so-so gesture with his hand. "Some cheeses and meats can cause migraines." This is true, and it's a good enough answer, so he could leave it there. But today he saw Charlie have some kind of panic attack, and he's inadvertently gotten some insights into Charlie's life that Charlie would probably prefer he didn't have. It feels like the scales have tipped uncomfortably, and if Simon doesn't even them, he'll lose the game of honesty chicken they're playing. Or that Simon is playing, at least. "Actually, my doctor doesn't think my migraines have anything to do with food. Caffeine doesn't even trigger them."

Charlie's slouched in his chair, a baseball cap pulled low on his forehead, his legs stretched out so far they're practically under Simon's chair. "What does trigger them?"

"Stress, allergies, bad sleep, skipped meals. Bright lights. But I avoid the foods anyway, just, like, as a show of good faith in case the universe is paying attention."

Saying it out loud like that—which he's never done except to his therapist—makes it sound even less rational than it already is. He's fully expecting Charlie to point this out, but instead Charlie just tilts his head and says, "Yeah, makes sense."

"It really doesn't."

"I mean, it makes sense that you'd want to control the things you can control."

Which is almost exactly what Simon's therapist says. It's also what she says about the rest of his rules, more or less.

Their food comes, and Charlie doesn't make fun of Simon for eating his fish tacos with a fork and knife.

It's a hole-in-the-wall restaurant, with stacking vinyl-cushioned chairs that have been repaired with duct tape and Formica tables with wobbly legs. The menus look hand-laminated. The tables are all occupied, and there's a steady stream of takeout orders being picked up at the counter.

"You ordered something from the menu," Charlie says.

Simon bristles. "There's a difference between a restaurant that sells twenty-five-dollar salads and a family taco place." Besides, fish tacos are basically fish tacos, no surprises, no matter where you get them.

"We used to come here all the time," Charlie says.

"You and Dave?"

Charlie hesitates. "Yeah. Sometimes my mom. One of my foster homes was just a few streets over, but we didn't come here." He's looking at his plate, only throwing a glance at Simon when he gets to the end.

Simon's never heard Charlie mention foster care. That isn't a surprise—most people don't go around talking to their least favorite coworkers about potential minefields of childhood trauma.

What's surprising is that Charlie's mentioning it now. Simon knows his reaction is important, but he doesn't know what the right reaction is. He doesn't want to alienate Charlie—the extent to which he doesn't want to alienate Charlie is something Simon's going to think about later. Like, maybe next month, when he's in New York. Maybe never.

The right answer is something like "Thanks for trusting me with that information," but Simon would need a solid hour with that before he could deliver a convincing line reading. If he tried now, it would come out somewhere between sarcastic and unhinged.

"Yeah?" It isn't exactly a meaningful response, but he nudges Charlie under the table, just a tap of his shoe against Charlie's ankle. He doesn't know what that tap means, or what he wants it to mean, just that he hopes Charlie figures it out.

"Yeah," Charlie says, kicking him back, very lightly. He isn't looking at his plate anymore, but at Simon, with an expression that Simon can't decipher, something that looks like a question.

There are years of irritations and grievances between them, built up like barnacles, a crust of ill will that makes it impossible to make out the shape of whatever's underneath. Simon can start to see it, though, and wants to look away.

Simon disentangles his leg from Charlie's when the waitress

comes to take away their plates. "My dad watches your show every week," she says, bending a little to peer under the brim of Charlie's cap.

"Is your dad Manuel?" Charlie asks, big smile in place.

"Manuel's my uncle."

"You tell your uncle he has the best taqueria on the west side. I used to come here after school."

She gets a calculating look. "Okay, so, you can say no, but would the two of you take a picture in front of the sign? Manuel will do something embarrassing with it, like put it on the website, but he'd love it."

Simon shrugs when Charlie raises his eyebrows at him. His face has been used to sell worse things than tacos.

They go outside to stand in front of the sign in the window. Charlie takes off his hat and Simon takes off his sunglasses.

"You should do the GIF," the waitress says.

"Which one?" Simon asks.

He's run across three GIFs that escaped containment from the fannish parts of the internet. One is mostly Simon. He's just rescued Charlie from space prison using math and the power of his intellect, and now he's demanding the heads of Charlie's captors. The GIF is Simon looking furious, one arm around a battered Charlie. The text reads "Just one? As a treat?"

Another GIF is Charlie excitedly explaining something while Simon examines his nails.

And the third—

"The space ghosts," the waitress says.

The context is that Simon's been taken over by dead aliens, and Charlie is shaking Simon's shoulders in a futile effort to get rid of the ghost. That episode had been fun to shoot—Simon always relishes a chance to be the villain.

Simon looks at Charlie. He might not want to reenact *Out There*'s gayest moments for a live audience, even in the service of good tacos. But Charlie just nods knowingly. "That's a good one. Simon?"

They get into position. Angela, the waitress, has no scruples about bossing them around, and enough confidence to make them both do whatever she says.

Charlie takes hold of Simon's lapels and gives him the world's tiniest, gentlest shake. When they were filming that scene, Simon nearly demanded a stunt double, Charlie had shaken him so hard. And here, outside a taqueria, after six hours in a car and two hours in an empty house, he's holding Simon like he's made of glass. The disparity strikes Simon as hilarious, and he starts to laugh.

"Space ghosts don't laugh," Charlie says, low, in Simon's ear.

Simon tries to rein it in, not very successfully.

"They don't giggle either," Charlie says.

"Take it back, I'm not giggling," Simon says while Charlie shakes him a little.

"No, shut up. We just need one good take," Charlie says, and he's shaking Simon's shoulders now. "Get it together, Hale!" he says in his Luke West voice.

Turns out Simon can't laugh and keep his balance, because he trips a little. Charlie gets an arm around his back almost instantly. Simon's holding on to Charlie's arms, which isn't even remotely necessary—not for this scene they're reenacting, and not to avoid the fall.

He catches Charlie's eye, which was the wrongest possible thing to do, because the look that passes between them is ... warm. It's no different from what Simon's seen in the eyes of all the other people who've been interested in him.

Simon knows what he looks like. Being sufficiently attractive is eighty percent of his job. It doesn't mean anything that Charlie noticed.

But this is Charlie Blake, and Simon's looking back.

Simon has to catch his breath because there's no way Charlie can look at him without seeing seven years of flaws and resentment, but Charlie's still looking at him like that. All the gears in Simon's brain grind to a halt as he tries to process the truth of this.

"Okay," Charlie says, letting go of Simon and taking a step back so quickly that Simon nearly stumbles again. "You guys can post that wherever you like. Go wild."

Chapter Nine

"A two-bedroom suite is always three times as nice as two single rooms," Simon explains as he unlocks the door to the hotel room he booked on the way from Dave's house to the taqueria. The real reason Simon wanted the two-bedroom suite is that he isn't sure Charlie ought to be left alone tonight. He's gone quiet and fidgety again.

The plan is to kill some time, order room service, go to sleep, and then in the morning—theoretically well-rested and less stressed—Charlie will go to the police station and file a missing persons report. Maybe by then, one of the old men Charlie contacted will get back to him with some idea of where Dave is.

"See," Simon says when they're standing in the main room of a fairly standard suite in a slightly upmarket chain hotel, "the kitchen is much better than in a single."

"You plan on a doing a lot of cooking tonight?" Charlie asks. It's the first mean thing he's said in hours, and it takes Simon about three full seconds to clock that Charlie isn't being mean at all. He isn't exactly smiling, but he looks like maybe he thinks it's funny that Simon is pleased about a kitchen he'll only use to brew stale hotel coffee.

Simon puts his bag in one of the two mostly identical bedrooms and shuts the door, then unpacks exactly what he'll need for the next twelve hours: phone charger, pajama pants and a T-shirt to sleep in, that book he's never going to finish, some clothes for tomorrow. In the bathroom, he lines up his lotions in the correct order.

There's something about the closed universe of one suitcase and one hotel room that makes Simon's brain shut up for a little bit. It's not that his house makes him anxious so much as it is that in new places his brain hasn't figured out what to be anxious about.

He takes a shower. When he comes out, he sees that Charlie has already done the same thing. He's sprawled across the living room's single couch, his hair wet, wearing sweatpants and a T-shirt.

"Edie already caved in and ate the scrambled eggs Jamie made her for dinner," Simon tells him.

"Is she going to be mad at you when you get back?"

"Oh, she won't talk to me for days."

Charlie grins. "Does she usually talk to you?"

Simon gives him the finger.

"Come on," Charlie says, getting to his feet. He stretches, and since he doesn't know how to buy clothes that fit, his shirt rides up. Simon doesn't bother looking away. "We need to watch some basic cable."

"Why on earth would we do that?"

"Because we're at a hotel. Gotta watch some weird television as part of the experience. Gotta use their remote control and see ads for local news teams."

That doesn't make the slightest bit of sense, but then again, whenever Simon's at a hotel in a new city, he finds himself watching the local morning news show, something that would never cross his mind to do at home. It's like when he's in a strange space, he forgets how to live his normal life.

Charlie's walking toward the bedrooms.

"There's a TV out here," Simon points out.

"You have to watch the television in bed," Charlie says. "That's part of the experience."

"Is mini-fridge wine part of the experience?"

When Charlie turns to look at him, there's an odd look on his face, and it's a few beats before he says anything. "For you, maybe."

"You don't drink?" Simon thinks back to all the times he's seen Charlie with a glass of clear liquid in his hand, and how it never once occurred to him that Charlie might be using the same trick Simon does: a glass of seltzer with ice and a lime wedge, a decoy for a mixed drink.

Charlie lets out an irritated huff. "You were there that first season. Rehab? Remember?"

"I knew there was . . ." Simon tries to phrase this as delicately and non-judgmentally as possible. "I knew there was a substance abuse issue going on. But I didn't realize there was any actual addiction."

He isn't even sure if there's a meaningful difference. All he knows is that it is, possibly, a little strange that it never occurred to him that Charlie was—what? In recovery? He knew Charlie must have made some changes, but never thought about what that might have looked like. "Good for you," he says.

"Good for me?" Charlie repeats, incredulous.

"For, uh. Dealing with the—thing?" Simon tries, cringing as soon as he says it.

"It's okay, people always say something stupid at this point in the conversation. You shouldn't feel too bad about yourself," Charlie says, punctuating it with a sarcastic little tap on Simon's shoulder.

"I'm trying to be nice," Simon complains.

"You're so bad at it. Have you ever tried before? Is this your first time? Should I be flattered?" Somehow, Charlie's managing to sound mean and hurt and fake-flirty all at once.

"Whatever. What's your situation with other people's substances? Do you need me to keep my pills someplace safe?" Simon's remembering what Charlie said in Simon's trailer about locking up his meds. Simon's emergency anxiety medication is infamously addictive.

Charlie closes his eyes, takes a deep breath, and looks like he's trying not to do something regrettable. "I'm not gonna steal your fucking pills, Simon."

"I wasn't implying that you were. But if you'd feel better if I flushed the benzos—"

"That's bad for the water supply," Charlie admonishes him. Simon wants to strangle him.

"Fuck the water supply and fuck you too. I'm trying to be supportive."

At the taco restaurant, when Simon hadn't been able to come up with the right thing to say, he'd touched Charlie. Well, he'd kicked him, but same difference. He figures it's worth another try in the name of not seeming like a jerk about literal addiction, so he squeezes Charlie's ridiculous arm. He does everything in his power to strip any bitchiness from his voice. "What you did—what you're doing—is hard. I respect it. Can you, just for the space of this conversation, assume I'm not a complete asshole?"

He's made his point, or at least he's tried to, so this is probably where he ought to let go of Charlie's arm. He thinks about it, even gets so far as to slide his hand maybe half an inch down toward Charlie's elbow, then gets distracted. They're about the same height, but Charlie's slouching against the door frame, looking up at Simon, bright blue eyes glittering in the unfortunate overhead lighting.

Charlie's gone very still, like maybe he's holding his breath. Simon watches his fingers attempt to span Charlie's upper arm, his own skin pale against the swirling black of Charlie's tattoo.

"You're impressed with me, are you?" Charlie says, voice quiet and smug and doing terrible things to Simon.

"You're so embarrassing." Simon still doesn't drop his hand. Charlie's so warm, and Simon wants to take a step closer. If he had to bet, he'd say that Charlie wants him to take a step closer too. He might be a basket case on a good day, but he can read a fucking room and he knows an invitation when he sees one. It's the same as that moment at lunch, a silent acknowledgment that they *could*.

It's still shocking, a piece of information that doesn't fit anywhere in Simon's brain, and so it rattles around. They could, and the reason they could is that they both *want* to.

"You," Charlie says, his voice a little rough. He reaches a hand out to Simon but pulls it back. "You have a gray hair."

"Ugh!" Simon spins out of Charlie's reach and throws his hands up. "Way to ruin a nice moment, Charlie!"

"Oh, were we having a nice moment?" Charlie asks. Simon wants to push him out a window. "No, shut up. I noticed it this winter. How could I not, dumbass? How many hours a day do I spend looking at you under studio lights? I'm not blind. Remember when I had that pimple?"

Does Simon ever. They'd had to re-block everything to keep that thing away from the camera. "It was the size of my car," Simon says. "How could I forget?"

"Anyway! My point is that I probably saw your stupid gray hair before you did."

Simon doesn't know what on earth that's supposed to mean, except now he feels almost nostalgic, like he'll have lost something by not having Charlie's eyes on him for hours a day.

SIMON TOOK THE room with two double beds and left Charlie the room with one king bed, on the theory that Charlie is bigger and could use the acreage. They pick Simon's room, with its two beds, to watch television.

Charlie flicks through the channels, changing before Simon even knows what he's watching. It would be annoying if Simon were paying any attention. Instead he's texting Jamie and trying not to think about Charlie, in bed, a few feet away.

"Oh, hey," Charlie says. "Look."

Simon knows what he's going to see before he even looks up, because he can hear Alex's voice as she shouts over the ship's communication system. Based on the red streaks in Alex's hair, it's an episode from the second season.

"She looks like a baby." Simon doesn't love the reminder that five years is a lot when your face is on a giant television.

He barely remembers this episode, so when the picture cuts to him harassing some actor he'd swear he's never seen before— "Get me the antidote, Callahan!"—he's unprepared. Charlie's on a stretcher.

It turns out that this is one of those rare episodes where he and Charlie aren't in practically every scene together, and that's only because Charlie's supposed to be dying while Simon's off finding space antidotes.

Unless Lian coerces him into attending a season finale watch party, Simon doesn't watch finished episodes of *Out There*. He's never seen this one, and for a minute it's like he's seeing something brand-new.

He's a little surprised to find that he likes it, that maybe it's a show he'd want to watch. Which is a stupid thought—he'd signed on for *Out There* precisely because it's the kind of show he likes. It's just that at some point he'd forgotten.

"My hair was so short," Charlie says, a little ruefully. On the screen, it's barely peach fuzz. Now, Charlie's hair curls at his collar.

If Alex looks like a baby, Charlie looks like a fetus. He's twenty-one or so in this episode. His shirt's off, of course, and he's missing half the tattoos that Simon's gotten used to seeing.

When Simon thinks of Charlie a year before this episode, arriving drunk to set and ramming his truck into the director's car, wrecking his trailer and punching people in bars, it feels like he's hearing about a kid stealing someone's blocks at preschool.

Twenty is more than old enough to be responsible for your actions. Still. That first season, Charlie wasn't much older than Nora is now, and the biggest problem Nora has in her life is what to major in at Brown. Simon, at that age, rage-cried when his roommate deleted a season of *Drag Race* from the DVR.

"You were a kid," Simon says.

Charlie makes a derisive sound and changes the channel. It's a commercial for a truck that somehow looks like it's going to eat all the other vehicles on the road.

"Is there anyone you want to see while you're in town?" Simon asks. "I can keep myself busy."

"God, no."

"Your mother doesn't still live here?" Simon isn't sure if this is a dangerous topic, but Charlie's brought his mother up a few times today.

"She's in Provo. Has a kid in first grade."

Simon's brothers are twelve and fourteen years older than him. They considered the age gap mortifying; Simon considered it solid proof that he was the midlife accident of a couple already well on the way to divorce court. A twenty-year gap is something else entirely.

"Was she very young when she had you?" Simon asks, with the feeling of stepping out onto thinner and thinner ice.

"Yup," Charlie says, no elaboration.

Simon might not have anything like social skills and he might not even be nice, but even he can tell that Charlie has practically handed him an annotated autobiography. There's a too-young mother. There's some time—more than once—in the foster system. There's a much older stepfather who didn't let Charlie eat his fucking food. There's no mention whatsoever of grandparents or a father or anybody else.

This is the fourth or fifth time today that Simon's had to come up with a non-asshole response when presented with some tragic detail of Charlie's childhood, and it isn't getting any easier. He rolls over so they're facing one another across the gap between the beds and just says, "Charlie."

"Yeah." Charlie's looking back at him, his expression serious. Simon doesn't know how he's supposed to look away.

Something on the television must catch Charlie's attention, because he sits up and leans in. Simon, curious, does the same.

It's the sort of homemade-looking commercial Simon hasn't seen in years. A pair of kids are eating corn dogs in front of a sky blue convertible that looks like it's from the fifties. Then there's a map of Arizona with a dot roughly in the center and text reading Classic Car Show, along with the dates for this coming weekend—tomorrow and the next day.

"I'm an idiot," Charlie says. "He goes every year. I don't know why I didn't think of that."

"Because there's no reason in the world for you to commit the dates of car shows to memory?" Simon suggests. "And also because cell phones still work at car shows? I mean, I'll be the first person to admit that I'm not familiar with the customs of the old car community, but I think you're still allowed to make contact with the outside world."

Charlie doesn't even rise to the bait. "It's five o'clock. I could be there by eight. Where are my shoes?"

Simon hears the *I* and doesn't know what to make of it, just that he doesn't like it. He also doesn't like the idea of Charlie getting behind the wheel of a car after spending an entire day alternately driving and panicking. "Or we could leave first thing in the morning, be there by ten, and you'll be able to search the place in daylight. But. If you want to leave tonight, I'm driving."

"I can't—"

"Bullshit."

"But—"

"It's final."

Simon doesn't know what it means that they've gotten so good at arguing that they can do a speedrun through a fight.

Charlie takes out his phone and—presumably—tries to call his stepfather again. He hangs up after ten seconds.

"Room service," Simon suggests. "Then sleep."

But Charlie's on his feet now, pacing as much as he can in a room that contains two beds.

"I didn't mean to steamroll you. Look, if you need to get on the road now," Simon says, "then that's what we'll do."

"No, you're right. There's no point going tonight. But that doesn't mean I can be normal about it." Charlie rubs a hand over his jaw. "I'm going downstairs to see how bad the gym is."

"Good idea."

"Want to come?"

"To the *gym*?" Simon doesn't recoil but it's close. "On purpose?"

Charlie appraises him, a skeptical once over, as if he doesn't already know exactly what Simon looks like.

"I swim," Simon explains, speaking slowly and calmly, because Charlie is laboring under a great deal of mental stress if he thinks Simon deliberately breaks a sweat. "I don't lift weights. Sometimes Jamie makes me do Pilates," he adds, aggrieved.

"Great news. If this is like most hotel gyms, there will be no weights to lift. Four treadmills and an elliptical, maybe a rowing machine."

Charlie's wringing his hands, and it hits Simon that Charlie doesn't want to go to the gym alone. Or maybe he just needs some kind of validation that going to the gym isn't a bad idea. Well, it's not like Simon has anything better to do.

"Okay, fine." Simon brought exercise clothes, mainly because Jamie helped him pack and Jamie has a lot more faith in Simon's interest in cardiovascular health than he has any reason to.

In the gym, Simon sets a treadmill to a speed slightly slower than he might use to walk Edie and tries to remain unaware of Charlie, three machines over, wearing a sleeveless T-shirt that isn't even a real garment. He texts Jamie, telling him that he's on a treadmill.

> **Jamie:** gonna need a picture of you with today's newspaper

> **Simon:** ha ha, it gets worse

> **Simon:** I think I'm here, on an actual treadmill, to give Charlie Blake emotional support

> **Jamie:** wow

> **Jamie:** everything ok?

> **Simon:** Yes, stop worrying and send me pictures of my dog

As Simon looks at two dozen pictures of an untraumatized and unbothered Edie, he realizes that what he told Jamie was the truth. Today has been . . . okay. Maybe better than okay. His anxiety is at a low ebb, which doesn't necessarily mean anything, but he'd expected it to be through the roof. Usually Charlie annoys him—or, maybe, unsettles him. And that makes him cranky, which makes it more likely that something will set his anxiety off. But none of that's happened today.

> **Simon:** Remember when you sprained your ankle at Coachella? And I wasn't a total wreck about it?

Jamie's then-boyfriend hadn't wanted to leave the festival, so Simon drove out to pick Jamie up, collected Jamie's belongings, told off Jamie's asshole boyfriend, drove Jamie to the emergency room, and brought him home. Usually, any one of those events would be enough to crank his anxiety all the way up to ten. But somehow, the fact that it was all for someone else changed things.

Right now, he's trusting that Jamie will be able to connect the dots without Simon needing to actually type "Charlie's pretty fucked up right now," because that seems like a breach of privacy.

> **Jamie:** first of all, you're never a total wreck. But, yeah, you've always been more patient with friends than you are with yourself.

Simon wrinkles his nose. That isn't the point he was trying to make at all. Nobody has ever called Simon patient. And implying that Charlie is his friend is objectively deranged.

This is all obvious to Simon, but he has a feeling that if he types it out, Jamie will call him and list all the ways he's being ridiculous.

From an *Out There* fan Discord

SpacePope: The other day we were talking about favorite episodes versus best episodes but I have one that isn't my favorite and it definitely isn't the best, but I guess it's the episode I think about the most often? It's Antidote from the second season.

DeathStarJacuzzi: Fandom's least favorite episode!

SpacePope: Exactly. I watched it with my dad when he was in hospice, and at that point we weren't really doing anything but watching television. We worked our way through all the shows we watched together when I was a kid—Deep Space Nine, Battlestar Galactica, Stargate. And we watched Out There every Thursday when it came out. So, in this episode, Luke's been dosed with space toxins or whatever, and Jonathan has to convince some shady aliens to get him the antidote. It's all about him negotiating with gangsters, buttering up diplomats, making promises he can't keep—all these bad choices to keep Luke safe.

GalactoseIntolerance: Right, this is the episode that people always complain about because everything Jonathan does is out of character. He's supposed to be this rigid rule follower, and here he is selling ammunition to arms traffickers. All the other million times Jonathan saves Luke's life, he's ethical about it.

SpacePope: But I'd have negotiated with space terrorists if that's what it took to get my dad healthy. When people complain about that episode, it's like: oh, so you're telling me you've never watched a loved one die. Anyway—not the best episode, but it lives in my brain rent free.

GalactoseIntolerance: oh honey

HowlsMovingSpaceship: I feel like "I don't know if it's good, but I watched it with my dad" is a recurring theme here. I mean, in my case it's my mom, but same difference.

SpacePope: dad (gender neutral)

DeathStarJacuzzi: When I was transitioning, my dad did NOT know what to say to me but he sure did sit there and watch all three Star Trek reboot movies without a single complaint

SupervillainApologist: My oldest memory is watching Battlestar Galactica—the original one from the seventies—with my older sisters.

GalactoseIntolerance: who authorized any of you to make me cry in the middle of a workday??

Chapter Ten

Simon checks out while, across the hotel lobby, Charlie talks to an elderly couple. They've been chatting for five entire minutes, and at one point Charlie's mouth makes the shape *California*, so these people probably have no idea who he is and are just talking to him as fellow visitors. Charlie's making friends with random senior citizens. And now he's bending over one of their phones, grinning at—Simon can only assume—photographs of grandchildren or the Grand Canyon.

As soon as Charlie waves goodbye to the couple, the smile drops off his face. His brow furrows and his lips press together in a tight line.

Simon *knew* that Charlie's nonstop good humor was an act. He knew it, and he's spent years wondering why nobody else could see through it. But it turns out that what lies behind the screen of affability is just a little less—less sunshiny, less gregarious, less charming. And also more—more thoughtful, more anxious. Nothing sinister.

They're loading their suitcases into the car by six thirty, Charlie looking rougher around the edges than he did yesterday. A few times last night, Simon woke to the sound of Charlie in the kitchen. He doubts Charlie got much in the way of sleep.

"Let me drive." Simon positions himself between Charlie and the driver's side door.

"I can—"

"Can you just for one minute remember the number of times that you've insisted on driving me home when I was in no shape to get behind the wheel?"

They're standing too close because they've been trying to maneuver one another away from the driver's side door. Charlie's quiet, scanning Simon's face. "You hate driving," he says eventually.

Simon didn't learn to drive until he moved to Los Angeles after college. It still doesn't feel natural. But he does drive, obviously. He doesn't even talk about how much he hates it, because he'll sound like the world's biggest baby, and everyone (Jamie) will yell at him to take more Lyfts.

"How do you even know that?" Simon asks, realizing too late that he could have just denied it.

Charlie shoves his hands in his pockets and looks up at the still-gray morning sky. "I noticed."

"Well, right now I'd hate even more watching you try to stay awake."

Charlie presses the key fob into Simon's hand, his fingers warm when they brush Simon's palm.

"You know what this means." Simon settles into the driver's seat. He taps the car's touchscreen, connecting his phone to the car's Bluetooth.

"Fuck no," Charlie says. "I'm not listening to your sad guitar music or whatever."

"I can't believe you think I'm emotionally stable enough to listen to sad music."

"I'll put on the same playlist as yesterday."

Simon clicks his tongue. "I'm driving. I get to pick the music. It's the law."

"No way."

"It's in the constitution, Charlie."

Charlie laughs, startled, almost a giggle, and Simon feels like he unlocked a door he wasn't trying to open.

Simon doesn't put on any music at all, because every few minutes, Charlie calls his stepfather. There's a rhythm to it—unlock the phone, tap the screen, listen to the call go straight to voicemail, end the call, sigh. Simon memorized it yesterday. But today he notices that this is all Charlie's doing with his phone.

"Why's your phone so quiet?" Simon asks.

"I silenced notifications."

"Why?" Simon wouldn't have thought Charlie ever wanted to be left alone. Then again, he'd never have thought Charlie would tell him about it, so who even knows anything anymore.

"I can't fake normal right now."

That's so uncomfortably relatable that Simon's at a loss about what to say.

"I swear to God," Charlie says, "if you tell me I'm supposed to be emotionally honest with my friends—"

"Have you *met* me? I'm on year six of a long con to convince Jamie I'm a functional human being."

"Is it working?"

"He installed a meditation app on my phone, so I don't think so."

Charlie cackles, fully laughing at, not with, Simon, and for some stupid reason Simon isn't mad about it.

Charlie calls his stepfather again and Simon pays attention to the road. They keep passing signs for towns that don't sound real. Bumble Bee. Flower Pot. The scenery is aggressively Old West, too green to be a desert but too brown to be chaparral. A range of mountains hovers in the distance, shadowy blue in the morning light, never seeming to get any closer.

"Are you going to Petra's wedding?" Charlie asks.

"I'll be in New York." He would have gone if he'd been in town—he'd have brought Jamie, stayed for ninety minutes, and left before dinner. That's how he deals with most *Out There*-adjacent social events, and it works well enough. Most social events, period.

Charlie shifts in his seat and unlocks his phone, and Simon doesn't think he can stand to hear another call go to voicemail.

"Put on *A Scorched Land*," Simon suggests.

"Really?"

"Do I make a habit of suggesting things I dislike? Have I ever, once, in the entire time you've known me?" Simon asks, and it's not technically a lie because it's in the form of a question.

"I knew you'd like it." Charlie sounds smug.

An hour later, Simon longs for the violent death of every single human character in this book, but he's overinvested in the fate of that dragon. He says as much to Charlie, who pauses the audiobook. Simon can feel the heat of Charlie's glare on the side of his face.

"That dragon is in *love* with the humans. Don't you want him to be happy?"

Simon is slightly, regrettably, charmed that Charlie has embraced the most unhinged interpretation of this book. "He'd be happier if he fell in love with someone smarter."

Charlie proceeds to tell him all the ways Simon's wrong.

Simon's heard Charlie charm people—hell, he's spent half his career being annoyed by it. But having it turned on himself is like being hit with a fire hose. Simon's physically incapable of doing anything other than driving and listening to Charlie. He doesn't hate it.

"I always loved dragon stories," Simon says. He wonders if he can convince Charlie to stop listening to this and put on *Temeraire* or *Dragonriders of Pern*.

"Well, yeah," Charlie says. "You were in a dragon show."

Tree of the Gods did, in fact, have a dragon subplot. Simon wasn't in any of those scenes, but he guesses he was, technically, in a dragon show.

"I can't believe that of all the space creatures I've had to pretend to fight on a green screen, we've never had a space dragon," Charlie says.

"It could have even been a nice dragon. Remember the lobster things that turned out to be like . . . pacifists? What *were* they?"

"A fucking mistake," Charlie says, and that's the first time Simon's ever heard him say a bad thing about *Out There*.

Heading north, the landscape gets greener and greener, pine trees on both sides of the road, until they're finally in the mountains. Charlie pulls up the map on his phone and gives Simon the shittiest possible directions.

"Turn—no not yet," Charlie says, after Simon already turned. "You're gonna need to pull into a side street to turn the car around."

"Gosh, wow, thanks for explaining how to make the car go in a different direction."

"Maybe you can keep your mouth shut for two seconds and get back on the road," Charlie says, but there's barely any heat in it.

It's still early—just past nine—but there are already plenty of people on the sidewalks of what turns out to be an alarmingly quaint town. Simon can't imagine how Charlie expects to find one old white man in a town that currently has about ten old white men for every person in any other demographic. Simon is a little taken aback, and he grew up in a part of Connecticut that's practically the old white man capital of the world.

He parks where Charlie tells him to, then ignores everything Charlie says until he's standing in line at what looks like a reputable coffee shop.

"Go walk around. I'll get your coffee." Simon waves Charlie off. "Go, go, go."

A few minutes later, holding two coffees that cost enough to suggest that this cute little town does a brisk tourist trade, Simon leans against the outside of the building. Old cars are parked along the streets for clusters of old white men to admire. As Simon takes a sip of coffee, a car that looks like the Batmobile from the old *Batman* TV show drives past.

"It was a stupid idea," Charlie says when he comes back. "I don't know how I thought I'd find him."

"Eat the banana bread." Simon shoves the paper bag into Charlie's chest. "We'll walk around."

The streets are lined with low-slung buildings, with lots of striped awnings and little American flags. Neon signs that straddle the line between seedy and quaint say things like HOTEL and GIFTS. Somebody here discovered vintage fonts and just went for it. Even not counting the old cars, the whole place is a little bit twee and one hundred percent camp, in a way Simon can respect.

"This town is what set designers are thinking of when they build generic main streets," Simon says when he realizes why it seems familiar. The design choices of a dozen movies suddenly make sense. They walk past a sign for a gas station museum. Simon would bet five hundred dollars they're going to see a soda fountain within the next fifty yards. "They can't get enough of Route 66 here." He's counted five signs in the past block.

"That's because you're standing on Route 66," Charlie says.

Simon, like an idiot, looks down at his feet. Charlie starts laughing.

"That's why they have the car show here."

"Vintage car aesthetic? Americana vibes?" Simon suggests.

"Something like that. Also you've gotta stop saying vintage cars. Vintage cars are basically Model T era. Antique cars are from before '75, and classic cars are more than twenty-five years old, but people fight about that all the time. A '98 Civic is not a classic car, don't embarrass yourself."

"How do you know all that off the top of your head?"

Charlie stops walking, so Simon swings around to face him.

"Seriously?" Charlie asks.

"What?"

"You know what I did before *Out There*, right?"

Simon apparently left his entire brain on the highway north out of Phoenix, because of course he knows that Charlie got his start on a show about car restoration. Teenage Charlie worked in a garage owned by a—"Dave owned the garage you worked at."

"You watched the show?" Charlie looks shocked and a little pleased.

"I watched everything Alex and Samara did too." There's no need to admit that he watched every scene Charlie was in at least twice, trying to figure out what Lian saw that made Charlie worth the trouble.

There's definitely no need to admit that by the end of the very first episode, the answer was obvious. Charlie is one of those people who have a magnet in them that makes it impossible to look away.

"And this isn't a stupid idea," Simon says. "You're doing due diligence before going to the police. This is the best you can do." He isn't in the habit of being reassuring to anybody but Jamie—and even then, it's hardly one of his strengths. But now he has to because there isn't anyone else around to do it.

"Okay," Charlie says, tossing his empty paper bag into the nearest trash can. "Let's keep walking."

"How many pairs do you have?" Charlie asks when Simon swaps out the sunglasses he wears to drive (not too dark, polarized) with the ones he wears when walking around outside in the sun (a bit darker, but not super dark).

"Six? Maybe seven. I don't fuck with sunlight."

When Simon realized that light—flashing light, bright light, light leaking through tree branches, the brake lights of the truck in front of him at a stop sign—can sometimes trigger his migraines, he splurged on a few pairs of sunglasses. He spent a dumb amount of money on Tom Ford Wayfarers, and an even dumber amount on a pair that's allegedly identical to what Cary Grant wore in *North by Northwest*. He even has a pair of aviators with pinkish-tinted lenses that he wears indoors when things are especially rough.

Simon and Charlie get recognized twice that Simon clocks, which is more than he might have expected, especially since Charlie is wearing a baseball cap and has a beard that ought to make him less immediately identifiable.

Charlie remembers why Simon's here in the first place, and they take a bunch of selfies, one inside a bright orange convertible that Charlie tells him is a 1970 Shelby, whatever that is. Charlie pets the car—actually pets it—and calls it a beauty, gorgeous, just look at her. Something goes fizzy and awful in Simon's stomach hearing the low rumble of praise. He decides that investigating this sensation is not compatible with sanity. Instead he lets himself get hauled into Charlie's side for picture after picture.

All Simon has to do is occasionally smile while Charlie asks car owners incomprehensible questions about engines and hubcaps and chrome. Whenever Charlie talks to someone who's part of this scene—for lack of a better word—he works in, "You haven't seen Dave Antonetti around, have you?"

Simon assumed Charlie's show was basically scripted, the sort of reality television that's an excuse to put attractive people in front of a camera. But Charlie knows about this stuff.

Simon has to watch a few of these interactions before realizing that he's... impressed, maybe? All he knows is that he kind of wants to keep hearing Charlie talk about sourcing old car parts.

"It's early," Charlie says after yet another person tells him they haven't seen Dave. "Not even noon on the first day. He might show up later."

None of that explains why the man hasn't answered his phone in a week, but Charlie already knows that, so Simon keeps his mouth shut.

Crowds of people, especially when they're milling around, make Simon anxious and disoriented. Today is no exception, but the fact that he doesn't have to do anything helps. Nobody has any expectations, and Simon has no goals, unless you count his secret goal of petting every dog that walks past—a goal Charlie facilitates by being the sort of person who can walk up to total strangers and ask about their dogs. Whenever Simon gets stuck in a sea of people who, somehow, never learned how to walk at a reasonable speed and keep to the right, for fuck's sake, there's Charlie's hand on the small of his back, steering him clear.

That hand—just the lightest pressure, barely even fingertips—is short-circuiting Simon's brain. He tries to make a list of reasons a person might repeatedly touch someone else's lower back. His list is one item long.

For lunch, they go to a restaurant that's clearly supposed to be the platonic ideal of American diners, with lots of chrome and red vinyl, a neon-lit jukebox, waitresses in gingham dresses. The aesthetic is appalling, and Simon says so, low and bitchy in Charlie's ear. Charlie steps on his foot.

"Is this—this perpetual hard-on that people have for the fifties—the explanation," Simon asks, turning in a slow circle as they wait for a table, "for why we keep electing shitheads?"

"No," Charlie says, "that would be racism. Hope that helps!"

"Is there a difference? Is there really?"

"This is cosplay. People can dress up as Darth Vader without being into fascism. Come on, you know this."

Simon slowly raises his middle finger, then catches a pair of teenagers with their phones pointing at him and jams his hand into his pocket. He was speaking quietly, almost whispering, so he doesn't think they picked up what he was saying. The owners of this restaurant probably don't deserve to be called out by minor celebrities. Simon can reluctantly admit that fifties-themed aesthetics maybe aren't conclusive evidence of actual evil.

"You look exhausted," Simon says after they've ordered.

"You say the sweetest things."

Simon rolls his eyes. "It's not an insult. It's—" What it is, is concern, but Simon feels weird saying so. Two days of peacefully not murdering one another does not constitute that kind of relationship. "I'm asking if you need anything. A nap. A break. I don't know."

Charlie takes a drink of his soda and starts twisting the straw wrapper around his finger. "So, I'm not great with stress."

"Wow, what must that be like."

Charlie kicks him under the table. "I mean, you were there that first season. I'm not gonna do anything stupid. I'm just saying that worrying about people I can't help is, like, a problem."

Simon's faintly disgusted that Charlie's managed to acquire an anxiety disorder or whatever fueled by kindness. Meanwhile, Simon's anxiety is fueled by absolute unadulterated frustration with the entire world, combined with a little bit of self-loathing, just for variety.

"Why do you look pissed off at me? What the fuck?" Charlie asks, loud enough that the people at the table across the aisle glare at him. Simon glares back.

"I'm not pissed off at you. I'm disgusted that you're *nice*. You're a *good person*. I've spent years wondering how you conned everyone into thinking you're a saint and it turns out it's just true. Gross. And boring."

Charlie's whole face scrunches into this expression of bewilderment, like he's not sure if what Simon just said was an insult. Simon wishes him luck in figuring it out; he doesn't have a clue.

"Anyway, you're doing well," Simon says. "A missing family member would be ten-out-of-ten stress for anyone."

Charlie gets very busy accordioning his straw wrapper. "Remember you mentioned your pills? Don't offer me any. Like, even if I freak out."

"Sure." Simon doesn't go around offering controlled substances to people, so this isn't a big ask.

"That stuff wasn't a problem for me. I've never even taken any benzos—it was just alcohol. Well, alcohol, a little coke, some pills. But I stay away from all of it now."

"I've seen you with a joint in your hand."

"Weed isn't a substance," Charlie says, frowning, like he can't believe the depths of Simon's ignorance.

"Sure," Simon says again, because he's the most magnanimous person alive and he isn't going to tell Charlie how to navigate his relationship with drugs. And also because he mostly agrees.

Charlie drags his fork through the puddle of ketchup on his plate. "I don't think it would take much to get me hooked on, well, basically anything." He flicks his gaze up to Simon and leaves it there, steady. "My mom was—anyway, you know how you stay away from more food than you have to? Same difference."

"Got it."

"I figure that if I ever need surgery and they want to give me narcotics, I'll decide then what I want to do about it. I don't need to decide now."

Simon isn't sure why Charlie's telling him all this. It's none of his business. In the past twenty-four hours, Simon has learned way too much about Charlie's private life. Charlie should be hitting the brakes, not dumping more sensitive information into Simon's lap. He studies Charlie's face, trying to figure out what's going on. "Why are you looking at me like you're expecting me to disagree?"

Charlie gives him an incredulous look. "I don't know, Simon. Maybe because I've spent seven years listening to you disagree with everything I say?"

The disagreement went both ways, but Simon won't say so, because that would be proving Charlie's point. Besides, he wants to make it clear that he *isn't* arguing with Charlie right now.

"Giving you shit is my favorite hobby, but not about this."

Simon doesn't know if it's a compulsion toward symmetry, or just not liking the sense that Charlie's somehow outdone him, but when he opens his mouth what comes out is, "My parents forgot to pick me up at school so many times, the principal used to just take me home with him. It wasn't, you know, neglect. It's just that with two parents, two stepparents, two brothers and three stepsisters with drivers' licenses, it was hard to keep track of whose turn it was to pick me up."

If Charlie's confused about why Simon's telling him this, he doesn't let on. He just kicks Simon under the table again. Simon kicks him back.

When they're nearly done eating—a hamburger the size of a hubcap for Charlie, a vegetable omelet, hold the cheese, for Simon—Charlie squints over Simon's shoulder.

"I know that guy." Charlie gets to his feet. "Hold on, be right back."

While Charlie's gone, Simon gets the check.

"That was one of Dave's friends," Charlie says when he comes back. He doesn't sit down. "He hasn't seen Dave but said that last year Dave stayed with a friend of his." He holds out his phone, open to the maps app.

"Okay, sure. Let's go show up at a total stranger's house."

"You can sit this out, you know."

Simon produces his most withering glare and heads for the door.

Chapter Eleven

They drive out of the little town and into the middle of nowhere. Fifteen minutes, and there aren't even buildings anymore. Half an hour, and the road unravels into a single lane.

Charlie turns onto a street that's just dirt and gravel and weeds, and which leads them up a hill to a house that looks like it was built from logs—like someone took the set of Lincoln Logs Simon never wanted to play with and used it to make an actual human-size house. It's a cabin, but not the kind of six-bedroom, plate glass wall overlooking a strategically landscaped brook kind of cabin that Simon's used to.

Parked in front of the house are two pickup trucks. Charlie engages the emergency brake, puts his head on the steering wheel, and lets out a breath. "That's his truck."

"If you want me to wait in the car, that's fine."

Charlie's head is still on the steering wheel, but he turns to face Simon. "If you want to wait in the car, that's fine too."

"If you think I'm passing up a chance to see what a man who doesn't answer his phone for a week looks like, guess again."

"Maybe something happened and he's in the hospital. And his truck is here because they didn't know what to do with it."

Recognizing an anxiety spiral when he sees one, Simon opens his door. "Only one way to find out."

Two golden retrievers come bounding across a hill to bark at them, delighted to say hello. When Charlie and Simon head toward the front door, the dogs trot happily beside them.

"Worst goddamn guard dogs," a man says from the front doorway. "And what do you want?"

"Is Dave Antonetti here? I'm Charlie. He hasn't been answering his phone."

"You're Charlie," the man says, like Charlie hadn't just said so. He steps out of the house, and Simon can see that he has black hair in a ponytail and brown skin. "I'm Mike."

"Are you the Mike who sold Dave that Impala about ten years ago? I worked on that bastard for months."

"He sold it for a mint," Mike says.

"I got seven bucks an hour."

"Yeah, well, if you're the Charlie I think you are, you aren't hurting."

"Can't complain." Charlie grins, and if it looks a little forced, then Simon bets he's the only one who can tell.

Mike turns into the house. "Dave! You've got company." Then, to Charlie, "You should come in. I'll get you a drink."

"This is Simon," Charlie says.

"Nice to meet you," Simon says, shaking Mike's hand.

Mike looks at Simon a second too long, which probably means he's watched the show.

Inside the house, every surface, including the ceiling, is made of broad pine slats. There's a huge stone fireplace and a wall of windows that Simon missed from the outside. If there's a hot tub somewhere on the premises, it's basically a four-hundred-dollar-a-night Airbnb in Aspen. Dave has not been living rough this past week.

At the kitchen table is a man with gray hair that's buzzed short, weathered tan skin, and two sleeves of tattoos emerging from a white T-shirt. He's clearly (1) alive and (2) fully capable of answering a phone. Simon hates him on sight.

Charlie opens his mouth and snaps it shut.

"What are you doing here, kid?" Dave asks, getting to his feet. He sounds confused. Disappointed. A little pissed off.

"You weren't answering your phone."

"What?"

"I've been calling you for a week. No answer."

"I left my charger at home."

"He has an iPhone," Mike explains. "This is an Android household."

"Wasn't gonna waste money on a new charger," Dave says. "We're not all rich movie stars."

Charlie, incredibly, doesn't rise to the bait. "I went to your house. I nearly went to the *police*. I was about an hour away from filing a missing persons report."

Dave takes a step back. "Why the fuck would you do that?"

Charlie's hands are balled into fists so tight that his fingers are white. The vein in his forehead is doing terrible things. "Because I thought you were dead. I was worried sick."

"What can I get you to drink?" Mike asks. His voice is low, the question meant for Simon.

Simon doesn't want anything but feels like drinks might be the kind of stage dressing that makes a situation feel more normal. "Water for me, and Charlie likes Coke, if you have it."

"How many times have I told you that you don't need to worry about me? I'm not your problem," Dave says.

"Only five-fucking-thousand times, but seriously, Dave, you don't get to decide who I worry about. If I'm not gonna worry about you, then who will?"

"He's got a point," Mike says. He hands Simon both the drinks, like he senses nobody ought to approach Charlie right now.

"None of your neighbors know you, which isn't any kind of surprise. Most of your friends are dead. When I drove by the garage, it looked like it was closed. When did that happen? You couldn't let me know? Whenever I talk to you, I ask about it, and you say everything's fine."

"None of your business, Charlie. Nobody asked you to stick your nose in."

"None of my business," Charlie repeats. "None of my *business*?"

"Drink." Simon hands Charlie the can of soda.

"And who the fuck is this?" Dave asks, looking at Simon. Simon doesn't believe for a single second that Dave doesn't recognize him. No matter how much of an asshole this guy is, no matter how little he thinks of Charlie, there's no way he hasn't occasionally watched an episode just out of curiosity.

"This is Simon," Charlie says, no explanation. Dave raises an eyebrow, and still Charlie doesn't qualify it with "from work," or "a friend," or anything else. It sounds like a dare.

Dave doesn't say hello to Simon, which is perfectly fine by him.

"It isn't your business," Dave repeats. "I'm not your father. It's not your job to keep tabs on me. You don't owe me that, and I don't owe you that, so you can quit this shit right now."

"Dave," Mike says, but Dave grabs a pack of cigarettes off the table and walks out the back door.

In the last five minutes, Simon's watched Charlie go from frantic with worry to incandescent with rage to just plain hurt. All this Dave fucker had to do was apologize, maybe even promise not to do it again, and Charlie would be completely satisfied. Charlie's expectations for this man are at rock bottom.

Charlie's jaw is clenched. There are divots in the Coke can where he's gripping it. This is the same Charlie who dumped coffee on that dickhead director. This is the Charlie who took whatever he was feeling and channeled it into bad ideas and self-destruction. Simon is flooded with shame to remember that he once saw this Charlie and thought he was being *tacky*, that Simon saw a crisis and thought it was in poor taste.

"We can come back tomorrow," Simon says, low, in Charlie's ear. "We can get out of here, take a break."

"Yeah," Charlie says, deflating a little. "Okay."

Simon takes the Coke can and his own glass of water and hands them back to Mike. "Sorry," he murmurs, because most people probably don't like drama unfolding in their homes.

Mike shrugs. "What can you do."

Simon gets into the driver's seat and Charlie doesn't even argue. "I'm going to get a hotel room unless you tell me not to," Simon says.

"Yeah," Charlie mumbles. "Fine."

Once they're at the bottom of the hill, Simon pulls over to the shoulder of the narrow road and takes out his phone. He has to lower his standards repeatedly before he finds a room, because apparently this car festival is a big deal, and all the decent places are booked.

Charlie doesn't seem like he's in any state to navigate, so Simon relies on GPS and luck to get them to the motel. It isn't as bad as Simon feared, at least not from the outside. They only had one room left, but he doesn't think Charlie will care. He isn't sure Charlie will notice.

"It's my own fault," Charlie says, once they're in the room. At least it has two beds. "He's right. He doesn't owe me anything."

"Bullshit."

Charlie flops onto one of the beds. "I'm so embarrassed that you were there for that."

"I bet," Simon says, because he'd have to murder anyone who got the kind of glimpse into his psyche that he's had into Charlie's.

"Thanks, Simon, you're helpful as always."

"No, I mean, I'd be dead from the shame."

"Maybe stop talking?"

"I'm trying to say that I get it." Simon sits on the bed and puts a tentative hand on Charlie's ankle. "I want to push Dave off a cliff," he says, which might not be comforting but is true anyway.

"We lived with him for a year when my mom was sober enough to have me but not sober enough to think twice about bringing me to live with strange men twice her age. In high school I worked at his garage. He was my boss. I'm not anything to him. I know that."

Something in Simon's heart gets pulled dangerously tight at that. Nobody should be able to say "I'm not anything to him" about someone they've spent days worrying about. Charlie is generous hearted in a way that Simon maybe couldn't understand and wouldn't think to value until he saw that same quality rejected and thrown back in Charlie's face.

"I feel like a kid who accidentally called their kindergarten teacher *Mom*." Charlie groans and puts a pillow over his face. "And you were there, which makes it a million times worse."

"If you want, I have three decades of embarrassing stories that are all yours, just say the word."

"That's nice."

"I know." He's sort of patting Charlie's ankle. Poor Charlie, stuck with nobody to comfort him but Simon, the world's least qualified person.

"Give me one now," Charlie says, the pillow still over his face. "Come on."

Simon has no shortage of embarrassing stories, but most are just incidentally embarrassing. He went on a date with a man who confused Simon with some other, more famous actor; once he got distracted and left Whole Foods without paying, just sailed right out the door with his cart until the security guard ran him down. "A few years ago, Jamie was having problems with his boyfriend, so I kept telling him to move out and stay with me. I bought all his favorite foods. I bought a new mattress for the guest room. I offered to put him on my car insurance."

"Your *car insurance?*" Charlie says from under the pillow.

"It made sense at the time." This is a lie, but also Simon's not totally clear on how car insurance works. "Finally he sits me down in a Panera and gives me this whole speech about how we can't get back together. Like, it was a *speech*. He'd definitely practiced. He probably had a PowerPoint presentation that he was going to use if he had to. I could hear the bullet points. One was sexual incompatibility. And I had to explain that, actually, I had no interest in getting back together, I was just lonely and missed him."

"That *is* embarrassing." Charlie's emerged from the pillow. "In a *Panera*."

"Yes, thank you, happy to serve. Do you want to call someone? Alex?"

Charlie tosses the pillow aside. "She doesn't know about this shit."

When Charlie said he wasn't texting people because he couldn't fake being okay, Simon gathered that Dave going missing—or at least Charlie's reaction to it—wasn't common knowledge. But he didn't think that included Alex. "Why not?"

"She needs things to be fun, or at least fine, otherwise she starts making flow charts and action plans, and the next thing you know there's an Alex-shaped hole in the drywall and she's gone."

Simon is surprised to realize he knows Alex well enough to see how this would be true. "Is there someone else you can talk to?"

"No, Simon, I try to keep my unnecessary feelings about my not-dad to myself, actually."

"It wasn't a criticism. I just thought you might want to talk to someone who could, like—I don't know—remind you that your worth doesn't depend on what some shithead in an undershirt thinks about you." Charlie doesn't say anything, so Simon just rambles on. "I mean, obviously it isn't as easy as that. If people could stop internalizing what their parents thought about them—no, shut up, Charlie. You obviously thought of him as a parent when you were a kid, so he counts. How old were you when you lived with him?"

"Eight."

Forget the cliff. Simon wants to feed Dave to sharks. "Right, so some part of your brain was like, 'oh, good, a dad,' and it stuck. That's *fine*, Charlie. It isn't your fault."

The awkward pats can't possibly be doing any good, so Simon just lets his hand rest on Charlie's ankle.

THE MOTEL DOESN'T have a gym, so Charlie puts on his sneakers and announces that he's going for a run.

"Do you mind if I borrow your car?" Simon asks. "I want to see what our dinner options are."

"Sure," Charlie says, handing him the key fob. He looks skeptical, which is fair since Simon's absolutely lying, but Charlie doesn't ask any questions.

As soon as Charlie leaves, Simon drives back to Mike's house. He still has the address in his phone, and he's still angry enough to make some questionable choices.

Usually, Simon is good at boundaries. He treats them like an electrified fence. He stays inside the lines, far from where any normal boundaries are located, not because he's just that respectful of other people's autonomy, but because he's anxious about overstepping and leery of anyone thinking he cares too much.

Right now, there's a good chance he's getting things wrong. He shouldn't do this without Charlie's permission. But *not* doing something is also wrong. Somebody needs to stand up for Charlie, and Simon's the only person around to do it.

"Yes, yes," he tells the dogs when they trot over to greet him. "I'm not mad at *you*."

Mike answers the door, and either he isn't surprised to see Simon or he's a very calm person, because he just opens the door and points to the rear of the house. "He's out back."

Simon thanks him and crosses through the house and back outside to a deck, where Dave is smoking, two empty bottles of beer on the rail in front of him and a full one in his hand.

"Oh, Christ. This again," he says when he sees Simon.

"As far as I can tell, you've done nothing to deserve Charlie caring whether you live or die—worse than nothing—and he still cares about you. He isn't going to stop, so you can either make sure he has whatever minimum information he needs not to spend an entire week of his life panicking about you, or you need to know that you're hurting him. Own it."

Dave doesn't answer. He isn't even looking at Simon, his gaze turned toward the empty hills that surround them.

A curl of anxiety wraps around Simon's stomach, but he reminds himself that he's doing a job. Playing a part. He has lines. The sense of doom recedes, the way it always does when he's acting.

He sits in an Adirondack chair and waits Dave out.

"He's done enough worrying," Dave says. "By the time he was ten, he'd done enough worrying about the fuckup adults in his life to last him a lifetime. I've told him that. I thought I finally got through that thick skull of his."

"Well, you didn't. And you won't. Charlie doesn't know how to not care about people, even when they don't deserve it." Simon thinks about Charlie hugging everyone at the wrap party. He thinks about Charlie explaining how he had to kiss that waiter so he didn't seem like a jerk. He thinks about Charlie driving Simon home while he complained in the passenger seat. "If you want to throw that away, that's up to you, but you can treat him like a person."

Dave swears under his breath and takes a swig from his bottle. "What are you, his boyfriend?"

"If you want to know about his life, you could pick up your phone." Simon doesn't know whether Charlie's out to Dave, but he does know that answering with an easy, honest *no* would be giving this man more information than he deserves.

Dave finishes his beer and drops his cigarette into the empty bottle. He still isn't looking at Simon. "I drove up here a week ago, left the fucking charger at home, and figured nobody would miss me for two weeks."

"I'm sure Charlie texts you more often than once every two weeks. When we went to your house, I think he was worried he might find your *body*. Do you understand what you put him through?"

"He went inside?" Dave asks.

"Don't worry, he didn't eat any of your food," Simon snaps.

"Oh, for fuck's sake, that was Krista's rule, not mine. She didn't want to freeload, and Charlie always ate like a horse."

Dave takes two more bottles of beer from the cooler at his feet and hands one to Simon. Simon doesn't like beer and he doesn't like driving when he's had anything at all to drink, but he knows a crucial prop when he sees one, so he takes the bottle.

"How is he?" Dave asks, passing Simon the bottle opener.

"You know, if you asked him that, you'd make his day."

"You think Charlie would give me a straight answer? He didn't even tell me about rehab until it was over and done with. You want to talk about someone not answering his phone, imagine what the fuck went through my head that month."

Simon tips the bottle back and drinks about a third of a teaspoon of beer. It's Heineken, which is the Devereaux family beer of choice for occasions that involve coolers filled with beer rather than caterers with trays of champagne flutes. It's the beer uncles drink while talking about fantasy football. Simon has an experience like a dolly zoom, a dizzying shift in perspective. He's the fantasy football uncle right now, having a man-to-man talk with another fantasy football uncle. The casting director really fucked this one up.

Simon gets to his feet. "Find a phone. Call him."

Back inside, Simon puts his bottle in the sink, then gives Mike Charlie's phone number and takes Mike's number to give to Charlie. If Dave pulls another disappearing act, Charlie has at least one person to contact.

Simon doesn't know if coming here was a mistake, but he doesn't think it made anything worse. Back at the motel, he'll come clean. If Charlie's upset, Simon will just have to deal with it.

At the bottom of the hill, Simon pulls over onto the same shoulder as a few hours earlier. His hands are sweaty on the steering wheel. He can't stop thinking about Dave saying that he didn't think anyone would notice if he was gone for two weeks.

When Simon isn't shooting *Out There*, he could absolutely disappear without anybody but Jamie noticing. His parents wouldn't be too surprised not to hear from him for a while. Nora would probably just think he was ignoring her. Everyone would think he was ignoring them, because that's exactly what he usually does.

Simon doesn't want to be the kind of person who pushes away

everyone who cares about him. He doesn't want to be able to disappear for a week and not have that matter to someone. He doesn't want anyone who cares about him to think they've thrown their feelings into a trash can.

He texts Jamie, asking if this is an okay time for a phone call. His phone rings fifteen seconds later.

"Everything okay?" Jamie asks.

"Yeah. I'm good. Promise. I'm leaving *Out There*."

Jamie doesn't say anything, and Simon hates himself for not having done this a few days ago, when they could have talked face-to-face.

"Okay," Jamie says. "This makes you happy?"

Simon opens his mouth to say *yes*, but he doesn't know. What if he only gets cast as variations on the theme of uptight doctor on a spaceship? What if his plan—which isn't even a plan so much as it is quitting his job and hoping for the best—doesn't work?

"I want something more challenging," Simon says, because that's true, at least.

"When did you decide?" Jamie asks.

"A month ago."

More silence. "Who else knows?"

Simon winces. "Lian and the producers. My agent. Someone told Alex. Alex told Charlie. I don't think anyone else."

"Wow."

"I'm sorry."

"What do you think you're apologizing for?"

"It would have been shitty if you found out from anyone but me."

"I'm not upset with you." Jamie sighs. "I understand why you didn't tell me. You didn't want me to have career feelings."

"Yes," Simon says, grateful, as always, that Jamie's able to do most of the emotional heavy lifting.

"Whatever I feel about my own life," Jamie says, "I will never not be happy about good things happening to you. Never. You know that, right?"

"Yeah." Now Simon's almost crying, because he doesn't deserve this, but he has it anyway.

"Is it time to call Margie?" Margie is Simon's therapist.

"When I get home."

"Can we talk about how you probably would have quit a few years ago—definitely after the space lobster season, you *hated* that—if you weren't afraid of your agent yelling at you?"

"No," Simon says, unprepared to engage with that on any level.

"So," Jamie says, in a we're-changing-the-topic tone, "you've been tagged in a bunch of pictures from a car festival. I'm sharing some on your Instagram because you look great."

"It's the sunglasses."

"No, it's that you're smiling with actual teeth."

"Gross."

"Charlie looks happy too."

"Charlie always looks happy," Simon says, even though by now he knows it isn't true.

"My point is, you and Charlie look like you're having a great time admiring old cars, which is not a sentence I ever thought I'd say, but here we are. *Are* you having a good time?"

Simon would not characterize the past few hours of his life as a good time, and he doubts the next hour or two is going to be any kind of picnic. But this morning, at the car festival? And yesterday at the taqueria? "Yeah," he says. "I kind of am."

"You look really, really happy in those pictures. Just something to think about."

After they hang up, Simon texts Lian to tell her that he knows he owes her a phone call. Then he texts Roshni to tell her that he can't get into that book she recommended because he's in his sexy dragon era. He texts Nora that he'll be at her graduation party. He opens one of the group chats he's been ignoring. This one's the main cast, and the first thing he sees is:

> **Petra:** Charlie, darling, did you kidnap Simon and make him look at cars?

> **Alex:** it was a mutual, consensual kidnapping, from what I understand

> **Petra:** That really shouldn't make sense. And yet.

> **Roshni:** 👀

> **Amadi:** who had this week in the betting pool

> **Amadi:** Charlie, if you steal Simon's sunglasses, I'll give you five hundred bucks

This is more than Simon can take.

> **Simon:** I will PRESS CHARGES, Amadi.

Roshni: Simon!

Alex: simon!!!

Petra: Simon ♥

Amadi: dude

Simon: For five hundred dollars, you can get your own pair. Look on eBay.

Because he's full of good will or something equally foreign, he does a quick search and pastes the eBay link into the chat.

Chapter Twelve

Charlie opens the door before Simon's even finished swiping his key card. He's wearing sweatpants and no shirt. His hair is wet like he just got out of the shower.

Charlie steps aside to let him in but then stops him with a hand on Simon's shoulder. He's staring at Simon so intently that Simon wants to look away. "What did he say to you?"

Simon takes this to mean that Charlie knows where Simon was.

"That's from talking to Jamie," Simon explains, waving a hand at his red eyes. "I told him I'm leaving the show."

Something complicated happens on Charlie's face, and Simon realizes too late that he just confirmed that he's leaving the show, not merely thinking about it. He's ready for an argument—about Dave, about Simon leaving the show, about Simon monopolizing the bathroom counter, about anything, because that would be normal. But Charlie doesn't look upset. Slowly, he lifts a hand to touch Simon's face.

"Everything go okay with Jamie?" Charlie's hand is big and warm and shocking.

"Yeah, very."

Charlie's thumb strokes Simon's cheekbone in a way that makes Simon's brain white out. He was so ready for Charlie to be annoyed, and this is so plainly the opposite of annoyance, that Simon is flooded with relief. Only when the relief hits him does he realize how very badly he didn't want Charlie to be upset with him.

Simon's spent seven years accepting Charlie's annoyance, Charlie's dislike, as the baseline standard state of affairs between them. At some point in the last day—maybe before that, maybe a while before—Simon started wanting something else, and now he has it in the form of Charlie's hand on his face.

"So. Dave called." Charlie's voice isn't any louder than it needs to be, with Simon just a few inches away. "He *apologized*. What did you say to him? Were knives involved? What did you *do*?"

Simon swallows. There is no way to tone down what he said to Dave. No way to make it sound like anything other than what it was.

"I told him he was lucky to have you and should stop being an entire bag of dicks about it." He swallows again, makes himself blink, tries to focus on something other than the blue of Charlie's eyes. "And he basically told me that he's trying to forcibly stop you from worrying about him because you've exceeded your lifetime quota of worrying about people. He is, obviously, a moron. But I don't think he's actively trying to hurt you."

Charlie's other hand settles on Simon's face, and Simon thinks he might die. There's no way he's breathing right now.

"Thanks," Charlie says, almost a whisper.

"It's nothing," Simon says. Or tries to say. He's a little distracted by the half step forward Charlie just took. The edge of Simon's cardigan is touching Charlie's bare chest.

Simon could move away if he wanted to, but he can't imagine wanting to, not when Charlie's leaning in, not when Charlie hesitates just a fraction of a second, his lips millimeters from Simon's.

They're so close, breathing the same air, the space between them warm and heavy with anticipation.

When Charlie's lips brush against his, Simon makes a sound. Not from surprise—he knew what Charlie was doing—but because he doesn't expect it to feel so immediately good. Kissing feels good; this is not news, even to Simon, to whom first kisses primarily feel anxious, like impromptu performances you can't rehearse for.

Kissing Charlie feels like he's finally let go of something heavy. Like he's filling his lungs after holding his breath. Charlie's lips are warm and a little chapped, and his beard is much softer than Simon thought it would be, and his hands are cupping Simon's face, and Simon's been waiting for this.

There's nowhere for Simon to put his own hands other than the naked skin of Charlie's back, so that's what he does, and now Charlie makes a sound, groaning against Simon's mouth.

Simon pulls back, just enough to talk. "Are you kissing me because I was rude to an old man? Is that what does it for you?" There's probably a less unhinged way to ask if Charlie's doing this out of something as unsexy as gratitude, but Simon's nowhere close to hinged at the moment.

He's near enough to feel Charlie smile. "Simon, I'm kissing you because I ran out of reasons not to."

That's insulting, Simon's sure of it, and later on, when his brain is back online, maybe he'll figure out why. For now, he presses in for another kiss.

When Simon's thought about how Charlie might kiss—in real life, not on camera—and Simon's maybe thought about this a non-zero number of times, he figured Charlie would be all in, right from the beginning. Teeth. A well-placed thigh. Definitely some groping.

But this—Charlie's hands cradling his jaw, Charlie's lips barely tasting him—is not that, not at all, and the gulf between expectations and reality is making Simon feel off-balance. Dizzy.

One of Charlie's hands disappears from Simon's face, and Simon doesn't like that, not at all. But then that hand lands on Simon's hip, and he's being steered backward until he hits the door. And that's—that's perfect, because it turns out that what Simon wants more than anything is to have the door behind him and the solid bulk of Charlie in front of him.

"Why do you taste like beer?" Charlie murmurs. "I've never seen you drink beer."

"I had to be super butch, so I drank two molecules of Heineken," Simon says into the corner of Charlie's mouth. He can feel when Charlie smiles.

When Charlie leans in again, Simon feels the muscles of Charlie's back shift under his hands. It jolts Simon's brain into remembering that he doesn't have to keep his hands politely at ten and two o'clock on Charlie's back. He's allowed to touch. Encouraged, even, if the way Charlie bites Simon's lip is anything to go by.

Simon is not unfamiliar with the shape of Charlie's body. He's not unfamiliar with how Charlie's body feels against his own or the smell of his skin. He knows what Charlie's shoulder blades feel like, the nape of his neck, the curve of his shoulder. It's different, obviously, like this, but the collision of familiar and brand-new is electricity under Simon's fingers, and he wonders if Charlie feels the same way as his hands map out the terrain of Simon's hips, his ribs, his shoulders.

"Fucking layers." Charlie pulls at the hem of Simon's shirt, sliding a hand underneath.

"Get rid of it." Simon could do it himself, but it's better when Charlie does it. Simon starts in on his buttons but only gets the first two open before Charlie's pulling it over his head, throwing it on the floor next to his sweater with the kind of disrespect fine fabrics don't deserve and which Simon is not prepared to do anything about. Then they're skin to skin, and it's a shock, new in every way. Charlie's mouth is hot and urgent on his neck, his body big and warm and heavy.

Simon's thoughts are honey-slow, and it takes a minute before he remembers he can put his mouth on Charlie too. So that's what he does, kissing Charlie's jaw. Simon is slightly obsessed with the place where the scratch of Charlie's beard meets the softness of his neck, the way Charlie's body goes taut at the contact, the sound he makes.

"We should get dinner," Simon says, feeling like somebody ought to make an effort to hit the brakes.

"Yeah, sure," Charlie agrees. "Just give me ten minutes." He presses his palm over the zipper of Simon's jeans. "More like five."

Simon, torn between arguing and the need to push into Charlie's hand, decides to split the difference. "Why aren't we on the bed? It's right there, for God's sake, Charlie."

The room is cramped enough that the bed is, in fact, *right* there. Two uncoordinated steps, and Simon's on his back, Charlie on top of him. Simon could stay like this, Charlie's weight pinning him to the bed, but he needs to know what's next. He's no good at surprises.

"What do you like?" Simon asks.

"Right now, I like kissing you."

It's a non-answer, and Simon could be annoyed that Charlie's missing the point. It's also not something Simon needs spelled out for him—obviously Charlie's enjoying this, because Simon's never been kissed so thoroughly in his life. But for some reason, Charlie's words send a warm rush of pleasure racing down Simon's spine.

"I like it too," he says. It feels like the darkest confession, something whispered and secret.

"I can tell." Charlie rolls their hips together.

"That's not what I—"

"I know. I just mean I can tell when you like something. All the rubber bands holding you together aren't strung so tight, just for a minute. That's how you get when craft services has those muffins or when someone brings their dog to set. Or when I kiss you right here." He kisses a spot under Simon's ear.

Simon can feel it, can feel himself slacken in Charlie's arms, then shivers when he thinks about Charlie noticing, knowing what it means, cataloging the things that make it happen.

"I like it," Charlie says. "It's one of the things I like the most about you. I just really do," he mumbles into Simon's neck, and Simon can't figure out how that relates to anything Charlie's been saying, so he puts two fingers in Charlie's mouth to shut him up, and also because he wants to, and things escalate from there.

Well, by escalate, Simon means Charlie pulls Simon's fingers out of his mouth and presses his hand to the bed, says, "For fuck's sake," and kisses him some more. Tomorrow, Simon's going to be red with beard burn and the thought makes him squirm, makes him think about even more places Charlie could mark him up, even more ways.

Simon's uncomfortably aware that he's not bringing much to the table, just sort of lying there and letting Charlie maul him, but in Simon's defense, he's stunned. Stunned, in the literal sense, like maybe he suffered a head injury at some point between walking through the door and now. Instead of thoughts, he just has nerve endings. He can barely move.

Still, for years now, he's been imagining—reluctantly, but it happens anyway—touching Charlie. And so that's what he does. But for some reason instead of getting a hand on Charlie's pectorals, like any sane person, or even his biceps, Simon reaches for Charlie's beard. Charlie goes still, then presses his face into Simon's hand like a cat. He turns his head to kiss Simon's palm.

Simon slides his hand lower, skimming his fingers over Charlie's chest, catching on a nipple and staying there for a moment when he hears Charlie suck in a breath. With his other hand, Simon tries to unfasten his own jeans.

Something in Charlie seems to snap, and he has the rest of Simon's clothes off before Simon can say much more than "hurry, please, hurry." He's staring at Simon, and Simon really likes that. Maybe he preens a little, but also he can't take another single second of this. "Why the *fuck* are your pants still on?" he asks, reasonably.

Charlie's sweatpants hit the floor. Before Simon can even properly look, Charlie is kneeling between Simon's legs, taking him in his mouth—and, yep, this is what Simon thought Charlie would be like, urgent and a little desperate. Eager.

Simon might be a little eager himself, because he isn't going to last long, especially not once he gets a hand in Charlie's hair, especially not when Charlie groans in approval. Charlie's hand is gripping Simon's thigh, his mouth is perfect, and Simon's orgasm hits him like a two-by-four to the head.

When he opens his eyes, Charlie's kneeling over him. "Do you need the paramedics?" He looks smug.

"Shut up," Simon says, and pulls him down, kissing him, stroking him lazily, then a little less lazily when Charlie clasps his own hand over Simon's. He gets distracted by the feel of Charlie's hand around his, the rhythm of it, the noises Charlie's making into Simon's neck.

"Come on, Simon, keep your head in the game," Charlie says when Simon gets distracted again. Simon tries to bite his shoulder, but it turns into a kiss.

SIMON'S EXPERIENCE IS that never, not once, has sex made things less awkward. He's sure that when he gets out of the shower, the fragile thread of civility he and Charlie have been relying on for the past few days will have snapped under the weight of We Just Had Sex.

But instead, Charlie starts reading aloud from the menus of the least-bad-sounding restaurants in the area. They wind up having adequate sandwiches while mutually bitching about the worst directors they've worked with over the past few years.

That lunch back home, when they'd stared at their plates and mumbled at one another and ultimately resorted to looking at dog pictures, now feels implausible. Of course they can make conversation. They have the same exact job. They know the same people. They both have personalities built on the shaky foundation of attachment issues. It would be bizarre if they couldn't find things to talk about. Part of it's just Charlie needing to be friendly with whoever's nearby, but friendliness doesn't come easily to Simon, and it's happening anyway.

"Why do you keep paying for my food? And the hotels?" Charlie asks after Simon's repeatedly smacked Charlie's hand away from the check.

"I don't want to owe you," Simon says automatically, because it's true, or at least not a lie. He doesn't think he could handle adding gratitude to the list of things he's feeling about Charlie Blake.

Charlie squints at him. "So now I have to owe you?"

"No, because I don't actually think you owe me."

"But I'm an asshole who's going to hold a couple hamburgers and a cheap motel over you? What the fuck."

"No, I mean—the money doesn't matter to me."

"We make literally the same amount of money."

"But I grew up with it. Like, a lot of it." Simon huffs impatiently because Charlie must already know this. "There is no universe in which the cost of a Caesar salad and a BLT could possibly matter to me or has ever mattered to me. So I make sure I'm the one who picks up the tab."

Charlie looks at him for a moment. "I can't decide if that's nice or some weird power play."

It's mostly Simon minimizing his own discomfort. "Let me know if you find out. I'd love to know."

Simon's sure bedtime will result in some other disaster, like maybe Charlie will try to sleep in his bed (absolutely not) or want to have more sex (undecided). But what happens is that Charlie takes the ruined bedspread off the bed they'd been in earlier, throws it on the floor, gets under the sheet, and says, "What time do you want to wake up?"

It's all suspiciously normal.

"Charlie," Simon says after turning the lamp off, the heavy curtains blocking the light from the parking lot.

"Yeah?" It sounds like Charlie's rolled over to face him, even though it's too dark to see one another.

"What are we doing tomorrow?" Charlie's going to try to see Dave again, but that won't take all day. "Are we going home?" He hopes Charlie hears that Simon isn't demanding to go back to Los Angeles. He isn't even asking to. He just wants to know.

"I want to stick around here for another day or two. If you need to leave, there's a tiny airport in Flagstaff. I can drive you. I'm not—I mean, it's up to you."

Simon thinks that's Charlie's way of making it clear that he isn't asking Simon to leave. He's also not asking Simon to stay—which is good, because Simon wouldn't know what to do with that.

They've already shared a bunch of pictures from the past two days, and Charlie put a few videos on his TikTok, including one Simon took of Charlie and the orange convertible, where you can hear Simon saying, very quiet, "Hand to God, Charlie just called this car *baby*." There's no need for Simon to stay.

Simon isn't sure why he wants to stay. They'll probably have more sex, which is in the pro column. But he feels like he's not going to be able to process what happened if Charlie's right there, because Charlie has a way of taking up ninety percent of Simon's thoughts when he's nearby.

"I'll stay," Simon says.

Charlie's quiet for a few seconds. "Good."

Chapter Thirteen

Hearing Charlie talk about cars doesn't get old, and today the car chatter is interspersed with finger guns and high fives and back slaps, all reminders that yesterday Charlie was subdued. Today, not worried about Dave, he's reverted to form. When Simon stops to pet a dog or text Jamie, and Charlie bounds off, Simon can track him down by following his voice. He's too loud. His crackling energy almost takes up physical space.

It's always driven Simon nuts, the way Charlie dials it up when he has an audience. He basks in attention. It's so—needy, maybe. People should see through it, should know it's an act. They shouldn't encourage him.

But, of course, Charlie likes attention. People don't usually go into acting if they hate attention. Simon spent high school and college with theater kids, and there's nobody who loves an audience as much as a teenager who just realized they're *good*, who just realized people *want* to watch them.

Simon started acting because pretending to be someone else—speaking someone else's words, moving his body like it belongs to someone else—made the more irritating parts of his brain shut off. But it hadn't taken long before he started craving that adrenaline rush of doing well, being seen, being enjoyed.

Charlie should have been a theater kid too. He should have spent his teenage years doing schlocky school productions of *Fiddler on the Roof* and *Godspell*, not living through whatever gritty reality he endured.

Instead of meeting for coffee like reasonable people while discussing their problems (or whatever, Simon doesn't know, he's never claimed to be reasonable), Charlie and Dave stand side by side, looking at the same car, complimenting it, then moving on to the next car. Simon rolls his eyes and leaves to buy two coffees. He doesn't get one for Dave. Instead, Dave gets some of Simon's best glares and some side eye.

"Jesus Christ, calm down," Charlie hisses.

"No," Simon says, and he doesn't.

When the crowds get thick, Charlie's hand lands at the small of Simon's back. Sometimes, when they're bending close to talk, he'll touch Simon's arm. Simon keeps leaning into it without meaning to. He has to check himself.

It's not that he minds being touched. He doesn't want to hug strangers and he doesn't like handshakes, but when it's someone he likes—

And that's a category Charlie falls into now.

Simon's going to need some time quiet and alone to make sense of the past few days. Tomorrow they're driving home and that'll be that. Charlie will go back to being the kind of person who doesn't touch Simon, and they'll only see one another when Simon is walking Edie during one of Charlie's runs.

But right now, none of that's happened yet, and Charlie has a hand on Simon's elbow, steering him toward a very eighties-looking sports car.

Charlie touches everyone. It doesn't mean anything. Simon's spent the morning watching him give high fives and back slaps to total strangers, shake hands with everyone he meets, lean close to a million people in a million pictures.

Simon usually tries to resist the urge to psychoanalyze people, mostly because he feels acutely nauseous at the idea of anyone trying to make sense of his own brain and pin it to the details of his life. But knowing what Charlie's childhood was like and seeing how he seems to crave physical contact now—well, Simon can't help but draw some conclusions.

Maybe as an experiment, and maybe because he's at some weird car festival in a town that's an Americana-themed Pinterest board and it feels like all rules are suspended, and maybe just because he wants to, he touches Charlie's hand when they sit down for lunch. When they're posing for yet another picture, Simon lets his arm linger a bit around Charlie's shoulders. Charlie goes still, a pause in the absolutely feral energy he's throwing around today. It's . . . good.

When it's time for Dave to leave, Charlie goes in for a hug. If Dave doesn't hug him back, Simon will simply push him into traffic. But Dave hugs Charlie and pats his back, and the hug passes muster. Dave gets to live another day.

Before Dave gets into his truck, Simon hands him an iPhone charger that he bought at a sickening markup at a shop catering to tourists hungry for Route 66 Christmas ornaments.

"Oh my God," Charlie mutters as Dave drives away. "Why are you like this?"

"Considerate? Generous?"

"I didn't know you could give someone a phone cord and make it look like a death threat."

"Thank you," Simon says, pleased to have communicated his intentions so clearly.

"Why don't you drive an old car?" Simon asks later that afternoon when Charlie's giving a blue convertible the kind of praise that makes Simon feel filthy.

"Airbags. Anti-lock brakes, crumple zone, fuel economy. They're pretty—I mean look at her, Christ—but not to drive on the freeway."

That's about the most boring answer that Charlie could have given, and Simon says so. Charlie rolls his eyes. "I mean it as a compliment," Simon says. It's true.

"Oh my God." Simon comes to a halt in front of a lime green car that looks like it was drawn by someone who'd only heard about cars second or third hand. It looks like a Honda Civic hatchback dressed up as a race car for Halloween. It's *The Island of Doctor Moreau*, but for economy cars. "What," he says, "is wrong with that thing?"

"There isn't one thing wrong with that car," Charlie says firmly. "Except the paint, which honestly should be brighter." If it were any brighter, Simon's retinas would disintegrate. "It's a Gremlin."

"It sure is," Simon agrees. There's something so fundamentally misbegotten about this car's design that Simon can almost respect it. It's a statement, if nothing else.

"An AMC Gremlin. From '73 or '74, I think. It isn't a muscle car, but some people will tell you it is." It's heavily implied that anyone who would say this is living in the darkest ignorance. This might be the most judgmental Charlie's been when talking about anyone other than Simon.

"Tell me more," Simon says, and is treated to a lecture about engine size, the 1973 oil crisis, and the 1970 passage of the Clean Air Act. Charlie doesn't have to look up any of those dates. He apparently just has that information sitting in his head.

"This is kind of hot," Simon observes.

"V-8 engines are hot, yes. That's the point of muscle cars."

"No, I mean you infodumping. You being. Smart," Simon concludes, because that's the word.

Charlie looks like his operating system is about to crash. "You—what. Shut up."

An off-leash corgi wanders over, so Simon pays it some attention instead of dwelling on whatever weirdness Charlie is committing.

They look at ten million more cars. Simon's in the kind of good mood that makes him feel like all those brain chemicals that are usually in too short supply, all the dopamine and serotonin and endorphins, are fizzing in his blood like bubbles in champagne. He knows it won't last. He isn't new here. The bad stuff comes back but then it goes away and he gets days like this.

He tries to take a mental snapshot—the buzz of conversation and the distant sound of a honking horn, the blue of the sky, the smell of corn dogs and cigarettes. Charlie, laughing, always in frame. He settles for an actual snapshot, even though it can't capture the lightness inside him.

It's closure, probably, that's prompted today's happiness. He's leaving *Out There*, leaving a chapter of his life that hasn't been all bad. Ending things on good terms with Charlie feels right. When, later on, he thinks back on the seven years of his life that he spent on *Out There*, maybe he can be glad about it.

When Simon's phone starts buzzing, he takes it out of his pocket, ready to show Charlie whatever picture of Edie that Jamie's just sent. But it's Nora.

> **Nora:** so I showed the video to my dad and he says he's never seen you laugh like that, not even when you were a baby

> **Simon:** video?

> **Nora:** the tiktok from the taqueria???

> **Nora:** have Charlie check his tiktok. that girl tagged him

Simon sits on a bench, tugging Charlie down by the sleeve so he follows. He shows Charlie his phone screen, and Charlie immediately checks his notifications.

"Oh, wow," Charlie says after a minute. "That's a lot of views."

He holds his phone up for Simon to watch the video of them trying to reenact that GIF two days ago. Simon thought the waitress would post a couple pictures to the taco restaurant's social media, maybe that three second clip where they finally manage to get it right, but now he's watching a video that's got to be a minute long, at least, of him and Charlie grabbing one another and cracking up.

"I told her she could post whatever she wanted," Charlie says, scrubbing his hand across his jaw. "I didn't think she'd post the whole thing. I didn't know she has like eighty thousand TikTok followers, or that it—" He clears his throat. "That it looked like this."

The video ends and loops back to the beginning. There's a lot of touching, much more than Simon remembers. There's also more eye contact. Simon remembers that moment when Charlie caught his eye, and Simon recognized a flicker of want there, but he doesn't think you can pick that up on camera, just a general sort of intensity. At least on Charlie's end.

Simon, though, looks—he looks fucking smitten. He looks like he's never seen anything as wonderful as Charlie Blake.

Something hot and panicky starts swirling around in his stomach and he forces himself to think about this rationally. Does this video change anything? Charlie was there, Charlie knows they were a little flirty. After yesterday, that's all out in the open, anyway. Nothing on this video is news to either of them, however embarrassed Simon might be at the moment.

The rest of the world may see this video and realize they're witnessing a not particularly heterosexual moment, but Simon doesn't think it will affect him. Some people will be assholes about it, but it isn't anything Simon hasn't heard before. He doesn't need to be convincingly straight to get the kind of roles he'd like to get in the future. He isn't looking to be a leading man in action movie blockbusters or superhero franchises. Mostly, Simon is annoyed that he has to think about this at all. It's like an emotional tax levied only on queer people.

Charlie, though. He may want the kind of roles casting directors equate with a certain kind of straight masculinity. If he's out, some doors will be closed—maybe not as many as would have been five or ten years ago, but it's still a problem.

"Are you okay?" Simon asks. Charlie must have watched the video five times by now. "For what it's worth, I think it mostly looks like I'm being gay *at* you, not like you're . . . complicitly queer, or whatever."

"Simon, can you just shut the fuck up?"

They've probably told one another to shut up a thousand times, and there's no reason this time should feel any different. Simon finishes his coffee and counts the number of cowboy hats in the crowd passing them by.

When he glances down, Charlie's still watching the video. Simon hears his own laugh. It's been a while since he's seen himself just being . . . himself.

"There isn't anything in this," Charlie says, tapping his phone, "that bothers me. It's two people having fun. It's cute. Flirty, sure, definitely. I'm glad I saw it. Don't treat it like a bad thing." He runs a hand across his beard. "I told you I'm not closeted. I'm not *not* out. I don't care about that. I'm not—I really fucking refuse—to make a big deal over being seen flirting with a man. For fuck's sake. If we were—I mean, if I were dating a man, I wouldn't keep it a secret, so."

Simon thinks about Charlie kissing that waiter, about him flirting with Jamie. Those aren't the actions of a man who's spending a lot of mental energy on staying closeted.

"Okay. Soft launching your queerness. Happy to help."

"Are *you* okay?" Charlie asks.

"I mean, this," Simon says, gesturing broadly at himself, "is not a secret and never has been. I don't love the idea of my personal life meaning something to total strangers, and that includes homophobes, obviously, but also people looking for queer inspiration or whatever. Sorry if that makes me an asshole."

"That isn't what makes you an asshole," Charlie says.

"Anyway, I guess we don't need to worry about people thinking we hate one another. I mean, mission accomplished."

"Yeah," Charlie sighs.

Simon's phone buzzes with another text from Nora. She's written, "It took my dad fifteen whole minutes to mention that if you publicly came out it would be convenient for his campaign."

"My brother's running for reelection," Simon tells Charlie, showing him the message. "He'd be so happy to be able to talk about his gay brother. Makes him sound like an actual person."

"That's . . . supportive," Charlie says, not sounding too sure about it.

"They actually are supportive. Always have been. My niece is out to everyone. I'm well-adjusted about this one thing and only this one thing."

Charlie doesn't say anything about his own situation. Simon knocks his knee against Charlie's.

"It's a good video," Charlie says.

"Good camera work," Simon agrees.

"She usually does eye makeup tutorials. Go figure."

"Jamie loves those." Simon realizes that Jamie probably saw this yesterday and didn't tell him when they talked.

> **Simon:** were you not going to tell me that I'm internet famous?

> **Jamie:** you're famous-famous you total dork

> **Simon:** TikTok young people love me

Jamie: you have a fucking emmy

Simon: the youths, though

Jamie: Simon Devereaux are you GIDDY?

Simon's smiling at his phone, and when he looks up, he finds Charlie watching him. "Jamie," he explains.

They sit there for a while, and Simon knows he has to say something because this is one of those silences that has edges, even though he doesn't know exactly why.

"What I want to know," Simon says, "is whether you bribed Laura from craft services to hide the blueberry muffins from me." He's been thinking about this since yesterday when Charlie said he knows Simon likes them—which, honestly, is exactly the kind of appalling thing Charlie Blake *would* think was appropriate dirty talk. His brain's put together a photo montage of all the times Charlie smugly ate one of those muffins right in front of Simon's face.

Charlie lets out a boom of laughter. "In my defense, they taste so much better when I know you don't have one."

"You are so fucking petty."

"Only to you."

There's no sane reason this should please Simon, but here he is, pleased. "I had no idea Laura could be bought."

"It's not her, I swear. The supplier started only sending a few every day, so I made sure to swing by early enough to snag one."

"One," Simon repeats, skeptical.

"Okay, four, but I gave three away. I didn't eat them all myself."

"And you waited to eat your muffin until you were in front of me?"

"Yup."

"That is so twisted," Simon says, and so what if it comes out fond.

THINGS HAPPEN FAST once they get back to the motel room, and that's probably Simon's fault. He has Charlie stripped to the waist as soon as the door's shut. He doesn't think he's getting this wrong, because all day long Charlie's been giving him these looks like he wants to eat Simon alive.

"What do you want?" Charlie asks, mumbling the words into Simon's neck as he works open the buttons on Simon's jeans.

"Well," Simon says. If this is the last chance Simon gets to have Charlie, he's not wasting it. They're driving back to Los Angeles tomorrow and normal rules will be back in effect.

Charlie pauses, his hands still on Simon's buttons. "Well?"

Look, Simon's kind of picky about sex, just like he's picky about every other thing in his life, and reciting the laundry list of things he doesn't like is a guaranteed way to kill the mood. "I don't like—" he starts. Charlie's looking at him. Simon shuts his eyes. "No hurting. No name calling. Nothing mean."

"You don't want me to be mean to you," Charlie says, and something in his voice makes Simon need to open his eyes.

"No judgment if you like that kind of thing. It's just not for me."

"I wasn't going to call you names, Simon."

"No, I mean—yes, please don't call me names. But the main thing is that I don't want to call *you* names." Charlie looks like he's trying not to look surprised, and it isn't working. "I don't want to be—"

Mean is the wrong word. Bossy is closer. He thinks of himself as sullen and bitchy, but knows it comes off, somehow, as quiet and stern to people who are optimistic about that sort of thing. He's eighty percent sure—a hundred percent, a hundred and twenty percent—this mistaken impression is what drew Jamie to him at first.

Anyway, he can't tell Charlie that he doesn't want to be bossy in bed, because he knows exactly how it'll sound. Whatever impression Charlie gets will be half right, but he'll probably conclude that Simon wants to be bossed around, which isn't right either. The truth is that he just likes the idea that someone wants to make him feel good, that he wants to make them feel good too. Obviously he can't say any of this.

"I think the men I sleep with expect me to be," Simon starts, "something I'm not? Aggressive? I have no interest in smacking anyone around. Also no interest in tying anybody up and telling them they're a good boy."

Charlie blinks. "Duly noted."

"I don't like being edged. Sertraline edged me for like ten years. I don't need that energy from amateurs."

Charlie lets out a crack of laughter.

"Sertraline's an SSRI," Simon explains.

"I know what it is. You don't take it anymore?"

Simon truly can't imagine a less erotic topic than his psychiatric history, but this conversation has already taken a sharp turn toward the unsexy, so why not just double down. "That class of drugs kept messing with my migraine meds. What sucks is that they were pretty good for my anxiety, but the migraines were making my life hell, so here we are."

Charlie's quiet for a minute, and Simon hopes he isn't casting his mind back, trying to identify the point when Simon went from being someone passably normal-adjacent to the person he is now. But Charlie just says, "Sounds hard."

Simon swallows. "Yeah."

"So, no edging. No pain or insults. No, uh, tying me up and calling me a good boy." He utterly fails to keep a straight face.

"Sorry to disappoint."

Charlie laughs again and pulls off Simon's jeans. "No, it's good. I am totally fine with those rules. But what do you *want*?" His voice goes so gravelly on that last word that Simon can almost feel it.

"I don't know." Simon knows exactly what he wants but can't bring himself to say it, not with Charlie looking at him. "Just normal sex please."

"Oh, *normal* sex. That kind of sex."

"Charlie." Simon pulls Charlie onto the bed with him, because they need to be done talking.

"No, really, how do you like it?"

"I told you. Very vanilla." Simon turns onto his side, away from Charlie, tipping his head into the pillow. He has a perfectly clear vision of what he wants right now and he doesn't know how he could possibly communicate that more clearly. Well, not without actually saying what he means, which is not an option. "Just. Nice."

"Nice. Why the fuck are you being shy all of a sudden. Just tell me where, in an ideal world, my dick is in all of this. I feel like you're telling me you want to get fucked but I literally do not know because you're being such a weirdo."

Simon is fundamentally incapable of answering any of this in a sane way. "I mean, I *could* fuck you. Like, if you really wanted me to. In an emergency situation."

"You'd fuck me to save my life."

"Yes. Exactly. You're welcome." This isn't even a fair characterization of what Simon likes. He doesn't hate topping, and even likes it under certain circumstances, but none of those circumstances are applicable when he has Charlie Blake in his bed for one night only. He knows exactly what he wants, and he does not have the faintest fucking idea why he's suddenly coy about it, except that he simply cannot open his mouth and ask Charlie to fuck him. "There's condoms and lube in my suitcase." He waves a hand and hopes Charlie realizes it's an order.

Charlie does realize it's an order. When he gets back into bed, he kisses the exposed side of Simon's neck, his hand sliding low on Simon's belly, his chest pressed against Simon's back. "What I'm hearing is that you want me to fuck you real nice."

Simon tries to smother himself with the pillow so Charlie can't hear whatever sound he just made, but there's no way Charlie missed the way Simon's body reacted to that. At least Simon doesn't need to explain anymore.

Charlie keeps kissing him, his mouth warm and slow on Simon's neck, his hips rolling against Simon's, his touch just a little too light, like he's being careful. It's exactly what Simon wants, and it's only a complete inability to be normal that makes him speak. "But what do you want?" Simon asks, his voice sounding far away. "We didn't talk about that."

"Oh my God," Charlie whispers into Simon's skin. "Can you get out of your own way for two seconds?"

"Probably not," Simon says, honest.

"Baby, what I really want is to see what happens when I give you what you want."

It's not the first time anyone's called Simon *baby*. It is, however, the first time it doesn't make him want to get dressed and go home. Usually, that sort of thing—sweetheart, baby, darling—makes Simon think he's dealing with a case of mistaken identity. Like they've forgotten who they have in their bed because Simon is just not the kind of person who inspires *baby*. He doesn't like being lied to.

But when Charlie says it, there's a bit of a tease, like he knows perfectly well that Simon's about to riot and is daring him to try. It's also undeniably *nice*, like Charlie's following orders while also being impossible. Simon buries his face in the pillow and groans.

Charlie's kissing the back of Simon's jaw, the curve of his shoulder, the spot behind his ear. He can feel Charlie, hard, pressing into the small of his back. He can feel Charlie's weight, and it sends a jolt of desire down his spine.

"What the fuck," he mumbles into the pillow. He keeps his face there, pretending he's invisible, and lets his universe collapse into the feel of Charlie's fingers, Charlie's mouth on Simon's spine.

Charlie doesn't make him roll over, just pushes him onto his side a little and gets a hand behind one of his knees. The intimacy of that—Charlie's hand on the back of his knee—is startling, somehow, despite everywhere else he's touched Simon tonight.

Simon moves where Charlie puts him, and if this is the most compliant Simon's been in his life, then that's just a coincidence. Nothing to do with Charlie, nothing to do with *that's it, baby, just like that, so good*. Simon asked for nice, but he didn't count on nice being weaponized.

And it is nice, it starts out really fucking sweet, and Simon's absolutely still hiding his face in that pillow, but he also flings a hand out, and Charlie grabs it, holding it to the mattress. It starts out nice, and maybe it even stays that way when Simon's on his knees, holding on to the headboard, his thoughts dissolving in the onslaught of *so good, look at you*.

After, he collapses, boneless, brainless. That was too intense. It was *tender*, which isn't even something Simon does. It shouldn't have been like that—it should have been fun. Yesterday was fun. He'll be embarrassed about it tomorrow. But they're leaving tomorrow, which is just as well.

Right now, though, Charlie's next to him, motionless, one heavy arm flung over Simon's back. It's not cuddling. It's one arm. And it's only there because that's where it landed.

Simon opens his eyes, takes in Charlie's profile. The only light is whatever's leaking in from the motel parking lot, around the edges of the curtains, but it's enough to make out the shape of the tattoos on Charlie's arm and chest, the one on the top of his thigh. He can see the flower on Charlie's chest. On the arm that doesn't have the swirl of stars, there are the two moons and a bird in flight that's the symbol of the rebel group on *Out There*. Lian locked herself in her office the day Charlie showed up with that one. Scattered up and down his left forearm are what look like stick-and-poke tattoos—vines, mountains, a wonky-looking lizard. Since they're all on his left arm, Simon guesses Charlie did them himself.

Simon's seen them all, even the tattoo high on Charlie's thigh, dozens of times, could map them out blindfolded. It feels a little dangerous, knowing that the map of Charlie's body has gotten into his mind without his wanting it, knowing that Charlie has tangled himself around Simon's psyche. It makes him wonder, for the first time, how hard it will be to cut himself free.

From an *Out There* fan Discord

DeathStarJacuzzi: Obviously we've all seen the video, but in case you didn't notice, that's a Tom Ford shirt Simon Devereaux's wearing at a taqueria in suburban Phoenix and—don't quote me on this—but I think those are Celine aviators tucked into his collar. It's killing me that his shoes are out of frame.

GalactoseIntolerance: Meanwhile, Charlie Blake, bless his heart, is wearing a t-shirt that looks like it used to say UCLA Women's Sports and has a hole in the armpit

SimonDevereauxsCheekbones: No offense but I give zero fucks about what they're wearing. I desperately need a reality check. After writing approximately a million words of fanfic about these guys my case of brain rot is too far advanced to tell if I'm picking up on a vibe or just hallucinating it as per usual

GalactoseIntolerance: def a vibe

HowlsMovingSpaceship: we can stop speculating on the private lives of actual people ANY TIME y'all

SupervillainApologist: No, sorry, I love you all but you're missing the point, which is that I think this is the first documented instance of Simon Devereaux laughing in public

GalactoseIntolerance: this is, in fact, exhibit A in re: The Vibe

SupervillainApologist: and, like, sure. I know they're actors, it is literally their job to convey emotions with their faces or whatever, but I've seen every episode of Out There an unhealthy number of times and also I've watched red carpet footage like it's the fucking Zapruder film and I have NEVER seen Simon Devereaux look that happy

SpacePope: Is nobody going to talk about Charlie Blake's BEARD? Explain yourselves.

Chapter Fourteen

In the morning, Simon wakes with the familiar sense that his brain is the wrong size for his skull, and like his skeleton has been taken apart and put back together with a few pieces forgotten along the way. It's been nearly a month since his last migraine—a personal best—but his luck was bound to run out. He has maybe an hour before things get bad. The smart thing to do would be to take his medicine and get on the road as soon as possible.

He can do that as soon as Charlie stops kissing the back of his neck. The problem is that Simon doesn't want to tell Charlie to stop. He's torn between the desire to go along with whatever Charlie has in mind and the need to get home as soon as possible.

Before he has to make a decision, his phone rings. With an actual telephone call. He takes it off the nightstand to see who's calling.

"Seriously?" Charlie asks, his mouth moving against Simon's skin.

It's from a contact labeled "Lucien from Restoration Theater" and it takes Simon a moment to figure out that he must have made the contact when he and Lucien were in the same class in drama school. Lucien is directing the play Simon's doing this summer.

"I should take it." Simon steps outside. Which, since it's a motel, means he's in the parking lot. He's wearing sleep pants and a T-shirt, which will just have to be good enough.

"Hi, Simon? It's Lucien from the—"

"Right. Good morning. Or—is it afternoon in New York?"

Lucien laughs, and it's the laugh that gives it away. There are so many kinds of laughs, and so few of them sound apologetic.

"You're not going to believe this, but Tom Brennan—you know Tom? He's been cleared by his orthopedist to do the show. He'd thought he'd be in that boot until August, but it looks like he can get around with just a cane. And there's nothing wrong with Prospero using a cane, you know? Sooo..."

All Simon can think is that this call should have come from his agent. Half the point of an agent is that you get bad news from someone who feels like an ally. They do the whole compliment sandwich thing. It's literally part of their job. You can cry on the phone, or you can badmouth everyone involved in the project that didn't want you. Not that Simon has ever cried on the phone to Ken. Ken would hang up and pretend the call got disconnected.

"Of course," Simon says, using his Jonathan Hale voice: confident, smart, not a garbage pail filled with nerves. "I completely understand."

"I knew you would." Lucien sounds relieved, very much like someone who did *not* know that Simon would understand. "Tom is *great*," he says, "just a great guy."

Simon doesn't know if he's imagining the implication that Simon is *not* great, which is true, obviously, but not what he wants to hear right now. He keeps thinking of that article in *Variety*. Tom is great. Simon has difficulties on set.

"Sure," Simon says. "Tom's great." He's never met Tom.

"I wanted to let you know myself. It would have been fun to have you on board, but..."

The word *fun* reignites all Simon's worries that he only got that part due to a combination of last-minute availability and the juxtaposition of an unserious actor with a serious role. (He knows this can't be true; he knows he's done serious acting; he knows that even his work on *Out There* isn't *un*serious. He knows these things on a rational level—a level that's completely inaccessible to him right now in the parking lot of a motel in northern Arizona.)

"No worries," Simon says, a phrase he's never before uttered in his life.

He ends the call.

Simon doesn't know why it never occurred to him that the actor who was originally cast might recover sooner than expected. Somehow, while he'd been busy worrying about everything else, he'd neglected to worry about that. People always say that there's no point to worrying, but it isn't true: one real advantage to comprehensive, thorough worrying is that you rarely get blindsided by a disaster you haven't already considered. That doesn't make it easier, but it takes the sharp new edge off and makes the problem into something worn in and familiar.

He considers opening the app that Jamie put on his phone, the one that tells you when to inhale and exhale in a way that's supposed to make you relax. But the idea of swiping through his phone and looking for an app when he doesn't even know what the icon looks like, then standing there while breathing exercises fail to work, makes him feel even worse.

How in hell is he supposed to go back inside? Charlie's there. He can't tell Charlie what happened. He can't make himself admit that he got . . . fired, basically. He got fired. He got fired, and it shouldn't matter, because it's just one role. But it does matter, because he wanted it. It was supposed to be the start of something. It was supposed to fix things, and without it, everything feels broken.

He can't tell any of that to Charlie. He can't even tell Jamie. Sympathy would be unbearable.

He makes himself turn around and use the key card to unlock the door. Inside, Charlie's already dressed and tossing things into his bag.

In some other universe, there's a better version of Simon who says something like, "Guess what. I have the next few weeks free. Let's get in the car and see where it takes us, you and me."

In this universe, Simon clears his throat. "Slight change of plans." He thinks he sounds normal. "I need to go right to New York."

His sublet starts today, technically, even though he hadn't planned on being there until the end of the week. Going to New York solves precisely none of his problems and probably causes a few extra ones, but it buys him a few days of quiet during which he doesn't have to talk about this to anyone.

Charlie's forehead creases.

"It's not a big deal," Simon adds. "But could you take me to the airport? I think you mentioned there was one nearby?"

"Do you have a ticket?"

Simon forces a smile. "On it." He takes out his phone and sees that in two hours there's a flight leaving for New York. He'll need to change planes in Phoenix, but that's fine. The app has his information stored so he can buy the ticket even though his thoughts are jumbled, even though his hands are a little numb.

He remembers Charlie, three days ago, in Dave's house, saying that his hands were tingling. He let Simon help. There's something wrong, something mean, about the fact that Simon can't imagine letting Charlie help, can't even imagine telling Charlie that there's anything to help with. But Charlie is better than Simon. He's known that for a while now.

He gets dressed and packs his suitcase, then manages to leave his charger and his pill case behind. Charlie finds them both and Simon crams them into his shoulder bag.

"Uh." Charlie looks acutely nervous. "Do you need to take . . ." He glances at Simon's bag, where he's just stuck his pill case.

Simon's best—his only—strategy for being anxious in public is to lock his emotions down under a layer of ice. He might feel like he's crumbling to pieces but on the outside he's smooth and cold.

"I don't know what you're talking about," Simon says, and walks out the door.

Charlie's quiet as they check out of the motel, and he's quiet for the first few minutes in the car.

"You want to tell me what's the matter?" Charlie asks.

"Everything's fine." Simon doesn't say anything for the rest of the ride.

Charlie parks the car, even though Simon asks to be dropped off at the curb. Charlie gets Simon's suitcase out of the trunk, glaring at Simon, daring him to protest.

"Look, I'm just going to say this once and you're going to stand there and listen, okay?" Charlie says. His fists are clenched, and that's where Simon looks instead of attempting eye contact. "I'm glad you came with me, all right? Like, yes, obviously because of the sex but also because if you hadn't been around, I'd have forgotten to eat and probably would have wound up sleeping on Dave's couch. I was fucked up and you helped me. So. Thanks."

"It wasn't anything," Simon says, when what he means is that he can't stand to hear it.

Simon has never seen an airport this small. The security checkpoint is basically right there as soon as they walk through the door.

"Text me when you land," Charlie says, his hands in his pockets.

"Sure."

Charlie frowns. "Simon—"

"I'd better go."

He makes himself walk through the tiny security checkpoint and into a terminal that has—he can't quite believe it—only two gates. He buys a granola bar and sits down, and at no point does he look over his shoulder to see if Charlie's still there.

Chapter Fifteen

By the time he boards the plane, Simon's head is already throbbing and there's an ominous blind spot in one eye. He'd known it was coming, but thought maybe it wouldn't catch him this time.

He spends the first leg of the flight participating in the fun little tradition of listing all the ways he deserves this migraine. Maybe it was the Parmesan on his salad last night, or that he skipped breakfast on Saturday. Too much coffee, not enough sleep, that glass of wine he had last week. Cigarette smoke at the car show. Pollen. Existing on a planet that sunlight can reach.

And, most annoying of all, even good stress—like whatever he and Charlie were doing—still counts as stress, at least as far as his body cares. He should have known he wasn't getting out of this weekend without a migraine.

By the time he lands in Phoenix, he's already put on his darkest sunglasses and taken his emergency migraine meds and an extra anti-nausea pill, because the thing about airplanes is that there just isn't anywhere reasonable to throw up. He figured that out at fifteen, on the flight home from his oldest brother's wedding, his mother's tentative hand on the back of his neck as she apologized to the flight attendants.

The meds don't completely wipe out the headache. When he

lands in New York, half his forehead is numb and there's a grenade of dull pain behind his left eye that detonates whenever light leaks in around the edges of his sunglasses.

By some minor miracle, he manages to look at his phone screen long enough to find the address of his sublet. He reads it to a cabbie who keeps looking in the rearview mirror like maybe he recognizes Simon, or maybe just like he's worried Simon's going to be sick in his cab. The cabbie takes turns too quickly, steps on the brakes too abruptly, leans on the horn. Charlie never does any of those things.

When he finally gets inside the apartment, it looks how it did in the pictures—minimal and tidy—and that's all he notices before he collapses on top of a fluffy white duvet and falls asleep.

He wakes up to his phone buzzing in his pocket. And since he has no idea how this apartment is laid out, he can't tell if the light slanting through the window is dawn or dusk; he doesn't know if he's been asleep one hour or ten. The migraine's mostly gone, but he's wrung out.

Wincing at the brightness of the screen, he checks his phone and sees that it's the middle of the morning on Tuesday. He slept for over twelve hours. He's grimy from sleeping in his clothes. His phone buzzes again. Jamie's texting, but Simon's head is too fragile to look at a screen for long, so he uses voice controls to make a call.

"Sorry," he says when Jamie picks up. "Just woke up."

"You went completely radio silent for twenty-four hours."

Simon texted Jamie from the airport to tell him he was heading to New York earlier than he expected. And then, not wanting to answer Jamie's questions about the change in plans, he'd put his phone into airplane mode a little earlier than necessary.

"Migraine," Simon says. "I should have let you know when I landed. Sorry."

"You want to tell me what happened?" When Simon doesn't say anything, Jamie goes on. "Theaters don't just randomly start rehearsals a week early without any warning. We both know this."

Simon still doesn't say anything.

"Was this just your best idea for getting away from Charlie?" Jamie asks. "I mean, who hasn't wanted to fly across the country to avoid someone they hooked up with."

Simon could just not correct Jamie. That would be easier than explaining that Simon doesn't want to talk about how shitty and lost he feels. It would definitely be easier than talking about how an empty, bland apartment three thousand miles from home feels safer than his own house.

He's not sure how he'd even put into words that what he wants is to pet his dog and curl up in his own bed, that he wants to hear Jamie tell him that everything's going to be fine, but that he doesn't think he can endure those things without shattering whatever flimsy scaffolding is holding him up. Even thinking about Edie makes him want to cry.

"You aren't denying that you hooked up with him." Jamie sounds scandalized and delighted.

"Like you didn't already know."

"I thought you'd deny it for a few weeks while you got used to the idea."

And that's why Simon can't go home right now. Jamie knows him too well. He'd take one look at Simon and see him for the mess that he is.

"I'm going to take a shower," Simon says. "And then figure out where the grocery store is."

"Do something nice for yourself, all right?"

"Why?" Simon asks, maybe a little defensive.

"Well. For one, because it's your birthday."

"Fuck." Between the time difference and losing a day to travel and a migraine, he's mentally a day behind.

"Don't take this the wrong way." There's something alarmingly careful in Jamie's voice. "But if I text you, I need you to answer."

"I always do." Simon's a little offended. Other than yesterday, he's never left Jamie on read, not even immediately after they broke up. He leaves practically everybody else on read, but not Jamie.

"While you aren't around for me to look at, I need proof of life. Just for the next day or two."

Simon winces. Even if Simon's never admitted it, Jamie still knows that sometimes Simon's anxiety takes over, grabs the wheel, and drives the car into the nearest ditch.

He might actively resent Jamie asking for this, but then he remembers Dave. Fucking Dave, who sails through life without a care in the world for the people who worry about him. Simon might not be the greatest friend, but he can do better than Dave.

"Okay," he says. "Sure."

After ending the call, Simon remembers that Jamie isn't the only person Simon disappeared on for twenty-four hours. He was supposed to text Charlie when he landed. Well, maybe Simon can't actually do better than Dave. Shit.

Squinting against the horrors of his phone screen, he pulls up Charlie's contact and types out "sorry, got here safe." It's not enough, but he doesn't know what would be enough, so he sends the text and goes back to sleep.

THE SUBLET IS in a fairly soulless Chelsea high-rise. It's a five-minute walk to Whole Foods, has a washer and dryer in the unit, and isn't cluttered with other people's belongings.

It would have been a short enough walk to the theater, but Simon isn't thinking about that right now. Instead, he's filling his shopping cart with premade salads and a random assortment of foods that he can't visualize forming any kind of meal. He may not have a plan for his career, but he does have a sixteen-dollar jar of almond butter and some crackers made from cauliflower, and that's going to have to be good enough for now.

As soon as he gets the groceries into the refrigerator, he's ready to fall back asleep. He doesn't know if he's tired from the migraine or if it's some kind of emotional hangover, but he makes himself have a glass of water and a few spoonfuls of almond butter before getting into bed.

When he wakes up, it's completely dark out, which means he's going to wind up fully nocturnal if he doesn't start paying attention to the time. There's a text on his phone from Charlie. It just says "Hey. Happy birthday."

There's no "how's New York" or "how was your flight," because Charlie doesn't expect Simon to respond. Simon disappeared in a way that Charlie probably took personally and then didn't text when he landed. Charlie has drawn some accurate conclusions about what kind of person Simon is.

He has a salad, a totally reasonable choice for—he checks his phone—one in the morning. But if it's one here, then it's only ten in California. He sends a picture of his salad to Jamie, the proof of life Jamie requested. "Alive and eating," he writes. Jamie sends a thumbs-up immediately, then sends a picture of Edie, fast asleep on Simon's bed.

The picture—and the fact that Jamie sent it—pierce the fog of doom that Simon's felt wrapped in since that phone call yesterday morning. He knows, logically, that this isn't the end of the world. He'll get more work. There's no urgency. He can afford to be choosy. He's good at what he does. But you can know something is fake and still feel it.

Simon's entire job is making people feel things that aren't based in reality. You can make an audience frightened, happy, triumphant, whatever, entirely from some made up dialogue and a halfway decent score. Right now all his brain chemicals are putting on a show and it's called *Everything Is Terrible and Nobody Likes You*. Simon knows it isn't real but it's a pretty convincing performance anyway.

Simon's spent most of the past twenty-four hours asleep. He's had—more or less—a normal number of meals today. He took his meds. He shaved off a gross three days' worth of stubble. He unpacked his suitcase, did a load of laundry, and lined up his lotions on the bathroom counter. Going to the grocery store and back probably counts as a walk. All the self-care boxes have been checked.

He may not be doing great, and he should seriously think about getting a therapist who does Zoom sessions, and who isn't seventy-five and basically retired, but he's doing as well as can be expected, if you're grading on a steep curve.

He's doing better than yesterday, at least. He's doing a hell of a lot better than he was when he asked Charlie to drive him to the airport. There's no way Charlie didn't know something was wrong. You don't spend seven years around somebody without knowing when they're upset.

As far as Charlie knows, Simon's still upset. As far as Charlie knows, something's seriously wrong.

Simon can be better than Dave. As far as affirmations go, this is a petty one, but it's also an attainable goal, which is good.

He opens Charlie's message and texts back a simple "thanks."

CHARLIE DOESN'T TEXT back.

It shouldn't bother Simon. He hadn't planned on staying in touch with Charlie anyway. When he imagined his future after leaving *Out There*, Charlie wasn't in his life. But that version of the future feels impossible now, because it all hinged on that one stupid play. And somehow, into the murky picture of his future that he's now trying to assemble, Charlie Blake has slipped in.

Or maybe Simon just can't imagine a future without Charlie in it anymore. Charlie's there because he couldn't be anywhere else.

And so Simon keeps checking his phone, expecting a text from Charlie, even though that isn't who they are. Of course Charlie isn't going to text back—he has no reason to believe that Simon will answer, so why bother? They have seven years of bad vibes, three days of civility, and two instances of above average sex. Charlie probably doesn't even want anything more to do with Simon, probably wouldn't even if Simon hadn't done the one thing Simon *knows* Charlie doesn't deal well with and disappeared on him.

Simon spends another two days eating prepared salads and

going on walks. He goes to the bookstore and he buys more groceries. His travel-size skin care routine is running out, so he goes to four separate stores to replenish his supply, instead of ordering it online like he usually does. He texts Nora.

Realistically, he should call his agent and explain what happened with the play, but he doesn't think he can handle Ken's rote assurances, the sense that he thinks of Simon as interchangeable with his other clients, when Simon's entire problem at the moment is that he isn't.

Instead, he calls his therapist, who agrees to do a phone session, and then spends most of the hour loudly blowing his nose while Margie says things like, "It sounds like you aren't being very gentle with yourself" and "This isn't the first time we've talked about what rejection means for you."

He shuts his eyes and remembers how happy he was on the bench at the car show, how he tried to store that feeling up so he could take it out later. Now's later; now's when he needs it. The closest he can get is the warmth of sunlight on his skin, the sound of Charlie laughing, the sense that the future was laid out in front of him, frictionless, easy.

He could look at that picture he took and try to recapture the feeling, but instead he can hardly bring himself to glance at the camera roll icon on his phone. He doesn't want to see Charlie's face. It's bad enough that he keeps wondering what Charlie's doing. Did he spend an extra few days in Arizona? Did he go back to Mike's cabin? Is he home?

For the past year, Simon's been telling himself that he's going to get better. He'll develop better coping strategies. He'll stop working on *Out There*, and whatever external validation he gets from his new roles will make him feel good. Someone will invent a new migraine medication or a new anxiety medication, or he'll discover crystals or magnets or a new strain of weed that fixes all his problems.

But this is it. His migraines are reasonably well managed. His anxiety isn't, but that's been a work in progress since the third grade, even when he was on his old meds. It gets bad, and then it gets better. It's a rhythm. A shitty rhythm, but he can work with it. He *has* been working with it. He's functional—even when he feels like he isn't, even when his brain insists that he isn't.

He makes himself tell Jamie the truth of what happened with the play.

"I know it doesn't matter," he tells Jamie. "But it feels like it does. Anyway, sorry I had to be a crazy person about it."

"Or," Jamie says firmly, "you need some space to process your shit."

"Most people manage to do that without running away."

"Most people can't afford last-minute airfare. Most people don't have entire empty apartments they can use. Most people don't have two months off. Who knows what most people would do in your shoes?"

"Still."

"Is it so different than checking yourself into a silent retreat or whatever? You didn't do anything harmful."

Simon isn't sure he agrees, but it's still nice to hear that Jamie thinks so.

He reads that book Roshni recommended, and it's boring but

not as boring as his brain and so he finishes it. Then he stays up until five in the morning—his sleep schedule is irredeemably fucked—finishing the horny dragon book.

The next afternoon, he texts Charlie a list of everything he hates about the book. Before hitting send, he really looks at it, thinking that before he sends it, he ought to at least know why he's sending it. But he doesn't have an answer, and he wants to send it anyway, so he does.

As soon as he taps the arrow, he realizes exactly how insane a text it is. It fills the entire screen. It's about dragons. It falls right beneath the other day's "thanks," making it a double text. Everything about it is appalling and he'd probably work himself into a spiral about it if Charlie didn't respond within five minutes.

> **Charlie:** okay, wrong

> **Charlie:** like, you're entitled to your (wrong) opinion but I bet you're going to read the sequel

> **Charlie:** wait, no, I bet you already bought it

Simon, a little high from the thrill of his deranged text not being treated as the lunacy it most definitely is, sends Charlie a picture of the sequel to *A Scorched Land* sitting on his coffee table.

Chapter Sixteen

So, now they text. Apparently.

It's nothing important. Charlie talks about whatever he's watching and occasionally sends TikToks. Simon sends detailed updates about the dogs who live in his building.

They aren't saying anything that matters. These are probably the most boring texts anybody's ever sent to someone they've had sex with, but the fact they're texting is more important than what's in them.

Simon can't bring himself to tell Charlie about losing the role in the play, so he mentions that he'll only be in New York for another week and trusts that Charlie's smart enough to take Simon's caginess as a sign he doesn't want to talk about it, and to google instead of asking questions.

Simon stays up way too late finishing the second book in the dragon romance series, then starts reading the third. He finds the subreddit for the series and gets sucked into a vortex of fan theories. Someone on the internet is *wrong* and Simon almost has to fight them. He preorders the fourth book and tries to decide whether it would be weird to go to a book signing.

This series maybe isn't what Simon would call good, or maybe his definition of good is useless. It's fun, the way novelty fringe is fun, the way Eurovision is fun, the way peculiar flavors of Oreos are fun. Simon is having fun, despite being a bit of a wreck, and it's because he's given his entire flawed brain over to another universe.

He feels like he's nurturing some freaky little part of his soul that he's neglected since high school.

"I forgot for an entire day that the humans aren't actually in love with that dragon," Simon tells Jamie. "You and Charlie have completely perverted my ability to read."

"You're welcome," Jamie says. "And also you're wrong."

"Sure, if you're playing make-believe."

"Yes," Jamie says. "Now you understand."

After nearly a week in New York, Simon calls Lian.

"Sorry," he says instead of leading with hello or anything passably normal.

But maybe Lian isn't normal either, because instead of anything polite or even intelligible, she says, "Come back as a producer."

"What?"

"If you want, we'll give you a producer credit."

Simon doesn't roll his eyes, but only because they aren't on a video call. After the third season, when *Out There* proved that it was, if not a huge hit, then at least a reliable success, he renegotiated his contract. So did Charlie and Alex.

At one point, instead of offering more money, they offered a producer credit. It's pretty standard to give stars that kind of title. Usually it doesn't come with any responsibilities or creative control, just gets tossed onto the negotiating table instead of money.

Simon turned it down, strongly preferring money to the uncomfortable feeling of permanence that would come with producing the show, however nominally.

"Why?" he asks.

"Do half a season. You can spend the other half stuck in space jail off camera. That would give you time to do other projects. Meanwhile, sign on as a producer. That way if the following year you only want to do a few episodes, nobody can stop you."

"One of us is confused about what kind of power an actor with a producer credit has, and it isn't me."

"Nobody wants you to leave the show. The network—they don't like it. Upfronts are in three weeks."

Every May, television networks and most of the streaming services put on a big show to pitch the upcoming season to advertisers. Simon's had to go to upfronts a few times, usually with Charlie and Alex too. They stand around onstage with a network executive, everyone engaging in the fiction that their weird little show is a great opportunity to sell car insurance and prescription drugs.

"The network wants to be able to show advertisers that *Out There* isn't changing," Lian says. "I'm just telling you, you have the upper hand, as long as what you're asking for isn't more money."

"When I asked for a few episodes off so I could do a movie, they said no." Technically, Lian said no. She's the show's actual executive producer. Over the years he's managed to squeeze in a few small projects, but it's rare that the scheduling works out.

"That was the year Samara left. I didn't want to run part of the season with half the original cast gone."

"Okay."

"I don't want you to leave. Personally and professionally, I want you to stay. You'll never know how pissed off I was when the network insisted on not one, but two white men as leads."

Since Lian makes sure to tell Simon this at least five times per calendar year, he very much does know exactly how pissed off she was, not that he blames her.

"But you *are* the show," she says. "For better or worse. You and Charlie. There isn't a show without you."

"Alex has as many lines as me or Charlie."

"Alex is leaving."

Simon is taken aback until he remembers the green makeup on Alex's face, the way her character spent the last few episodes of the season in a hospital bed. This must have been in the works for a while. "Does Charlie know?"

"You'd have to ask him."

Simon's going to miss Alex. It doesn't make sense—he's known for months that he was leaving the show. The idea of missing her shouldn't feel new.

"You told Alex I was thinking of leaving," Simon says, piecing it together. "When she didn't sign, you let her know that I wasn't signing either. Did you make her the same offer? Producer credit? A seat at the table?"

"I don't think the show can survive losing both you and Alex at the same time," Lian says, which is its own kind of answer. "Listen. This show is going to be my legacy. And it's probably going to be yours too. You might want to think about what that means."

Simon knows she doesn't mean it to come off as vaguely menacing, but it does anyway. It's possible—probable—that *Out There* will always be what he's best known for, that it will haunt the rest of his career.

Still, there's something about the word *legacy* that shifts his perspective. This show matters to people. He always feels a little let down when a show he likes ends abruptly, or when a character leaves without a satisfying resolution. Maybe, if he's leaving, the least he can do is give the writers time to give his character a good send-off.

"Can I tell the network you'll do next season?" Lian asks. It's a testament to how well she knows Simon that she isn't fazed that he hasn't said anything in about five minutes.

"I need to think about it."

"You have a week."

After ending the call, Simon has to pace the apartment for a little while. Doing half a season feels manageable. He isn't sure he'll *enjoy* it, but he can get behind the idea of finishing things right. Closure, maybe. Narrative closure for his role on the show, professional closure for Simon.

It occurs to him that this is another conversation he should be having with his agent, and the fact that he hasn't even talked to Ken about the entire play debacle is—well, Jamie may be onto something when he says Ken is useless, or at least useless for Simon. But right now, Simon is still mentally awarding himself star stickers for eating three meals a day. He's counting binge reading romance novels as radical self-care. Firing his agent—and, oh God, finding a new one—does not feel possible.

Instead he emails Ken and asks him to see what they can get from the production company. Seeing it in writing, he feels . . . not great, but optimistic. That's enough, for now.

THE IDEA THAT Charlie might not know about Alex leaving is bothering Simon more than he knows what to do with. He can't just tell Charlie—at least, he doesn't think he can. It's too messy to throw a bomb into somebody else's friendship.

Instead he goes right to Alex, texts her what Lian told him, and then sends what might be the most incriminating message he's ever written: "Does Charlie know?" He feels like his intentions are in flashing letters all over his phone screen. Only "give Charlie a hug for me" would be worse, and maybe not even that, because if anybody got that message from Simon, they'd assume his phone was hacked.

A few minutes later, he gets an answer from Alex: "yeah, told him as soon as I started thinking about it."

So, back when Charlie was carjacking Simon to deliver a lecture about the importance of giving people a chance to say goodbye, he already knew Alex was leaving. He wonders if Alex got the same lecture and doubts it. Their friendship is so light, so . . . breezy. Simon's never had a light and breezy friendship in his life.

His phone buzzes with another message: "so are you two talking?"

In order to answer that, Simon would need to define some terms. Does forwarding Charlie the pictures of Edie that Jamie sends him constitute talking?

But of course it does. Just because nothing's being said doesn't mean they aren't talking. It makes the fact of their talking more significant—they're finding things to say, pulling them out of thin air, just so a day doesn't go by without some kind of contact. He texts back "yes." He doesn't qualify it, doesn't explain.

"You're both really dumb and I hope you know that," Alex writes.

SIMON HAS NOTHING at all to do other than eat expensive salads and occasionally replenish his supply of face serums. So he takes out his laptop and starts watching *Out There* from the first episode of the first season.

He'd forgotten that right from the beginning, he and Charlie were in nearly every scene together. At the time, he assumed this was Lian putting them in the narrative equivalent of a get-along shirt. Now, though, he can see how well he and Charlie played off one another. These days, when a scene comes together, Simon assumes it's due to the kind of chemistry you earn after putting in thousands of hours.

But it was like this from the start. They never had to do dozens of takes. It just worked, even when Charlie was drunk and Simon was irate, even when production was so behind schedule, they only had time for a single take.

Right now he's watching his character learn that the mysterious passenger who altered the ship's landing gear to avoid a fatal crash is a teenage escapee from a prison colony, not a trained engineer. They're both shouting, their dialogue overlapping, but mingled in with the anger and frustration is a grudging mutual respect. Something crackles between them.

By the third episode, it occurs to Simon that maybe when the network said they wanted more Charlie, what they really wanted was more Charlie *and Simon*. That's what Lian gave them. That's what audiences have been watching for seven years. When Lian said the show can't stand to lose both Simon and Alex, she wasn't wrong. It's a show about a crew. It's a show about a family.

He's always known that—about *Out There*, but also about pretty much every show he's ever enjoyed. *Out There* is about people who belong together, or at least are stuck together, which is more or less the same thing. That's how a certain type of science fiction narrative works: you put people on a spaceship and it's the emotional equivalent of a locked-room murder mystery.

Halfway through the first season, there's an episode—written and directed by Lian, so it's all her fault—where Charlie's and Simon's characters are stranded on one of those ice planets that are apparently scattered across every fictional galaxy. They're stuck in a cave, fighting hypothermia, huddled together.

Maybe Lian thought a couple days of that and they'd stop bickering, that being forced together would work as some kind of team building exercise. Instead it just infuriated them both. Charlie's hair stuff gave Simon a headache. So did the smell of alcohol layered under mouthwash. Simon's constant complaining—always under his breath, generally about Charlie—made Charlie red-faced and bad-tempered. It didn't make them like one another, but by the end of that episode there's something worn in and comfortable about their dialogue. It's the patter of people who are used to one another.

He texts Charlie, not to tell him any of that, but to make fun of his hair. "Why didn't you have any hair until season 3?"

The response comes almost immediately.

Charlie: I was so bald

Charlie: I set the clippers too low and decided to own it

Simon: I'm not saying it didn't work for you.

He's two-thirds of the way through the first season before he realizes that he's texting Charlie all day. And Charlie's texting him back. They are, basically, having a nonstop conversation about the show they're both in, and it's either the most narcissistic thing Simon's done in his life or—just maybe—he's processing this experience with the only person who could possibly understand.

He almost asks Charlie what he thinks about the show's flagrant homoeroticism but can't figure out how to phrase that without asking if Charlie believes they've been playing out a love story all along.

> **Charlie:** oh shit, we're about to hit that episode

Simon hadn't realized there was a *we* in this binge watching. But he knows what episode Charlie means. It's the one with the dickhead guest director.

They skip it. Simon doesn't want the reminder of the way that guy needled Samara and Alex that in retrospect seems more than a little racist in addition to the obvious sexism. He doesn't want the reminder of his failure to speak up. He doesn't even want to label what was wrong with what the guy said to him. Obviously it's homophobic to tell a gay actor that he isn't being masculine enough for the role he's already done for most of a season. But it's also something else. Femmephobic? There's nothing about his character that's ever needed to be masc. Nobody else ever said anything, but that asshole's comments echoed in Simon's head for a while.

But if that director said bigoted things to Simon and Alex and Samara, he must have said something to Charlie.

> **Simon:** you can tell me to shut up but did that guy ever say anything to you?

The dots appear and disappear, then reappear.

> **Charlie:** just what you'd expect—trailer trash, amateur, etc.

Simon winces, because he's definitely called Charlie an amateur, behind his back and to his face and muttered under his own breath.

But that was a lot of typing and deleting for one sentence. It's none of Simon's business, but they've been making things one another's business since Arizona. Simon's been trying to keep things friendly, neutral, light, to act like they didn't spend two days presenting one another with secrets like outdoor cats gently placing mangled rodents at one another's feet.

> **Simon:** did something else happen?

There's a long pause before the dots even appear.

> **Charlie:** He kind of kept messing with my shirt. I mean, costumes messes with our clothes all day and it's fine. It's not a thing. But he kept adjusting it? Kind of gropily. The first twenty times I thought it was in my head.

Simon's taken aback. Not, unfortunately, about a director getting handsy with the cast—that's a tale as old as time. But that he hadn't noticed.

> **Simon:** I'm so sorry that happened to you

> **Simon:** Really glad you fucked his car up

> **Charlie:** It didn't help that I was extremely not sober and not in a place to come up with ideal strategies for dealing with workplace harassment or whatever

> **Simon:** did Lian know?

> **Charlie:** Only after the car incident. That's why she didn't get rid of me

Charlie apparently doesn't want to talk about it anymore because he starts sending Simon sweaty gym selfies. Simon isn't complaining.

By the end of the second season, he realizes he and Charlie have been watching *Out There* for four days. It's basically the length of time they spent together in Arizona, but they're doing it on opposite sides of the country.

> **Charlie:** this is my hottest season

> **Simon:** no

> **Charlie:** okay, tell me what IS my hottest season

> **Simon:** also no

> **Charlie:** your hottest season is this last one

> **Charlie:** it's the gray hair

> **Simon:** blocking your number

> **Charlie:** no shut up we're getting to the space snakes now

This latest season is Charlie at his hottest to date, because he's clearly on an upward trajectory. He has the features to pull off some weathering.

Those first few seasons, Simon obviously *knew* Charlie was attractive, but it hadn't really registered. Charlie had been twenty, twenty-one, *young*. Only in the last few years has Simon's awareness of Charlie shifted, and even then, it happened gradually enough that Simon could pretend it wasn't happening.

The next episode is another alien diplomat love triangle. He wants to know who in the writers' room got hurt by a diplomat. It's not the best episode, so he keeps one eye on the show and texts Charlie.

> **Simon:** are you okay with Alex leaving?

> **Charlie:** I'm happy for her

The response is immediate but doesn't answer the question. Simon isn't sure if he should press it. A friend would ask, even though Simon's no good at being a friend, and even though friendship doesn't fully explain whatever he and Charlie are.

> **Simon:** but are YOU okay

> **Charlie:** I knew it was coming. I'll miss her but I really am happy for her

That still isn't exactly an answer, but Simon gets it. He tries to imagine Jamie getting a job that meant they didn't get to see one another much. He'd miss Jamie but he'd be happy for him.

And now he feels like a fool because *of course* that's how Jamie feels about Simon's career. You can be happy for someone and also not feel great about yourself.

> **Charlie:** are you gonna get mad if I ask you something

> **Simon:** I mean, probably? But now you have to ask anyway

> **Charlie:** are you okay? I thought you might be staying in NYC because you're having fun but you're on your couch all day

Simon could answer with a dishonest "yes" or a more honest "almost" but he doesn't think that's what Charlie's asking.

Simon: did you ever read The Yellow Wallpaper?

Charlie: are any dragons in it? Because if not, you know the answer

Simon: ha

Simon: it's about a woman in the 1800s who (supposedly) had some kind of mental episode and her doctor husband makes her stay in the attic and not do anything as "treatment"

Simon: (but he's totally just locking her up)

Simon: anyway, she has nothing to do but look at the yellow wallpaper (she loses her mind, obviously)

Simon: but when my anxiety's really bad, I want nothing more than to be stored in an attic where nobody expects me to do anything and I don't have to interact with anybody

Simon: (to be clear, this is the worst take on literature anyone's ever had)

Charlie's quiet. Simon doesn't know if that's simply because everything he said was completely unhinged—which it was, that's just factual—or if Charlie's googling "The Yellow Wallpaper."

Still, Simon got the basic facts out there: he's dealing with some anxiety and this is just what he's doing to feel better. Look at that, actual communication.

> **Charlie:** so, like, instead of yellow wallpaper it's Out There. And instead of an attic it's a furnished apartment in one of New York's nicer neighborhoods.

> **Simon:** Yes, exactly. I'm probably going home next week. Rest cure: accomplished

But if he agrees to do another year of *Out There*, there's no point in going home, because he'll only be in California for a week before he has to fly back east for the upfronts.

> **Charlie:** will you kill me if I tell you I was worried

Simon thinks Charlie already knows the answer, and that he wouldn't have asked if he thought it would seriously bother Simon. It does bother Simon, in that he'd prefer to pretend everyone in the world thinks he's fine, but that ship has sailed. That ship is at the bottom of the sea.

> **Simon:** it's objectively worrisome, so whatever

He wants to take it back as soon as he sends it, mostly because the knowledge that people (*Charlie*) know exactly how messed up he is makes him want to hide under the duvet until the heat death of the universe, but also because somehow they now have the sort of friendship (or whatever) that implies *caring*.

It's Simon's own fault. He started it by storming off to yell at Dave. Even at his most self-delusional he couldn't convince himself that he was motivated by anything other than caring about Charlie, and Charlie knew it (and then they had sex). And now Simon has to just *deal* with it when Charlie cares about him? And they aren't even going to just have sex about it. Awful.

And now he's just sent a weird text that leaves Charlie with no possible non-weird way to respond, so he flings his phone onto the couch and eats a salad.

SIMON'S SETTLED INTO a routine during the two weeks he's been in New York. He wakes up, has breakfast, takes a walk, eats lunch, takes a nap. That's a great routine for babies and old people and thirty-four-year-olds who recently had some kind of episode.

After his nap, he watches *Out There* with Charlie. And all day long, he and Charlie text.

Simon's decided not to bother himself with insane little questions like when he started missing Charlie, or liking Charlie, or hoping it's Charlie whenever his phone buzzes. Maybe Jamie's right, and Simon's been mildly obsessed with Charlie for seven years. Maybe a little bit of obsession minus severe dislike equals ... whatever this is.

Charlie's gym selfies become frequent enough that Simon starts to wonder if Charlie has a special setup in his gym with tripods and ring lights. He wonders what these pictures mean, then figures they mean exactly the same thing most shirtless pictures mean. This is not subtle. This is not in code. He lets himself look.

He's been trying not to think about the sex. That goes about as well as it ever does, because if Simon could even slightly control his thoughts, he'd choose not to have opinions on things like the correct angle for coffee cup handles and the necessity of counting objects in multiples of three. He keeps remembering Charlie saying things, pressing his hand into the mattress. What's the difference between having your hand held and being held down? And which is more devastating to Simon's well-being?

He finally opens up his photos and looks at that picture of Charlie at the car show, and he knows immediately that he was right to avoid looking at it. He's hit with a wave of fondness. It isn't even a good picture. It's just Charlie in three-quarters profile, his mouth halfway open because he's talking about where to source Chrysler hubcaps, a bunch of cars in the background.

It isn't the context of the picture that's making him feel things, it isn't the memory of how blissed out he'd been when he took that photo. It's Charlie's stupid face.

He opens Instagram and goes to Charlie's profile, testing his hypothesis. Sure enough, there's Charlie with a picture of yet another dragon romance novel resting on his chest, one hand behind his head, the camera catching all his best angles and a good portion of his triceps. Simon might actually be smiling right now. It's terrible.

Charlie posted a few pictures from the car show, including one of Simon petting a dog. The picture of Simon isn't flattering—it's a bad angle and his mouth is doing something stupid because he's using his talking-to-dogs voice. He looks happy and uncomplicated. That green Gremlin is in the background. It isn't even interesting. He can't stop thinking about why Charlie posted it.

THEY'RE IN THE middle of the third season—one of the two seasons that got delayed and shortened because of Covid and the writers' strike—when Simon realizes he's having fun.

He isn't convinced that *Out There* ever lived up to Lian's pitch of *Twin Peaks* in space, but it does deliver an ensemble of characters with secrets that range from dangerous to bizarre. Charlie's character escaped from a prison planet. Simon's character is at least partly a cyborg, on the run from his old owners. Alex's character is a rebel spy who may or may not have traveled from the future. Scattered among the body swap episodes and threaded through the love triangles are mysteries that don't quite make sense and never exactly get solved.

In the universe of *Out There*, space is populated by moody weirdos and nobody is who they seem.

On the sofa, under a blanket, the laptop balanced on his knees, Simon feels like he'd probably have watched *Out There* if he weren't on it. He'd get on the forums and complain about plot holes. He'd peer pressure Jamie into watching it with him.

Instead, he's watching it with Charlie, complaining to Charlie. He feels the way he did when he was thirteen and discovering that there were entire websites full of *Lord of the Rings* fanfic, thousands of people who liked the same things he did for the same reasons he did, and who maybe took refuge in the two-dimensional safety of online interactions for the same reasons he did.

This time, instead of that internet full of like-minded fans, it's just Charlie. It's the realization that he's living from text to text. It's the same Charlie he's known for seven years, the same Charlie who's currently heckling him for having paid twelve dollars for sprouted amaranth crackers. It's the same Charlie from that Arizona motel room. But contained on the screen of his phone, there aren't years of professional grudges or weeks of confusing sexual tension, and there's no escaping how much Simon likes this.

Chapter Seventeen

When Simon signs his contract for half a season, he isn't ready for the rush of relief. Partly he's just glad to have made a decision. But mostly he wants to see what happens to his character; after a week on the couch watching *Out There*, he's embarrassingly invested.

"Did you tell people?" Jamie asks. They're on FaceTime so Simon can watch Edie take a nap on Jamie's lap.

"It's weird because I didn't officially tell them I was leaving. So how do I announce that I'm not leaving?"

"Group chat. Just say hey, I'm not leaving after all, looking forward to shooting the new season, exclamation point." He reaches for his laptop, types something, and a minute later an email pops up in Simon's inbox. It's word-for-word what Jamie just said. "Copy and paste," Jamie says.

"You don't need to be my assistant."

Jamie frowns. "Noooo. I don't think of myself as your assistant."

"I know!" Simon's face is hot. "I know you aren't." Then again, Jamie's spent the past few weeks dog sitting for Simon. He goes with Simon to every event that involves a plus one and acts as a social buffer. He's run Simon's errands and filled his refrigerator a non-zero number of times. He does all Simon's social media. This isn't the first time he's drafted texts or emails for Simon. "Am I treating you like my assistant?"

"If you were crossing a line I'd have told you. I like helping. You help me too, you know. Knowing that I have a place to stay is huge."

"I can pay you."

Jamie throws up his hands. Edie startles in her sleep. "And I can pay rent."

"Are we bartering? Is this, like, a trade? You help me in exchange for housing?" There's nothing wrong with that kind of arrangement, probably, but he doesn't want to be Jamie's landlord, however informally.

"No!" Jamie is visibly pissed. Simon can see him bite back a comment and take a cleansing breath. "You have room in your house, and I need a place to stay. I have time in my day to do things you don't have the mental bandwidth for. But those two things aren't related. We're helping one another because we can help one another."

"Okay. Good."

"I'm not broke."

"I'm glad."

"I can show you my bank statements. I can afford an apartment. I'm not here because I'm homeless."

"Jamie."

"Sorry, sorry."

"No, I'm sorry. I'm being weird about this."

"Actually, no, you really aren't. I think this is all on me. I feel wrong not paying rent. Not morally wrong, just unsettled. I have basically no expenses right now? It's insane. So, uh, thank you."

"You're welcome. And thank you." Simon manages not to offer

to put Jamie's name on the deed to the house, because that's probably weird and also not going to help.

"A real assistant might be a good idea, though. Someone who does that as their job will think of things that wouldn't occur to me."

Simon is a little taken aback. "I'm not busy enough to need an assistant."

"It's not about how busy you are. You have a—" He breaks off. "I'm not sure if disability is the right word."

It's not a word that's come up before. Not with Jamie and not with his therapist. Debilitating, yes. But "debilitating anxiety" sounds like something you should figure out how to cope with, not something you should get an assistant for. *Disability* feels more accurate when he's thinking about his migraines, even though they're reasonably well controlled right now. Maybe it's the combination of the two things that pushes the entire situation over the edge into unmanageability? Or maybe Simon's definition of disability needs work.

"For the past few weeks," Jamie says, very gently, "would you have been able to go to work if you had a regular job?"

The answer is yes, obviously, Simon could have gone to work. It just would have been agony.

When they end the call, Simon opens the main cast group chat and pastes the message Jamie drafted. The responses start coming in almost immediately.

Alex: !!!

Petra: ♥♥♥

> **Amadi:** wait were you NOT going to sign?
> I thought only alex was leaving, wtf

> **Alex:** we've been through this babe

> **Amadi:** I figured if he didn't leave after the space lobster season he was here for life

> **Roshni:** Yay!!!! So glad, Simon!

An hour passes, and there's no response from Charlie, even though Simon can see when he scrolls up that Charlie's in this group chat all the time.

When two hours pass, Simon wonders if Charlie's offended that Simon didn't tell him first. But that seems pretty out of character for Charlie. If he's pissed off at Simon, he'd probably just say so. Maybe he's annoyed that he didn't get offered the same deal Simon did? Maybe he has a deep-seated desire for a mostly meaningless producer credit?

Around this time of day, they're usually watching *Out There*. At least they have been every day for over a week. They're on season four now. So he texts Charlie, just "wasn't sure if you'd seen the group chat" followed up with the same message of Jamie's that he'd copied and pasted.

The text is marked as delivered, but Charlie doesn't answer. The little dots don't even appear.

He scrolls up. That morning, Charlie had been painstakingly explaining to him the difference between a chin-up and a pull-up and the different muscle groups involved—not a topic Simon cares about, but there had been visual aids in the form of sweaty gym selfies with arrows pointing to different muscle groups. It had been light and—okay—flirty, for the very limited definition of flirtation that Simon's capable of.

No matter how critically Simon reads those texts, he can't find anything he did that would make Charlie want to stop talking to him.

Maybe Charlie just doesn't want to work with him. Maybe the entire almost-friends thing they have going on depends on never having to see one another again. That's not unreasonable of Charlie. It's not like they enjoyed working together.

It still stings.

If anyone told Simon a month earlier that he'd be severely stressed by going less than a day without a text from Charlie, he wouldn't have believed it.

When he wakes up and still doesn't see a message from Charlie, he feels like—not like he's been broken up with. They weren't together, or anything like together. And even if they had been, twenty-two hours without a text doesn't mean anything.

Texting pretty frequently for a couple weeks doesn't mean anything. The fact that they had sex twice also doesn't mean anything. Simon's had sex with plenty of people he didn't get emotionally invested in—people he didn't want to be emotionally invested in and would have cringed to think they felt anything at all about him.

But just the other day, Charlie said he was worried about Simon. And now Charlie stopped talking to him and Simon's feelings are hurt. This is not an emotion-free situation.

The problem is that Simon doesn't just like people. He's either indifferent with extreme prejudice or greedily overinvested. Clingy. Needy. When he cares about someone—when he lets himself admit that a person matters to him—he needs constant reassurance that he matters to them. He works so hard to keep that under wraps, to keep his mouth shut and his attitude icy. That's what he needs to do now.

But he thinks about Dave, alone with his dusty paperbacks and the collar of a dog who isn't around anymore. Dave, who didn't think anyone in the world would care if he disappeared. Simon wants better for himself, and he wants better for the handful of people he cares about, and so he waits until it's nine A.M. California time and sends Charlie a picture he took yesterday of a dog in a raincoat.

Then he sticks his phone into the bottom of his bag and makes himself go out for a walk. The looming specter of Nora's graduation party is only made bearable by how it's an excuse to buy her something nice, but he still hasn't found the right present. He also needs a gift for Jamie to thank him for being Edie's parent this month. Maybe he'll get something for himself that isn't the same two pairs of pants, two sweaters, and four shirts he's been wearing for nearly three weeks. It turns out he just doesn't have what it takes to survive indefinitely with a capsule wardrobe.

He's on Prince Street, in the kind of store that makes him feel old and déclassé, but like maybe spending five hundred dollars here would solve those problems, when he hears his phone buzz. He finishes picking out peach silk pajamas for Jamie—very old Hollywood, he'll love them—then makes himself wait until he's on the sidewalk before checking his phone.

It isn't Charlie. It's Nora with a picture of today's outfit. He responds, asking about brands in a way that probably makes it obvious he's trying to figure out what to get her.

The weather's decent and he needs the distraction, so he walks the half hour back to his apartment, stopping to get himself a salad that's slightly—but not stressfully—different from all the other salads he's been eating. He passes a woman walking two dachshunds that are obviously inferior to Edie and he's hit with a pang of homesickness.

He'd thought being in New York would feel comfortable, like coming home. He spent four years here for college, but either the city changed or he did, and his memories aren't mapping onto the landscape. The city he's walking through feels like a LEGO model of a city he used to know. He wants to go home.

He's . . . fine. Not any worse than yesterday, except he's sad about Charlie and a little homesick. But it's almost a relief, this reminder that he can have a normal human emotion without spiraling about it. It's okay to miss your home. It's okay to not enjoy being rejected. It's okay—maybe—to have the sort of feelings that you want to be returned, even if you don't want to put a name to any of those feelings.

Back at the apartment, he opens his laptop and puts on the next episode of *Out There*, even though Charlie isn't watching it with him.

It's midnight when Charlie finally texts. It reads, ominously, "This a good time to talk?" Simon can't imagine a universe where this leads to a conversation anybody wants to have.

Something hot and nervous and terrible fills his chest, but he types back, "sure." When his phone rings, he answers it with a normalish voice.

"Okay," Charlie says. It sounds like normalish is the best he can do too. "Sorry."

Simon wasn't expecting a sorry, isn't quite sure he wants a sorry. "Okay," he says.

"I didn't think you were doing another season."

"Yeah. I got that." So, it's like Simon suspected: Charlie can be friendly with him, but not if they're forced to see one another every day. That's fine. Simon knows he's a lot. He knows he isn't fun or easy to be around.

"Two weeks ago, you said you weren't."

Simon had come back from Dave's and let it slip that he told Jamie he was leaving the show. "Lian offered me a shorter season and, well. I want to end this right."

"Oh. So you changed your mind."

"Yeah—wait, did you think I lied?"

"No! I just didn't know."

They've hardly said anything to one another. At least half the duration of this phone call has consisted of awkward pauses. But there's a heavy subtext that's making Simon feel like he's in over his head. The fact of this conversation at all is an admission that whatever is going on between them is important enough that they need to be clutching their phones, sweaty and nervous, making things right.

"I think," Simon says slowly, "that I was supposed to tell you right away, as soon as I realized I was considering staying. I think that since we were talking, I should have mentioned it." *Talking* is doing a lot of heavy lifting in that sentence, standing in for everything that happened in Arizona, everything that's happened since.

"You didn't owe me—" Charlie starts, but Simon has to cut him off.

"I did. Or—maybe I didn't, but I don't want to be the kind of person who thinks like that." He's squeezing his eyes shut, like maybe that'll stop Charlie from seeing what's happening here, like maybe it'll stop himself from seeing.

Charlie's quiet for long enough that Simon wonders if he's gotten things completely wrong.

"Okay," Charlie says.

"Okay?"

"I wasn't upset about that." There's the tiniest emphasis on *that*.

"Did I do something else?" It wouldn't be hard for Simon to believe. At any moment he's prepared to accept that he's done something unforgivable. That's the easiest proposition in the world for Simon to accept.

"No, Simon," Charlie says, sounding awfully gentle in a way that Simon doesn't know what to do with. "I just don't want to fuck things up on set."

Oh. "But we're getting along." Simon feels very small. "I know I'm easier to take in small doses, but I think we can still be—" He wants to say civil, or maybe friendly, but those are wrong and he can't make himself say them.

"I'm not saying this right," Charlie says. Simon can hear him rub his palm over his beard. "When Alex ended things with me, it was so much work at first to stay friendly."

Simon tries to remember when Charlie and Alex broke up. It must have been during the writers' strike, so he wasn't seeing them every day. They showed up at an event with different dates, but he'd have noticed if there was any tension. He remembers them arriving together at the picket line.

"I didn't realize," Simon says.

"That's because I worked my ass off to make sure she and I stayed friends. It was *hard*."

Simon has never thought of Alex and Charlie's friendship as anything but effortless and easy. They always look like they're having fun. But—how had Charlie put it—*when Alex ended things*. In Arizona, when he'd said something about Alex needing things to be light and fun, he'd sounded . . . hurt, maybe. Simon can put that together and draw some conclusions.

"And you thought," Simon starts, but can't finish the sentence because he's afraid to say it out loud. Charlie was worried that things would get ugly after he and Simon were done with—whatever this is. Charlie had been thinking of a future—something like a breakup, which implies that whatever they're doing is real. It's enough to make Simon need to hide in the bathroom, still holding the phone.

"Yeah," Charlie says, answering the question Simon didn't ask.

"Oh."

The silence stretches out dangerously. Simon sits in the corner of the bathroom, the tile cold beneath him.

"When Jamie and I broke up," Simon says, "the first month was excruciating. Awkward check-in texts. Hideous attempts to get coffee. He insisted on giving constructive criticism on my Grindr profile."

Charlie lets out a bark of a laugh. "Please send me a screenshot immediately."

Simon ignores this. "I can do that. I mean. If we—I can be friendly." He's writing checks he can't cash. But he made it work with Jamie, and with nobody else he's ever been involved with—

actually, with nobody else ever, period—because the idea of Jamie not being in his life made his heart ache in a way that breaking up with him never did.

Simon remembers how he'd felt at the idea of Charlie not being in his life, of how impossible it had been to imagine.

Simon presses a palm against the smooth tile floor.

"Are you saying," Charlie asks, "that when—if—Jesus Christ, Simon," he breaks off, exasperated, like this is Simon's fault, like Simon even knows what he's talking about. "Are you saying that if—whatever—things end, you'll be *nice*?"

It only occurs to Simon now that a normal person would have insisted that nothing needed to change between them just because they had sex, and that it isn't a problem because they won't do that again. For fuck's sake, Simon. That's what people *say* in these situations. There's practically a script for it. They don't promise to have a nice breakup.

Simon's making it so obvious, so embarrassingly obvious, that he wants this. It didn't even occur to him to pretend that he doesn't want it.

He wants to throw his phone out the window. He wants to hide at the bottom of the sea.

"Yep." Simon figures that owning his dumb offer is his only move.

"That," Charlie says, his voice gone all warm, "is really sweet."

"Oh, shut up." Simon presses his hot face against the cool glass of the shower door.

"You've been returning my texts in like thirty seconds."

It should be a non sequitur, but it isn't, and Simon's face gets even hotter. At first, Simon started doing it because he felt guilty about not having texted Charlie when he landed in New York, and wanted Charlie to know—he wanted Charlie to know that he mattered, which is bad enough. But now he just answers quickly so Charlie will get back to him sooner.

"Maybe I do that with everyone," Simon says. "Maybe I'm great at texting people back."

Charlie laughs, probably because he's close friends with half a dozen people who can confirm exactly how bad Simon is at returning texts.

"Closer to fifteen seconds, really," Charlie says.

"Do you have a stopwatch?" Simon means it to sound testy but it comes out breathless, probably because he's almost hyperventilating. In his bathroom, at midnight, because someone noticed something they were fully intended to notice and interpreted it correctly.

Charlie's quiet for a minute, and Simon has the horrible conviction that he's about to start asking some pertinent questions, like what are they doing here, and what does it mean? It's what anyone would ask. Simon might die.

But when Charlie speaks, what he says is, "I've been returning your texts in about ten seconds."

"Embarrassing for you," Simon says immediately, awash in gratitude that of all the things he could have said, that's what Charlie went with.

"I think I'll keep doing that."

Simon feels like he might throw up, but he knows he's smiling, and those two things don't belong together. "Me too."

Only later, when Simon's trying to fall asleep, does he remember what Charlie said in the motel room after learning that Simon was planning to leave the show. He'd said that he was kissing Simon because he ran out of reasons not to kiss him. As if—maybe—it was something he'd wanted to do for a while, but waited until Simon wasn't on the show.

He stows it away, puts it in the emotional piggy bank: a good thought, something to come back to.

From an *Out There* fan Discord

DeathStarJacuzzi: It's three a.m. and I got a notification that a fic was updated for the first time since 2019. I think I've unlocked a new kind of high.

SpacePope: which fic?

DeathStarJacuzzi: The infamous ice planet AU. Three hundred thousand words. The slowest of slow burns. Written with all the style of a Booker Prize finalist.

GalactoseIntolerance: I opened this app to say the same thing! Is it insane if I take a sick day to read the update?

DeathStarJacuzzi: babe, read it AT work

GalactoseIntolerance: true, reading gay fanfic on company time is praxis

DeathStarJacuzzi: the author's note was like SORRY I lost my job and got covid and moved across the country and had a baby and got divorced but here's four chapters of Luke West and Jonathan Hale under the influence of ice magic sex pollen

SpacePope: WAIT is this the one where there are like . . . ice fey?

DeathStarJacuzzi: YES

GalactoseIntolerance: YES!!

SpacePope: And there's something about the shuttle crashing into a temple (??) and Luke is now in charge of some weird alien cult and has to marry someone? (you'll be shocked to learn it's Jonathan)

DeathStarJacuzzi: No no, that's a different one. This is the fic where it turns out that all along Luke's parents were ice fey and now he has magic and has to learn to lead this planet of weird little ice guys

GalactoseIntolerance: This fic is one of those where, like, is the author a time traveler? A mind reader? Because they predicted Luke West's leadership story arc a full year before it even crossed the writers' minds.

DeathStarJacuzzi: and let's be honest this fic does a better job with that arc than the show does

HowlsMovingSpaceship: I'm not taking the day off, but I'm working the circulation desk, so if anybody tries to interrupt my reading to borrow a book, I'll simply engage them in conversation about space boyfriends until they leave.

SpacePope: I love this for you

HowlsMovingSpaceship: ♥

Chapter Eighteen

"You have veto power," Jamie says when Simon answers the phone. "She's your dog. But you miss her. You're over there, having a mental health episode or whatever, pining for your dog, and there's an easy solution."

"What's happening right now?" Simon asks, confused. "And I'm not having a mental health episode anymore. I mean, my life is kind of an ongoing mental health episode, but what does Edie have to do with it?"

"Charlie's flying to New York in a couple days. He got an extra seat, so she won't even need to stay in her carrier other than during takeoff and landing, and we both know Charlie can probably charm the flight attendants into looking the other way if there happens to be a dachshund buckled into the seat next to his. There's no reasonable objection."

Simon feels certain there are plenty of objections, but he can't figure out what any of them might be. Jamie's right that he misses Edie. Buying a first-class seat—he doesn't even seriously consider that Charlie might not be flying first class—for a *dog*, however wonderful that dog might be, is a ridiculous expense. And that's not even getting into the hassle of finding an airline that will let you buy an empty seat.

"Whose idea was this?" Simon asks.

"Charlie, hundred percent. It would not occur to me to ask Charlie, of all people, to fly your dog around."

"He already bought the ticket?"

"Yes. Non-refundable."

Jamie's probably lying about this last bit, but Simon doesn't care. If Charlie wants to spend some of his money on Simon's dog, that's Charlie's own business. "Okay."

"Okay?" Jamie asks, like he wasn't expecting it. "You trust Charlie Blake to be, like, in loco parentis to Edie for a cross-country flight?"

No objections on those grounds even crossed Simon's mind. "Yes. Shouldn't I?"

"Holy shit, Simon, you know better than I do. But you paid some guy to run a background check on Edie's groomers. Your house is wired like a fucking bank, with drop cams in every room so you can watch your dog while you're on set. You use preservative-free toothpaste when you brush her teeth. *Your* toothpaste isn't even preservative-free."

"You've been reading my toothpaste ingredients?" Simon sputters, torn between laughter and indignation. "And you know I turn all the cameras off when you're there, so don't act like—"

"There's nothing wrong with preservatives, you snob."

"It's the only brand she likes!"

Now they're both laughing, and Simon gets to see his dog in a few days, and he thinks he found a perfect present for Nora on eBay of all places, and Charlie—*Charlie*—

It's one of those rare moments when everything in his life fits where it belongs, when his skin is the right size and his brain isn't a total liability. He lies down on the couch and lets himself soak it in.

The only problem is a new flavor of awkwardness when he's texting Charlie. It's been two days since their mortifying conversation, and things have pretty much gone back to normal. They text on and off nearly all day and watch a few episodes of the show together.

> **Simon:** Thanks about Edie. I'll probably cry when I see her and you'll need to pretend it isn't happening, fair warning

> **Charlie:** I get to cuddle your dog for five hours so who's the real winner here

> **Charlie:** I thought about surprising you.

> **Simon:** Absolutely not

> **Charlie:** I know! I thought about it for maybe three seconds, then remembered that this is you

> **Simon:** What's that supposed to mean?

> **Charlie:** It means I will personally fight anyone who tries to surprise you

Simon has to put his phone down and pace around the apartment a bit. He'd been expecting some roasting—he knows he's not spontaneous and he's starting to get to a place where he doesn't mind Charlie making fun of him, just like he doesn't mind Jamie making fun of him because he knows it's done with—affection, or whatever.

But Charlie is upping the ante and Simon isn't ready for it. Simon doesn't have a lot of people in his life who would offer to have fictional fights for him. He doesn't have a lot of people who know what he'd want them to fictionally fight about. For Charlie it was probably a throwaway comment but for Simon it feels like something more.

SIMON ARRIVED IN New York with a suitcase and a shoulder bag. It took him about sixty seconds to unpack. Even with the blankets and extra clothes he's bought, the apartment is essentially empty.

Still, he manages to spend the two hours before Charlie's due to arrive tidying up. For the two hours before that, he went to the grocery store and bought things that Charlie might like but Simon likes too, so he can maintain plausible deniability about what he's doing.

He doesn't know where Charlie's staying. The network will put him up at a hotel, but obviously he needs to come to Simon first to bring Edie. Will he want to stay with Simon? Will Simon want him to stay? Simon has no answers.

Halfway through wiping down the inside of the refrigerator with cleaning spray that smells like juniper and costs as much as a bottle of midrange wine, he realizes Charlie might not have meant to come here at all.

> **Simon:** Do you want me to meet you at the airport to get Edie?

Charlie: I'm landing in an hour. You'll never get to the airport in time.

Simon: Sorry, I should have thought of that.

Charlie: I can drop her off and go, no worries

Simon: ok

Charlie: or I can stay

Simon: ok

Simon reads Charlie's messages six times, trying to figure out what Charlie wants, before realizing that Charlie's probably trying to figure out what Simon wants. Good fucking luck to him; Simon has no clue.

Simon: I have donuts

Simon: and coffee

Charlie: I like coffee and donuts

Simon: I know

Charlie texts when he's ten minutes away and again when he's downstairs. Simon waits in the hallway for the elevator to arrive.

He notices Charlie for as long as it takes to see him drop Edie's leash.

Edie is so happy to see him that Simon instantly feels guilty—what kind of monster abandons his dog for no reason at all? He scoops her up and lets her lick his face while he tells her how good she is at being a dog.

They eventually make it into the apartment, Charlie rolling two suitcases behind him. Edie squirms to be put down, and proceeds to zoom around the apartment, circling back every five seconds to make sure Simon's still there. Simon puts out a bowl of water for her, shows her where she can sleep (a stack of folded blankets with a pillow on top, which Simon rearranged six times that morning), then watches as she lies down on a totally unrelated part of the floor and passes out.

"She didn't sleep much on the plane," Charlie says.

Only then does Simon really look at him. It's been less than a month. Nobody looks different in three weeks, unless they've cut their hair off or something, and Charlie's no exception, but somehow he looks better than he does in Simon's memory. He's wearing actual jeans and a hoodie that, on anyone else, Simon would suspect was made of cashmere.

"You're wearing clothing that looks like it came from a store," Simon says. "I bet none of it was free."

"I went stress shopping while you were, you know, missing in action. I never did that before."

"It shows," Simon says with feeling, instead of trying to address the rest of the sentence.

"Jesus Christ," Charlie mutters.

"You look good, is the point. That's all."

Charlie stuffs his hands in his pockets and looks at the ceiling, like that's where he's going to find an explanation for why Simon is the way he is.

"Not that you look bad in the rest of your clothing." Simon manages to ruin this by putting air quotes around *clothing*. "The internet's full of people who'll tell you so. There's an entire Tumblr about your flip-flops, but those are probably fetishists. Which is fine," he adds, feeling magnanimous. "I support that."

"You support people jerking off to pictures of my feet," Charlie says, incredulous. "You know, you're kind of sweet over text."

That's just factually incorrect—Simon's never been sweet in his life—and he's about to say so when he notices that Charlie's stalking across the room toward him.

"I forgot what a fucking gremlin you are," Charlie says, stopping about six inches away. "How do people not realize you're a gremlin?"

"You missed me." Simon's smug and a little giddy and absolutely unsuccessful at hiding his own smile. Honestly not bothering to try. "That's what you're trying to say."

"I'm trying to say that I want to kiss you, but you just let your dog slobber all over your face."

"That's where you draw the line? You fill the internet with pictures for foot fetishists to masturbate over, but this is a bridge too far?" But Simon's already halfway to the bathroom, and when he shuts the door behind him, he hears Charlie laugh.

He washes his face, which gives him just enough time to be filled with doubt and nerves, but then Charlie's knocking on the door. "How the fuck long does it take to wash *one* face, Simon?" So Simon slows down and brushes his teeth too.

He thought there'd be a lead up. Donuts. Small talk. Lots of awkward dancing around the issue of what they're doing together. Plenty of time for Simon to worry. But Charlie apparently decided to steamroll over that entire process.

When Simon opens the bathroom door, Charlie's there, waiting, impatient and fake-angry, and it's so easy—Charlie's made it so easy—for Simon to grab him by the sleeve (it *is* cashmere) and kiss him.

He tastes like airplane pretzels plus one breath mint. In the interest of justice and fair play, Simon should insist that Charlie brush his teeth, but his hands are on Simon's face, and Simon's brain empties out, thoughts swirling down the drain. There's nothing in the world but the scratch of Charlie's beard, the softness of his sweater, the slide of their lips.

They're good at this. It's not like he didn't already know, but the reminder is a bit of a shock anyway. He doesn't know if Charlie's kissing him slow and deliberate because he knows that's what Simon likes, or if it's what Charlie likes too. And it is Charlie who's taking the lead here. That's fine—being with Charlie always makes him feel slightly concussed and, honestly, he's not smart enough to navigate a kiss right now. The best he can do is keep up.

Everything slows down even more, syrupy and almost sleepy, and it takes Simon a minute to realize that it's not because he's slipping into some kind of altered state where time doesn't work right, but because Charlie's barely kissing him now. Their lips are only skimming one another's. They're just sort of standing there, breathing, Charlie's hands holding Simon's face exactly where he wants it.

"You said you had donuts," Charlie says, just above a whisper, his voice gravelly enough, and Simon close enough, that he can feel the rumble in Charlie's chest.

"Your priorities are terrible," Simon informs him, because somebody has to.

"I don't think they are." Charlie punctuates it with a kiss to Simon's temple. Simon's face goes hot.

In the kitchen, Charlie sits at a barstool, not even pretending not to watch as Simon puts on the coffee maker and gets out the bakery box. Simon tries to look like someone who isn't thinking about Charlie's priorities, and what that means in the context of a man flying your dog across the country and kissing you like you're . . . precious or whatever. There's only one way those pieces fit together, and Simon knows it, and it sort of makes him want to lock himself in the bathroom.

Simon brings over the box, but he doesn't open it, just clutches it to his chest even after Charlie reaches for it. He makes a belated attempt at normalcy and drops the box on the counter. Charlie opens it, and Simon can't look at his face, but does see that instead of taking one of the donuts he picks a blueberry muffin.

Charlie doesn't say anything about it, because it's just a muffin and not, like, an encrypted message. This is not a stained-glass window. This is not a text rich in symbolism. Simon got a food that he knows Charlie likes, and it's only in the morass of Simon's mind that the muffins have any meaning other than that he's currently at peace with refined sugar and gluten.

Simon takes the other muffin like he's a person in a play about normal people eating normal foods. He sits on the stool next to Charlie's—just following the stage directions—and tries not to think about the gap between Charlie's thigh and his own, tries not to notice that Charlie has one foot hooked around the leg of the stool while the other taps on the floor, tries not to notice the way Charlie's folding up the paper muffin liner.

But Simon does notice, because you don't spend as much time together as he and Charlie have and not pick up on someone's nervous tics. The idea that Charlie is nervous is unbearable and, somehow, temporarily shoves Simon's own thoughts to the side.

"How was your flight?" Simon asks. It's probably the first normal thing he's said since Charlie walked through the door.

"Edie wants to file a lawsuit against every person who walked past us without trying to pet her," Charlie says, correctly guessing that what Simon's really asking is how Edie tolerated the flight. "And she's not a fan of altitude changes. Other than that, she was fine."

"Thank you."

Charlie folds the paper into the narrowest possible isosceles triangle. "You've already thanked me."

"Well, I'm thanking you again and you can just deal with it."

Charlie doesn't say anything, not even to make fun of Simon. Instead he takes the triangle of paper and rolls it up like he's making a croissant.

Simon presses his palms against the cool marble of the counter. There isn't any reason for Charlie to be nervous right now. But there's rarely any reason for Simon to be nervous and God knows he manages it anyway.

It's probably standard to be a bit awkward when you see someone after a few weeks, especially if during that time apart you've . . . escalated things. Especially if you don't know where you stand. That kiss answered some questions for Simon, and probably the same questions for Charlie, but there are still a host of issues left undecided, starting with where Charlie is sleeping and ending with what all this means.

The coffee maker clicked to a stop a few minutes earlier, so Simon gets up and pours Charlie a cup, adding some white sugar that he bought at the store that morning. Then he pours some for himself, because even though it's four in the afternoon, Simon's still on California time. No—he's been sleeping such bizarre hours that he's no longer affiliated with any time zones. He's been liberated from the concept of the twenty-four-hour day, from the earth's rotation itself, and he can drink as much coffee as he wants, whenever he pleases.

"Come on," he says, handing Charlie a mug. "Let's sit in the living room so I can stare at my dog."

THEY WATCH AN episode of *Out There*, the laptop balanced on Simon's lap and Charlie leaning close. Their arms are pressed together, their legs touching, but it's the same thing they've been doing for weeks. It's just Charlie.

"This is the episode where I started to play it—" Charlie starts but cuts himself off.

In this episode, Alex's character is stranded on a planet that's about to get bombed while the rest of the crew tries to rescue her. It's one of the get-along shirt episodes—Charlie and Simon are in literally every scene together.

There are fifteen, maybe twenty, episodes with this basic structure. The threats vary, but in a show that's about a group of fractious outcasts and weirdos learning to function as a family, coming together to save one another is going to be a pretty core theme.

Simon can't see that there's anything about this episode that sets it apart from all the other episodes just like it.

"Started to do what?" Simon asks.

"I figured, if they were going to give me ten romantic lines per episode, then that's what they were going to get."

"You started playing it romantic. I fucking knew it."

"You and the whole internet."

"Why this episode, though?"

"It started to bother me. Alex and you were out at work, so two-thirds of the main cast is openly queer, and I'm secretly queer but at that point, like, *actively* queer for the first time in my life. We're being given these lines that should land as romantic, and they're written by a bunch of people with pride pins on their tote bags. So I figured, I'm going to assume the best of everyone involved."

"And nobody ever told you to play it straight."

"No! If Lian got shit from the network, she didn't say anything to me."

"So weird." Simon puts the laptop on the coffee table and crosses his legs under him. "Technically, I have a producer credit this year."

"Yeah, they offered me one too."

"Did you take it?"

"Once I heard you did, yeah. Insisted on it, actually."

Perversely, Simon likes the reminder that Charlie can be petty and jealous and competitive, that the Charlie who flies dogs across the country is the same Charlie who spent months doing muffin heists.

"I'd like to know whether I'm producing a show that's being actively not great about queer stuff or if they deliberately wrote a seven-year-long will-they-won't-they arc."

"What are you thinking of doing?"

Simon wasn't thinking of doing anything, and he almost certainly *won't* do anything, but now that Charlie's put the idea in his head, he'll at least feel bad about it.

"It'll probably be my last season," he says, and it isn't exactly connected in his mind with what they were just talking about, but it isn't unconnected either.

"Figured." Charlie looks like he wants to say more, but when he speaks again it's just, "You mind if I use your shower?"

Simon shows Charlie where the spare towels are, then points out the bath supplies he's stocked the place with, as if Charlie needs to be personally walked through Simon's lineup of shampoos and exfoliants.

While Charlie's in the shower, Simon washes the coffee mugs and wipes down the counter, then scratches Edie behind the ears when she wakes up just long enough to find someplace else to nap. Then he doesn't have anything to do but decide whether he's supposed to keep his clothing on.

The water in the bathroom turns off, and Simon sits on the edge of the bed, playing with his phone and trying to look like someone who has actually had sex before, with this very person, more than once even, and knows how to be normal about it.

Charlie comes out with his towel around his waist, not fully dry, like maybe he was in a hurry, and Simon should probably stand up but instead he's glued in place. When Charlie crosses the room, Simon's still sitting there. And when Charlie reaches out to tilt Simon's chin up, Simon's still clutching his phone.

This is probably a good time for some kind of discussion about what they're doing here. He doesn't know how Charlie even approaches dating or sex or whatever. Maybe Charlie's here out of inertia. Maybe he flies everybody's dogs across the continent. Maybe he's here to be polite, like kissing the waiter at Lian's party.

Simon's relationships, if you can even call them that, have mostly been casual, but not in a fun, carefree way. They've been brief. Short enough that nobody has time to get tired of him, or to notice that he's conducting the whole relationship at arm's length. Short enough that Simon barely has time to decide whether he's disappointed not to be feeling whatever he's supposed to be feeling.

Well, he's feeling a whole bunch of things right now, mostly terror, but also something warm and fond and new. He wants to keep it hidden away where Charlie won't see it, maybe somewhere he doesn't have to see it himself.

"Hey." Charlie holds Simon's chin so he can't look away.

Simon's sure the next words out of Charlie's mouth are going to be "we don't have to" and Simon doesn't think he can handle that right now, so puts his phone aside and makes himself look up. He's seen Charlie shirtless so many times—who hasn't—but never let himself really look. Late afternoon sunlight slants through the window, making Charlie golden. He runs his hands over Charlie's chest.

"You are," Simon starts, but he has no plan for how to end that sentence, no exit strategy whatsoever. The fact that he nearly said *beautiful* and would have meant it is just something he's going to have to live with. He swallows. "Those sweaty gym selfies you sent me? I saved them to a special folder on my phone."

Simon tugs impatiently at Charlie's towel, letting it fall to the floor. Then he bends his head to kiss Charlie's hip, slow and with intent, because he may have plenty of problems but not knowing what to do with Charlie Blake when he's naked and standing in front of him isn't one of them. Charlie makes a sound as soon as Simon's mouth touches him. Both his hands land in Simon's hair, and then there's nothing to worry about.

He's lazy about it, mouthing at Charlie's skin in an aimless sort of way. "I can't work with this angle," he says after a minute. He reaches for one of the bed pillows to throw on the floor. Charlie swears, appreciative, like Simon kneeling on the floor in the fussiest possible way is more than he can handle.

Simon's been thinking about this, about how it would feel to have Charlie's hand in his hair, hear the sounds he makes. He wants to make it good, wants to pull out all the stops. But as soon as he has Charlie in his mouth, Charlie's hand slides to the back of Simon's neck, and Simon just . . . stops. His operating system undergoes a complete reboot. He lets himself get lost in it—mechanics, sensation, no decisions to be made.

Charlie's hand tightens in Simon's hair, followed immediately by a muttered "sorry" and a tragic slackening of his hand.

Simon rolls his eyes, very deliberately makes what he hopes is a pleased sound, and lets Charlie draw some conclusions.

"Oh, really?" Charlie asks, and Simon should have guessed that he'd be capable of being a smug pain in the ass even now. "Well, well, well, you're just full of surprises."

Simon pulls off and glares up. "You know I could just bite this thing off."

"Hot."

Simon cannot believe he has to give a blowjob under these conditions. But when Simon puts his hands on Charlie's hips and pulls, Charlie gets the message, does as he's told, and Simon just—lets it happen.

Charlie swears a little, which is gratifying, but then he starts running his mouth and Simon nearly loses his concentration. It's the usual Charlie Blake sex monologue—gorgeous, so good, etc.—but Simon isn't ready for "Aren't you pretty like this, honey."

Simon thinks his heart might skip a beat. He glances up at Charlie, meaning to glare but knowing that isn't what he's doing. Charlie looks stricken, like a man who's run a stop sign and sees flashing lights in the rearview mirror.

Simon doesn't like that look on Charlie's face, not ever but especially not now, so he just—makes a sound and unzips his pants.

"You like this," Charlie says, a little wonderingly, as if the fact that Simon is literally jerking himself off right now isn't proof of that. As if the fact that Simon's even doing this in the first place isn't proof.

Simon pulls off long enough to say, "I hate you," but his point is probably undercut when he goes right back to what he was doing, definitely undercut when he comes a full minute before Charlie does.

Chapter Nineteen

"I'm starving," Charlie says. Simon isn't quite sure how he got into bed, under the duvet, but he's still floating, his entire brain hidden away somewhere he doesn't have to deal with it.

"Mmm," Simon says.

"God, you're useless after sex," Charlie says, not sounding at all bothered. "I mean, even more useless than usual."

"There's a restaurant," Simon says. He's thinking of this place on Tenth Avenue that has dog-friendly sidewalk seating and a menu Simon can work with. Instead of explaining this, he keeps his eyes shut and drifts some more.

Charlie prods him in the ribs. "Do you want to come with me or am I going by myself?"

"Rude to go without me," Simon mumbles into the pillow.

"Okay, pal, time to get up. I'm walking out the door in fifteen minutes."

Simon pries his eyes open. "The fact that you think a person can get ready for anything in fifteen minutes explains so much."

"Fourteen minutes and fifteen seconds." Charlie taps his wrist. "Clock's ticking."

Simon hauls himself out of bed and into the shower. Twenty-five minutes later, they're in the elevator, Charlie holding Edie's leash because Simon can be generous like that. While Simon was in the shower, Charlie put on jeans and an actual honest-to-God linen shirt, which he mostly ruins by wearing it over something that came out of a T-shirt cannon, but the look is overall more than acceptable.

"Stress shopping really works for you," Simon observes.

"So close to a compliment. And yet," Charlie says, but he looks pleased.

When they get to the restaurant, it's eight o'clock, already dark. The tables on the sidewalk are lit with candles and strings of lights, and the mood is more overtly romantic than it seemed in daylight. Simon's embarrassed, but it's not like he can say, "Sorry, change of plans, I'm not sure the vibe of this restaurant exactly matches the vibe of our relationship, if it even is a relationship, so let's find someplace else."

The hostess recognizes them and they get a table right away. Simon might feel bad about it, if he were a much better person, and if Charlie weren't twitching with hunger.

Simon watches in amazement as Charlie puts away the entire contents of the breadbasket. "I couldn't eat on the plane," Charlie explains. "Your dog kept looking at me like I was doing war crimes by not giving her half my sandwich. And I didn't know if she was allowed to eat people food."

Simon stares. "So you just didn't eat?" Charlie needs to be fed every two hours, like a newborn baby or a bacteria sample in a lab.

"I don't want her to hate me."

"All dogs do that. When you're eating, they give you the saddest possible eyes. They put their chin on your leg, they cry like they're being tortured. Every dog on the planet is working from the same playbook."

"Excuse me for not being a fucking dog psychologist."

Charlie's said a couple of things that make Simon suspect he knows next to nothing about dogs. He probably just didn't grow up with pets. Plenty of families don't have pets, but with Charlie, it feels like more evidence of a deprived childhood. Charlie should have had two golden retrievers at all times and at least one cat. It's appalling that the universe didn't give him that.

"If you give her some bread, she'll love you forever," Simon says.

Charlie does, and Edie situates herself so she's basically sitting on Charlie's foot. Charlie looks smug about this, so Simon doesn't tell him that Edie has identified him as a soft touch and will now extort him for food at every opportunity.

When Simon orders something *mildly* off menu—like, it's practically on the menu—Charlie looks a touch apoplectic, but maybe fondly irate?

"I'm never stopping," Simon says. "Get over it."

"No," Charlie says, but he's kind of smiling. Simon might be smiling back.

"Upfronts are in three days," Charlie says.

"I need something to wear." Simon could make do with what he has, probably, but can't think of a single reason why he ought to.

"Oh, I forgot. Jamie sent a suitcase full of clothes. He also packed a weighted blanket. I had to pay thirty whole dollars to check that suitcase, it was so heavy."

The idea that Charlie's bitching about a thirty-dollar fee when he must have spent upward of five hundred dollars on the empty seat for the dog is too much for Simon. He takes out his wallet and counts out a twenty and two fives, then deliberately slides the bills across the table.

Charlie looks like he isn't sure whether to laugh or flip the table, but he takes out his own wallet and shoves the bills in, then puts the wallet back in his pocket, never breaking eye contact.

"I already bought a weighted blanket," Simon says, "as soon I could look at a screen long enough to order one."

"You had a migraine when you got here?"

"Not the greatest day of my life."

Charlie looks acutely unhappy, like he's found a whole new thing to worry about and now has to go back over the past few weeks and factor it in. "Is that why you didn't text me when you landed?"

"I should have just used voice controls." Simon resists the urge to press his glass of ice water against his face. "I'm sorry."

Charlie's quiet for long enough that Simon's sure he got this wrong. Was an apology too much? Not enough? Should he explain that it wasn't personal, that Simon also didn't text Jamie, and he is in fact just like this, possibly permanently?

"Apology accepted," Charlie says.

"I wonder what Jamie packed," Simon says, desperately changing the topic.

"He seemed pretty sure it would be what you wanted."

"He knows me well."

"Why did you two break up?"

Simon already told Charlie the story of Jamie, post-breakup, sitting Simon down in a Panera and delivering a bracing speech about sexual incompatibility, so this isn't a question Charlie should need to ask. Simon produces the same version of the truth that he gives anybody who asks. "We work better as friends."

This is where normal people let it drop, but Charlie is not normal people. "Right, but why?"

Charlie might just be making conversation, or he might be nosy, but Simon's dealt with more than a few men who were suspicious that he was about to run back to Jamie. Usually he lets them stay suspicious.

He gives Charlie a level stare and holds it. "Of the people at this table," he says, gesturing between them, "only one of us has hit on Jamie in the past five years."

"I wasn't hitting on him," Charlie says, slouching, looking caught out.

"Sure you were. You have good taste. In men. And literally nothing else, just to be clear. Anyway, the main reason we didn't work out is that we have no chemistry. The sex was just—"

He doesn't finish the sentence, partly because they're in public, but mostly because it occurs to him a little belatedly that Jamie might not love this conversation. "I mean, it was my fault," Simon adds quickly, because he's not such a bad friend that he's going to go around implying that Jamie's bad at sex. "Because, you know." He gestures at himself.

"I do?" Charlie asks, eyebrows all the way up.

Simon squeezes his eyes shut and shakes his head. He hears Charlie laugh, the sound closer than it was a minute ago. When he opens his eyes, Charlie's leaning forward, delighted. "I am begging you."

The way the table's set up, there's a wooden railing separating them from the street, and Charlie has one arm resting on it, his fingers almost touching Simon's shoulder.

"I—" Simon starts, but gets distracted by the brush of Charlie's thumb against his sleeve.

"Are you being shy? About sex?" Charlie whispers, thrilled. "Oh God, you were like this in Arizona too. I want to go back in time and tell 2019 me that Simon Devereaux is—"

"Shut up, shut up." Simon's laughing despite himself. He leans in even more, close enough that nobody at any nearby tables will be able to hear. "What I'm trying to say is that I'm *lazy*," he hisses, and Charlie bursts out laughing, head thrown back, the sound ricocheting off buildings and asphalt.

"Who told you that?" Charlie asks when, eventually, he gets himself under control.

"Uh, my *brain*? Reality?"

Charlie covers his face with his hands, his shoulders shaking. "Okay," he says, wiping a literal tear from his eye. "Not even two hours ago you let me—You realize that wasn't exactly low effort, right? I know what you mean, but *lazy* isn't the word I'd use."

Simon's not sure it's the word *he'd* use either, but it's the only one he can think of that isn't *passive*, which is too loaded for Simon to consider. "Fine," he says, throwing his hands up, "what word would you use?"

Charlie leans back now and looks at Simon. The idea that Charlie's thinking about him, thinking about what they've done together, makes Simon's face heat.

"Well," Charlie says, quiet and a little rough, "you don't like to be the one doing things."

Simon gives him an extremely unimpressed look, because if

Charlie thinks he's made a big discovery by noticing something anyone could have learned from his short-lived dating app profile, he has another think coming. "My God. You've cracked the code."

Charlie laughs. "No, no, I don't just mean that."

The waiter brings their food, so Simon can't ask exactly what else Charlie means. Instead they talk about the movie Alex is doing this fall, and Charlie seems so genuinely happy for her that it's like some of his happiness slips into the small space between them and gets absorbed into Simon's skin, because he starts to feel it too.

They're talking so much and eating so slowly that Simon's linguine gets cold. The tables around them start to empty out. Simon gets his credit card to the waiter before Charlie even sees the check coming.

"But," Charlie starts.

"My treat," Simon murmurs, and Charlie doesn't protest.

Edie, who'd fallen asleep at some point, her head on Charlie's foot, wakes up and decides she's had all her rights violated by being forced to sleep on cement, so Simon picks her up. She sits, aggrieved and alert, on his lap.

"She's tired," Simon says. "She's being so heroic. I should get her home."

Charlie, who'd been tracing a pattern in the condensation on his water glass, goes perfectly still. Once you know that Charlie's always moving, always fidgeting, never fully at rest, you notice those pauses. Then he starts rolling his napkin into a tube.

"It's stress origami," Simon says.

"What?" Now Charlie's rolling the tube into a spiral, like he's making spanakopita on one of the YouTube baking channels Simon watches as ASMR.

"You only start with the folding and rolling when you're nervous."

"It's satisfying," Charlie says.

"I can't even tell you how much you don't need to explain that to me, a man who doesn't know inner peace until all the mug handles are at four o'clock, but what did I do?"

Charlie's head snaps up. "What are you talking about?"

"You were fine, then you weren't. I'm the only one here," Simon explains. "So, out with it. What did I do? If you tell me, I won't do it again. I'm trying, here." It's such a stupid thing to say. It's a bit passive aggressive, to start with, but what's worse is how much it exposes Simon.

"It doesn't have anything to do with you," Charlie says. "I mean, it does, obviously, but it isn't your fault."

"Come on, out with it."

"Where am I sleeping tonight?"

"Fuck if I know," Simon says, startled into honesty.

Charlie snorts. "Any ideas?"

It's such a relief that *this* is what's bothering Charlie, the same thing that worried Simon all morning until Charlie's presence temporarily jostled it out of his mind. Charlie doesn't have any more of a clue than Simon does.

If Charlie stays with him, then Simon doesn't know how he'll keep his wrecked little emotions under wraps. But the idea of Charlie at a hotel thirty blocks away makes Simon want to kick things.

"Sharing space with you isn't terrible," Simon says, figuring that if Charlie wanted to stay at a hotel, he'd have said so instead of doing terrible things to his napkin. "We did okay in Arizona."

"I was going to stay in town for four nights."

Apparently they're going to decide this by throwing barely connected statements at one another and flagrantly avoiding question marks.

"I'm here until next week because my niece is graduating high school and I'm making an effort." For reasons Simon can only blame on literal mental illness, he makes air quotes around *making an effort*. "I mean, I *am* making an effort. I like her. But having a family member who likes me back is enough of a novelty that I feel like I need to go."

"How did you wind up with a niece old enough to be graduating high school?" Charlie asks, like this information isn't easily available by comparing the birth dates on his and his oldest brother's Wikipedia pages.

"I was your classic midlife surprise. My parents had already filed for divorce by the time I was born." Again, all of that is basically public. There are pictures of him, still a baby, at both his parents' remarriages. It's an explanation he's made dozens of times, usually when people realize that the age gap between him and his brothers isn't filled with the evenly spaced births of six other siblings.

None of it's a secret, but saying it out loud to Charlie feels—not like an admission or a confession, but like he's handing over a document to someone who will be able to read the invisible ink that's all over it.

It's not that Simon thinks he is the way he is because of how he grew up. He's met enough aunts and grandparents to know that weird shit is simply in the gene pool. Uncle Clement's house is filled with two decades' worth of newspapers. Grandmother Devereaux spent some time at a special hospital in the sixties. Simon's own mother has been on SSRIs practically since they were invented, a fact that came as a bit of a shock when he learned this from Nora, of all people.

Still. Sometimes, when he's feeling sorry for himself, he wonders if things might have gone a little differently if he hadn't known all along that he wasn't part of the plan, hadn't spent most of his childhood reading that meaning into everything that happened. He knows—this is what a couple decades of therapy will buy you—that his automatic assumption that people don't want him around is part of a well-worn thought process, rather than anything based in reality. He knows this, but knowing things isn't the same as believing them.

"Are they nice to you?" Charlie asks.

Simon isn't expecting that; he is honestly too much in his head right now to expect anything at all. "Oh, *very*," he says, and it comes out weird and wrong. He doesn't even know what he means, why there's a slightly nasty edge to his words. Charlie nudges him under the table, his shoe connecting with Simon's calf, and Simon remembers the taqueria, remembers everything he knows about Charlie's childhood, and could not possibly feel stupider for bitching about his own family.

He isn't sure what, exactly, is playing out on his face, but whatever it is, Charlie rolls his eyes and starts kicking him in earnest.

The waitstaff is snuffing the candles and sweeping the floor. It's time to go. Edie fell back asleep, so Simon carries her home.

At an intersection, while they're waiting for the light to change, he catches Charlie looking at him—at him and the dog—with an expression Simon hasn't seen before. And, sure, a man carrying a dog around like an infant isn't something you see every day, but Charlie doesn't look embarrassed to be seen with him. And if he has a problem with Simon being an overly indulgent dog owner, he probably wouldn't have flown that dog across the country, first class.

It's more like he's looking at Simon like he's doing something much more wonderful than carrying his geriatric dog.

"Come on." Charlie's hand is on the small of Simon's back, his eyes still on Simon's face. "We have the walk signal."

Chapter Twenty

The next morning, Charlie's already awake when Simon stumbles into the kitchen.

"It's six in the morning your time," Simon says. "What are you even doing."

"I wake up early." Charlie's even wearing *shoes*.

They're both used to early call times, but there's something disgustingly *responsible* about waking up early on a day off. But—Charlie is responsible. After that first season, he never showed up late, never missed a day. Simon thinks of Charlie asking whether he can pet Edie. He thinks of how Charlie drives, his meticulous parallel parking and obsession with correct mirror orientation. He recalls that Charlie has a particular strategy for getting rid of people who sleep at his house after parties. He remembers the party itself, which wasn't boisterous and full of crime but instead featured snacks from Trader Joe's, carefully labeled as gluten-free or vegan.

Simon has personally witnessed Charlie put Alex in a headlock no fewer than twenty times, and seen Alex put Charlie in a headlock at least twice as often. He's been the irritated bystander of a years-long prank war Amadi and Charlie have been waging. Charlie is loud and sometimes he's . . . exuberant. He's kind of a pest. But underneath all that is a core of something steady.

Charlie hands him a cup of coffee. "Drink this. I think you just fell asleep standing up. I already took Edie out."

They stand there awkwardly in the kitchen for a minute, not touching, not talking, until Charlie clears his throat. "I'm going for a run."

By the time he gets back, Simon is maybe thirty percent awake. He's dressed, at least. He wants to spend the day with his face pressed into the microfiber of the sofa—he had too many emotions yesterday; it can't be healthy—but Charlie probably wants to do things.

Simon's still figuring out how to explain that if Charlie wants to do anything fun, he's on his own, because Simon doesn't participate in "fun" or "doing things," when Charlie gets out of the shower and sits on the couch. Simon moves his feet about four millimeters to give Charlie room, but Charlie just swears and hauls Simon's legs onto his lap.

"What do you usually do?" Charlie asks.

"I go for a walk. I eat lunch. Sometimes I lie on the couch facing the other direction." This is a lie: the other direction is for feet, and Simon could never. "I'm full of surprises. Spontaneous."

Simon sits up, as if demonstrating that he's capable of movement, has a sip of the coffee that's gone lukewarm on the end table, and collapses back down. Charlie's fiddling with the television remote, something it hasn't occurred to Simon to figure out since he can watch things on his laptop or phone.

"What episode were we on?" Charlie asks.

"We just finished the planet full of old people. Season four, episode . . . ten, maybe?" He watches as Charlie logs into the streaming service. "I was mostly joking. We can go do things."

"I just ran three miles, up and down the High Line. I want to sit. We'll go out to lunch."

"I like lunch." That was all suspiciously easy. Obviously Charlie doesn't depend on Simon for his entertainment. He's twenty-seven and rich and probably has a dozen friends in the city. He's capable of getting off this couch and doing whatever he pleases.

"You've spent the past three weeks watching television and playing on your phone," Charlie says as the *Out There* theme music plays. "I know you weren't, like, at the club."

Simon isn't sure whether that's supposed to be insulting or reassuring, but the episode starts and Simon gets distracted because it's one of his favorites. It's the body-swap episode, which means he essentially got to play Alex's character and spend the episode authoritatively colluding with space pirates. It was fun, a chance to do something new.

"You're so good in this episode," Simon says halfway through. Charlie's gotten switched with Petra's character, so he spends the episode acting like a serene and vaguely feline telepath.

"What?"

"I mean, you're always good. But this one is special." Charlie's just looking at him, so Simon reaches for the remote and hits pause. "Okay, what did I say wrong?"

"Nothing. You don't need to patronize me. That's all."

"I wasn't." Simon doesn't exactly think Charlie Blake is a generational talent but he's good at what he does.

But of course Charlie doesn't believe him. Simon's spent years rolling his eyes and sighing loudly and being, in general, pretty appalling about everything Charlie's done on set. Simon can't think about any of that right now.

Simon puts the show back on. Before, Charlie's hand had been on Simon's ankle. Now he's using it to hold an electrolyte drink.

It's the first time Simon's seen the finished episode, and this part is better than he remembered. Charlie's character needs to negotiate a hostage exchange. He's angry, obviously, but he's also frightened. He can't let the person he's talking to figure that out, but the audience has to be able to tell, which is tricky. There's a lot of overlapping dialogue, which is never easy, and it ends with Charlie getting stabbed. And he's doing it all while conveying that he's Petra's character pretending to be Charlie's character. It's a good performance—maybe even a great performance—in a good scene in a good episode.

"This is the part I was talking about," Simon says. "I remember when we shot it, I thought, God, Charlie figured out how to be subtle."

"Okay, yeah, that's a Simon Devereaux compliment." Charlie doesn't seem mad—maybe even slightly amused—but there's something brittle in his voice, and Simon doesn't like it.

"I'm not trying to be mean."

"I know, Simon."

Simon sits up and swings his legs to the floor. "You learned on the job. If you compare what you were doing in the first season to what you're doing here"—he gestures at the television—"you can see. You started out with limitations, but that was because you were new and you had no training at all. You have fewer limitations now. In a few years you'll have even fewer. But even at the beginning you were charismatic and—"

"Simon, just stop." Charlie slouches and sort of knocks his head into Simon's shoulder. Before Simon can ask what on earth is going on right now, he realizes Charlie's *cuddling* him.

"It isn't going to work," Simon tells him. "I'm too bony." But he puts his arm around Charlie's shoulders, his fingertips landing on the inside of Charlie's elbow.

"Shut up and let it happen," Charlie says into Simon's clavicle, and Simon does.

THEY GO OUT for a late lunch, or maybe an early dinner, and they spend so long at the restaurant that they wind up getting takeout for dinner on the way home. Back at the apartment, Simon unpacks the suitcase Jamie sent, then sends Jamie about ten thousand heart emojis and one thank-you.

He takes pictures of all his clothes laid out on the bed and sends them to Nora, asking her to tell him what to wear to her party, upfronts, and just in general.

When he finishes, he finds Charlie lying on the couch, shirtless, Edie on his chest. He has one arm cushioned behind his head, and with the other he's holding a book. Attractive Man with a Dog and/or a Book is a particular weakness of Simon's, so he has to take a moment, and it's even worse when the dog is his dog and the man is Charlie and the book is—

Simon has to sit down on the arm of the sofa.

It's a book he mentioned offhand, in a series of semi-deranged four A.M. texts when he'd been listing all his favorite dragon books. Honestly, he hadn't expected Charlie to pay any attention, and even less to read any of those books. But here he is with the book that was Simon's favorite from ages eight to fourteen—Patricia Wrede's *Dealing with Dragons*.

Twenty years later, he can see that part of the book's appeal is that it's a wish-fulfillment fantasy of running away to live in a cave with a dragon for a roommate, nothing to do but organize books and treasure. That, and there's something going on with gender that spoke to him when he was starting to understand that he wasn't particularly interested in masculinity, or at least not in performing it.

But now, seeing Charlie with that book, he has the same feeling he did at the restaurant yesterday, where he's sure Charlie can see the invisible ink all over him.

"Take a picture," Charlie says. "It'll last longer."

"You know what you look like." Simon refuses to be embarrassed by finding a hot thing hot. But his phone is already in his hand, so he does take a few pictures. He tries not to think about how he's going to feel in a few months when he comes across them in his camera roll.

"Lemme see," Charlie says, holding out his hand for the phone. Simon passes it over, and watches as Charlie taps the screen a couple times. On the coffee table, Charlie's phone vibrates, so Simon guesses he sent the pictures to himself. "You mind if I post one? Edie's in them."

"You have permission to post whatever pictures of Edie you like."

Charlie gives him an odd look, but he reaches for his phone. Simon moves closer, sitting on the edge of the couch, his hip against Charlie's thigh, and scratches behind Edie's ears.

"What about this one?" Charlie turns his phone so Simon can see a selfie Charlie must have just taken—Edie on his bare chest, Simon's hand on Edie's head. It's just Simon's hand and wrist, his cuff folded back twice. It could be anyone's hand, but if someone recognizes Edie from Simon's own social media, they'll guess who the hand belongs to. Simon doesn't object to any of that, but he's surprised Charlie doesn't.

"Sure." Simon gets up, a little overwhelmed and not interested in thinking about why. He crosses the room to look out the window, but it's dark out and it's bright inside, so all he sees is Charlie's reflection looking at him. "Are you enjoying the book?" His voice is weirdly small. He makes himself turn to face Charlie.

"Yeah. I should probably just stick to kids' books."

"Nothing wrong with kids' books."

"I mean, I can get through this without the audiobook."

"Nothing wrong with audiobooks either. I like audiobooks."

"And *you* aren't stupid." There's an edge to Charlie's voice.

A few years ago, they were doing press at a hotel—probably something to do with Comic-Con, if Simon's Xanax-filtered memories are anything to go by—when they wound up on the same elevator. Charlie looked him dead in the eye and pressed the button for every single floor, just smearing his palm along the panel until all the buttons were lit up, never breaking eye contact. Simon had simply gotten off at the next floor and taken another elevator, but he'd felt unsettled the rest of the day, like he'd missed a cue.

The look Charlie had on his face when he pressed all those buttons is the same look he has now. This is some blatant shit-stirring, maybe even picking a fight. Simon shouldn't be humoring him.

But he remembers that awkward moment this morning on the sofa and figures he can either deal with this now or Charlie's going to keep poking at it.

"Maybe I spent seven years treating you like you were dumb and talentless," Simon says, "but in my defense that was because I didn't like you." It was also because Charlie has these alarming gaps in his knowledge that have more to do with a total lack of education than they do with anything else. He seems to have switched schools often, and, ultimately, just stopped going.

Charlie gives him an incredulous look. "In your defense you didn't like me," he repeats.

Simon rolls his eyes. "Are you going to tell me it wasn't mutual?"

"A little," Charlie says, not meeting Simon's eyes. "At first."

"I was there. It was more than a little, and longer than at first."

"In *my* defense, you were really mean."

"I'm not going to apologize for my personality."

Charlie's sitting up now. "But it isn't. You aren't like that with anybody else. You singled me out."

"It was mutual!" Simon says, in case Charlie missed it the first time, or during the seven years it was happening.

"And now?"

Simon's too stunned by the honesty of Charlie's question to come up with an answer, so Charlie's words hang in the air while they stare at one another.

"Oh my God, shut up," Charlie says, even though Simon hasn't said anything. He flops backward and throws an arm over his eyes. "This is so embarrassing. Can you forget that happened?"

"Embarrassing?" Simon asks, trying to keep up.

"Stop."

"Can you help me out here?"

Charlie does not remove his arm from his face. "I thought I didn't care what you thought as long as you were nice or whatever, but it turns out I do, and now you know."

It truly is mortifying to care about someone's opinion of you, and even more mortifying if they find out. This maybe isn't the healthiest attitude, but at least he and Charlie are on the same page here.

"God, I know," Simon says.

"Thanks," Charlie says, his voice full of venom.

"No, I mean—" Simon doesn't know how to show someone he cares about them and how to let them know he hopes they care about him. He shut down that part of himself years ago. Decades ago.

He wonders if Charlie would notice if Simon took a little break from this conversation to google how to convince someone you like them, or maybe to consult with Jamie. Simon wants to cross the room and kiss Charlie, but that might just cement whatever absolute bullshit is going through Charlie's head about Simon's real reasons for wanting to spend time with him.

This is where, in a script, Simon's supposed to say something decisively affectionate. *I like and respect you. Being mean is my only reliable coping mechanism; sorry about that!*

Simon tried compliments earlier, when he was praising Charlie's work on *Out There*, and Charlie hadn't believed him, so that's out.

There's only one thing Simon can do here. He grits his teeth. "Me too. I'm ready to die of embarrassment about it."

Charlie lowers his arm and looks at him. "Yeah?"

"God. Yes. How can you not tell? Are your eyes broken?" Edie makes a discontented sound. This quarrel, or whatever it is, is interrupting her nap. Which reminds Simon—"Do I really seem like I'd trust my dog to someone I didn't like *and* respect?"

Charlie doesn't look totally convinced.

"Look," Simon says. "I've fucked plenty of people I don't like."

"You are so good at this," Charlie says. "Wow."

"Shut up. What I mean is that's not what this is. For me, at least.

I'm, like—" He makes a vague gesture between their bodies, a Rorschach blot of a gesture that he's hoping Charlie will figure out how to interpret. "So you can just deal with that. Fuck off."

He feels like he's taken a few internal organs and tossed them on the floor for Charlie to step on. He feels like Charlie's now the proud owner of a functional MRI scan of Simon's brain showing all kinds of terrible truths, the active parts of his brain lit up like a Valentine's heart.

Charlie's face is unreadable. "Yeah?"

Simon thinks he might throw up. There are sirens going off. Red flags. Flashing lights. "Yes, you nightmare."

"Sorry for being like this." Charlie doesn't look sorry at all. He looks a little smug.

"You should be. Now I'm all sweaty. I'm dying, here." Simon runs a finger under the collar of his shirt. "I'm not built for this."

"Alex says I'm needy."

"Pfft. She doesn't know what she's talking about." Simon is a global market leader in nuclear-grade neediness and Charlie's running an adorable little lemonade stand. "Is that why you broke up?"

"Yep."

The surge of irritation Simon feels toward Alex makes no sense at all. If they hadn't broken up, Charlie wouldn't even be here.

He takes a few steps toward Charlie. Charlie holds out a hand and Simon takes another few steps.

"I really am sorry for, you know. My personality."

Charlie wraps a hand around Simon's wrist and tugs. Simon goes alarmingly easily. "I like your personality."

"Nobody likes my personality. *I* don't like my personality."

Charlie lets go of Simon's wrist long enough to put Edie on the floor, which is animal abuse, but whatever; Simon's okay with it because he knows what's coming next. Charlie tugs Simon onto his lap. "Is it my turn to say nice things about you?"

"I will literally gag you and lock you in the bathroom."

"That's what I thought." Charlie pulls Simon down for a kiss, then just rearranges him until Simon's sprawled across Charlie's chest.

"You like the book?" Simon asks into the skin of Charlie's neck.

"Yeah, Simon. I like it." One of Charlie's hands is on Simon's neck, the other big and heavy on his lower back.

"You should read *Howl's Moving Castle* next. There aren't any dragons, but there's dragon energy. Bitchy wizard plus his extremely competent housekeeper, basically."

"I saw the movie."

"He's bitchier in the book, trust me."

Charlie's fingertips drift under the hem of Simon's shirt. It's been a while since Simon had a make-out-on-the-couch kind of relationship, but apparently that's what they're doing, and Simon doesn't hate it. He just sort of lies on top of Charlie, not even bothering to hold himself up, and kisses the hinge of Charlie's jaw, the place where his neck meets his shoulder. He smells like Simon's bath soap mixed with whatever laundry detergent Charlie uses at home. Simon breathes in the scent like he's chasing a high.

Charlie's hands skim over Simon's back, his fingers slipping under the waistband of Simon's pants, but without any real intent. His hands are big and warm and a little callused, presumably from whatever he does at the gym and also a catastrophic failure to use moisturizer.

Simon's coming to accept that he has a full-blown thing for Charlie's hands.

"Is this how weighted blankets work?" Charlie asks, his mouth moving against Simon's ear.

"I mean, my blankets don't usually try to rub off on me but I'm not an expert."

Charlie groans. "Let me see."

For a minute Simon thinks Charlie wants to see his weighted blanket. Then—"Oh."

"Or not," Charlie says, because he's slept with Simon three times, which is more than enough to have gathered that Simon's comfort zone for sex (and also everything else) is not exactly broad and expansive.

Simon thinks about it, thinks about Charlie's eyes on him, and nothing about that image doesn't work for him. Simon sits back enough to undo his belt, to shove his pants down. Charlie does the same thing, scrambling a little, then tugs Simon back down so he face-plants into Charlie's neck.

Then Simon just . . . does what he was doing before, except he pushes himself up on one elbow to give Charlie room to watch. He's lazy about it—in this instance, that's absolutely the right word—letting his pleasure build slowly, feeling up Charlie's chest with his free hand.

The whole situation is completely no frills, utterly basic, two people getting one another off in the least creative way possible. When they came back home, Charlie turned on every light in the apartment, so they don't even have the lighting working for them. Most of their clothes are still on, and not even in a sexy way.

Simon can't think of a single reason why it should feel like more than all that. It might have something to do with the fact that Charlie's running his mouth, telling Simon what he looks like. But even that's pretty standard, as far as dirty talk goes, nothing Simon hasn't heard before.

But it feels . . . safe? Simon has never, not once in his life, felt *un*safe during sex, so he has no idea why this is new or surprising.

When Charlie says, "Come on, show me," it shouldn't feel like a fuse has been lit. When Charlie says, "All right, there you go, just like that," Simon's sure he should feel condescended to but instead he comes almost immediately.

Simon drifts, lets himself be moved around while Charlie picks his dumb free T-shirt off the floor and uses it to clean them up.

"Can I," Simon mumbles, his eyes still shut, making a gesture in the direction of Charlie's crotch.

Charlie snorts. "In a minute. Are you always like this?"

Simon's face is smashed into Charlie's shoulder, but he can open one eye, so that's what he does. "Like what?"

Charlie laughs, low and rumbly. Simon can feel it against his skin, so he presses closer, burrows a little deeper, and stays there until Charlie drags him to bed.

Chapter Twenty-One

"How do the mugs go?" Charlie asks after breakfast. "You said the handles have to go a certain way."

Simon pauses in washing the pan that he used to cook scrambled eggs. "I'm not supposed to make this other people's problem."

"Tell me anyway."

Simon dries his hands on his pajama pants and shows Charlie how the mugs in the cabinet are arranged, all the handles pointing in the same direction, each mug equidistant from the mug next to it.

"Got it," Charlie says.

"The real issue is stuff on the counter and in the sink. It's not such a big deal here, but at home I start to feel like..."

"Like what?"

"Like there's contamination. Germs? Not actual scientific germs, but like. Germ energy."

"Anything else?"

The rest of Simon's rules are self-contained inside his own mind—the right number of times to do certain things, items that need to be counted, some rituals. But that's probably not what Charlie's asking.

A few years ago, Simon paid for an evaluation, a couple thousand dollars out of pocket. He was sure there was something critically wrong with him, possibly something brand-new and mysterious that the psychiatrist would want to write papers about. In the end, she'd told him that it was anxiety and mild OCD. Simon had been dubious. "You're telling me I'm fine?" he'd asked. The doctor had blinked at him, tilted her head, and said, very slowly, "No, you have an anxiety disorder and OCD."

"It's mild OCD," he says now, because Charlie already knows about the anxiety. "It's worst when I'm already anxious or stressed." When things are going well, the compulsions fade to a background hum, and Simon spends a delusional few weeks thinking he's been cured.

"It costs me literally nothing to make sure the sink is empty or whatever the fuck," Charlie says. "Just, like, FYI."

The only person he's talked to about this, other than his therapist, is Nora, and that's because she has it too. Jamie knows, probably, just because he spends a lot of time with Simon and has eyes in his head, but he doesn't know the details, or he'd never leave stuff all over the kitchen—which is partly why Simon's never told him.

"I'm going to the hotel," Charlie says.

"Oh." Simon should probably have figured that a guided tour through his brain's more ludicrous features would make anyone need a little space. Hell, Simon wouldn't mind a little space from his own bullshit.

"For the gym," Charlie says. "The gym in this building is even worse than the hotel gym. Want me to pick anything up while I'm out?"

"Take my key. I'll probably be asleep when you get back."

Charlie goggles at him, likely because he knows Simon slept for ten hours last night.

"Oh, whatever. If I want to sleep twelve hours a day, who does that hurt?"

Charlie laughs and kisses him and gets ready to leave.

Simon goes through what's become his usual morning routine. A walk—this time with Edie—followed by lunch, then burrowing under about fifteen blankets and reading until he passes out. Sometimes he doesn't fall asleep, but he figures that if his body needs this much rest, that's what he's going to give it. He gets more migraines when he isn't well-rested, so maybe the inverse is also true.

He wakes up to Charlie sitting on the edge of the bed.

"Someone took a picture of us the other night at that restaurant," Charlie says, and it's the edge to his voice more than the words he's saying that wakes Simon all the way up. "They put it on their Instagram and now it's every-fucking-where."

"Show me."

In the picture, they're sitting outside at the restaurant the night Charlie arrived. The photo quality is better than Simon would have thought, given that the only lighting is string lights and candles.

Simon can tell right away when the picture was taken. They're leaning toward one another, both grinning. Simon has recently declared that he's lazy in bed and Charlie just finished laughing at him. The way the picture is angled, Charlie's arm, resting on the rail, looks like it's touching Simon's shoulder.

It looks like a picture of a date. It looks like a picture of a very good date.

It wasn't *not* a date. It was date adjacent. One might even call what they're doing dating. Maybe.

In terms of, like, the sheer homosexuality of things, it's not much more than the taqueria video. But Charlie hadn't cared about that video. He'd even been kind of annoyed with Simon for suggesting that he might be bothered by it. Right now, the irritation—maybe even anger—is rolling off him.

The main difference, as far as Simon can tell, is that in this picture they look like they're together. In the video, they just looked flirty.

Simon sits all the way up. "I can see why this would bother you."

"Are you *not* bothered?"

"It doesn't matter as much for me." Simon thought they'd covered this ground already. Photos can surface of Simon on ten thousand gay dates and it won't change his life in any meaningful way.

"What are you even talking about?" Charlie sounds mean and impatient and it's an unpleasant reminder of the way they used to be. It sets Simon's teeth on edge. It makes him want to back off, to settle into their old pattern of nastiness. It would be easy, like what they're doing is so fragile that all Simon has to do is look away for a second and it'll crash to the ground, splintering into pieces.

Simon isn't going to do that. He wants to fight everyone who's ever hurt Charlie and he doesn't have the energy to be mad at himself. "I'm going to get a glass of water. You want anything?"

Charlie shakes his head but follows Simon into the kitchen. He takes the glass of water Simon hands him and eats the granola bar Simon unwraps and slides across the counter.

They stay like that for a moment, in the silence of Simon's sublet, the only sound the hum of the refrigerator and city noises from twenty stories down.

"What's the worst part of it?" Simon asks.

"Sleazeball motherfuckers," Charlie says immediately, his mouth still full of granola bar. "How did they find us? Who the fuck was even looking for us?"

"Chances are, some random person saw us, realized who we are, and snapped a picture." Simon's not totally sure about that, but doubts paparazzi were staking out a medium-nice Italian restaurant. "Okay, what's the next worse thing?"

"It's an invasion of my fucking privacy," Charlie spits out, like he's annoyed to have to explain it to Simon.

"Our privacy," Simon says, knee-jerk, irritated.

"Okay, yes, sorry, whatever. This was *private*." Charlie taps the screen of his phone.

Simon isn't going to point out that they were in public. He doesn't want to argue about the ethics of photographing celebrities—however minor—in public. He doesn't want to argue about anything. "It sucks."

Charlie rolls his eyes, like *duh*.

Simon was wrong before, because it turns out he does have the energy to be mad at himself. He thinks Charlie is just upset, not upset with Simon, but there's a pool of anxiety gathering in Simon's stomach and it's telling him that this is all his own fault.

The thing with anxiety is that every attack is a clone of the last one. It's always the same—the conviction that he messed up, the sense of impending doom, the overwhelming loneliness. His hands are sweaty, his lungs useless, his heartbeat too fast. It isn't a panic attack, but it's definitely something he could take his meds for.

He looks at the clock on the oven. Two forty-five. At two fifty he'll take his pills if he still needs them.

His poor dumb brain tries to activate the usual defenses—be quiet, act calm, because then at least nobody will know he's a mess inside. He could lock himself in the bathroom, turn the faucet on for some white noise, achieve mental anesthesia via crossword puzzles.

He can do all that five minutes from now. First, there's one possible solution to this problem and he needs to make sure Charlie's aware of it.

"I'm going to talk for thirty seconds," Simon says, feeling like he's balanced on the edge of a ravine. Everything in him is telling him to turn back. "And you're going to try not to get pissed at me until I'm done. If you want to go get photographed kissing women or whatever people usually do in these situations, I get that."

They haven't had any kind of conversation about exclusivity—for all Simon knows they're just having sex and hanging out while confessing embarrassing feelings to one another—and Simon isn't sure how to navigate any of this with a pissed off Charlie. The safe thing would be to say nothing, to assume nothing, to act indifferent to the idea of Charlie being with other people.

But he's never been indifferent to Charlie, and faking it now—letting Charlie think he cares less than he does—feels cruel. He takes a deep breath and forces himself to look Charlie in the eye.

"I would consider that, like, work," Simon says, and it isn't a heartfelt declaration but he thinks he got his point across.

"Fuck no. Thirty seconds are up. That's gross. And just . . . wrong." Charlie makes a frustrated sound. "I know you think I'm a complete fucking idiot, but I've thought this through. I know that homophobes exist, Simon, and I know I'll have to deal with some bullshit, but this"—he holds up his phone—"is not about me being *outed* or whatever's going through your head right now. It's never been a secret. I knew it would happen if I lived my life and that's a choice I made a while ago. I just didn't expect it to feel gross. The TikTok didn't feel gross."

"I don't think you're an idiot. But you *were* keeping it a secret. You flipped out at Jamie when you thought he told me."

"It was only a secret from you, Simon." Charlie scrubs his hand across his beard and squeezes his eyes shut.

Simon winces. "Did you think I was going to be shitty about it?"

"Simon, for fuck's sake, I thought that if you knew I was into men, you'd figure out right away that I had this massive embarrassing crush on you."

"You *what*?"

"Don't worry, it was only physical."

"I mean, obviously."

"I didn't like you or anything."

"Who would?" Simon says reasonably.

"Anyway! My point is that I don't give a fuck about anyone knowing I'm queer. It's just—it was private," Charlie repeats, seemingly to himself. Simon finally understands what Charlie's getting at: what happened between them the other night was private. When they got to the restaurant, Simon hadn't been sure whether it was too romantic a setting. By the time they left he'd thought it was just right. Something had settled during the course of that dinner and Charlie's bothered because it was reduced to a photograph for people on the internet to speculate about.

The anxiety drains away, a little. "It was," Simon agrees.

"How the fuck are you so calm about this? Not being calm is, like, your whole thing."

That startles a laugh out of Simon, which makes Charlie's mouth twitch in a way that's vaguely in the direction of a smile. "I'm not,"

Simon admits, and watches as Charlie's gaze narrows, taking in the whole of Simon.

"Shit," Charlie says.

"I'm okay. It was just a bad"—he glances at the clock—"four minutes."

Charlie takes Simon's half empty glass and fills it with water from the refrigerator, then puts it in Simon's hand. It looks like glasses of water are doing a lot of symbolic work this afternoon.

"I genuinely don't care about the photograph, though," Simon says. "It's a good picture."

Charlie sputters.

"I'm serious," Simon says. "We both look great. I'd be livid if I had food in my mouth." He takes a deep breath. "Is the problem that we look like we're together?"

"No. Obviously not." Charlie still sounds pissed, but Simon's starting to see that he isn't pissed at Simon, or even about Simon. "We still should have been able to choose. I mean, I haven't even told Alex."

"You haven't?"

"Well, you know, because she has eyes and a brain she knows what—" Charlie lets out a breath and gives Simon an exasperated look. "She knows how I feel. And I told her about the sex. I mean, I told her we had sex, not *about* the sex. I've also told her everything you've ever done or said so we could analyze your motives."

Simon scoffs. "I think my motives have been embarrassingly obvious."

"That's what Alex says. She actually used the word embarrassing," Charlie says, sounding pleased, both about Simon being embarrassing and about Alex being right. "Anyway, I haven't told her that we're ... dating?" He gestures at his phone, presumably meaning the frankly romantic picture. "If we even are?"

"We are," Simon says, very firmly, and refuses to add, *unless you don't want to*, because every single thing about Charlie's body language—and, like, *language* language—is saying that he wants to. "Together," he adds, for clarity.

"Okay, good," Charlie says. And he *still* sounds pissed. He looks like he'd probably punch whoever took that photograph, or at least dump coffee on them and drive a truck into their car, but like he'd do it while being, apparently, in some kind of relationship with Simon.

"You did post that picture," Simon points out. "The one with my hand in it." He feels stupid as soon as he says it. The picture is cozy, even suggestive—Simon's hand inches from Charlie's bare chest—but it isn't exactly an announcement. Charlie didn't necessarily mean anything by it.

But Charlie just lights up. "You're right." Grinning broadly, a finger pointed at Simon, he says, "I told you I'm not closeted."

"Go take a shower. Honestly. You stink," Simon says, because maybe some insults will restore a bit of normalcy. "And I can't believe you appeared in public wearing a crop top and basketball shorts."

"It isn't a crop top," Charlie says, pulling at the hem of what is, tragically, a crop top. "And I didn't mean to, but my agent called when I was on the treadmill. I came back here right away."

"Not that you aren't making it work," Simon says, leering, because Charlie deserves a little compliment, "for a given value of work. But: bathe." He waves Charlie toward the bathroom. "Like, twice."

While Charlie's in the shower, Simon checks his phone. It probably says a lot about his career trajectory and general outness that his agent hasn't gotten in touch. Or maybe it just means Ken's useless. And it says a lot about how obvious he's been about Charlie that Jamie's only message is "if you got Charlie Blake to wear real clothes that truly is the power of love."

Simon opens the cast's group chat, but he isn't backscrolling to read a million messages, and he probably should leave it to Charlie anyway, so he closes it.

Knowing it's a bad idea, he searches for his name on a few social media sites and sees that there's a lot of commentary. Discourse. Whatever. Most of it's intrusive and creepy, some of it's hateful, and then there are the people tagging him in posts about how celebrities deserve private lives. He deletes several apps.

His phone buzzes with a message from Nora: "fair warning, I'm calling him Uncle Charlie at graduation."

Simon can't imagine where Nora got the idea that Charlie's going to her graduation party, so he just responds with an eye roll emoji.

Simon would have liked to spend the rest of the day lounging around, but Charlie looks like he's ready to climb the walls, so they put on Edie's leash and head out with no real goal. This is like when Edie was a puppy and had to be taken to the dog park, although Simon isn't going to say so out loud. Probably. Not yet, at least.

Chapter Twenty-Two

"Is Edie coming?" Charlie asks while they're getting ready to go uptown for network upfronts.

"She can stay here alone for a few hours. It's fine. She has water and about fifteen hundred pillows."

"No, I mean," Charlie starts. "You're happier when you have her with you."

"I like my dog. Everyone likes their dog. But there isn't anywhere to put a dog during these things. I can't bring her out onstage."

"You could have a PA hold her leash for five minutes. If someone brought a service dog, that's what would happen."

"But she isn't a service dog."

Charlie doesn't say anything. Charlie does, however, put on the sweater they bought yesterday during their stress shopping expedition. Technically, Simon bought it while Charlie waited outside with Edie: a sea blue crew neck sweater in a cashmere and linen blend, lightweight enough to wear all year. His thinking is that it's emotionally identical to a T-shirt.

It's also almost indecently soft, so Simon spends most of the car ride petting it. He's decided to deal with upfronts using the time-honored maladaptive coping mechanism of taking an edible and dissociating, so it isn't his fault if the weave of Charlie's sweater is just really important to him right now.

Simon is perfectly comfortable being onstage and reading lines. He doesn't care whether the audience is filled with people who bought a ticket to see a play or advertisers trying to decide whether *Out There* is worth spending money on. It's just that in order to project an unholy level of excitement and charisma for five minutes, he doesn't need to be his smartest, soberest possible self. He can space out fully, be a passenger for this whole experience.

When they get to the theater, he and Charlie get hustled through a mysterious back entrance and dragged off for makeup, because apparently they should have had that done at the hotel. This would ordinarily annoy Simon—they knew he wasn't going to be at the hotel, so don't make this his problem—but instead he sips his iced coffee and wonders why oat milk tastes different in New York than it does at home: a mystery.

He shakes hands and he smiles, and some man he's probably met before acts like they're friends. Simon just kind of stares at his teeth—they're amazing, science can do such wonderful things—until someone with a clipboard and a headset tries to corral them toward a step-and-repeat backdrop so they can get photographed.

Simon feels a hand on the small of his back.

"First, we have to go to the other place," Charlie says.

"The other place," Simon says knowingly. "There."

Charlie brings him to a mostly empty hallway. His sweater is the softest object on the planet. Simon knows this because he's leaning against it.

"Oh, buddy," Charlie says, holding Simon at arm's length and peering at him. "How many did you take?"

"Just one. I'm not—fuck off. I'm not *high*. I take this exact dose when I have a migraine coming." Or sometimes when he has an anxiety spike or the urge to repeatedly check his cabinets for rogue mug handles. "I'm just leaning into it."

"Leaning into it," Charlie says, amused. "Listen, I wanted to ask if it's okay if I do this." He puts his arm around Simon's shoulders. "Or this." He drops his hand to Simon's waist.

"Are you getting affirmative consent for putting your arm around me?" Simon asks, stunned.

"Babe, you can't consent to shit right now."

Simon gives him what he hopes is a scathing look.

"I meant, on camera," Charlie says. "I would have asked before but I didn't think of it until now. And, um, you didn't seem bothered by the picture yesterday."

It slowly clicks into place what Charlie's asking.

Yesterday, Charlie said he wasn't specifically bothered by their relationship—or whatever—being made public, but he'd also said that he wished he'd been able to choose who knew. This, apparently, is him taking control of the narrative. Or trying to, at least.

It's not like Charlie's doing this in front of a huge audience. Nobody pays attention to these things, except for the live audience and some media journalists. But the media journalists, bored out of their minds, are looking for anything even mildly interesting to write about. If Charlie's giving them that, they'll take it.

Simon spends a solid two, maybe three, seconds deciding whether he has any objections to Charlie's plan. Does he care whether Charlie feels him up, subtly, on camera? Not really. Does he care that every journalist he'll talk to this summer for promo is going to say something like, "So, you and your costar Charlie Blake seemed awfully cozy," and Simon will have to come up with professional ways to say *what does it fucking look like?*

"Sure," Simon says. One thing about Charlie is that it's never boring.

Charlie beams at him. It's a smile Simon's seen before, on the show, this whole face situation that unfurls slow and a little crooked, crinkling his eyes. Even on set, it makes Simon feel drugged. And now that he is, in fact, slightly drugged, the effect is too much.

"Oh my God, are you telling me that thing is real?" Simon asks, poking at Charlie's face, like he might discover that the smile is a hologram. "You're just walking around with that inside you?"

Simon proceeds to put his entire being on autopilot while he smiles for the photographers. Occasionally Charlie's arm is around Simon's shoulder, super casual, except for how sometimes he slips a finger beneath Simon's collar. And sometimes his hand lands at the small of Simon's back. It's exactly the same way Charlie's been touching Simon in the apartment and on the street for the past few days. Affectionate, but not overtly sexy. It just barely crosses the line out of platonic territory. It's nothing new.

Usually, what Simon does at this kind of event—anything where he has to appear as himself—is still acting: he's playing the role of Simon Devereaux. But today, every time Charlie touches him, the persona drops away, and he's left there, under too-bright lights, as nothing but himself.

He doesn't know what to do with his face or his voice, doesn't have the faintest idea what the blocking for this scene should even look like, so he has to get rid of the persona completely and just be Simon. And if that means he has a hand clutching Charlie's sweater, if it means he can't quite stop looking at Charlie even when he's supposed to be looking at the camera, then so be it.

When they go onstage and act wildly enthusiastic about the upcoming season of *Out There*, he must look nervous, because Charlie shoots him a questioning glance, an obvious *should I back off*. He doesn't want Charlie to think that, not for a minute, so there's nothing to do but double down. By the time their bit is done, Simon's plastered against Charlie's side and the network guy with all the teeth is looking at them with—well, Simon's about sixty percent sure it's amusement, which could be worse.

After they're done and the PA unclips their microphones, Charlie follows Simon into a bathroom, where Simon takes a face wipe from his bag and uses it to get rid of the makeup. The products the makeup artist used today are different from what he's used to on *Out There*, so a full sensory nightmare is unfolding on his face. Charlie watches him like he's doing something fascinating.

"How much of that was an act?" Charlie asks. "Here, give me that, you're missing a spot." He takes the wipe and dabs at Simon's temple.

Simon would laugh if it weren't for how much he hates that this idea even crossed Charlie's mind. "There was no acting involved, except me acting like a—" Like a lovestruck idiot, but he isn't quite ready to say that out loud. "I just didn't hide anything."

Then Charlie's kissing him, or as much as you can kiss someone while you're smiling. He tastes like terrible wrong-brand setting spray, so Simon shoves a wipe at him until the makeup is gone, then lets Charlie press him up against the sink and kiss him some more.

"I NEED TO wash my hair," Simon protests when Charlie has him up against the wall before the apartment door is even shut behind them.

"You need to wash your *hair*?"

"Whatever spray they used, I can feel it on my scalp." Also, that makeup wipe was insufficient, and Simon's skin is crawling.

Charlie follows him into the shower and proceeds to interfere with all Simon's attempts at self-care.

"I swear to God, Charlie, if you can't keep your hands to yourself for thirty seconds." It's not exactly unflattering just how much Charlie can't keep his hands off him. Simon's not under any illusions that he looks his best soaking wet and lit by an overhead blue-tinged CFL bulb.

Charlie makes it fifteen seconds, but Simon manages to get some conditioner in his hair.

When Charlie's reasonably clean, Simon kicks him out so Simon can finish his shower in peace. Two minutes later, there's knocking on the door.

"Come *on*, you're clean enough. What are you even doing?"

Simon attempts to ignore him. There's more knocking. Edie barks. Simon starts laughing. There's some pounding that at first Simon thinks is Charlie escalating the bit, but which he then recognizes as the downstairs neighbor banging on the ceiling. Charlie shouts, "Oh, calm down," and now Simon's laughing hard enough that he's in pain. His sides ache. His face hurts. He's out of practice.

He's glad to have the door between them because he doesn't know what to say, doesn't know what to do. He's never felt so wanted, or so happy with it, and that's probably because he's only been with normal people who don't bang on doors and make the neighbors mad, and honestly that's on Simon. Why would he ever think he could make anything work with normal people?

He turns off the shower.

The only way they even wind up seventy percent dry before getting into bed is because Simon does the job himself. Then Charlie's on top of him, and Simon stops complaining.

It's easy. It's so straightforward with Charlie. Charlie *knows* him. Simon doesn't need to be anyone he isn't. And he doesn't need to wonder whether it's working for Charlie, because Charlie can't shut up about it.

Right now—Charlie over him, almost inside him, one hand on Simon's knee—Simon feels untethered. He's floating through space, Charlie's body the only real thing in the universe.

"This is what I was talking about," Charlie says. "Not lazy. You just want to be taken care of."

Simon goes hot with embarrassment—what the fuck, Charlie—and is about to argue, but then Charlie presses in and he gets distracted. Also, maybe Charlie's right. Simon just wants to drift and know that Charlie's going to make it good for both of them. He's slightly resentful to be discovering this about himself in his thirties, years of merely satisfying sex put into context.

After, Simon pointedly steals the duvet and attempts to pinch Charlie's shoulder, but he's tired and his hand lives on Charlie's shoulder now.

"Jeez," Charlie says, his face buried in the pillow. "It wasn't an insult."

"I know. I, uh. Thanks for that. I mean." He isn't going to say *thanks for taking care of me*, because he hasn't grown a new and better personality, but he trails off in a way that lets Charlie fill in the blanks.

Charlie flops half on top of him.

"It's nice," Charlie says. "I mean, taking someone who's usually a bit cold and making them *beg*?"

"I wasn't begging."

"Yes, you were."

"Mmm, no, that must have been somebody else."

"Anyway, that's not some niche fantasy that I just invented. It's an entry-level sex fantasy at best."

"You're great at sex compliments."

"Every single fucker," Charlie says, sounding a lot more pissed off than he should, considering, "who thought you'd call them *names*? How fucking dumb do you have to be?"

"Don't kink shame," Simon says automatically.

"I'm idiot shaming," Charlie says into Simon's clavicle. "Like, I get the appeal. You're snotty and mean and rich, and then there's the whole clothing situation. That dynamic would work if you were a totally different person."

And instead, Simon's apparently someone who likes being taken care of, a phrase that now lives in his head, spoken in Charlie's voice, rough with want. He shivers a little and lets Charlie forcibly cuddle him.

"Do you ever do it the other way?" Charlie asks. "You said you'd fuck me to save my life. What do you need? A doctor's note? A prescription?"

"A court order," Simon suggests. "A petition with ten thousand signatures. No, it's good. I like it, sometimes." He shuts his eyes, lets himself imagine it, feels his body react. "As long as you don't mind doing all the work and me coming in two minutes." He's mostly joking, but it's important not to oversell the experience.

When Simon opens his eyes, Charlie's grinning at him, like Simon isn't being actively unsexy and relentlessly weird.

"My flight leaves tomorrow at noon," Charlie says. There isn't a question in there, but he doesn't sound entirely sure about it either.

"I'll go with you to the airport," Simon says, even though he's never gone to the airport for anyone's flights but his own. That must have been the wrong thing to say, because Charlie doesn't answer. "Or," Simon says, getting with the program. "You could change your ticket. Stay. If you wanted."

"You wouldn't mind?"

"I mean, it's your funeral." Simon can't imagine that spending an entire week in close quarters with him is any kind of fun. "I'm going home on Monday. I just have to go to Greenwich on Saturday for Nora's graduation."

The truth is that Charlie gets on Simon's nerves less than he'd have thought. That morning, Charlie was listening to music loud enough that Simon could hear it from Charlie's earbuds. Simon simply announced that he was about to commit homicide, fair warning, and Charlie gave him a thumbs-up and lowered the volume, not even pausing in between sit-ups. When Charlie encroaches on Simon's side of the bed in the middle of the night, Simon pokes him until he moves.

And it goes both ways—when Simon monopolizes the bathroom performing his skin care regimen, Charlie harasses him until he gets out. When Simon gets cranky about overdone eggs or makes the barista show him the carton of oat milk, Charlie doesn't hesitate to tell him what a pain in the ass he's being. It's almost like after griping at one another for seven years, they can handle minor domestic bullshit without much drama.

It's not that Charlie has thick skin—Simon doesn't think anyone who experienced the Dave affair could think Charlie was thick-skinned. Nobody who saw Charlie on Simon's couch, needing to be told he isn't dumb, could think that.

And anyone lying next to Charlie in bed, when he's gone suspiciously quiet and still, would know something was wrong.

"That was an invitation," Simon says. "But if you want to go home tomorrow, I won't be insulted." That's probably a lie. Simon will be insulted. But he isn't going to throw a fit about a person needing space or wanting to be in their own home. *Simon* wants to go home.

"I'll switch my ticket. Send me the details for when you're leaving, and I'll get on your flight."

In case he hasn't made things abundantly clear, Simon kisses him.

From an *Out There* fan Discord

SimonDevereauxsCheekbones: BIG DAY FOR SPACE BOYFRIEND TRUTHERS!!!!!

DeathStarJacuzzi: Congrats @SimonDevereauxsCheekbones, long-awaited, well-deserved.

SimonDevereauxsCheekbones: I think this is how my mom felt when I got married. I'm so proud of them!!

SpacePope: first, can we stipulate that speculating about celebrities who are literally on a stage in front of cameras is maybe not as tacky as speculating about what was going on in a paparazzi photo??

GalactoseIntolerance: I just don't think it's reasonable to look at any of this—the TikTok, the restaurant photo, the thing at upfronts—and say hey, nothing to see here. Like, if I saw any two human beings acting like that, I'd assume they were together.

SpacePope: for real, I've been to weddings where the couple was less handsy than those two

HowlsMovingSpaceship: okay, sure, but why does it even matter??

SpacePope: HMS, I love you with my whole heart, but if you don't understand being overinvested in the lives of celebrities, then that's on you

HowlsMovingSpaceship: okay, okay, honestly I'm only here to talk about the show but carry on you total weirdos 🖤

DeathStarJacuzzi: Obligatory mention that Simon's wearing a leaf green linen suit from Percival. I think Charlie's wearing a Ralph Lauren Purple Label sweater in a blue cashmere linen blend, which makes this the first time we've seen him at one of these things looking like he didn't just step out of Men's Wearhouse.

SupervillainApologist: the way Charlie keeps touching Simon's back in every picture is killing me. The way Simon keeps looking at Charlie like he's a walking miracle is killing me even more. What the fuck. This is not allowed.

HowlsMovingSpaceship: This is off brand for me, but something SupervillainApologist said reminded me of when we were all losing it over how Jonathan Hale kept looking at Luke West at the end of the Season 4 finale rescue mission. For your consideration:

[image from *Out There* of Jonathan Hale gazing adoringly at Luke West side by side with a photograph of Simon Devereaux gazing identically at Charlie Blake]

GalactoseIntolerance: I am UNWELL

SpacePope: I am IN MY GRAVE

SimonDevereauxsCheekbones: I am UPDATING THE RED TAPE CONSPIRACY WALL

Chapter Twenty-Three

"What is this?" Simon asks after five consecutive days of Charlie dressing like a civilized member of society and not an extra in a dystopian drama. "That has a collar."

Charlie looks down at his shirt, like he needs to refresh his memory even though he put it on four seconds ago. "You don't like it?"

"I like it a lot. But I'm used to seeing you in—" Simon decides *rags* might be a tad judgmental. "Other things," he decides on.

"You always look," Charlie says, and now it's Simon's turn to glance stupidly down at his own clothes. He's wearing black jeans, a black T-shirt, and a fuzzy gray cardigan. It's not his best effort. "Nice."

"I look nice," Simon repeats.

"I didn't want to look . . . not nice."

"You mean, if another creep takes our picture."

"No, I just. Like. Maybe wanted to make sure you knew . . ." He trails off and goes silent long enough that Simon gives up all hope of that sentence ever developing another clause.

Simon is getting familiar with Charlie's weird lapses into silent nervousness. He moves so he's standing in Charlie's space. "What did you want me to know?"

"That I'm, you know." Charlie looks at the ceiling and sighs. "A whole entire adult.

Simon wrestles himself away from demanding exactly how old Charlie thinks Simon is. "I know you're an adult. An adult with terrible taste, but a functional, responsible adult with a mortgage—"

"I paid off my house."

"And a steady job." The correct, therapist-approved next sentence probably goes something like *and even if you didn't have those things, it wouldn't matter*, and that's true, sure. But it's going to sound like bullshit. "You've worked hard to become that person. Your clothes are usually"—Simon heroically refrains from saying *literal garbage*—"not what I personally would choose, but you look good in them and you know it. You know exactly what your"—he starts to gesture at Charlie's chest and arms but then thinks better of it and feels him up, because anything else would be disrespectful—"threadbare T-shirts look like on you."

Charlie blushes, which is what Simon was going for. "It's sometimes weird for me to spend money on things."

Charlie has two reasonably fancy cars and a house that's nicer than Simon's. He goes on vacations whenever they aren't shooting, and from the intensive study of Charlie's social media that Simon's conducted over the past few weeks, they don't look cheap. He tips heavily—even more than Simon, who considers tips combat pay for service workers who have to deal with him.

But that's just Charlie spending money on things that matter to him. Clothes don't matter to him, but they do matter to Simon, and so Charlie spent the money.

Simon knows—mainly from Jamie, but also from, like, being alive—that people who grew up never having enough are going to have a different relationship with money than Simon does. Obviously. Charlie spending that money anyway makes Simon feel—something. Pleased, but also a little ashamed, because Charlie should already know that Simon likes him despite his shitty clothes, and if he doesn't know it, that's . . . not great.

"You were wearing your usual, um, ensembles, when we were in Arizona and that didn't stop me from . . ." Simon makes a gesture that he hopes signals something like *developing feelings or whatever*.

"Didn't stop you from what?"

Simon takes a moment to arrange the collar of Charlie's shirt so it looks less like he's on his way to his job fixing computers at an investment bank. "Obviously I'm attracted to you no matter what you're wearing. And that's some self-knowledge I didn't want, so thanks for that. But also—you know it's not just that. Right?"

They've been circling around the state of their relationship like it's an undetonated grenade that might explode if the conversation gets too close. They've agreed that they're "dating" and "together," but you can date and be together in a casual, short-term kind of way. Simon's pretty sure you can date without feelings being involved, but then again, he's overthought this so thoroughly that "date" and "together" have stopped meaning anything at all.

It should be obvious, surely, that nobody acts how Simon's been acting unless they're invested on, like, a feelings level.

Charlie relaxes enough that Simon can only conclude it was not, in fact, obvious. Or maybe it was obvious, and Charlie needed to hear it anyway. Maybe, when you have the kind of history they do, you have to constantly remind one another that things are different now.

Simon tips forward, resting his forehead against Charlie's shoulder. The horrible truth is that they're going to have to keep doing this. Emotional honesty isn't one and done, which is terrible news for everyone in this relationship.

"I know," Charlie mumbles into Simon's hair. "I just—sorry about being needy."

Simon nearly tells him he isn't being needy, but they'd both know it was a lie. "That doesn't bother me," Simon says instead, which would come as a surprise to everyone he ghosted as soon as they looked like they were feeling things about him, as soon as Simon worried he was feeling things himself. "It's okay to need things. It's okay to need more than other people do." And that would come as a surprise to his therapist, who's been trying to get Simon to accept that about himself for years.

He doesn't say that he wants to give Charlie whatever he needs. He doesn't say that he's at least ten times as needy as Charlie could ever be. He doesn't say a lot of things, because even though he knows what he feels, it's staying in the privacy of his own mind until he's had some time to get used to it.

"And, you know—me too," Charlie says. And Simon, who hadn't known he had any doubts, feels himself sink against Charlie's body.

THE ONE HUGE downside to that picture circulating on social media is now people know Simon's in New York. His phone keeps buzzing with variations on "hey we should get a drink while you're in town."

"Oh no," Charlie says when Simon complains about this. "People want to see you. It's terrible."

"They don't really want to see me. It's the kind of thing people have to say." Simon doesn't expect Charlie to understand—people *do* want to see Charlie.

"What would they say if they did want to see you?"

"Oh, fuck off." Simon sees where this is going.

"Because it would be the exact same message, right?" Charlie picks up Simon's phone and holds it in front of Simon's face to unlock it, slow enough that Simon could grab the phone away if he wanted to. "How does a person even get four hundred unread text messages?"

Simon drops his book and stands up only to climb into Charlie's lap. "I don't want to go out for dinner with friends from college or people I worked with ten years ago. I want to have dinner with you."

He doesn't mean anything by it, not really—but he doesn't mean nothing by it either. Charlie raises his eyebrows. "You can't help it; you're obsessed with me." He kisses Simon's neck.

An hour later, Simon's in the bathroom, still wearing a robe, trying to get ready.

"What's that?" Charlie asks, coming up behind him and sticking his entire finger in the pot of moisturizer.

"What is *wrong* with you?"

"I just washed my hands. Why is this stuff blue?"

"There's some kind of plant in there that's supposed to reduce redness, and redness is a real problem in my life right now because you're a total freak who can't stop leaving beard burn all over the place." He pointedly dabs some cream onto his neck.

Charlie, because he really is a freak, slips a hand under Simon's robe and starts pawing at Simon's chest, his stomach, his inner thighs—all red from Charlie's beard.

"You want me to stop?" Charlie murmurs into Simon's neck.

"Stop groping me right now or stop mauling me with your beard?"

"Both. Either. I could shave."

"No," Simon says, far too quickly. "But how bad are your feelings going to get hurt if I need an hour alone?"

"Not at all."

"You sure?"

"Gotta wait for you to come to me, like when someone's trying to lure the raccoons to the bird feeder."

Sometimes talking to Charlie is like entering another dimension where words have different meanings. "Someone? Why on earth would 'someone' want raccoons at the bird feeder?"

"Why wouldn't anyone want raccoons at the bird feeder?"

Simon's going to have to figure out a casual way to bring up the existence of rabies. "You know you can't cuddle a raccoon, right, Charlie?"

"Not with that attitude you can't."

Simon decides not to be bothered that he's the raccoon in this metaphor, and instead closes the bathroom door in Charlie's face. When he's sufficiently moisturized, he finds Charlie sprawled on the sofa, on a video call, not pouting or sulking or whatever Simon was worried about in the back of his mind.

"Gotta go in a sec," Charlie tells whoever he's talking to, already on his feet, already across the room. "This is so slutty," he says approvingly, one finger pressed against the exposed vee of skin at Simon's collar.

"I really hope that's Alex," Simon says, because he didn't see Charlie disconnect the call.

Into the phone, Charlie says, "He has three buttons undone on his prissy little linen shirt."

Simon grabs the phone. "It's the shirt's fault," he tells Alex, angling the screen so she can see. "Two buttons and I look like a golf dad."

"Slutty's a good look on you," she says.

"You too," he says absently, because Charlie's mouth is on his collarbone.

"Oh gross," Alex says, and ends the call.

"You're really not mad?" Simon asks.

"That you're going out to dinner with your whole chest out? No, I'm into it."

Simon rolls his eyes. "That I kicked you out of the bathroom."

"I know I'm clingy as fuck but come on, give me some credit."

"You aren't—that's not what I mean."

Charlie studies him. "Did somebody make you feel bad about wanting time alone?"

"No, no. It's just. Not everybody likes being told to go away." He says the words to the stretched-out collar of Charlie's T-shirt, but it feels like Charlie's looking at him very carefully, not groping anymore, his hands on Simon's hips. "I thought maybe you also—I don't know. Never mind."

"I know the difference between someone asking for space and someone telling me to go away," Charlie says, not offended, just— too gentle.

It's the gentleness, the idea that Charlie thinks he has to be gentle about this, the fact that he's right, that makes Simon snap. "Okay, well, congratulations."

"Hey." Charlie's thumb traces Simon's cheekbone.

Simon was trying to be *nice*. He started this entire cursed conversation because he wanted to make sure Charlie's feelings weren't hurt, and now he feels like his skin is see-through, everything important just sitting there, out in the open. This is why it's better to keep his mouth shut, a lesson he thought he learned half a lifetime ago.

"I'll be careful," Charlie says.

"We aren't talking about me."

"If I want space. I'll be careful."

"Still not talking about me."

Simon doesn't know if Charlie's remembering Simon being the first to leave parties and dinners, doesn't know if he's thinking about four hundred unread text messages, doesn't know if Charlie can extrapolate exactly how much Simon prefers to *be* alone over being *left* alone.

Simon doesn't want Charlie to become one of the unread texts on his phone. He twists the fabric of Charlie's T-shirt around his fingers like that will somehow stop himself from ruining this.

CHAPTER TWENTY-FOUR

"Will you stay with Edie while I'm in Greenwich?" Simon asks while he's attempting to rewrap Nora's present. "The car gets here at noon and I'll be back by seven."

"Why don't you just take her?" Charlie asks.

Simon doesn't have a good answer to that, except that it hadn't occurred to him. He's seeing his entire family in a few hours and the idea of adding anything new to the mix feels impossible.

"Are you going somewhere?" Simon feels a little off-balance because Charlie usually narrates all his plans as the ideas occur to him. *Maybe I'll go to the gym, how about I pick up dinner, do you need anything sent to the dry cleaner.* "I didn't mean to assume you'd babysit my dog."

Charlie gives him a look that Simon can't read. "I mean, I'll go to the gym for an hour, probably. But I don't have plans. And I'll babysit your dog whenever you want me to."

"I didn't check to see if the car service allows dogs."

"What's the name of the company?"

Charlie calls while Simon wrestles with the Scotch tape.

"They allow dogs."

"Why are you pushing me to take Edie?" Simon asks. He's already overwhelmed by knowing he's about to see his family, by wrapping paper that rips too easily, by doubt over whether Nora's going to like this jacket.

"You're happier with her," Charlie says. He's said it before. "Calmer."

It isn't fair for Simon to immediately assume he's being criticized, but he's doing it anyway. His face is hot, his hands sweaty, and he tears another piece of wrapping paper.

"People have emotional support dogs," Charlie says.

Simon crushes the ruined wrapping paper into a ball. "She isn't—"

"I know. But she helps, right?"

Simon doesn't know how he thought Charlie could live with him for a week and not notice this. "Yes, but—"

But what? It would take nothing to bring the dog with him. It's a garden party, not a sit-down dinner. Both his brothers and both his parents have dogs, so Edie probably wouldn't even be the only dog there. She would love meeting new people and smelling new smells, and she'd love all the bits of food that people would undoubtedly slip her.

And he would feel better. He knows that. She's a buffer between him and the rest of the world. Sometimes Simon simply talks about her instead of attempting to navigate actual conversation. Sometimes people will talk about their own dogs, which Simon is always happy to hear about. Worst-case scenario, she's a get-out-of-jail-free card: Sorry, better see what the dog needs!

"It's just—" Simon's about to say that it's just his family, but they both know there's no *just* about it. He's wrapped and rewrapped this present no fewer than four times—he isn't exactly projecting normal at the moment.

What Charlie's saying makes sense. Simon can either argue, or he can go along with it. His whole entire faulty brain wants to argue.

Charlie hands Simon the scissors so he can trim another rectangle of wrapping paper, and doesn't say a single thing as Simon wraps the box again. When Simon's done, Charlie takes the present away and puts it on the table by the door, which is just as well because now Simon's out of wrapping paper.

"I could come with you too," Charlie says, his back to Simon.

"Why on earth would you want to do that?"

Charlie knocks his forehead into the frame of the mirror that hangs by the door. "Are you going to try to tell me it would be worse with me there? I mean, maybe it would be. I don't know your family. But would it be?"

"No," Simon concedes.

"If you don't want me there, that's fine." Charlie doesn't sound like it would be fine, but he turns around, at least. "I mean, I'm visiting my mom next month. I need to do that alone. Having you—or Alex, or anyone—with me would make it worse. My feelings won't be hurt if that's what you need too."

He kind of sounds like his feelings would be hurt, though.

When Simon's anxious, he's not great at figuring out what's going on in other people's heads. But he's spent enough time with Charlie that he doesn't even have to do any deciphering. It's all right there, out in the open.

Simon has this sense that if Charlie meets his family, he'll *know*—know what exactly, Simon isn't sure, except that Charlie will see Simon for the mess he is. All Simon's weaknesses will be right there, under a spotlight for Charlie to see.

"You'd probably like my family," Simon forces himself to say. "Most people do."

"That's not the point."

"I know." The point is that Charlie wants to make things better for Simon, and that's a thought that Simon wants to push away from himself as hard as he can. It's worse than conceding that he could bring Edie.

What Charlie's offering is no more than what Simon did by interfering with Dave. It's not so different than all the little things Simon did in Arizona to make Charlie feel less terrible. It's less than what Charlie did by bringing Edie to New York.

They've spent weeks doing this, showing one another their weaknesses. Falling in love, probably, although that's at the top of the list of things Simon isn't thinking about.

So, right now, he can ask Charlie for help, when it's so clear that it's what Charlie wants from him, and—and it doesn't mean that Simon's clingy or pathetic. Or it does mean he's a bit clingy and there's nothing wrong with that, because Charlie already knows.

"Nora would love to meet you," Simon says.

"Yeah?"

"I should have asked you before." It's true, even though it feels all wrong in Simon's mouth. "I think I don't like asking for things."

"I don't know how the fuck a man who can demand to read nutritional labels at restaurants can't just ask his boyfriend to go to a party with him," Charlie says.

Simon *should* have asked Charlie to come with him, just like he should have asked Charlie to stay with him, instead of leaving Charlie guessing. Charlie doesn't seem upset, but maybe he should be. Simon feels like he's been carelessly stingy.

Charlie's face is pink, and it takes Simon a minute to rewind and figure out why. That's the first time either of them has said *boyfriend*.

"I can ask a barista about the brand of oat milk because that's her *job* and also I tip extremely well," Simon says.

Charlie obviously wants to argue about every single syllable in that sentence, but instead he jams his hands in his pockets and looks at the ceiling. "It's my job. Just—let it be my job."

Simon can hardly breathe. "Okay," he says. "Okay."

SIMON FEELS WILDLY self-conscious rolling up to his brother's house with a dog and a whole extra person, but there must be a hundred people on the lawn, an entire flock of waiters, and a couple of men who look a lot like bodyguards. Nobody's paying attention to Simon.

"I should have written her a check," Simon says, clutching the present. "That's what people do for graduations. What was I thinking?"

"Doesn't look like this kid's hurting for money," Charlie observes, taking in the house, the crowd, the entire spectacle. He's right. "How rich *is* your family?"

"Everybody has a real job and nobody has a private jet." These are crucial bits of information in Simon's classification of rich people, but Charlie looks like he's ready to storm the winter palace. "Private school but not boarding school. Martha's Vineyard, not Dubai. Upper middle class, really, when you think about it," he adds, mainly to get that vein in Charlie's forehead to do its thing.

Simon's sister-in-law, Nora's mother, greets them, and Simon goes through the motions of introducing Charlie and *good to see you* and *you must be so proud* and a couple of air kisses.

It's more of the same with Simon's oldest brother, who inflicts the usual hearty handshakes and back slaps. George, who's never seen Charlie in his life, unless you're counting television screens—and Simon doubts he has much time these days for anything other than C-SPAN—greets Charlie like he's never been so happy to meet anyone in his life. Assuming someone on his staff has a news alert set for Simon's name, he already knows precisely who Charlie is to Simon.

Simon's fine with this part. It's acting. Which doesn't mean it's fake—Simon means what he's saying, mostly, but he needs a layer between himself and the role. His brother is acting too.

When George crouches to let Edie sniff his hand, Simon has a dizzy little moment, remembering George showing him the right way to greet a dog. That's something he hasn't thought about in a couple decades. It's probably sweet, right? An older brother teaching a preschooler how not to get mauled by strange dogs. Simon doesn't know why he has that sorted in with the sad memories.

He doesn't know why he has his entire family sorted in with the sad stuff.

Simon must be radiating bad vibes, because Charlie's hand lands at the small of Simon's back, and he's close enough that Simon can feel the heat coming off him. Or maybe Charlie just wanted to touch him. Either way, Charlie's here.

George clocks it immediately. His grin somehow doubles. "Simon never brings *anyone* to meet us."

Simon is about to perish, but Charlie just grins right back, wattage cranked all the way up, and says, "I guess I'm just that lucky." He pulls Simon a little closer. "Hey, babe, let's go find somewhere to put this present." A neat extraction.

Simon's sister-in-law points them toward Nora. It's not like they've never met in person. Simon does show his face at family events, at the rate of once every eighteen months or so, or however long it takes to forget just how unsettling these things are. But when your relationship consists of words and images on a screen, the leap to face-to-face interaction isn't always smooth.

Nora looks awkward enough for both of them, though. She's wearing a pale-yellow dress that Simon would bet a literal million dollars she didn't pick out herself, her makeup looks both subdued and professionally applied, and there are no visible piercings except for a tiny pearl in each earlobe.

"Oh, darling," Simon says, taking in the entire look. "It'll be over soon."

She doesn't exactly launch herself at him, but she takes a smidgen of a step forward and Simon recognizes what an enormous effort that is from a tiny goblin child. So he does the rest of the work and bends to hug her. She's nearly a foot shorter than him. He's careful not to wrinkle her terrible little dress.

"You brought Uncle Charlie," she says, absolutely loud enough for Charlie to hear.

"And you can behave yourself or I'll donate this to a thrift store." Simon lets go of her and gestures at the box Charlie's still holding. "Charlie, this is Nora. I've shown you enough pictures of her for you to know you can't hold this look against her."

"We follow one another on TikTok," Charlie says, because of course they do.

"Come on, open the present so I know whether I have to sell it," Simon says.

Nora leads them inside through a kitchen filled with caterers and into an empty living room. Simon's seen the house before, in person and in the background of Nora's pictures, but it isn't familiar. Neither are his parents' houses, or his other brother's house. The houses where he grew up have long since been sold. There's nothing connecting him to this place—or to these people—except this one teenager and a whole bunch of neutral-enough feelings toward everyone else.

Nora tears open the present and takes the lid off the box. Simon watches her face for the three seconds it takes her to realize what she's looking at.

"Oh, shit," she says, holding the jacket up.

"I measured it," Simon says. "But if it's the wrong size we'll find something else."

"What am I looking at?" Charlie asks.

"A motorcycle jacket," Simon says, at the same time Nora says, "Vintage Vivienne Westwood."

"If you don't like it—" Simon starts.

"Oh, shut *up*," Nora says. "Thank you." She puts it on then gets out her phone to use as a mirror.

"I wouldn't," Simon says. "Not with that dress. You'll just get depressed. *I'm* a little depressed." She does a little twirl, holds the camera out as far as she can to get a better angle. "Seriously, if you change your mind, it's fine."

She rolls her eyes.

She keeps the jacket on while Simon asks when the graduation ceremony is, who the bodyguards belong to, when she starts her summer internship.

"Nora!" calls a voice. "People are wondering where you are."

Nora scrambles out of the jacket. "Sorry, Gran."

"I've been sent to collect you," Simon's mother says as she enters the living room. "Oh, Simon, there you are." She says this in the same tone of voice she'd use if they'd seen one another earlier that day, rather than two Christmases ago.

The last few times he's seen her, he's been a little startled by how old she is. She's seventy-five. It shouldn't be a surprise. Her hair, which used to be as dark as his, is steel gray. Her closet used to be full of dresses, but at some point she shifted to flowy pants and tunics, everything soft and neutral. Today she's wearing a scarf he got her for her last birthday, pale blue silk with ivory embroidery. Like he always does when he sees her, he thinks he might have missed her, but maybe didn't notice until now.

"Hi, Mom," he says.

"I'm going to hang this up and then I'll go outside," Nora says. "Thanks, Uncle Simon." She usually leaves off the *uncle*, so Simon assumes this is part of whatever normie drag she's performing today.

"Mom, this is Charlie. Charlie, this is Paulette Robins, my mother."

Charlie shakes hands and beams. Simon and his mother jointly remember that they're supposed to hug, so that's what they do for about two seconds, his mother's shoulders fragile under Simon's hands.

Edie is winding around Simon's feet like she thinks she's a cat, so Simon picks her up. As soon as he has her in his arms, it's like the edges of his mood get sanded off. He doesn't even know what his mood *is*.

"We've heard so much about you," his mom tells Charlie.

Simon winces. He calls his mother every other week. Usually they talk about clothes. Sometimes she monologues about azaleas and her grandchildren and the woeful ineptitude of the board of directors she serves on. Simon monologues about Edie's latest exploits and whatever annoying things Charlie's done.

Charlie has to know that anything Simon told his mom about him before this spring would be negative, but he keeps on beaming.

"Cucinelli?" Simon's mother asks, taking in his outfit. It's a shell-pink linen suit he bought on a deranged whim two years ago, and which he wears whenever it's even remotely plausible to wear a pink suit.

"Naturally," he says, inordinately pleased she recognizes it, the first real thing he's felt in what seems like hours. Next to him, Charlie sucks in a breath like he's figured something out, and—it's fine.

"Your father's around here somewhere. Peter and Sarah too, and Bill and Lauren," she says, listing Simon's middle brother and sister-in-law and both his stepparents. He assumes various stepsiblings and nieces and nephews are also around. "And, well, everyone. If you want to say hello."

She says this like Simon's a visitor from an alien planet where saying hello might not be customary, and she's trying hard not to cause a diplomatic incident. It's kind. She's kind. They've all always been kind. Something's horribly wrong with Simon that it doesn't make him feel anything.

Simon doesn't particularly want to say hello, but he doesn't want *not* to say hello, so he follows his mother outside. "I'm so glad you brought someone," she says, quiet, when Charlie's dropped a few paces behind.

There's nothing he can say to that, so he doesn't try. He's sure she means it, and he guesses he's pleased, but he doesn't know. His feelings are all situated behind a nice, thick fog.

Outside, Charlie takes Simon's hand. That's new. They don't do that, except in bed, which is a little different, and also not a direction Simon's brain is capable of going right now.

His dad comes over, then his middle brother, then fifteen consecutive Devereaux and Devereaux-adjacent people. It turns out that when you're holding a dog and your boyfriend's hand, nobody can hug you.

Charlie million-dollar smiles his way through the entire ordeal. Simon's seen the Charlie Blake charm offensive dozens of times before, all loud good humor and booming laughter infused with what he now knows is genuine warmth. At one point, Charlie, Simon's stepfather, and one of Simon's brothers are talking about some kind of sport. Hockey? Basketball, maybe? Simon feels like he's watching the entire thing on a tiny screen. It's an episode of a show he's not sure he wants to watch.

Charlie steers Simon toward one of the little tables scattered around the garden. Simon wonders what they would have done if it rained. Not that there would be any trouble fitting a hundred-odd people inside the house, but at what cost to the aesthetics? Charlie disappears, then comes back with a bowl of water for Edie and a plate of fruit and some bread for Simon.

"They're all happy to see me," Simon says, voicing the one thought that keeps scrolling through his head as he watches family members assemble and reassemble in various configurations. Everyone's either having a good time or doing a professional quality job at faking it.

"I can tell."

"You can go have fun if you want." Charlie is like these people, gregarious and cheerful, full of the right things to say. They'd like him. He'd fit right in.

"Look at me," Charlie says. Simon does. "Don't be a fucking idiot. I didn't come here to hang out with your family."

"You could, though."

"You could fuck yourself." Charlie slings his arm over the back of Simon's chair, not touching him, but there for Simon to lean into.

Simon watches Nora talk to her mother, to Simon's mother, to some cousins. Whatever dynamic his family has cultivated, the dynamic that's made Simon a spectator for thirty-four years, doesn't exclude Nora. She's a part of it. Maybe the family dynamic has broadened, or maybe Nora's better at this than Simon ever was.

Either way, he's relieved. Maybe she put on that dress and took out the piercings in order to cooperate with her parents, not because she got browbeaten into it. He'll find out later.

He doesn't know why being near his family feels like wearing clothing tailored for somebody else, pinching and pulling ever so slightly, never a chance to forget that it isn't his own. They love him. Even his brothers. Even his stepparents. Probably even his sisters-in-law, both of whom have known him for going on twenty years.

Three children are hovering near Simon's table. They're younger than Nora, but old enough to be in high school, or close to it. One of them looks enough like a Devereaux that he's probably a nephew. The others might belong to his stepsiblings.

"Hey, you guys," Charlie says. "What's up?" Simon had planned on ignoring them, but Charlie's a better person.

The tallest one takes a step closer. "How long have you been boyfriends?" she asks.

"Oh my God, Emma, no," Nora says, swooping in.

"No, it's okay," Charlie says. "A month. A month?" he repeats, lower, for Simon.

"Yes. A month," Simon agrees. It's been about five weeks since that motel in Arizona and a week since Charlie arrived in New York. The truth probably lies somewhere in the middle, but a month will do.

"Are your characters gay?" asks a kid who Simon has no trouble identifying as a theater kid of the presumptively queer variety. Simon remembers the absolute wasteland of gay representation that was television during his own ghastly adolescence. It's better now, but not perfect, and he imagines kids still watch shows like they're reading tea leaves, looking for any sign a character might be like them.

"Well, bi," Charlie says.

Simon whips his head around, but Charlie looks perfectly placid.

"The writers might disagree," Simon says.

Charlie shrugs. "I said what I said."

Out of the corner of his eye, Simon sees two adults approaching the fringes of the little group clustered around their table. He thinks—hopes—it's some parents come to collect their nosy offspring, but it's just Simon's father and George.

"Do you remember when Simon used to sneak into the living room to watch—what was it?" his dad asks. "We should have known this is what he'd do with his life."

"*Deep Space Nine*," George answers.

"*Voyager*," Simon says, under his breath.

"In his little pajamas," Simon's dad says. "When he should have been in bed."

"We always caught him," George says.

Simon feels like some part of his psyche has been cracked open in front of Charlie and a couple of teenagers he may or may not be related to. For a moment, he's in his dinosaur pajamas, thinking that if only he's quiet enough, he might be able to have a place on the couch with everyone else.

The hand that Charlie had on the back of Simon's chair now lands on Simon's neck, warm and dry.

"Every foster home I was in," Charlie says, loud enough for everyone nearby to hear, oozing enough charisma that nobody can help but give him their attention, "there was someone who needed to watch their spaceship show." He pauses, holding the crowd, all the focus on him and far away from five-year-old Simon. "I think that's why I've stayed on *Out There* so long. One of the reasons, at least."

"That's what I think about when I have to cry on camera," Simon says after Charlie's made some excuse to pull Simon into the house, around a corner, into what turns out to be a laundry room. "Not being allowed to watch television with my brothers and my dad. I feel like if you needed proof that I had a good life, the fact that this is the worst thing I can drag up is it."

"I don't think that means what you think it means," Charlie says.

Simon doesn't know how many times he's seen Charlie hug people—friends, coworkers, literal strangers—but somehow this is the first time he's ever hugged Simon. He's known, just from watching, that Charlie's good at it, and he was right. It's because Charlie likes hugging people, that has to be the reason, because it feels right—safe and solid and normal—even though Simon isn't sure where to put his hands. Charlie's arms are tight around him, tight enough to crush, a three-dimensional weighted blanket. Simon feels surrounded—he isn't in a laundry room, he isn't in Connecticut, the only location that matters is Charlie's arms.

"Why isn't it enough?" Simon asks when they're in the car heading back to the city, Edie passed out on the back seat between them.

"What isn't enough?"

"They love me. And I love them?" He doesn't mean for it to be a question. "I mean, I do. But not, like, actively. Except Nora." He tries to fill his lungs. "And my mom?"

Charlie doesn't ask what it means to love someone but not actively love them, which is good because Simon doesn't have any answers. All he knows is that he's unsatisfied down to his bones, greedy for something he can't identify.

He's not sure he's ever felt this exposed. In a few days, they'll be back home and it won't be like this, but Charlie will still know all Simon's secrets.

"Is it always like that?" Charlie asks, quiet enough that the driver can't hear. "Like you aren't—I don't know—part of the main cast?"

Simon is speechless for a minute, because he's never told Charlie that. Sometimes he wonders if he dreamed it all up, and his family is normal and the problem is, as usual, Simon.

But if Charlie saw it—

"Sorry, shouldn't have said that. I don't know what I'm talking about," Charlie says easily.

"It's always been like that. I must have had bad vibes even as a little kid."

"You've never had bad vibes, what the fuck."

Maybe that's the moment Simon knows that Charlie loves him, and is a little stupid with it, because Charlie is America's greatest living expert on Simon's bad vibes. "Okay," he says. "If you say so." They're both petting Edie, and Simon lets their fingers tangle.

Maybe Simon's operating on a different definition of love than most people. Maybe he needs the kind of love that won't let him forget it, not for a minute. Maybe he needs the kind of love that flies your dog across the country after a seven-year-long fight.

"I never had a bad foster placement, but the worst ones, for me, were when the parents had kids of their own. There was this whole family and there I was. Not their fault, not my fault, just a shitty situation." Charlie rubs his thumb over Simon's wrist. "In your case, though, it's definitely your family's fault. I'm gonna fight them. Don't care if they're old."

"I think you can take them," Simon says, a little overwhelmed.

Chapter Twenty-Five

Jamie picks them up at the airport. Simon hugs him hard enough that Jamie's feet leave the floor.

"You messaged me literally half an hour ago," Jamie says, but it's not like he's letting go either. "We FaceTimed every day."

Then Jamie hugs Charlie, which might have been a surprise if Simon hadn't seen Jamie's name on Charlie's phone from time to time. It makes him feel warm. Maybe this is how people feel when they think about family. He doesn't know.

They manage to get all their luggage into Jamie's car. Charlie climbs into the back seat with Edie and Simon gets behind the wheel.

"You're making Simon drive?" Charlie asks Jamie. "Wow."

"Oh, honey," Jamie says after he finishes laughing. "Don't you know—"

Simon gets a hand over Jamie's mouth and Jamie stops talking, but in the rearview mirror he sees Charlie looking thoughtful.

On the ride home, Jamie fills him in on the minutiae of his life, as if they haven't been talking the whole time Simon was gone, but Simon doesn't mind hearing it all again.

"That was the turn for Charlie's house," Jamie says after they've turned into their neighborhood.

Simon doesn't know why he didn't think of it. Charlie's going home to his own house, and Simon's going to *his* own house. They've spent the past week in a six-hundred-square-foot apartment. The idea of Charlie not being there is a little strange, too abrupt.

"You probably don't have any food in your house," Simon says, even though it can't be true. A week isn't even long enough for eggs to go bad. And whoever cleans his house could have brought groceries, for all Simon knows.

"You're right," Charlie says from the back seat, absolutely lying.

"You probably want coffee," Simon goes on. "Jamie made cupcakes." He'd gotten the pictures somewhere over Colorado.

"It's true," Jamie says, sounding like he's trying not to laugh.

"I'd love coffee and cupcakes," Charlie says.

"Okay, it's settled," Simon says, relieved.

Simon doesn't know how much he's missed his house until he walks through the door, but now that he's home, it's going to take a court order to get him out again. He wants to pet every wall, every bookcase, every piece of furniture. He wants to jump into his pool and stay there until tomorrow. Edie obviously feels the same way, rolling around on the sofa and sniffing everything.

Then he turns and sees Charlie standing in the doorway, and it hits Simon that Charlie's never been here. They've lived a few minutes away from one another for years, but Charlie's never been here. Until last month, Simon had never seen Charlie's house either.

It would be so terrifyingly easy to just . . . stop. To go back to the way it used to be. Maybe the thing that exists between them depends on being away from their normal lives.

Maybe they'll forget how to be together or why they want to be. Maybe Charlie will realize he doesn't have patience for Simon's nonsense, not when he has dozens of easier friends nearby. Maybe Simon will forget how to be the person he is with Charlie—a little less guarded, a little more generous. He likes that version of himself.

Hoping he looks like someone who isn't mid-crisis, Simon goes to the kitchen and puts on coffee. The kitchen is kind of amazingly clean, but then again, Jamie always does clean up after he cooks, just not within the thirty-second time frame mandated by Simon's rogue synapses. He opens the cabinet to take out mugs, and the handles are all fucking over the map, so jarring it's almost a jump scare.

He feels Charlie come up next to him, one hand landing heavy on Simon's shoulder.

"Do you want me to go?" Charlie glances at the cabinet and starts rotating the mugs. Simon takes his hand, pulling it away from the mugs and keeping it in his own hand. Charlie's trying to help, and Simon's almost convinced himself that he can live with people knowing he needs help. But fixing the coffee cups isn't the solution.

"You're freaking out," Charlie says.

"It's a day ending with Y." He leans against Charlie for a minute. "I realized you've never been here."

"You should give me the tour." It's not a huge house. You can see about eighty percent of it from the kitchen. "No, seriously, show me around. I mean, I'm coming back, so I need to know where everything is, right?"

It's not quite a rhetorical question. "Yes," Simon says, firmly, and proceeds to show Charlie around.

SIMON DRIVES CHARLIE home.

"I'll talk to you tonight?" Charlie asks. Simon leans in and kisses his cheek for some cursed reason, like that's something they even *do*.

Charlie gets out of the car before Simon can do anything even weirder, like follow him inside. Simon waits until the front door shuts before pulling out of the driveway.

Back home, he sits on the sofa next to Jamie. "I missed you."

"Me too," Jamie says, closing his laptop and tossing it onto the cushion on his other side. "But we don't have to pretend I wasn't getting on your nerves before you left."

"No—"

"Don't lie."

"It isn't you. It's my brain."

"Your brain is, in fact, attached to you."

"It's a real shame."

Jamie sighs. "I've been looking at apartments, so I'll be out of your hair soon."

"It isn't you that's bothering me."

"Okay," Jamie says, sounding dubious. "Then what is?"

Simon buries his face in a throw pillow and explains about the sink and the dishes, the rituals and routines, the way his nerves sometimes feel fried, like one additional stimulus is going to tip him into oblivion. "Until you came to stay, I didn't even realize how bad it'd gotten. You being here set off trip wires I hadn't even known about."

"When did it get bad? When you went off the meds?"

"The whole last year was . . . really not good. But it got worse as the season was winding down." He'd known that he was facing a big change, and it didn't matter that it was something he wanted—his brain doesn't know good stress from bad stress.

"So, I'll clean as I go when I'm cooking, not leave anything in the sink, et cetera. Earbuds on low. And you'll tell me if there's anything else."

"I'm not asking you to cater to my whims."

"You mean, take an extra two minutes to help my friend with an actual health issue?"

"I'm not supposed to make it your problem. Margie's orders."

Jamie's quiet for a minute, his fingers tapping a rhythm on his thigh. "Why didn't you tell me all this months ago?"

"Mostly because I didn't want to think about it. And I didn't want you to know what a wreck I am. Sorry."

"You aren't a wreck."

"I think, sometimes, maybe I am? Or at least it feels that way? And I've tried not to let you know."

"Then you're a generous, funny, loyal wreck and I love you," Jamie says, no hesitation. Simon kind of slithers a little closer, so his head is in petting range of Jamie's hand. Jamie takes the hint and strokes his hair. "I thought you wanted me to go away."

Simon winces. "I'm sorry." He should have guessed that Jamie might take it that way. It's what anyone would think if a friend started acting irritated and refused to talk about it. And Simon's spent so much effort driving people away that it's no surprise Jamie thought Simon was up to his old tricks.

It's kind of a stark wakeup call.

Simon takes a deep breath. "Remember when I asked if I was treating you like my assistant, and you said it was okay because we're helping one another? You help me out and I give you a place to stay?"

"That's not exactly how I remember that conversation," Jamie says. "I have some names for you, by the way, if you do want to hire someone."

Simon manages not to point out that assembling a list of potential hires is something an assistant would do. "What I mean is that I'm not giving you a place to stay. You live here. I think you've spent more time living here than you have anywhere else in the past few years."

Jamie looks stricken. "I'm sorry."

Simon is somehow still getting this wrong. "I love having you here. If you want to leave, I won't be weird and sad about it—well, I won't *act* weird and sad, at least—but it's your home, permanently, unless you don't want it to be."

"You mean that?"

"I've meant it for a while." Simon just hadn't known that it was something he could say, something he could ask for.

"And when things between you and Charlie get more serious? You'll want the place to yourselves."

Simon's less sure about that. There is nothing about that man that says *I need privacy*. "Charlie has a house."

"Most people would not be okay with their partner's ex living with them."

"Charlie isn't most people. And I don't even mean that as a compliment. He's a total weirdo."

"I've never seen you like that. You were almost clingy with Charlie."

Simon's mortified, but it's not like he can deny it. Without a few helpful layers of armor, Simon's . . . affectionate? He's a little affectionate with Jamie now, but Simon didn't let his guard down until he realized that Jamie wasn't going anywhere. It took years for him to redraw his boundaries with Jamie in a slightly less constricting shape than he's used to.

This thing he's doing with Charlie depends on Simon keeping his guard down, on Simon letting Charlie in past his defenses. It's possible that human relationships, in general, depend on not being covered in ten layers of spikes, but that's a mystery for future Simon.

"It was nice," Jamie says. "Seeing you like that. I'm happy for you."

"It's only been a little while."

Jamie raises his eyebrows. "What, are you planning on ending it?"

Simon shakes his head.

"Do you think Charlie is?" Jamie asks. "He seemed pretty happy to have you hanging off his sweater."

Simon's face heats. "I don't want to ruin it."

"Then don't ruin it."

"I'm not great at relationships. You know this."

"Have you ever really tried?"

The truth is that he's done the exact opposite of trying: he's done everything in his power to make sure people know he doesn't care what they think of him, that he doesn't need them.

"I know this isn't exactly true," Simon says, "but sometimes I think you're the reason I know what it's like to feel loved. Not to *be* loved, maybe, but to feel it. You're the only point of reference I had for a while."

Jamie whips his head around. "Are you okay?"

"I don't mean it as a bad thing." Simon's been thinking a lot about this since Nora's graduation. "You never let me forget that I'm important to you. I think—" This is too heavy, and all Simon's instincts are screaming at him to stop, but he's starting to figure out that with people he cares about, he has to take a good look at where his instincts are pointing him and throw himself in the opposite direction. "When I need to figure out how to treat someone like they matter to me, I just imagine what you'd do."

"I have to do this video in five minutes and if you make me cry, Simon, I swear to God," Jamie says, but he's already hugging Simon.

SIMON GOES TO bed early, partly because his body has no idea what time it is, and partly because he feels like he's been awake for days. It's seven o'clock.

While he's brushing his teeth, he looks in the mirror and presses a finger to the lingering beard burn on the corner of his mouth and the side of his neck. There's more in places he can't see. He wonders how long it will take them to fade, how long it will take before Simon can feel comfortable in his body without thinking of all the places Charlie touched him, how long it will be before they can see one another in the neighborhood without it being strange.

But Charlie said they'd talk tonight. He wanted a tour of Simon's house because he's coming back. Charlie isn't acting like it's going to be over anytime soon, and Simon doesn't want it to be, so he doesn't know why every molecule in his body is telling him that he's just had a breakup, that something terrible has happened.

Maybe it's because he feels, deep down, like he should have pulled back days ago. Weeks ago, even. He shouldn't have let it get to this point, shouldn't have let himself care, shouldn't have let Charlie *see* him. His brain is trying to do what it always does, keep him safe, only it's decided safety means keeping everyone away. Nobody can hurt you if they don't matter to you. It's . . . really fucking dysfunctional, actually, but that's nothing new.

His phone is heavy in his hand. The idea of calling Charlie—something Charlie explicitly asked for, something Simon actively wants—feels daring and impossible.

Simon spends a moment staring at his phone, trying to figure out which time zone he should use to determine whether it's night yet, then gives up and calls Charlie. Texting would be normal, but he can't imagine what he would even write, and the one single advantage of a phone call is that he doesn't have to plan further than "hi."

"Oh, hey," Charlie says, answering the phone. He sounds like he's home, not out doing whatever it is he does in his regular life.

"Everything okay at your house?"

"Yeah, no surprises."

Simon knows it's not possible to run out of things to talk about after spending four hours apart, but he can't think of one single thing to say other than *tell me how not to ruin this.*

"Did you call because you miss me?" Charlie asks, sounding intolerably smug.

"No, shut up," Simon says immediately. "God."

Charlie just laughs. "Yeah, you missed me." There's a rustling that makes Simon think Charlie's lying down on his bed or getting himself settled on the couch.

"Are you in bed?"

"Is this going to be *that* kind of phone call?"

"I'm about to fall asleep, so that's a pass."

"So are you in bed, then?"

"No, I'm hanging upside down like a bat. Yes, I'm in bed, that's how I sleep."

"Gray duvet, white pillows, approximately seventeen blankets," Charlie says, because he apparently memorized Simon's bed linens when he saw the house earlier. It's a good reminder that Charlie is maybe as deranged as Simon.

"I'm only under four of the blankets right now."

"Black T-shirt?"

"White. You haven't seen this one."

Charlie makes a dissatisfied sound. "Hate it. Switch to FaceTime."

If Charlie needs to know exactly what Simon looks like at that moment, Simon can go along with that. "There." He holds the phone at arm's length so Charlie can see his shirt and the entire blanket nest situation.

"You look cozy," Charlie says, and only then does Simon pay attention to his phone screen. Charlie doesn't have a shirt on, and if there's anything in the world that should be less surprising, Simon doesn't know what it could possibly be, but he still hears himself make a noise. Charlie raises his eyebrows.

"Shut up," Simon says. "*Switch to FaceTime.* You knew what you were doing. Okay, your turn. Show me your bedroom."

"Come see it yourself."

"I'm already in bed."

"Come over tomorrow." Charlie winces. "No, sorry, forget it."

Simon's stomach twists. "What, did you have plans?"

"No. I mean, I'll probably go over to Alex's at some point but that's not what I meant."

Simon stares at the image of Charlie on his screen, trying to figure out whether Charlie just told him he doesn't want to see him tomorrow.

"I'm trying to give you space," Charlie says. "Trying to follow your lead."

"My lead is terrible. It's a path straight to hell."

Charlie's quiet for a moment. "Simon, I've been following your lead from the beginning."

"Explain."

"You seem like you don't actively hate me, I spend more time with you. You flirt with me, I flirt back. You harass my stepfather, I assume you might care about me. You stand around biting your lip and ogling me, I kiss you. You text me, I text you back. You say shit like you promise to be nice *if* we break up—no, shut up, you said *if*—and I start to get some ideas about what it is we're doing."

That's a bracingly accurate summation of their relationship, even if Simon might fight about the lip biting thing, just on principle.

But what's Charlie counting as the beginning? The way Charlie says it, it's like he was looking for an opportunity to spend more time with Simon. Charlie'd said he had a crush, but Simon believed him when he said it was only physical. This all sounds a lot more involved than that.

"If I need space, I'll tell you," Simon says, instead of asking Charlie for a detailed written timeline of every feeling he's ever had.

"Will you, though?" Charlie asks, skeptical. "Will you really?"

"Like, fifty-percent odds."

"Okay, we can work with that." There's something about the way Charlie says it, so casual about dealing with Simon's bullshit, that makes Simon feel panicky at the idea of losing it.

"Also I actively hate space most of the time," Simon says. He shuts his eyes and tries to astrally project to somewhere he isn't doing this. "I mean, yes, sometimes I need half an hour to think about redundancies in my skin care regimen, but in an ideal world I'd have one of those shock collars like Alex's dog has and I'd get zapped whenever I get too far from—well—basically you or Jamie."

He opens one eye. Charlie's staring at the camera, his mouth a little open.

"I realize that's not healthy," Simon says. "I'm not going to microchip you. Or myself. My point is that I don't think you need to worry about me needing space."

"You are . . ." Charlie shakes his head, but his expression is all goofy and fond. "You are a mess. A disaster. And that fact is so special to me."

"Oh my God, just die please," Simon says, but he knows Charlie means it. "I don't want to ruin this," he says in a rush. "Don't let me ruin it."

"Okay," Charlie says.

"Okay?"

"I won't let you ruin it."

"What's your plan? Give me, like, a flowchart."

"If you're being a dickhead, I'll say, 'Hey, Simon, you're being a dickhead and it's making me sad,' and then you'll fall all over yourself trying to make me feel better. Off the top of my head. Just brainstorming."

Maybe Simon did something like that once or twice. Charlie didn't have to point it out, though. God. Also in none of those instances was Simon being a dickhead. He'll take being called a dickhead over accuracy, though, because accuracy probably involves uttering phrases like "meeting one another's emotional needs" and Simon might never recover. Still, he switches back to a regular audio call because actions have consequences, Charlie.

"Or, plan B, I just fuck you, because that's a battle-tested strategy to get you in a better mood," Charlie goes on happily.

"Oh my God," Simon says, a little faintly. "You're a monster."

He thinks of how he is after sex, warm and dumb and not quite there. He thinks of Charlie asking *are you always like this*.

"You started it," Charlie says. "But I'm not wrong."

"No," Simon agrees. "You aren't."

Chapter Twenty-Six

"Do you want to go to Petra's wedding?" Charlie asks.

It's bright in Charlie's bedroom, the curtains wide open. "I RSVP'd 'no' already," Simon says. "I thought I'd still be in New York."

"I meant, do you want to come with me?"

The truth is that Simon doesn't want to go to Petra's wedding, or any wedding, or possibly anywhere at all, basically ever. But Charlie's going, and maybe he doesn't want to go alone? Simon doubts his company will improve anything, though.

"Do you want me to come?" Simon asks.

"That is literally why I'm asking you. But if you don't want to, it's okay."

"Sure. Why not."

"Alex is coming by in an hour if you want to say hi."

Simon props himself up on an elbow so he can look down at Charlie. "Are you arranging playdates for me? Do I seem lonely? What's going on here?"

"Just giving you a heads-up," Charlie says. "You can stick around, or you can split."

Simon spends a few minutes trying to find any hidden meaning in all that and concludes that Charlie is saying exactly what he means.

Charlie's refrigerator is stocked with a bunch of the same salads and bottled water that Simon had been buying in New York. On the counter is a box of his favorite brand of granola bars. Simon feels mildly nuts about it all.

When Alex walks in, Simon doesn't know what to expect. He's braced. Well, he's sitting on the sofa holding Edie, wearing his indoor sunglasses, but same idea. Simon wants to murder Jamie's boyfriends on first sight, and he wouldn't blame Alex for being suspicious of Simon's ability to make Charlie happy—Simon's suspicious of his ability to make Charlie happy.

"What does it take," Alex says to Simon instead of *hello*, "to get you to respond to your texts?"

"You're not going to like the answer to that," Charlie says. "Okay fine, don't hug me, see if I care," he adds when Alex makes a beeline to the sofa, plopping down next to Simon, stealing Edie, and supervising him while he reads the past week's worth of messages in the group chat.

It's eighty percent small talk and inside jokes that Simon barely understands, along with Charlie telling everyone to shut up whenever a picture surfaces of him wearing real clothes.

"Why are you even in this group chat?" Simon asks her. "You quit."

"Tough shit, you're stuck with me."

"Fair."

"Give me your phone. No, unlock it first."

Not liking any of this, Simon hands her his phone, then watches as she makes herself a favorite contact. Which means she sees that his current favorite contacts are Jamie, Nora, and Charlie.

"Why?" he asks, gesturing at his phone.

"Because I'm going to miss seeing you every day."

That seems highly unlikely, and he tells her so.

"Fine. You'll miss seeing me, then," she says.

The worst part is that she's right. Simon remembers Charlie insisting that Alex and Simon are friends. He supposes, looked at from certain angles, it's true. They've spent a lot of time together, and even though most of it's been on set, Simon hasn't minded it. He's looked forward to it, maybe. Or he's gotten used to it. He isn't sure there's a difference.

"Tell me about the movie," he says, because that seems like a normal thing to ask a person, and also because he's curious.

She tells him, and then they talk about how brave Edie was on the airplane, and it's all . . . nice. She doesn't warn him off Charlie. She doesn't even say anything about him and Charlie.

"Do you like your agent?" Simon asks, the words out of his mouth before he's made up his mind to say them. "I think I need a new agent."

"Hey," Charlie says. "You didn't ask whether I like my agent."

"Probably because your agent is mean," Alex says.

"She's so mean," Charlie says, a little dreamily. Simon grins up at Charlie—he can't help it—then catches Alex's eye and she's grinning too. His phone buzzes with contact info for Alex's agent.

"Want me to ask her to get in touch with you?" Alex asks.

That sounds like the next best alternative to doing nothing at all and hoping the situation magically resolves itself, so he says, yes, he'd love that, thank you.

Simon stays long enough to finish his coffee and eat a granola bar. He doesn't have any interest in watching them play video games, but it's nice seeing Charlie happy, nice hearing the two of them laugh. Simon keeps waiting to feel jealous, and it doesn't come.

He keeps thinking about how Charlie said that Alex needs things to be fine, needs to keep things light. Now that he knows Charlie better, he can see the work Charlie puts into it. But work doesn't mean it's fake. The fact that it isn't perfect, isn't ideal, doesn't mean it's fake either. It just means that Charlie's taking care of his friend the best way he can, and that feels like a very Charlie thing to do.

When Simon leaves, Alex squeezes him on the shoulder, a humane alternative to a hug. But Simon's trying here, he's making an effort, so he leans over and gives her an actual hug.

Then he grabs his phone and leaves before anyone can say anything.

"I COULD KISS you both," Lian says when Charlie and Simon sit down. They're at a French restaurant that's always Lian's first choice for expense account lunches. "You can't buy this kind of publicity."

That TikTok is still doing the rounds, and so is the picture from the restaurant, a handful of pictures and a clip from upfronts, and a few pictures someone took of them in the Chelsea Whole Foods arguing in the pet supply aisle about the ethics of spending thirty-eight dollars on three pounds of dog food.

"Are you getting shit from the network?" Charlie asks.

"No," Lian says, after a tiny hesitation that probably means she's getting questions from the network, maybe *concern*, but no actual trouble.

Obviously, bigots exist, and so do tinfoil hat conspiracy theorists who think he and Charlie are engaged in a publicity stunt, so their social media is a disaster zone. Simon can't even look at it, and it's too homophobic in there to ask Jamie to help, so he finally hired an assistant.

Charlie posted a video explaining that if anyone thought he was straight, "that sounds like a *you* problem," and another video apologizing, and then a third saying that anyone who doesn't like it can die mad, all within twenty-four hours. Neither of them are getting through the rest of June without agreeing to some terribly earnest pride month social media content.

"What're you planning to do about it?" Simon asks. Charlie's hand comes to rest on the back of Simon's chair.

Lian takes a sip of ice water and looks like she's counting to ten. "Actors become involved all the time without it changing the trajectory of the show."

"Lian," Charlie says. "Come on. It's not about us being involved. It's about us being *out*. There's an element of, like, responsibility here."

This is mighty rich, since Charlie's spent the past few weeks telling Simon that he's never not been out, but Simon can respect the pivot. He butters a piece of bread just for the sake of doing something. He agrees with Charlie's point. But he also feels like he should have had this conversation with Lian years ago. He's a bit ashamed that he didn't.

"Wait a minute," Lian says, sitting up even straighter. "Do you think you need to persuade *me* that we need to do a romance storyline? After I've spent the past seven years being cyberbullied by gay teenagers who want to see your characters together?"

"Um," Charlie says.

"Keeping the network happy and making the show I—*we*—want to make is a tightrope walk. I wasn't going to commit to a queer romantic storyline between two of the show's main characters unless I had your full support. This time last year, would I have had your full support?" She doesn't wait for an answer. "I was afraid one of you would quit. Or burn the set down. Or commit actual murder. Nobody on this show is paid enough to deal with what would have happened if I told you to *kiss*."

"We're both professionals," Simon says, mildly affronted. "Romantic leads have hated one another since acting got invented."

Lian looks like she might be praying. "I was trying," she says after a moment, "not to be an asshole. Do you remember when I told you *Out There* wasn't going to be like *Tree of the Gods*? This is what I meant. No toxic power dynamics. No nasty comments about weight or shooting outside for twelve-hour days during heat waves or firing the intimacy coordinator in the middle of shooting. Just, in general, treating the cast and crew like people instead of like bodies that I hired to move around like little dolls."

"Ah," Simon says. "Thank you?"

"Besides, we didn't want a romance between the central characters. That kills the tension. If we got Luke and Jonathan together, then we'd have to break them up, and this is not a prime-time soap," Lian says, despite having very much written the episode in which Amadi's character turns out to have a secret space baby with a sexy alien amnesiac.

"I think that what Charlie and I are trying to say is that you have our support, one way or the other."

Simon doesn't say much for the rest of the meal. Charlie and Lian are more than capable of keeping a conversation going. Simon's had dozens of similar meals where he mostly keeps quiet, but this feels different—the press of Charlie's thigh against his, the knowledge that at least one of the people at the table wants to be there with him. Both of them, if he's being his most truthful self.

After he finishes eating, Charlie peers over Lian's shoulder. "I see someone. I'll be right back."

Simon watches distractedly as Charlie hugs two people he dimly remembers having seen on set. One of them, he thinks, was a space pirate in season three.

"I was all set to tell you not to fuck up my show," Lian says, following the direction of Simon's gaze. "I was going to tell you that you'd better be good to him."

"Yes, thank you, it's about time someone threatened me." He kind of means it.

"I was going to say that, but I don't think I need to."

"I want him to get hurt even less than you do," Simon assures her. "I've got that covered."

Lian gives him a complicated look, and Simon has a horrible certainty that she's going to say something kind or meaningful, so he blurts out, "Vintage J.Crew. Your cardigan." He's being very charitable in calling it vintage instead of just old. He remembers buying the same exact sweater for his sister-in-law his freshman year of college.

She looks down at what she's wearing. "Did you rummage through my closet and memorize all the labels?"

"You left it on the back of your chair once and I checked the label," he admits. This probably isn't much more normal than snooping in her closet, but at least they aren't talking about feelings anymore. "You know Alex's agent, right?"

"Claire? Sure, why?"

Claire got in touch with Simon that morning and they're meeting for lunch tomorrow. Simon feels a little sick about it.

"I've had a kind of shitty year." It feels bizarre to say it out loud. It feels dangerous admitting that he's full of flaws and weaknesses, that the face he tries to show the world is a flimsy screen. But Lian doesn't look surprised. "It would have been less shitty if I had an agent I felt comfortable being honest with."

"I think you'll like her. Her wife was in my prenatal yoga class. They have a pair of those dogs that herd you when you walk into the house." Lian pauses for a moment. "She has multiple sclerosis."

"I know."

"A tick in the plus column," Lian says, and it isn't a question.

"Yeah." He thinks, maybe, that it's a good idea for him to work with people who already understand that sometimes you need to play the hand you've been dealt.

"Good."

"Would you tell me if you thought she'd be a bad fit for me?" Simon doesn't know why he's looking to Lian for reassurance, except that he's known her for longer than anyone else he trusts, and she knows both him and the industry.

Lian raises her eyebrows. "Yes. Simon. I want things to work out for you."

She says it so deliberately, he can't help but hear the implied *of course I care about you, Simon, you idiot* that maybe she'd say out loud if she didn't know it would send Simon running to hide in the bathroom. A year ago, he wouldn't have heard her meaning, let alone believed it. The fact that he believes it now feels like something good and solid that he can hold in his hand.

"Me too," he says, and hopes she understands.

From an *Out There* fan Discord

SimonDevereauxsCheekbones: Some reprobates have been sending Charlie and Simon links to explicit fanfic about them. Not about their characters, but about them. I'm embarrassed to be alive.

HowlsMovingSpaceship: I'm usually against incarceration but some people just need to be removed from society

SimonDevereauxsCheekbones: God is sorry he made us

GalactoseIntolerance: Charlie, at least, seems pretty unbothered

SupervillainApologist: Charlie Blake's entire social media presence this summer has healed me. Fifty percent five-minute-long videos of Simon Devereaux's dog, fifty percent responding to homophobic comments with "get well soon, I guess." A blessing.

DeathStarJacuzzi: Personally I'm focusing on every picture that surfaces of Simon and Charlie together with Simon looking like he's putting on his own personal production of The Talented Mr. Ripley while Charlie is wearing swim trunks, a t-shirt with the sleeves torn off, and a backward baseball cap advertising a car wash.

SimonDevereauxsCheekbones: I know you all think I'm even more delusional than usual but I REALLY think we're going to see a Luke/Jonathan relationship happen on-screen?

GalactoseIntolerance: You're probably right, but I kind of hope you're wrong. Luke and Jonathan will get together in forty-five nuance-free minutes and it'll make me mad every time I think about it.

HowlsMovingSpaceship: There is nobody in that writers' room I trust with this story more than I trust the strangers on the internet writing about it for free.

SpacePope: Seriously. I've read about these guys falling in love hundreds—thousands?—of times and I will keep doing exactly that. Sometimes Jonathan is a space vampire and sometimes Luke is a war hero and sometimes they're both working in a coffee shop on Earth, and all those stories live in my heart and are just as true as whatever the literal corporation in charge of Out There decides to put on television.

DeathStarJacuzzi: gonna be honest, I've been pretending the show got canceled after the space lobster season. Everything after that just didn't happen.

HowlsMovingSpaceship: Is now a good time to mention that @SpacePope and I got a cat?

GalactoseIntolerance: Wait. Got a cat, as in got a cat TOGETHER?

SupervillainApologist: 👀

DeathStarJacuzzi: pics or it didn't happen

SupervillainApologist: cat tax, payable now

SpacePope:

[photograph of cat]

SimonDevereauxsCheekbones: I think I manifested this. You're welcome you crazy kids

Chapter Twenty-Seven

When Simon wakes up, the room is pitch black, no light seeping in around the edges of the blackout curtains. He reaches for his phone. It's ten in the morning. He's been asleep for over twelve hours.

He and Charlie had been on their way out to dinner when his vision went swimmy. The culprit: the setting sun coming through the window at an odd angle, flickering through gaps in the palm trees. Charlie turned the car around. By the time they got back to Simon's house, a ball of pain had gathered behind his left eye. He took his migraine meds, drank a glass of water, and went to bed.

This was his first migraine in more than six weeks, and it wasn't brought on by stress or missed meals or fatigue or sharp smells or sudden movements or any of the other things he can control—just the same sunlight he sees practically every day.

He feels hungover, and like he's probably going to take a nap later today, but all that's left of his headache is the feeling that his brain's been lightly scoured. He's a little nauseous, and his body feels like it's been ransacked for parts and left on the side of the road, but the medicine did its job. He's counting it as a win, or at least not a loss.

He heads out to the kitchen, hoping there's some coffee left in the pot. The entire house is dark—not pitch black like his bedroom, but like someone went around and shut all the blinds halfway. Jamie and Charlie are in the living room, talking quietly enough not to have woken Simon.

"Hey, you," Jamie says, seeing him first. "Feeling better?"

"Yeah. Wrung out, but okay." Simon gives up trying to make it to the kitchen and plops down next to Charlie. He's wobbly. When he tips onto Charlie's shoulder, he can't think of any good reason to sit back up. Charlie puts an arm around him and Simon shuts his eyes.

"Coffee or that ginger tea?" Jamie asks.

"You don't have to," Simon mumbles into Charlie's T-shirt.

"I'm making myself something. So, what do you want?"

"Can I have both?" The tea is supposed to help with nausea. Simon wouldn't know, because boiling water is too much work when he's in this state. "Like, not in the same cup, please."

Jamie snorts. "Got it."

"Thank you."

Last night, Jamie had taken out Simon's sleeping clothes and put all Simon's pills directly into his hand. And Charlie fixed his blackout curtains. Simon usually wakes up to daylight spearing through his eye sockets.

It's a little embarrassing, knowing they fussed over him. No—it's embarrassing that he apparently needs all that fuss.

He's awful at dealing with his migraines on his own. Sometimes he forgets to take all his pills. He never remembers the blackout curtains. Usually he passes out in his clothes, then wakes up miserable, Edie pawing at his shoulder to be let outside.

"You didn't have to stay," he tells Charlie.

"I didn't. Not the whole time. After you fell asleep, I went home, ate, got changed, brushed my teeth, and came back. Jamie let me in."

"You know," Simon says, trying to sound like he just had an amazing idea, "you should keep some stuff here."

Charlie gives his shoulder the gentlest of pinches. Two days ago, he shouldered his way into Simon's closet, opening and shutting drawers, declaring "you never wear any of this," and shoving a bunch of Simon's less favorite bathing suits in with his second tier T-shirts, then dumping the contents of a duffel bag into the empty drawer.

Simon stood in the doorway to his closet, fully aware that this was a dare, Charlie escalating the situation and waiting for a reaction. Simon grabbed Charlie's empty duffel bag, threw two changes of clothes and some travel-size toiletries into it, and shoved it back at Charlie.

"And I could keep some things at your place," Simon goes on. "That could be something we do after talking about it like normal adults."

"I don't see any normal adults in this relationship," Charlie says, and he has a point.

"Fucking sunlight," Simon mumbles into the worn cotton of Charlie's shorts.

"How does that work? In the car, you didn't have a headache yet, but you knew it was about to happen."

"That's the aura. My vision gets weird fifteen or so minutes before the headache starts. But sometimes I feel off for a couple hours even before that. That's the prodrome."

"Huh. It's kind of cool that your brain lets you know ahead of time."

Simon needs a minute to process that. The aura and other assorted bullshit aren't actually his brain's early warning system, they're just part of the trash can of neurological symptoms that make up a migraine. And yet—the image of his brain, a poor dumb lump of cells, trying to warn him the only way it can? That does something to Simon. He's picturing his brain like a wounded animal, trying its best. He shuts his eyes and sniffles as discreetly as possible.

"Hey, hey," Charlie says, "I didn't mean—obviously there's nothing *good* about your headaches—"

"No, I like it," Simon says. "I like it." He shuts his eyes, threads his fingers through Charlie's, and lets himself drift for a minute. "You like taking care of me," he says, as quiet as he can. And what he means is something like, I'm trusting you with all the parts of myself I don't even like.

"What if," Simon says, "hypothetically, someone were to throw you a birthday party?" Charlie's birthday is just over a month away.

"Hypothetically, who's asking? You?" They're walking Edie, who's dedicated to her project of memorizing the unique smell of every blade of grass between Simon's and Charlie's houses.

"Yes?" Alex had texted Simon, "so are you doing C's birthday this year or what." Simon promptly had a crisis about it.

"I like birthday parties," Charlie says. "I like all parties." Simon already knew this. Charlie is being the opposite of helpful.

They run into one of Simon's neighbors. When they got back from New York, every neighbor he ran into stopped and said hi. Well, they said hi to Edie. For years, he's been exchanging low-effort small talk with them—mostly about dogs, but that's still talking. Simon is, somehow, a person who knows his neighbors. He keeps coming back to Charlie's notion that Edie is similar to an emotional support animal. *It's like a wheelchair,* Charlie and Jamie keep saying. *Wheelchairs are good.*

After the neighbor drags her dog away from Edie, Simon says, "So do you want me to throw you a party?"

"Do you want to throw me a party?"

Simon doesn't want to throw anyone any kind of party. The idea of it—who to invite, where to find a caterer, how do parties even work—is enough to make his heart race. But he wants to do right by Charlie, and if that means a birthday party, then he's going to throw a fucking birthday party.

"I don't want anyone else to throw you a birthday party," Simon says.

"I usually do it myself. Because I like to. If you really wanted to take over, I'd say sure, but you don't—no, shut *up*, Simon, you should see your face—so I'll keep doing it."

"Okay," Simon says, unconvinced. He'd sort of thought that he'd go out of his way to make sure Charlie had the birthday he wanted, and then Charlie would know Simon—well, he'd know that Simon means it, that Simon's disgustingly invested in this. It seems like the sort of grand gesture that would appeal to Charlie.

"What I want," Charlie says, and Simon's ready to agree to anything, "is just for you to come."

"Obviously I'm coming," Simon says, a little offended.

"I know, but you never did before."

Simon's stupid face goes hot with shame.

"No, I mean, shit. I'm getting this wrong." Charlie gets a thumb under Simon's chin, which shouldn't even work, since they're the same height, but somehow Simon's looking up at him now. "I just always kind of thought it would be cool if you showed up and it meant—I don't know—that we could stop fighting and just be normal. But also I kind of wanted to keep fighting with you because it's fun."

"Fun," Simon repeats. He wouldn't say that quarreling with Charlie was fun, but it was easy in a way talking to people rarely was. He never had to plan, never had to pretend.

"Anyway, now you'll be there, and you fight with me all the time, so there's nothing left for me to want. You can just get me a present. Expensive clothing, since that's your love language."

"Love languages are fake," Simon says, because he heard that on a podcast, and also because if Charlie wants fighting, Simon can do that.

"That doesn't change the fact that buying people expensive clothing is your love language," Charlie says, and he's right, but whatever.

"I'll get you more sweaters." Simon means it to sound like *and then you'll be sorry* but instead it comes out a little breathless, maybe because Simon's looking forward to both buying the sweaters and seeing Charlie in them. Maybe because Charlie's hand has moved so he's cupping Simon's cheek.

"Yeah, you will," Charlie says, low and about an inch from Simon's mouth. He pushes Simon's hair off his face.

"Let's see how you like it if I put my finger under your chin and tell you things." Simon maneuvers Charlie's chin in the least romantic way possible, then gets distracted by the need to paw at Charlie's beard a little. "I just want you to have a good birthday," he says, right before Charlie kisses him. Just a little kiss, because they're in the street. "And a good, you know, everything."

When they continue walking, somehow Simon's holding Charlie's hand.

"What about this one?" Simon traces a finger over the lizard on Charlie's forearm. They're in Simon's pool, Charlie on a float, Simon attempting to do laps but mostly cataloging Charlie's tattoos.

"It's supposed to be a dragon, but I was sixteen and a little high."

Simon needs not to think about Charlie, sixteen and high, tattooing himself, or he's going to start hyperventilating. There's an actual dragon—professional, unmistakable—on Charlie's thigh, and Simon takes the opportunity to give it a squeeze.

This might be the first time he's seen it in broad daylight at a distance of less than six inches. "Is that the dragon from *Tree of the Gods*?"

"Yup."

The float starts to drift away, so Simon hauls it back. "I didn't realize you were a fan."

"I used to watch it every Sunday night, on Dave's old couch. He always had all the streaming services."

Simon still isn't capable of hearing about Dave without wanting to snarl, but Dave is returning Charlie's texts almost immediately, which is at least something. Simon can feel at peace with Dave's continued existence, because there he is, an object lesson in what happens when you push people away. Dave, Simon's patron saint of isolation.

"And then a few years later I was on the same show as you," Charlie goes on.

Simon ducks under the water for a minute, wanting to sink lower, into the bedrock, into the Earth's molten core. "And I was an asshole," he says when he has to come up for air.

"You were *queer*. It blew my whole mind. I mean, yes, sure, you were a dick." Charlie sighs happily. "Bitchy and hot and good at your job. Nothing not to like."

Simon's face must be doing something against his will, because Charlie shoves him with his foot. The float goes sailing toward the other end of the pool. "I mean, I wasn't in love with you or anything. I wasn't pining. I have feelings for a lot of people, fuck off."

It's easy to imagine Charlie with half a dozen simultaneous crushes. Charlie's heart is expansive, generous.

Simon paddles over and drags the float back to the shady half of the pool. "I don't. I mean, I don't have feelings for a lot of people. I try not to. I've known for a couple years that I like all this . . ." He gestures at Charlie's body, his face. "But anything more? That wasn't until Phoenix, I think."

"I call bullshit," Charlie says, sliding off the raft and landing next to Simon, shoulder deep in the water. "It was before that."

Simon should have kept his mouth shut. "Not really."

"You don't let anyone drive you anywhere," Charlie goes on. "Jamie says you only got into his car a year ago. You barely use rideshares."

"What does that have to do with anything?" Simon asks, baffled. "Jamie's a terrible driver. I've never seen him use a turn signal. You should see him try to park in the Trader Joe's lot. Mayhem."

"You've been letting me chauffeur you around for years."

"You kept kidnapping me!"

"Simon." Charlie's hands are on Simon's hips, so Simon can't even swim away. "All I'm saying is that even when you didn't like me, some part of you knew better."

It's sweet, probably, that Charlie thinks there's a secret part of

Simon's brain that knows what's going on. Simon's well aware that his brain is three unreliable narrators stacked in a trench coat.

"But I don't give a shit, except for how I like when you're wrong and I'm right," Charlie goes on. "I don't care if you figured it out last month, as long as you did figure it out. So you can stop arguing with me."

"You're the only person in this pool arguing."

"I can see you arguing in your head."

"That's called thinking," Simon says, defaulting to bitchy without even meaning to.

Charlie gets Simon backed up against the side of the pool, kissing him, shutting him up in the most efficient way.

"I did figure it out," Simon says, his lips moving against Charlie's.

"I know," Charlie says. "I know."

"No sex in my pool," Simon says a minute later.

"Okay but what about sex on the lounge chair?"

Simon thinks about explaining that the way hills work is that the people higher up can see into the yards of people lower down, but decides to save his breath. "Jamie could come home anytime. I'm trying not to traumatize him." Charlie knows that Simon's trying to make it so Jamie stays if he wants to.

Charlie reaches for the sunblock on the edge of the pool and slathers some on his own shoulders haphazardly. Simon bats his hands away and does it himself. It's not like it's a hardship. He gets a little distracted at the biceps—who can blame him—and spends some extra effort rubbing the sunscreen onto Charlie's most intricate tattoo, the cloud of stars wrapping around his biceps.

Simon used to think it was such a boring tattoo for an actor on a show set in space, but now he gets it. *Out There* was—is—a meaningful experience for Charlie. He's done it for most of his adult life, and it's how he met most of his friends. There's meaning in making something other people enjoy, something they look forward to, and talk about, and write their own stories about.

And now Simon can't look at that tattoo without thinking about Charlie on the couch at a foster home, Simon sneaking into his father's living room, Charlie with his shithead stepdad, Simon making Jamie watch the original *Star Trek* until Jamie started to enjoy it. Simon keeps thinking of the weirdly wholesome TikToks he and Charlie keep getting tagged in. Simon's left with the impression that the entire app is nothing but crying queer sci-fi fans. And also eyeliner tutorials. It's kind of heartwarming.

Simon figures there are worse legacies.

He hasn't decided what he's doing next, but the first script Claire sent him is for the adaptation of *A Scorched Land*. They're asking Simon to read for the role of a cape-swishing, Cruella De Vil-esque dragon hunter, so it might be a decent amount of fun for a few months' work. Lian's been hinting that she has some new project up her sleeve. It's entirely possible that Simon will spend his career following Lian around, which actually doesn't sound so bad.

Sure, he wants to do more challenging roles, and he hopes he gets that chance, but he also hopes he gets to work on projects that mean something to fans, projects that fans have fun with. And maybe he'll have fun with them too.

"Why are you smiling?" Charlie asks, a little suspicious.

"I think it might be optimism." Simon has no idea why it feels embarrassing to admit that. "What are you going to do after this season?"

Nobody's said out loud that this will be *Out There*'s last season.

But with Alex already gone and Simon only doing half a season, it's at least the end of *Out There* as everybody knows it. Eight years is a long time for any show.

Charlie pushes a wet piece of hair off Simon's forehead. "I'll stay for as long as there's a show." He's quiet for a moment. "After that, I don't know. I, um. Alex thinks I'd be good in romcoms?"

"Yes," Simon says immediately, because it's obvious that this is what Charlie wants to do. "You're funny and you're good at smoldering."

"Not sure I have the range."

"Don't say that about yourself," Simon says, even though he spent years complaining about Charlie's lack of range. "That might have been true at first, but it isn't true now. Also, I just told you that you have the range. Funny. Smoldering." He ticks them off on his fingers. "Keep up."

Charlie rolls his eyes in a way that makes Simon pretty sure he's heard all this before—maybe from Alex, maybe from his agent. Good.

That afternoon while Charlie's swimming laps, Simon curls up on the couch and watches the last few episodes that he and Charlie never got around to watching.

"It's a love story," Simon tells Charlie when he's finished the final episode. He sits on the edge of the pool, his feet in the water, Charlie's hand around his ankle. "From season one onward."

It isn't just a collection of throwaway romantic lines. There's something more than that, and Simon can see the story arc in a way that he couldn't when they were filming it. It doesn't matter whether the writers intended it or whether he and Charlie intended it: it's still there, plain as day.

Maybe acting it out for years etched the truth of it into his body, into who he is. Maybe that's why this thing with Charlie feels right.

Or maybe it feels right because he's spent those same years at Charlie's side. Maybe Charlie's known him better and longer than anyone else, even the mean parts, even the sad parts, even the things he's tried to hide. If Charlie wants him anyway, likes him—probably loves him—then that's proof of Charlie's terrible judgment, clearly, but it's also proof that he isn't going anywhere. Proof that this is real.

Charlie splashes Simon's legs. "Obviously," he says. "How are you the last person in the world to realize this?"

Chapter Twenty-Eight

"The flight doesn't leave until two," Charlie says. "Don't rush me."

Charlie's suitcase is open on his bed, a truly random assortment of unrelated clothes strewn on top of it. Simon doubts he could assemble a single coherent outfit from the entire pile, not that coherent outfits are much of a priority for Charlie even at the best of times.

"Okay," Simon says, instead of pointing out that there very much is a rush: it's noon, and you can always count on there being some kind of traffic disaster on the way to the airport.

"I visit twice a year," Charlie told him a few days ago. "Summer and Christmas." He said it like he was talking about mandatory community service hours, not visiting his family. Although, it's exactly how *Simon* talks about visiting his family.

"She wasn't a bad mom," Charlie says now. It's the fifth or sixth time he's said this since they woke up. It isn't Simon he's trying to convince.

"Bring this sweater in case you go somewhere nice." Simon folds the cashmere sweater they got in New York and puts it in the suitcase, next to about seventeen USB cords, a full-size bottle of shampoo, and a pair of flip-flops. "How about you untangle these wires," Simon suggests.

While Charlie's distracted, Simon packs one pair of jeans, two of the less seedy pairs of cargo shorts, three T-shirts, gym clothes, running shoes, underwear, and socks. Then, from the bathroom, a beard trimmer, a toothbrush, and some deodorant. That's enough—Charlie can buy whatever else he needs. They have drugstores in Utah.

"What are you doing?" Charlie asks when Simon's zipping the suitcase. He sounds pissed.

It's perfectly obvious that Simon's packing Charlie's things because Charlie isn't going to do it himself. "Come on. There's probably some room for protein bars if you want to get some from the kitchen."

"I can pack my own suitcase."

"Good for you. Now get those protein bars. They aren't going to pack themselves."

Charlie looks like he wants to have a fight about it, but he leaves the room, and when he comes back, he's carrying a Costco-size box of protein bars. Simon opens the suitcase just enough to slide in six bars, unwraps one for Charlie to eat now, then zips the suitcase back up.

Simon doesn't usually think of himself as patient. Part of him wants to tell Charlie he's being a big baby. If he doesn't want to see his mom, he shouldn't go, and bitching at Simon won't get him anywhere.

But none of it's that simple, and honestly Simon doesn't give a shit if Charlie has fifteen cranky minutes every now and then. Simon is no stranger to being mean when he's upset. Simon's no stranger to *Charlie* being mean when he's upset. He's spent seven years in training for this.

Simon rolls the suitcase out to his car—Charlie was going to drive himself, but Simon has no faith in that ending with Charlie at the airport. Charlie follows, his jaw set and his fists clenched. But he gets into the passenger side of the car when Simon opens the door.

They're nearly at the airport before Charlie says anything.

"I probably won't be very nice when I call. If you don't want me to call, I'll see you next week."

"You'd better call," Simon snaps. It's probably the first time all morning he's let himself sound annoyed. "Also, you don't need to be nice. Give me some credit. You think you'll scare me off? I'd like to see you try."

Charlie's quiet for too long. "I don't want to be mean to you," he says, like he really does think he's going to scare Simon off. For fuck's sake.

"This is barely even rude. You aren't as scary as you think you are. Text me or I'm getting on the next flight to Utah, are we clear?"

Charlie texts when he lands, but there's nothing else until Simon's getting ready for bed. Charlie's sent a picture of one of those doodle-type dogs wearing the kind of bandanna dogs get at the groomer. No comment, not even an emoji. Just a dog.

Simon asks the dog's name, and in return gets a FaceTime request.

"I'm flossing my teeth," he says after accepting the call, the phone on the counter, its camera pointing at the bathroom ceiling.

"Yeah, whatever, your teeth will wait," Charlie says. So, still in a shitty mood, then.

Simon takes the phone into bed and props it up on his knees. "Well, you're in a state."

It looks like Charlie's also sitting in bed, but that's all Simon can make out. "I can hang up," Charlie says.

Simon has a moment of emotional double vision, where he can see perfectly clearly the other version of himself that takes the out, that seizes the excuse. *We'll talk later*, that other, worse Simon says, effectively creating a nice, safe barricade between himself and other people's feelings. Between himself and other people, period.

But he hasn't done that with Charlie since New York, maybe not since puttering around Dave's living room.

Maybe Charlie's right and, on some level, Simon already was thinking of Charlie as an ally. Maybe he already trusted Charlie enough that he could pass out as soon as he got into the passenger seat of Charlie's car, and so he trusted Charlie enough to let himself care.

All that matters is that he does care and that he wants Charlie to know it. He never wants Charlie to doubt it. Maybe that's the trick to relationships—with friends or lovers or colleagues who become something like family. Simon just needs to occasionally do the opposite of what all his defense mechanisms want him to do.

And so Simon fills the air with nothing: what he had for dinner, a meme Nora sent, a movie he wants to watch.

"This kid," Charlie says when Simon winds down, "isn't fucked up at *all*."

Simon assumes "this kid" is Charlie's half sister, and that if Charlie sounds pissed about her being well-adjusted, it's a lot more complicated than that. "How old is she?"

"Seven. They have a *pool*. Brad—his real name, swear to God—is a chiropractor. I just—what the fuck. Every time I come here it's something else—Haley goes to ballet class. Brad has opinions about lawn care. My mom volunteers at Haley's school."

And Charlie didn't have any of that. Charlie's mentioned sleeping in his mother's car.

"When did she get sober?" Simon asks, because he thinks that might be the real issue here.

"When she turned thirty. I was in eighth grade." He scrubs a hand over his beard. "I lived with her the last two years of high school, then she moved back to Utah and I stayed in Phoenix. She met Brad."

And Charlie started *Out There* the same year his sister was born. Simon can only imagine what it was like for Charlie to see his mother settle down and raise a baby in a house with a pool and a lawn and what appears to be a tastefully appointed guest bedroom, when Charlie had just come out of a very different kind of childhood.

"I'm happy for them," Charlie says. He sounds painfully honest. "But, like."

"I know."

"Sorry, I'm not fun tonight."

"Well, I'm never fun, so."

"Being here makes me remember the shitty things. And I think that when I'm around, my mom remembers the shitty things too. But what are we supposed to do? I *like* my mom. I like seeing her. I like seeing Haley. Fuck's sake, Simon, I even like Brad."

Maybe this is why Simon is able to let his guard down around Charlie. They're both coming from a place of unbelonging. Simon's dealt with that feeling of being perpetually outside by turning everything inward and protecting it with the only armor he could find. Charlie learned how to make everyone like him, how to make sure he always belongs.

"I think you're doing great," Simon says.

"Thanks," Charlie mumbles. He's slumped low enough on the bed that he's basically talking into his shirt. "They all want to meet you."

Simon offered to come this time, when he realized how Charlie felt about this trip. "Anytime," he says. Maybe he'll convince Charlie to stay at a hotel. Maybe he'll stay in the guest room of a suburban house with what seems to be inspirational text art on the nightstand.

"I can't be this shitty to anyone else," Charlie says. "Everyone else needs to think I'm fine or they'll worry I'm off the wagon, or, like, hate me."

Simon gets a greedy little thrill at the idea that he has this part of Charlie all to himself, but he reins it in.

"First, you aren't being shitty to me. You're upset. That's not the same thing. Second, it hasn't really occurred to me to worry that you're going to start drinking," he says, because he doesn't think Charlie would have thrown in that sentence if he didn't want to talk about it. "You've handled it for six years. That doesn't mean I think it's easy for you. I just—" He doesn't know how to communicate that he thinks this is Charlie's business, without implying that he's washing his hands of it. "So, if you told me that you trust me to manage my anxiety, I'd change the locks. But—something like that? I . . . believe in you?" He manages not to make any air quotes whatsoever.

"Wow. Gross," Charlie says, but he looks pleased, so Simon hopes he got that right enough.

For the rest of the week, they talk every night, their conversations steadily decreasing in grumpiness and unprocessed feelings. At one point, a little girl with light brown hair appears on the screen, only long enough to wave and run.

When Simon picks Charlie up at the airport, he brings Edie because obviously she'll improve anyone's mental state. Charlie gets into the car and goes quiet and fidgety right away.

Simon drives them to Charlie's house, entering the code on the keypad himself and turning on the lights. The house somehow feels emptier than it ever has, abandoned, like Charlie's been away for months. Charlie sprawls on the sofa, taking up enough space that Simon has to pretty much plant himself on top of him.

"Sorry," Charlie says, his eyes shut. Simon doesn't know what he's apologizing for. Charlie probably doesn't know either. One of his hands is on Simon's back, heavy enough to hold him in place.

"I missed you," Simon says, because it's true and he hasn't said so yet, even if the fact that he's burrowed himself into Charlie's chest might have made it obvious.

"You probably liked having some space."

They've established a few times that Simon doesn't want space. Space is Simon's enemy, and Charlie knows it, so this is just Charlie asking for reassurance.

"God no," Simon says, his lips moving against Charlie's T-shirt. "I complained to Jamie until he suddenly remembered something he had to do in San Diego for a few days." This is a slight exaggeration. Jamie probably did have something to do in San Diego, but Simon's not imagining the way he ran for his car like a fugitive fleeing police dogs.

Charlie starts laughing, always cheered by stories of Simon being embarrassing. "Does that mean your house is empty?"

Simon can't imagine who else Charlie thinks would be at

Simon's house. "Sure. Want to come over?" he asks, assuming this is what Charlie's getting at.

Charlie's quiet, still except for his fingers tracing circles on Simon's lower back. "I kind of hate it here. I mean. Not all the time. But right now it's empty, and tonight..."

"I wasn't going to leave you alone," Simon says, a little offended. He brought Edie's bed and some dog food. "But please come to my place. I have ingredients for you to make smoothies, and I bought a few extra of those bath sheets you like." He was going to bring the bath sheets to Charlie's, but he's getting the feeling that isn't the right move at all. "And I want you to come over, so you should, just to make me happy."

"Yeah?" Charlie sounds perfectly casual. Only his hand, tightening on Simon's hip, gives anything away.

For Charlie, being welcomed into someone's home—being asked, being wanted—might mean something different than it does for most people. Simon thinks about Charlie sitting at the kitchen counter of Simon's sublet, nervously waiting for an invitation to stay overnight. Or, later, waiting for Simon to ask him to change his flight and stay a few more days. Simon feels like his heart is being run over by a car.

Simon gets it together and lifts his head up so he can see Charlie's face. "I gave you the code to the door and cleared out half the garage for your car. I don't keep enormous canisters of bespoke protein powder in my kitchen for just anyone."

"Did you get the chocolate flavor?"

"Obviously." He slips a hand into Charlie's pocket and pulls out his phone, then shoves it toward Charlie's face. "It's your turn to pick where we order dinner from."

"Why do you look like you're about to cry?"

"A trick of the light. An optical illusion. Come on, let's get out of here."

"I can't get up if you don't let go of me."

"Sounds fake."

Charlie gets to his feet, hauling Simon along with him.

Only later, after they've had dinner and watched an unmemorable movie, and Charlie's unpacked his suitcase directly into Simon's washing machine, does Charlie start to unwind. The grumpiness and prickliness gradually slough off.

"Thank you," Charlie says, low, grabbing Simon's arm as they're passing one another in the kitchen. "Nobody's ever done this for me before."

Simon doesn't know exactly what Charlie means, but he's probably referring to how Simon basically grafted himself onto Charlie's body for a few hours.

"I want you to have what you need," Simon says. "Because when I think of you not having what you need, I feel—" His voice is wobbly and he takes a minute to steady himself, his fingers hooked tight in the belt loops of Charlie's jeans. "The idea of you being eight or twelve and not knowing whether there's a place where you belong or a person who's going to take care of you—that's the worst thing I can think of, okay? Is this too much? I don't need to emote all over you."

Charlie uses Simon's arm to reel him in, close enough that Simon doesn't have to make eye contact anymore. "You. Uh. You can keep going," Charlie says. There's a hint of a question in there, the faintest doubt, like maybe Simon won't keep going, like there's any universe where Simon isn't going to do whatever Charlie asks right now.

"Is this because you want me to say nice things or because you want to hear me embarrass myself?"

"Yes," Charlie says.

"Look. I'm glad I get to know this side of you. This part of you is worth knowing. I think you don't know that." Simon would like to hide right now, but he can't, so he buries his face in Charlie's neck. "And that part of you deserves a place to belong and be looked after." *Thank you for letting me do that*, is what he's supposed to say. "And if you think I'm letting anyone else do that," he says instead, "you're out of your fucking mind."

Maybe he got it right, because Charlie lets out a sound that's almost a laugh, and his arms tighten around Simon.

"I DIDN'T REALIZE she was pregnant," Simon says about an hour and a half into Petra's wedding, when he finally realizes what's going on with her dress.

"She said so in the group chat," Alex says from the seat next to him. "Like five hundred times. She has a registry."

"We got her crib sheets from that linen place all your podcasts are obsessed with," Charlie says.

The vows portion of the event is over, thank God, because even Charlie's arm, steady on the back of Simon's chair, isn't enough to make the spectacle of people voluntarily crying in public something Simon wants to experience.

He says as much to Alex as they're eating tiny little pastry things the waiters are bringing around on trays.

"You're a dick," she points out. "But, like, same."

"I love weddings," Charlie says.

Alex boos him, so Simon doesn't have to.

They're at a giant house on the beach that gets rented out for weddings. Petra's new husband has approximately five million family members and they're all here. An elderly Filipino woman called Simon handsome, so Simon thinks Petra's married up.

"It's an excuse for dressing up," Charlie says. He's wearing a suit that looks like it was tailored by someone who knew what they were doing. "And dancing."

It's true: people are, unfortunately, dancing. Charlie raises an eyebrow and tips his head to the dance floor.

"I can be obvious and slutty standing perfectly still," Simon says. "It's a gift. Dance with Alex."

Charlie's driving home, so Simon takes a flute of champagne from the next tray that passes by. He puts on his migraine glasses, even though he knows it's going to make him look like an asshole, but there's too much happening at this party, lighting-wise.

Then he finds a seat at an empty table and settles back in his chair, watching Charlie dance with Alex, with Petra, with a bridesmaid and two of the groomsmen. He dances slow songs, he dances fast songs. He twirls the flower girl around. It takes about four songs for his jacket and tie to go missing, and another for his sleeves to get rolled up.

There's something about the sight of Charlie having fun that beams joy directly into Simon's dopamine receptors.

People from the show, or who used to be involved with the show, keep coming up to say hello to Simon but they don't linger (probably because of the glasses, and also his body language and entire personality). He says what he's supposed to say and tries to look friendly about it.

It turns out that he knows a lot of people who want to talk

to him, or at least want it enough to cross a room. He's been experimenting with the idea that maybe not everyone resents being around him. Maybe his coworkers like him. It's possible.

Lately, Simon feels like he's taking up more space, spreading out, letting himself care about people, letting himself think he might matter to them too.

But, right now, what he has is a handful of people he loves, and who love him back, and that's enough.

On the way home, Charlie starts clenching the steering wheel and cracking his knuckles and finally comes out with, "I don't think I'll ever want kids."

Simon's glad they aren't looking at one another because he doesn't think anyone ever needs to bear witness to whatever his face just did. He's never had this conversation with anyone he's been involved with. He's not sure what made Charlie say something, whether it's Petra being pregnant, or if he's worried Simon saw him dancing with the flower girl and got some ideas. All that really matters is that Simon answers the implied question.

"Well, I definitely won't, so that works out nicely."

"I didn't think so, but. You know." Meaning, Charlie wanted to check because that's mission critical information in a long-term relationship. Which, obviously, is what this is, but any verbal reminder of this sends Simon into emotional outer space for a few minutes.

But Charlie shouldn't have to be the only one dealing with this sort of relationship housekeeping, if for no other reason than that Simon refuses to let Charlie be better at relationships than he is (even though Charlie is absolutely better at relationships than he is). Probably there's some normal and sane way to share your feelings but Simon isn't normal and he's pretty sure he's only part-time sane, so his current strategy is to occasionally take the entire garbage can of his thoughts and feelings and dump it into Charlie's lap.

"I kind of don't see the point of marriage," Simon says, and Charlie makes a sound that's somewhere between a laugh and being strangled to death. And, okay, they've been together for two or three months, depending on who's asking. Maybe it's too soon to talk about this, but Charlie started it. "Just going through the list of stuff you're supposed to talk about when you're in love or whatever," Simon says, a little defensive. "You started it."

"Serious question: Are you trying to kill me?"

"What can I say, I'm playing a long game, Charlie. When seven years of bickering didn't end your life, I had to get creative."

"Do you want to stop at that food truck with the lobster rolls? I think it's open late."

Simon does, so he takes out his phone and puts in their orders, plus another to bring home to Jamie.

"I don't really care about marriage either," Charlie says.

"It's administratively convenient," Simon points out, feeling like maybe he shouldn't disparage the institution on the way home from a wedding. "I've never lived with a partner."

"I haven't slept at my house in weeks."

"Mmm," says Simon, who's pretending to be very chill and relaxed and normal about how, after coming home from Utah, Charlie's been a fixture in Simon's house.

"I only go home to use my gym."

"Mmm," Simon repeats.

"My PlayStation is in your living room. I keep waiting for you to tell me to go home."

Simon gives up. "Do you not remember what I said about wanting to keep you locked in my basement?"

"You don't have a basement," Charlie says, sounding like a man who'd happily fling himself into the first available codependence dungeon. Like he'd dig one himself.

Jamie's still living with Simon, which means there are two people around to see the truth, two people who see all the cracks in the facade. Which is terrible, obviously, and Simon wants to hide in the bathroom on an existential level, but also—it's two people he doesn't have to pretend around. It feels like a secret club.

When they pull up to the food truck, Simon waits in the car while Charlie gets their food. Simon lowers the window and takes a minute to watch Charlie walk away, handsome in his suit. Halfway there, he turns around and grins at Simon over his shoulder. It's one of those rare, easy, sunshine moments, even in a dark parking lot, bad music playing tinnily from inside the food truck, no aesthetics whatsoever.

When Charlie gets back into the car, he drops the food into the back seat, puts his soda in the cup holder, and gives Simon a funny look. It's only when he leans in for a kiss that Simon realizes he's smiling. Just sitting in a parked car in the middle of the night, smiling like a loon.

But why shouldn't Simon smile? He's happy, and Charlie's smiling back—a little tentative, like he can't quite believe this.

"We're good," Simon says, not quite sure what he means, but knowing that Charlie will hear everything behind it.

"Yeah, I know," Charlie says, kind of wonderingly, so Simon kisses him again.

Acknowledgments

It seems to be traditional for me to use the acknowledgments section to apologize to my family for spending a year inflicting my research on them, but this year I'm unrepentant. You're welcome for all the *Star Trek*. Still: thank you to my family for tolerating (to various degrees) a tour through all my favorite sci-fi shows, even when I paused every three minutes to point out queer subtext. At least you enjoyed *Lower Decks*.

Katie Welsh read an early draft and provided invaluable advice, but most importantly they came up with *Out There* as the perfectly terrible title for the show in this book. Megan Tomkoski read the first few chapters and said something that will stick with me for the rest of my career: make them worse.

I'm grateful to my agent, Deidre Knight, for putting in my head the idea that I could write a contemporary. I'm thankful to everyone at Avon who took a chance on me writing something a little different, especially my editor, Tessa Woodward.

I'm enormously grateful for the readers who've stuck with me through various permutations of the genre, through weird little novellas and hundred-thousand-word character studies about sad journalists. You all make writing into storytelling; thank you.

This is probably a good place to point out that Simon's experience with anxiety and migraines isn't meant to be universal or exemplary; he's a work in progress, like most of us.

About the Author

CAT SEBASTIAN is an award-winning author of queer romance. Cat's books include *We Could Be So Good* and *You Should Be So Lucky*, and have received starred reviews from *Kirkus, Publishers Weekly, Library Journal,* and *Booklist*. *We Could Be So Good* won a Lambda Literary Award in 2024. In her spare time, she acquires too many houseplants and misplaces things.

Read more from critically acclaimed author
CAT SEBASTIAN

"Cat Sebastian is an author at the absolute top of her game."
—ERIN STERLING,
New York Times bestselling author of *The Ex Hex*

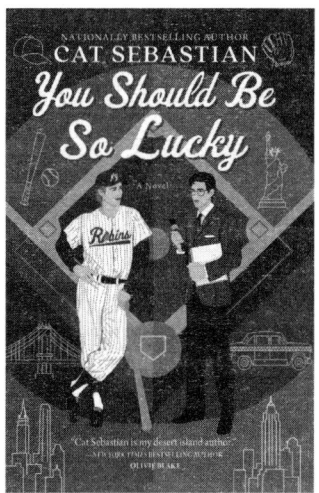

DISCOVER GREAT AUTHORS, EXCLUSIVE OFFERS, AND MORE AT HC.COM.